SONG OF THE SEA

A LITTLE MERMAID RETELLING

THE SINGER TALES
BOOK 2

DEBORAH GRACE WHITE

LUMINANT PUBLICATIONS

SONG OF THE SEA: A LITTLE MERMAID RETELLING

By Deborah Grace White

Song of the Sea:
A Little Mermaid Retelling
The Singer Tales Book Two

Copyright © 2022 by Deborah Grace White

First edition (v1.0) published in 2023
by Luminant Publications

All rights reserved. Without limiting the rights under copyright reserved above, no part of this publication may be reproduced, distributed, transmitted, stored in, or introduced into a database or retrieval system, in any form, or by any means, without the prior written permission of both the copyright owner and the above publisher of this book.

The characters and events portrayed in this book are fictitious. Any similarity to real persons, living or dead, is coincidental and not intended by the author.

ISBN: 978-1-922636-64-5

Luminant Publications
PO Box 305
Greenacres, South Australia 5086

http://www.deborahgracewhite.com

Cover Design by Karri Klawiter
Map illustration by Rebecca E. Paavo

For my parents
Thanks for loving me simply for my own sake.

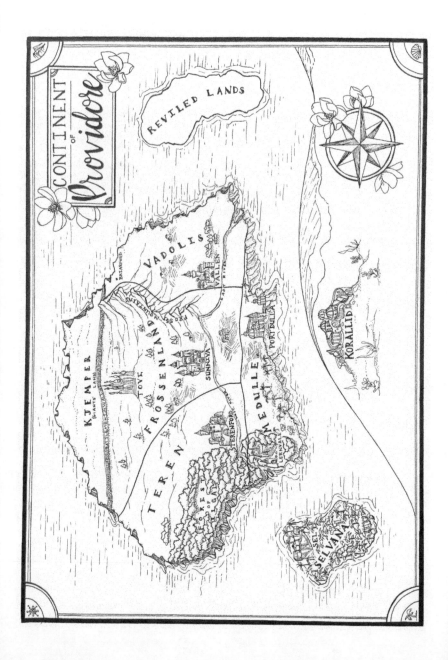

CHAPTER ONE

Estelle

Estelle nodded to herself as she rose gently in the water, pleased with the results of her efforts. Opening her mouth, she sang gently to the plants below, watching critically as they responded to the power that surged from the seabed into their fronds. The scraggly ones expanded, and those growing too enthusiastically came back into line.

She pushed a strand of pale blue hair out of her eyes to better study her little coral garden. It was neat and thriving once again. She'd neglected it for too long, and it had begun to show. She knew it didn't really matter—with everyone finally gathering to celebrate her fifteenth birthday, she could only assume she would be forming a marriage alliance and leaving the palace imminently. But she would still prefer to leave her garden in good order.

Her eyes passed wistfully to the patch alongside hers. Eulalia's garden still showed signs of care to the careful observer. Estelle could almost see the outline her sister had tried to shape the garden into, in the form of a large scallop shell. But it had mostly grown wild. After all, it had been ten years since Eulalia turned fifteen and was married. Eulalia's husband's family ruled the southernmost province of Korallid, far from the palace, so Estelle had seen her sister infrequently in that time. Still, she cherished the memories of her early years, when Eulalia had been one of her chief companions, the ten year age gap making her more carer than playmate.

The garden beds of her other sisters were all fully wild by now, but they evoked little emotion. Etta, Emilia, and Eilise were forty, thirty, and twenty years older than Estelle respectively. They had all been married at the traditional age of fifteen, well before Estelle was born. Etta was the only one to still live in the palace, given her position as their father's heir. But she had never been a close companion to Estelle. After all, most of her children were at least twice Estelle's age.

"Princess Estelle."

Estelle turned to see a servant swimming toward her across the sandy stretch of ocean that separated the sprawling garden from the palace.

"Yes, I'm here," she called.

The servant pulled up as he approached, his eyes straying curiously to Estelle's garden bed.

"Do you like it?" she asked, trying not to laugh at his bemused expression.

"It's lovely, Your Highness," he said quickly. His tone turned hesitant. "Is it...is it an urchin? Too many spikes for a starfish, I think?"

Estelle chuckled. "No, it's not an urchin. It's the sun, see?" She pointed to the center of her garden, where the circular rows of anemones increased in size, forming a large circle. Brightly colored fish darted in and out between the fronds, enjoying the shelter of the plants.

"And these parts," Estelle pointed to the lines of coral jutting out from the central circle, "are the rays of light coming from the sun."

The servant was silent for a moment.

"You can't see it?" Estelle asked, a little crestfallen.

"No, I can," he said. "It's just...forgive me, Princess Estelle, but...I thought you'd never seen the sun. I thought...I thought you'd yet to ascend to the surface."

"I haven't," she admitted. "But I've heard my sisters talk about it, and sometimes I almost think I can see a bright spot through the water, on a very clear day. To tell the truth," she smiled disarmingly, "my garden is based more on depictions of the sun in artwork than on the sun itself." Her gaze suddenly keen, she looked him over. He was certainly much older than fifteen. "Have *you* seen the sun?"

"Well...yes," said the merman, his tail flicking slowly back and forth. "That is, I've seen the sky, and the sun's light. But you can't look directly at the sun, you know. It's too bright for our eyes."

"Is that so?" Estelle asked, fascinated. "How have I never heard that before? What about the moon? Is that too bright?"

"No," said the servant. "At least, I don't believe so." He sounded uncomfortable, like he regretted entering into the conversation, but Estelle pushed on, eager for the opportunity.

"Have you been to the surface many times since your first ascension? Have you seen humans?"

"I...uh...I've been once or twice." The servant's discomfort was painful to watch now, and Estelle realized it was cruel to press him when he clearly wasn't supposed to say more.

With a sigh, she abandoned the topic. She was very used to her questions being turned aside anytime she showed interest in the world above the surface. Her father was positively fierce about it when she did so in front of him. This wasn't the first time she'd suspected that the emperor had instructed the servants not to engage in conversation regarding his youngest daughter's unhealthy level of interest in what lay above the waterline.

"Did you come with a message for me?" Estelle prompted the still-squirming servant.

"Yes," he said, straightening. "The first of your sisters has arrived."

"Which one?" Estelle demanded, the previous topic forgotten as her fins quivered with excitement.

"Princess Eulalia."

The words were barely out of the servant's mouth when Estelle took off in a shimmer of pale blue scales. The palace's colorful walls rose rapidly before her, the coral just as alive as that in her garden. Her sudden approach startled a clown fish, which darted out of the wall, skating over a lazily drifting turtle as it hunted for a better haven. Estelle had almost reached the palace when she realized she'd left her gardening satchel nestled among the coral behind her. Pausing, she began to sing idly, the sound reverberating through the water as the currents shifted responsively. In moments, the satchel came into view, carried gently right to her outstretched hand. The moment she grasped it, she let her song drift into stillness, and the currents returned to their usual pattern.

Estelle smiled as she slung the satchel over her shoulder. She was getting better, even without training. No doubt it was another area her father would chastise her for if he realized she was practicing her singing when she wasn't supposed to be trained in it for another decade at least. But what else was she supposed to do with her time while she waited for him to decide she could actually claim her fifteen years?

When she reached a side entrance of the palace, she nodded to the guard on duty and sped through the waving seaweed curtain that provided a semblance of privacy over the doorway. She flicked her tail to put on more speed, eager to reach the interior courtyard where she knew her parents would be receiving Eulalia and her family. It had been a year since Estelle had last seen her closest sister, and in that time, Eulalia had added a second child to her family. There would be so much to discuss.

Guards straightened in the water as Estelle passed, their eyes following her progress attentively. As a daughter of the undersea emperor, she was so used to the scrutiny that she didn't even notice it. The corridor leading to the interior courtyard was curved, and Estelle slowed as her destination neared. She didn't want to surge around a corner into some unsuspecting servant carrying a turtle shell bowl full of food for the evening's reception. It wouldn't be the first time.

The doorway to the courtyard came into sight, flanked by two guards. As Estelle neared, she realized one of the guards looked familiar.

"I've seen you before," she commented, pulling up. "Demetri?"

"Demetrius, Your Highness," he said, bending his upper body in a bow.

"That's right," she said, smiling brightly. "I knew I'd met you. You're a friend of Esteban's, aren't you?" She named the third child of her oldest sister, Etta.

"I have that honor, Your Highness," said the guard, for some reason looking uncomfortable at her mention of Esteban.

Esteban was Estelle's nephew, but his relationship to Estelle was nothing like that of Eulalia's new baby. Etta was in her mid-fifties, so her third son was twenty, about five years older than Estelle.

The guard before her looked to be a similar age, which was why he'd stood out. Estelle looked him over thoughtfully, noting the dark amber color of his hair and scales. It was unusual to see such a young guard attending a member of the royal family, and Estelle was fairly certain these guards were present thanks to her family being in the courtyard. As the door was an internal one, it wasn't usually manned.

"Have you joined the royal guard?" Estelle asked him. "I think I remember Esteban mentioning that you were training to be a guard."

There was a moment of silence, during which the other guard cast Demetrius a sideways glance. "Yes, Your Highness," said Demetrius at last.

Estelle nodded slowly, still unsure why he seemed unhappy about her question. "Well, perhaps I'll see you around more in future," she said. She tilted her head toward the doorway. "I heard that my sister Eulalia is here?"

"That's right, Your Highness," said the other guard, a green-tailed merman in his young middle age. "I believe you're expected."

With a nod, Estelle swam past them, her outstretched arms pushing the seaweed curtain aside to reveal the courtyard within. The stately figures of Emperor Aefic and Empress Talisa dominated the space, a ring of guards placed at a respectful distance around them. But Estelle had no attention to spare for her parents, not when she caught sight of a flash of purple scales behind her mother.

"Eulalia!" she cried, swimming forward eagerly.

The older mermaid turned, her lips stretching into a smile as her sister approached. Her sleek nose crinkled with the motion, the gills that scored it seeming to lengthen. It was an endearingly familiar expression, and it lifted Estelle's heart.

"Little sister," said Eulalia, holding out one arm to embrace Estelle. "It's been too long."

At sight of the bundle in Eulalia's other arm, Estelle pulled herself up so abruptly, her fins flicked into her father's face.

"Estelle," the emperor chastised. "Can you not move with more decorum?"

"Sorry, Father," said Estelle, her eyes still on the infant in Eulalia's arms. "I just didn't see her at first. She's so beautiful, Eulalia!"

"We think so," said Eulalia, beaming first at her infant child, then at her husband.

Estelle smiled at him as well. She liked Eulalia's husband. He was nice, unlike Emilia's, who was always aloof, or Eilise's, who was downright grumpy.

The couple's eldest child, a ten-year-old boy, tried to look disinterested in the whole exchange, but Estelle could see the warmth even in his eyes as he glanced at his baby sister.

"I remember when you were that small," Estelle teased her nephew. "You were very cute."

He gave her a long-suffering look. "You would have been only five, Aunt Estelle. Do you really remember?"

"I do!" she assured him. "I'd been very sad about your mother moving away from the palace when she married your father, but then they came back to visit after you were born, and I could see why it was worth it after all."

Her nephew's gaze drifted back to his new sister, a smile tugging at his lips. "Babies are pretty cute," he acknowledged.

"If you were a girl, you'd be having one of your own in about five years," said Estelle, nudging him with her elbow. He looked horrified, and she couldn't help laughing. "Don't worry," she said reassuringly. "You're a boy, so you'll probably get an extra ten years compared to us girls."

His forehead crinkled as he thought this over. "Aren't you already fifteen, Aunt Estelle? Shouldn't you be getting married and having your first baby?"

Estelle felt her pale cheeks heating, and although she opened her mouth, no words came. She shot a look at her parents, and saw that her father looked disapproving and her mother uncomfortable.

"Why don't you go find your cousins?" Eulalia urged her son, hastening to fill the awkward silence. "I'm sure Aunt Etta's children aren't far away."

The ten-year-old's face lit up, and he darted off, followed closely by a pair of guards.

Estelle watched him go, smiling a little at his eagerness. He had a contemporary among Etta's children, and once Eilise and Emilia arrived, each of their ten-year-olds would be able to join the crew. It was one of the convenient things about the way mermaid fertility worked, with each mermaid only able to bear a child every ten years. Estelle and her sisters were all ten years apart, almost exactly. And since her sisters had all married at fifteen and had their first children soon after, the family was full of aligned cousins. Once everyone was present, there would be not one but four new babies to admire.

Estelle's heart twisted uncomfortably as it washed over her, yet again, that her own first child should be adding a fifth to the number around now. It wasn't that she was devastated—in fact, if she was honest with herself, a significant part of her was relieved that her betrothal hadn't been announced on her fifteenth birthday, as she'd expected. But another part of her felt embarrassed about the omission, and the discomfort only grew as the months went by. Her parents had never explained why they hadn't yet chosen her a husband—she didn't even understand why her birthday celebration had been so long delayed. She was halfway to her sixteenth birthday, and her family was only gathering to mark the occasion now.

Nerves rushed over Estelle. Would her parents announce a betrothal at tomorrow night's celebration? They'd said nothing about it, but that didn't mean anything. Emilia's marriage alliance had been planned since her infancy, from what she'd heard, but Eulalia's had been decided behind closed doors mere weeks before she turned fifteen.

Knowing the matter was entirely out of her control, Estelle pushed those thoughts aside. Instead, she focused on a much more exciting aspect of her birthday celebrations. She was finally to experience the rite of passage that should have occurred when she turned fifteen. It was at last her turn to ascend to the surface. She could barely wait for the following day. Young as she'd been, she could still remember Eulalia's fifteenth birthday dinner with perfect clarity, when she'd listened, along with all the guests, to the princess's account of what she'd seen on her first visit to the surface hours before.

Estelle had been absolutely rapt, and had been longing for her turn ever since.

"Estelle. Did you hear me?"

"What? Sorry, Father." Estelle returned to the present with a shake of the head. Clearly the conversation had moved on while she'd been lost in her thoughts. "What did you say?"

"I was telling your sister," her father responded, his voice tight, "of your interest in learning more of the southern province."

"Oh," said Estelle blankly, her eyes traveling to her brother-in-law. "Yes, my tutor has been teaching me about abalone exports, and she tells me that your province is the main provider. She suggested I ask you more about it."

With her thoughts still on the surface, she didn't manage to insert any enthusiasm into the question, and she saw her father's tail flick in irritation. Estelle sighed. She seemed capable of nothing but disappointing him. Clearly he'd wanted her to pose the question more naturally, and give her brother-in-law the impression of genuine interest. But she wasn't speaking to him as the son of the southern province's rulers. Did her father really have to use her first meeting with her sister in a year as an opportunity for diplomatic flattery?

"We can discuss it further once we've settled in if you wish," said Eulalia's husband, his sympathetic smile telling her that he wouldn't really subject her to a lecture on abalone once her parents weren't present. She smiled gratefully at him. He was definitely the nicest of her brothers-in-law. If her parents chose someone like him, it wouldn't be so bad.

Nerves once again coiled in her stomach, and she hastened to push them aside with their most reliable counter.

"You'll come with me tomorrow, won't you?" she asked Eulalia eagerly. "To the surface?"

"Of course," smiled Eulalia. "It's tradition. We'll all come—why do you think the whole family is gathering for the celebration?"

Emperor Aefic cleared his throat meaningfully. "As to that, we're getting ahead of ourselves. It hasn't been absolutely determined that Estelle's first ascension will happen tomorrow."

Estelle's mouth fell open with horror, and she could see her sister staring at their father as well.

"What do you mean?" Eulalia demanded. "The first ascension always happens the day of a mermaid's fifteenth birthday dinner. When else will we all be gathered to hear her impressions of the surface?"

"Estelle's case is a little different," said their father stiffly. "Tomorrow is not actually her birthday. There is more flexibility in—"

"Father!" Estelle cut him off, heedless of politeness. "You can't be serious! I've been waiting my whole life for my ascension, and I've already had to wait half a year longer than I should have!"

Her father frowned at her. "It's that kind of talk, Estelle, that confirms my impression that whatever your literal age, in truth you are too young to celebrate your fifteenth birthday. You speak as though a mere half year is a great expanse of time. Do we not have three hundred years to our lives? What is one more year here or there?"

"You're going to make me wait another whole year?" Estelle demanded, aghast.

Humiliation washed over her at the confirmation of one of her fears—that her parents hadn't formally marked her fifteenth birthday and all the associated rites because they thought her too immature to be considered fully grown. But even her embarrassment paled next to her horror over the news that she might be denied her long-awaited ascension. It was what she had most looked forward to, not just in the lead up to this celebration, but for as long as she could remember. She'd been so disappointed to have it denied her on her real birthday. And now it was to be postponed further still?

"Father, you can't do this to me."

She knew at once that she'd gone too far. Her father's brows drew together, and by Estelle's judgment, he was prevented from an angry outburst only by his wife's hand laid on his arm.

"Come on, Estelle." Eulalia jumped in yet again, linking her free arm through her sister's. "Why don't you help me get settled in while Mother and Father talk?"

Gratefully, Estelle took the offered escape, swimming from the courtyard with her sister.

"What was that about, Estelle?" Eulalia asked, once they were out of hearing of the emperor and empress. "Why is Father so angry about you coming of age?"

"I don't know," said Estelle miserably. "The way he's been speaking to me, you'd think I'd been attacking people, or trading in black market talismans. But I haven't done anything different from normal."

Eulalia frowned. "Something is clearly bothering him. Do you know why he's so reluctant to let you ascend tomorrow?"

Estelle shook her head. "That's the first I've heard of it. It must be the same reason they've delayed marking my birthday half a year. You heard Father—he doesn't think I'm mature enough."

Eulalia's frown grew, her eyes straying to her husband, who was swimming ahead, led by a servant. "That doesn't seem reason enough." She clearly saw Estelle's distress, because she squeezed her arm reassuringly. "I'm sure Mother will talk him down."

"I don't know if she will," Estelle said gloomily. "She's been as strange as he has any time I've asked why my birthday celebrations have been delayed. But she doesn't seem to find me irritating like Father does—I don't understand her reluctance."

"Don't you?" Eulalia's expression was thoughtful as she studied her sister. "I think I do."

"What do you mean?" Estelle demanded, following her sister through a doorway into one of the palace's most elaborate guest suites. The bed, carved from stone from the seabed, was studded with pearls. For a moment Estelle was distracted by the sight of the area prepared for the newborn. "Oh, look, Eulalia! That's for the baby, isn't it? It's so cute."

Eulalia smiled as she cast an eye over the enormous clam shell that had been secured to the ceiling with thick seaweed ropes. It swayed gently in the current, the curved shape perfect to lay the infant in.

"And that's why Mother isn't in a hurry to mark your birthday," said Eulalia with a smile. Estelle stared at her in confusion, and Eulalia exhaled a long stream of water. "Sentiment, Estelle. Try as we might not to give in to such folly, we're all prone to being a little emotional about our young. You're Mother's last. She's seventy, now, past the sixty years of fertility. Once you marry and move away, that will be it. She'll miss you," she clarified, seeing Estelle's frown.

"Perhaps you're right," Estelle said thoughtfully. She bit her lip, her tail swishing slowly from side to side as she thought. "But I doubt that's the cause of Father's hesitation."

"No," Eulalia acknowledged. "Probably not." She gave her sister a reassuring smile. "I'll speak to Etta as soon as I'm settled, and Eilise and Emilia will be here by dinner tonight. We'll raise the matter at the meal, and Father won't be able to resist all of us combined. We'll sort it out before tomorrow, don't worry."

Estelle did her best to return her sister's smile as she listened to Eulalia begin to sing to her infant. Estelle could feel the power drifting up from the seabed, wrapping around the child and lulling him to sleep as surely as the rocking of the current.

But Estelle could feel none of the soothing effects herself. She could only hope Eulalia was right, because in the ordeal of coming of age and facing her future, ascending to the surface at last was all she had to look forward to.

CHAPTER TWO

Demetrius

Demetrius shifted his fins rhythmically, keeping himself in position in the water with the minimum movement, as he'd been trained to do. The last thing he wanted was to draw attention to himself. He knew the private family dinner—which still involved over thirty people—was nothing compared to the morrow's formal celebration of the youngest princess's coming of age. But the gathering of the emperor's entire family was still a significant event. Half the royal guard were required in order to provide the necessary ceremonial ring around the edges of the enormous dining hall. That was the only reason Demetrius had the chance to guard the emperor himself so soon after joining the royal guard, and he didn't intend to waste the opportunity.

Princess Estelle's comments earlier in the day came back to him, and he groaned internally. It was so like royalty to speak their thoughts without any awareness of the impact for those beneath them in the social order. Esteban, good-hearted as he might be, was just the same at times. Had Princess Estelle truly not seen the way the other guard looked at him? No doubt that merman had reported the incident back to the rest of the barracks by now, and Demetrius would have even more of a struggle to gain the respect of his fellows.

A current of bitterness flowed over Demetrius as he thought of the snide comments he'd heard in his first weeks among the royal guard. The worst part of all of it was his fear that the gossip might be right—*had* he gained his position so young only because of his friendship with Prince Esteban? Had Esteban, unbeknownst to Demetrius, pulled the captain of the guard aside for a word, and asked him to take Demetrius on?

It was an awful thought. Demetrius had worked hard for years to reach his position, and no one had been more surprised and delighted than him when he'd been selected from among older applicants to fill a vacancy. It was only afterward that he heard the mutters that disseminated through the water when he swam past groups of other guards, that he'd been given his position rather than earned it. If Esteban had spoken for him, Demetrius hadn't asked for it. But it was immaterial—no one would ever believe that.

And just when the mutters had died down, and Demetrius was settling into his place, Princess Estelle had to remind one of the guards' worst gossips that Demetrius was such a close friend of Prince Esteban that he was recognizable even to the prince's youthful aunt, whose contact with Esteban was minimal.

Demetrius was pulled from his thoughts by a noticeable lull in the constant flow of sound that filled the water in the dining room. The throbbing noises of the ocean remained, of course. His ears were still full of the tide's dull and comforting roar, the unsteady, constant crackling of the sea life, the distant call of a blue whale. And of course there was the periodic hum of the guards' quiet song, as they pulled power from the ocean floor to regularly reinforce the protective barriers they'd placed around the royal dining hall. He could even hear the distinct popping sound of a mantis shrimp on the hunt somewhere in the reef outside, frightening its prey into immobility with the sudden noise.

But inside the royal dining room, conversation had stilled, and a glance at the emperor showed Demetrius why. Chastising himself for not noticing that Emperor Aefic had risen in the water to address his family, Demetrius schooled his features to look as if he wasn't listening.

"Welcome, my family," said the emperor formally. "Talisa and I are pleased you have joined us, to mark the milestone of our family passing forever from the stage of childhood."

Being a guard, Demetrius showed no reaction, but inside he was surprised at the emperor's wording. Emperor Aefic spoke as if the event affected all the family generally, rather than being the most significant moment of Princess Estelle's life. The emperor hadn't even mentioned his daughter's name. If Demetrius hadn't been so rigidly trained to keep his gaze straight, he would have glanced at the emperor's youngest daughter to see how she responded.

The emperor's welcoming speech was brief, and he'd barely drifted back down to the seabed when a whole school of servants began swimming into the room, moving low in the water under the weight of so much food. Even with his eyes carefully straight, Demetrius caught a glimpse of the dishes as they passed him. Turtle shell bowls overflowing with mussels of every variety, at least a dozen types of fish, more plants than he'd known were edible, octopus tentacles, whole slabs of squid...the array seemed endless. Demetrius thought of the simple meal of cod he'd shared with other guards in the barracks before commencing duty. Royals truly lived far from the reality of their subjects. Really it was no wonder they didn't think to consider how their words and actions might affect the less fortunate.

"Father. Thank you for your welcome."

Demetrius's peripheral vision showed him that another of the princesses was speaking. Her bright purple hair and scales were unmistakable—it was Princess Eulalia, the one whose family he'd been assigned to guard since her arrival.

Emperor Aefic inclined his head in recognition of his fourth daughter's words, but it seemed she wasn't finished.

"We are all glad to be here to celebrate Estelle's birthday—however belatedly—tomorrow night. But you made no mention of her ascension. We are to assume it will take place tomorrow?"

Judging by the new level of hush that fell over the room, Demetrius wasn't the only one surprised by the direct approach. In spite of himself, his gaze flicked to the long stone table, and he was intrigued to see that not only Princess Eulalia, but Princess Estelle's other three sisters had risen in the water, the better to get their father's attention.

Emperor Aefic's voice was hard as he replied. "That is a matter for your mother and me to decide, Eulalia. The circumstances of Estelle's coming of age are unusual, and it is therefore natural that her ascension has not followed the usual traditions."

"We're all family here, Father," cut in another of the sisters. Princess Emilia, Demetrius was fairly certain. "We can speak freely."

Demetrius's eyebrow went up. Family the group might be, but was the princess really oblivious to the fact that the husbands of the various princesses represented the ruling families of every province of Korallid? It was the last assembly in which he would wish to speak freely.

"We're all parents," Princess Emilia went on, gesturing to herself and the three sisters who'd risen with her. "We understand how difficult it must be to say goodbye to your last child. But Estelle deserves to—"

"Difficult?" The emperor's tone was incredulous. "Do you

imagine that Estelle's coming of age has been delayed due to sentiment? Not on my part."

Demetrius couldn't help but notice that all of the sisters' eyes flew to their mother. Following their gaze, he saw that the empress looked a little embarrassed, her pale face tinged with color.

"Then why?" asked Princess Eulalia bluntly. "Why are we celebrating Estelle's birthday half a year late, and why is there discussion of delaying her ascension still further?"

Princess Estelle's head whipped around to face her father. Demetrius had the impression she'd been waiting a long time for an answer to this question.

"If I were to consult my own inclination alone," said Emperor Aefic, "we would not be celebrating her birthday until all the arrangements had been made. As to the matter of the ascension, I have no doubt Estelle knows perfectly well why I'm reluctant."

"But I don't, Father!" Princess Estelle burst out, rising up to join her sisters at last. "I don't understand at all. Why has there been such delay? You know how much I long to visit the surface. I want to see the human world more than anything!"

"Estelle," said Eulalia, a hint of warning in her tone. "Leave it to us."

The youngest princess sank back down and, in spite of himself, Demetrius felt a stirring of sympathy at the look of confusion on her face. She was so young, and clearly her cloistered life had done her no favors. Even he could tell that she was harming her own cause by expressing her eagerness to explore the world of the humans. It was a rare sentiment among merfolk, most of whom preferred the deeper parts of the ocean to anywhere the destructive sun could reach. Demetrius could only assume that the emperor of the undersea domain wouldn't be pleased to hear his own daughter speaking in such glowing terms of the world of the despised and mistrusted humans.

"Thank you, Estelle, for illustrating my point so clearly," said the emperor, as if in confirmation of Demetrius's thoughts.

The look on Princess Estelle's face suggested that she'd finally caught up.

"But, Father," she pleaded. "I'm fifteen now, whether you wish it or not. The tradition of our people is that the first ascension happens at fifteen. You didn't deny any of my sisters their opportunity."

"Had any of your sisters displayed such unseemly fascination with a world which is in every way inferior to ours, I would have felt the same hesitation in their case," said the emperor.

"Father, I agree with Eulalia." The no-nonsense voice of the emperor's eldest daughter and heir, Crown Princess Etta, brought a frown to her father's face. "I understand your feelings," the middle aged mermaid went on. "But you know my views. Preventing Estelle from partaking in the ascension tradition will only increase her curiosity. Let her rise to the surface tomorrow, and she will see what those of us who've come of age already know—that the world above the water has nothing of especial value to offer. She can give her impressions publicly at the dinner, as per tradition, and move forward with her life."

"If that were possible, I would have allowed the ascension half a year ago," the emperor acknowledged. "But until she can move forward, there seems little point in indulging her curiosity."

Against his training, Demetrius's gaze strayed back to Princess Estelle. She was floating just above the seabed, her eyes still a little desperate, but her mouth determinedly shut. What must it feel like to have someone as powerful as the emperor discuss your fate in such a large gathering, speaking of you as if you weren't present? For the first time, Demetrius felt a surge of gratitude that he hadn't been born royal.

"Why can't she move forward?" Princess Eulalia demanded. "What are the arrangements that haven't been—oh." Sudden comprehension crossed her features. "You're speaking of her marriage. No betrothal has yet been formed."

She exchanged a glance with the sister floating closest to her, and Princess Emilia spoke up, her tone matter-of-fact.

"If you don't make the arrangements soon, Estelle will miss her first cycle of fertility. She will be unable to bear a child until she is twenty-five!"

Again, Demetrius couldn't help his eyes flying to Princess Estelle. Her gaze was on her lap, her pale cheeks suffused with color. His weren't the only eyes on her. Many members of the extended family kept shooting her looks, and the younger children among them were openly gawking.

"I am aware of that," the emperor told his daughter, a snap in his voice.

"Then why the delay?" asked Princess Eulalia. "Surely there must be many eligible mermen of noble birth here in the capital. Can you not—"

"Enough, Eulalia," said the emperor, in a voice as cold as the deepest trench. "This is not a matter for you to decide. Each of my daughters has brought honor to our family and our empire by strengthening the ties between all our provinces. Estelle must do no less."

"Father, I'm ready to do my part for our family," Princess Estelle declared, once again propelling herself upward. "I have always expected to marry for the sake of our empire."

"So I should hope," her father said tersely, "given it is the only substantial means you possess of enlarging the honor of our family." His voice dropped, as if he was speaking to himself. "An unfortunate reality, given the lack of opportunity."

"Again, Father, I disagree," said Crown Princess Etta. "There are other types of alliances that might be beneficial. Estelle can still make you proud."

"There are no provinces left," said the emperor, the exasperation in his tone suggesting that he and his heir had engaged in this debate before. "We will discuss the matter no further here."

Demetrius drew in a thoughtful swirl of water through the gills that stretched across his nose. So that was the source of the emperor's annoyance. A basic understanding of the capital's politics was a necessity for a royal guard. Accordingly, Demetrius was fully aware of the significance of each of the other princesses' marriages. It was the first time in many generations that the imperial family had marriage alliances with the ruling families of each of the three provinces that made up Emperor Aefic's domain. The eldest princess, needing to remain in the palace in her role as heir, had made a political marriage within the capital. But the next three sisters had each performed their part in tying their father's family to one of the provinces, weaving the empire together more securely than in living memory.

It seemed that no less exalted marriage would satisfy Emperor Aefic for his youngest daughter, which left Princess Estelle in something of a difficult position. It was no secret that the emperor had been bitterly disappointed when the last child born to his wife in her final window of fertility had been yet another mermaid. A merman would have been much more welcome.

Again, sympathy stirred within Demetrius, much as he tried to quell it. It seemed absurd to him to hear all her family speak of the young princess being ready, even overdue, to bear her first child. She was little more than a child herself, and she looked so small and powerless in this room full of important rulers. When her sister had declared Princess Estelle in danger of being twenty-five before she bore her first child, she'd said it as though the age was ancient. Demetrius suppressed a shudder. He'd only just turned twenty himself, and he doubted he would be ready to become a father in ten years, let alone five. But it was different for mermaids—they didn't have the same luxuries of choice as mermen.

The thought brought his eyes back to Princess Estelle. Surely she must have opinions of her own on the matter. Her demeanor supported the idea—she was having little success in hiding her frustration.

"Father," Princess Estelle said, her tone determined. "Although I am ready to marry as you wish, according to tradition and honor, I am more than content to wait until you form a betrothal with which you are satisfied. But please, in the meantime, don't make me wait longer for my ascension."

"She's right," said Princess Etta briskly. "The matter of her marriage aside, the question of her ascension must still be determined. Father, it's time to end these delays. She must be allowed to ascend tomorrow."

The emperor was silent for a moment, his gaze passing slowly over his daughters. All five of them were still floating a full tail length above the rest of the merfolk present, staring him down. His eyes moved to his wife, and the empress gave the barest of nods, indicating her agreement with her daughters.

"Very well," said Emperor Aefic, not very graciously. "Estelle, you will ascend tomorrow in accordance with tradition."

Princess Estelle's face lit up like a luminous jellyfish. It made her look more a child than ever, as eager as a little one receiving a gift on their decade day.

Demetrius's gaze strayed to Princess Eulalia, who was squeezing her younger sister's arm supportively. He knew the tradition—all of Princess Estelle's older sisters would accompany her to the surface, to provide guidance and protection on what could be a perilous journey. It was a ceremonial gesture, of course. As the mermaid in question was a princess, she would float in no need of her sisters' protection. She would be accompanied by a veritable swarm of guards, not to mention her sisters' guards.

Which, thanks to his current assignment of guarding Princess Eulalia and her family, would include Demetrius.

It had been a couple of years since his last trip to the surface, and Demetrius found he didn't mind the idea. Perhaps Princess Estelle's enthusiasm was catching, because he even felt a small stirring of excitement.

It was time to feel the warmth of the sun on his face again.

CHAPTER THREE

Estelle

Estelle spun in the water, her motion so quick that she couldn't tell if the flash of pale blue before her eyes was her scales or her hair.

It was finally time. She was finally going to the surface.

"Calm down," laughed Eulalia, swimming up alongside her. "If Father sees you frolicking like a dolphin in front of all this gathered crowd, he might just change his mind."

The comment had been light-hearted, but it sobered Estelle at once. A quick glance in her father's direction showed that he was currently distracted by a discussion with the head of Estelle's personal guard, but she shouldn't take any chances. As pleased as she was that Eulalia had been right, and their father had been unable to withstand semi-public pressure applied by all of his grown daughters, she knew the emperor wasn't truly convinced of the wisdom of all this. He'd been surly all morning, and he was sending double the number of guards necessary.

"Are you ready, Estelle?" Eilise smiled as she swam up, her burgundy tail flicking briskly. "I'm quite looking forward to that fresh morning air. It's been a long time."

"I've been ready for years," Estelle responded eagerly. She studied her sister's serene expression. "Has it truly been so long? Once you've made your first ascension, can't you go up whenever you want?"

"Of course," said Eilise.

"Then why don't you?" Estelle pressed. "Why don't you go up every day?"

Her sisters laughed. "There's really not that much to do up there, Estelle," said Emilia, joining them. "You'll see."

Estelle was unconvinced, but at that moment she heard the bubbling blast of a conch shell, and she made no reply. A tangle of excitement and nerves rose up in her. At last, at last, it was her turn. She barely heard the formal announcement by her father, or the polite celebration of the crowd. Her eyes were focused upward, locked on the lighter water above.

At a nod from her father, the head of her personal guard began to rise, checking the water on all sides. Estelle fell into position beneath him, trying to hide her impatience at his glacial pace.

Her sisters surrounded her, their own guards joining Estelle's to form a protective sphere that enclosed them on all sides. Estelle knew her place at the center of the bubble was a position of honor, one she'd waited all her life to fill. But the truth was it chafed her to be hemmed in. It wasn't the ceremony she'd looked forward to, but the exploration. She wished she could streak ahead, break the surface first, or better yet, alone. She wanted to take it all in properly, not catch the odd glimpse through the shield of merfolk surrounding her.

Estelle forced these thoughts down, refusing to let anything sully this triumphant moment. She gazed excitedly at their surrounds. Everything was becoming gradually lighter as they rose, and she could see further than usual through the clear water.

Her sisters chatted on as they continued to rise, moving at a steady pace, if not as quickly as Estelle would like. When they'd been swimming for half an hour, Estelle realized what felt so different.

"The water is getting warmer," she said eagerly.

Eulalia nodded, her smile indulgent. "It'll get much warmer before we reach the surface. It's a shame Father didn't let you ascend on your actual birthday, Estelle. It would have been winter above, and the temperature wouldn't have been much different from underwater. Now it's summer—the sun will be very hot in the middle of the day."

Estelle laughed aloud. "A shame?" she repeated incredulously. "Eulalia, do you really think I would consider it a benefit for the surface to be more like our world? The more dramatic the differences, the better, as far as I'm concerned."

Eulalia's smile became a little rueful as she shook her head. "Your obsession with the world above will never make sense to me, Estelle. What's wrong with our world?"

"I didn't say anything was wrong with it," Estelle said vaguely, peering upward through the water. It was continuing to steadily lighten, but she couldn't yet see the sky above. "But there isn't a great deal to get excited about, is there? I mean, a political marriage at fifteen, then five decades of pressure to produce heirs for your husband, then another two hundred years of everything the same, but no one having any use for you since you have nothing more to contribute."

"Thanks, Estelle," said Etta dryly.

Estelle gave an uncomfortable laugh. She'd forgotten for a moment that, given Etta was fifty-five, the child she'd just had would likely be her last.

"I'm sorry, Etta, I spoke thoughtlessly," she said. "I meant no offense. I just meant that from what I can see, the ability to go to the surface at will is the only truly good thing about reaching adulthood."

"Getting married isn't so bad, Estelle," said Eulalia.

"That's right," agreed Etta. "Just because it's a duty doesn't mean it's unpleasant."

Glancing at the eldest and youngest of her sisters, Estelle could see that they meant it. But she also noticed that neither Eilise nor Emilia said anything. She wasn't deceived—the pleasantness or otherwise of marriage depended entirely on the temperament of the merman in question. And since it wasn't something Estelle would get to choose, she felt she would be wise not to count on any particular good fortune in that area.

But, she reminded herself happily, married or not, as a fully grown mermaid, she would retain the right to ascend to the surface whenever she wished. No matter how dreary her future, she would always have that to look forward to.

As the conversation lagged, one of her sisters began to sing. Soon, they'd all joined in, Estelle gladly adding her voice to theirs in a wordless melody that wove and danced as joyfully as a seal pup. Many of the guards added their deeper strains, the harmony filling Estelle's ears as it blended seamlessly with the constant sounds of the underwater world. She felt the power respond, not as quickly as normal, as it danced its way up from the ocean bed. But soon enough, the currents bent to their direction, aiding in the swimmers' ascent.

Their speed doubled, and when a strange sound met Estelle's ears, it had been considerably less than the additional half hour she'd expected.

"Did you hear that?" she demanded suddenly, her head jolting up. "What was that shrieking sound?"

"I believe it was a sea gull," said Emilia, smiling at her enthusiasm. "We're getting close."

Fins quivering in excitement, Estelle propelled herself upward. The group had ceased singing, and now she was listening, she could hear more than just the gull's cry. The whole quality of the sound was different. There was less crackling, and the water barely pressed against her ears. All sorts of strange noises were reaching her from above, as the world beyond the surface splashed and rushed and went about a life of its own. Everything looked different as well. The water was incredibly light now, almost the color of her scales. Peering around the guards above her, she realized she could actually see the surface.

"You can *see* the currents," she breathed, her eyes as round as pearls. "They sort of...billow."

"Those are waves," said Eulalia. "The movement comes from the current, but those little ripples—the shapes the water makes—are caused by the wind."

"It's so beautiful," said Estelle, her voice a little choked. "It's almost like the ocean itself has scales on its skin."

Eilise chuckled. "That's an interesting way of putting it."

Estelle's eyes were drawn to a huge white splotch above them which was almost painful to look at. "Is that the sun?" she asked, awed.

The others all nodded. "It's time," said Etta solemnly.

Eulalia glanced at her youngest sister. "Are you ready, Estelle? You'll have to hold your breath."

Estelle nodded, too overwhelmed to speak. She knew what to do—she'd asked anyone who would tell her about a hundred times. She drew in water through her gills, the pulls deeper and deeper as she prepared to immerse herself in pure air. Her eyes were riveted on the serene blue she could see above the water as they traveled the last distance. The water was so warm now, she almost felt like she was back with her tutor, touring the fissures to the west of the capital, where warm water poured impossibly out of the seafloor, thick with the power that all merfolk could feel and harness throughout the ocean. Her skin crawled with the sensation, but not in an unpleasant way.

The guards in front had stopped now, allowing her to catch up to them. With a thrill, she realized she would be allowed to break the surface first after all. As she drew her last breath of water before reaching the air above, she cast one quick glance around the group. Her sisters were all smiling indulgently, but most of the guards looked indifferent, and some were visibly tense. She knew most merfolk didn't like to be so far from their usual domain. Estelle started slightly as she caught sight of an unusually young guard, and realized she recognized him. It was Esteban's friend, Demetrius. He stood out, not just because he was familiar, but because he was the only one who actually looked like he was enjoying himself. There was even a faint hint of excitement on his face as his eyes flicked up toward the surface above.

Looking suddenly down, he caught Estelle watching him, and instantly schooled his features into the impassive mask usually worn by guards. She felt a flicker of regret at the loss of fellow feeling, but the thought didn't hold her attention for more than a second. Turning her face upward, she gave her fins one final, powerful flick, and broke the surface at last.

There were no words for the maelstrom of sensations that washed over her when her face felt air for the first time. The sun seemed to kiss her skin, its warmth somehow overwhelming and comforting at the same time. The surface of the water looked surprisingly similar from above to how it looked from below, except the billows were rougher than the smooth ripples she'd seen as she rose.

And the colors were all different. Everything was so bright, she could hardly bear to look at it. But she most certainly couldn't bear to look away. The water stretched out in an endless expanse before her, no landmarks or features to mark location like there would be in the equivalent underwater stretch. A light wind played around her face, attempting to lift strands of her wet hair from her cheek. Speaking of her hair, it felt oddly heavy, pulled irresistibly down instead of floating gently around her.

In spite of what the servant had told her the day before, she snuck a glance up toward the sun. She saw what he meant—instinct prevented her from looking right at it, her eyes smarting as they darted quickly away. She spun in a slow circle, her tail working steadily to keep her in position, then bobbed in excitement at the sight of a small pillar of rock jutting out of the water some distance away. She knew that underneath, the rock would continue down onto a substantial shelf. Excitement rushed over her at this image of the worlds above and below water meeting.

Estelle was burning for breath by this time, and she ducked her head back under the surface to pull water through her gills.

"Well?" demanded Eulalia, the moment her head was submerged. "What do you think?"

"It's incredible," breathed Estelle. Her sisters chuckled, and this time when she pushed back upward, they all followed.

Five heads broke the surface together, and Estelle's heart warmed. They were finally all together, and the moment was everything she'd dreamed it would be. Soon many other heads appeared, as those guards at the top of the formation joined them in the air.

Continuing where she'd left off, Estelle completed the rest of the circle, her whole body bobbing in excitement when she caught sight of a dark mass in the distance. She would never be able to see that far underwater, but looking through the air, she could make out not only a rocky ledge of some kind, but what looked like an intentional structure perched atop it. As she stared, something glinted off the building, reflecting the blinding rays of the sun.

Excitedly, Estelle let herself drop back into the water. Eulalia followed, the other sisters not far behind.

"Was that land?" Estelle asked eagerly. "Did I see a building made by humans?"

"That was probably the castle of the humans' royal family," said Eilise, nodding.

"It's so far away," said Estelle, trying not to let her disappointment show. "I thought we'd be closer."

"My ascension point was quite a lot closer," acknowledged Emilia. The others nodded in agreement.

Estelle let out a bubbling breath. It was utterly unsurprising that her father had chosen a point this far out into the ocean for her ascension. She supposed she should be grateful she could see land at all.

"Did any of you actually see humans on your ascensions?" she asked her sisters.

"I did," said Eilise. "But not on land. They were passing, in one of their ships."

"What was that like?" Estelle demanded, fascinated. "Did they see you?"

Eilise laughed. "Of course not. I stayed below mostly."

"I wonder if humans have ever seen merfolk during an ascension," mused Estelle.

"My mother-in-law swears she was seen once, about six decades ago," Eulalia said. "She was visiting the capital and went to the surface to see the land—we're so far from any land in the southern province, you know. It's quite a novelty for us. She said she went close enough to shore to see fishermen in their little boats. Claims they just about fell into the water in their shock."

The sisters all laughed, with the exception of Estelle, who was too rapt to take her eyes from Eulalia's face.

"I'm sure everyone they told just thought they'd lost their minds," Eulalia said comfortably. "We've become a legend to the humans, nothing more."

"And that's the way we like it," Etta said firmly.

Estelle's eyes traveled upward. "I want to hear more, but I'm wasting my time at the surface. I wish our voices worked above water." She looked back down at the closest of her sisters excitedly. "Eulalia, you're old enough now that you must have begun proper training in harnessing the ocean's power. Have you learned a way to make your voice work above water?" She grew more excited as a thought occurred to her. "Or to breathe pure air like the humans do?"

"Of course not," said Etta, her disapproving expression increasing her resemblance to their father. The other sisters wore similar looks, even Eulalia looking a little alarmed at the rapid pace of Estelle's thoughts.

"You've forgotten your lessons, Estelle," continued Etta reprovingly. "The power in the ocean can't affect things outside its realm. Only power from the land can have an effect up there, and we can't access that. There's no way to make a mermaid breathe or speak when out of the water."

"Well, as far as we know," amended Eulalia. "I suppose it's possible there are talismans on the black market that might allow—"

"Nonsense," said Etta sharply, her gaze shooting a warning at Eulalia. "A feat like that would be beyond the power of any talisman. Not that the matter has any relevance to Estelle's question. The creation of talismans is a disgraceful crime, and no member of the royal family would ever consider accessing one."

"Of course," Eulalia agreed, her tone apologetic. "I didn't mean to suggest otherwise, and I'm sure Estelle didn't, either."

She sent her youngest sister an indulgent smile. "Go on, Estelle. Go get your fill."

"Will you come with me?" Estelle asked, shelving her curiosity about the conversation for a time when the surface wasn't so tantalizingly near. "How long will it take us to swim close to the land?"

The head of Estelle's personal guard cleared his throat. "I'm afraid that won't be possible, Your Highness. The emperor's instructions are that you approach no closer than this."

Estelle scowled, disappointed but not surprised. "Were your ascensions this restricted?" she asked her sisters.

They exchanged glances. "Well, no," Eulalia admitted. "But it doesn't matter, Estelle. You've seen the surface. Going closer to land wouldn't gain you much. It's not like you could go up *onto* the land to actually see anything."

Estelle remained silent, feeling disheartened. She appreciated the support her sisters had shown her in making this ascension happen, but it was clear none of them really understood her curiosity. It seemed that everyone but her was fully content with the occasional glimpse of the sky.

"Don't you want to know more about the humans' world?" she asked, unable to help herself. "Don't you wonder about their lives, and what it's like to live out of the water?"

"Why would we?" Eilise asked.

"Well, they're supposed to be much like us, aren't they?" Estelle pressed. "But with such a different environment, who knows how much we might have to learn from them?"

"They're not like us," Emilia said dismissively. "Humans are an inferior species, Estelle. There were good reasons for the decision to withdraw from any contact with the world above. Surely your tutor taught you that."

"Nothing he said was very compelling," Estelle said shortly.

"Estelle, it's questions like this that caused Father to delay your coming of age for half a year," Eulalia reminded her. "I know you're unusually curious by nature, but can't you direct your curiosity at a different target? Father would probably love you to take an interest in the fissures, or investigate one of the rarer species of crustacean."

"But that's not how curiosity works," Estelle protested. "I'm interested in the human world, not the fissures. I can't just decide to change the subject of my interest."

"Estelle, I've stood against Father on your behalf in this matter," Etta said, a stern note to her voice. "But if you keep on like this, you'll make me wonder if he was right. Humans have nothing of substance or value to offer us. On the contrary, they've only ever given us bad things, and getting too close to their world could be dangerous for us."

"Why?" Estelle demanded.

"What if you get tangled up in the nets of their fishermen?" Eilise said. "Or speared by a whaler?"

"Come on, Estelle," said Eulalia coaxingly. "If you want another look, this is the time. Then we should really start our descent."

Estelle glanced around the ring of guards surrounding them, her eyes catching on Demetrius. His inexperience was once again showing. She had no doubt the guards were hearing every word she and her sisters said, but they were all trying to look as though they weren't listening. Only Demetrius wasn't succeeding.

For the briefest of moments, the young merman's eyes met Estelle's, and she had the sudden uncomfortable conviction that he heard more than she'd said. Feeling faintly humiliated, she propelled herself upward, taking a last opportunity to feel the wind in her hair.

She was disappointed at the reminder that she seemed alone in her dissatisfaction with life in the depths of the ocean.

But more than that, she was annoyed with herself for letting that disappointment sully her long-awaited ascension.

Lifting her face to the sunlight, she reminded herself that while she might have no choice but to live in the chill of the seabed, that restrictive life would now be brightened by trips to the surface—as often as she could manage them.

CHAPTER FOUR

Estelle

Estelle barely saw the ornate doors right in front of her face, her thoughts too focused on the world far above her. She pulled up just in time to avoid swimming right into them, casting an embarrassed look at the guards on either side of the doorway.

They were both experienced royal guards, their faces familiar to her in light of the fact that they'd been guarding the royal family since before her eighty-year-old father was born. Neither of them showed the faintest flicker of response to her clumsiness.

When she'd composed herself, one of the guards let out a single baritone note, his voice reverberating through the water. Estelle felt the currents respond, and the door clicked gently open. With a nod of thanks, she swam forward into the vast expanse of the royal ballroom.

The space was filled with merfolk, scales glistening in the light of the luminescent plankton that lined every wall. Glowing jellyfish also moved randomly around the space, their billowing movement seeming in time to the music that resonated throughout the room.

The music came from the merfolk themselves, of course. Anyone who wasn't actively engaged in conversation was either singing or humming, the effortless harmony as necessary a part of any celebratory event as the food. Estelle's heart swelled at the comforting substance of the communal song. It pressed against her ears in a continual reminder of what a special night it was. She was officially coming of age, a full member of the merfolk's empire.

Power swirled invisibly through the water, harnessed by the many servers and guards who were on duty. It was pleasantly warm in the room—after feeling the true warmth of the sun, she'd never been more grateful that some servants were trained in that particular use of power. The glow of the living lanterns was also brighter than she imagined it would be without the magical aid. And she knew that the guards' song wasn't for the purpose of entertainment. They were trained to manipulate the power of the ocean in many indispensable ways, from repelling sharks and other predators to harnessing currents to warn of incoming merfolk.

For no reason she could articulate, Estelle's eyes scanned the guards that lined the room in search of Demetrius. She saw him positioned against the far wall, behind Eulalia and her family. His mouth was open in song, although she couldn't identify his voice among so many. As she watched, he flicked one shoulder slightly, dislodging a curious little cleaner shrimp which must have crawled from the coral wall behind Demetrius, bent on investigation.

Estelle turned away with a smile. She supposed there were reasons such young mermen weren't usually given guard positions, but she was glad they'd made an exception. It was entertaining to watch someone still learning to swallow all visible reactions.

A hush fell as she entered the room, and her parents rose in the water. Instantly the song of the guests ceased, only the background hum of those on duty continuing. All attention flicked to the emperor and empress, and Estelle held herself proudly as her father spoke the formal words of welcome and presentation. As soon as he was finished, the guests burst back into sound, this song one of celebration and congratulation. Estelle added her voice to theirs, her heart light as her sisters swam forward to join her in the center of the enormous room. Soon they were surrounded by many laughing merfolk, and the dancing began.

Estelle surrendered herself to the sensation of motion, the current holding her up as she spun effortlessly. She remembered how it had felt when she'd raised her arm above the water, moving it in a wide arc to see how the air felt. It had been strange and wonderful—there was very little resistance to the movement, and yet the arm had felt so heavy. What would it feel like to dance above the water? Did the humans dance?

She supposed it would be difficult to move gracefully without fins to provide stability and balance. Rising in the water, she performed a somersault, her pale blue hair billowing around her face as she came right way up again, to see Eulalia laughing delightedly back at her.

The first hour of the celebration went by in a blur of dancing and food, Estelle quickly losing count of all the friends and strangers who congratulated her on coming of age. She heard a number of mutters steal through the water about the lack of a betrothal announcement, but she refused to let it trouble her. Not tonight. After all, embarrassed though she might be about the abnormality of it, she thought the extra time of freedom was probably worth the embarrassment. She was in no hurry to be married to a stranger.

She was enjoying a break from the motion, adding her voice to the song from the sidelines with Eulalia, when her parents drifted over to her.

"Well, Estelle," said her mother, smiling at her. "Your father might disclaim sentiment, but I will own up to it. It is strange to think that my youngest has come of age."

Estelle returned her mother's smile. "It's strange for me as well," she admitted. "But it feels like time."

"It is," said Eulalia, giving Estelle's shoulder an encouraging bump. "Time and more."

"Yes, it is past time," their father said, in the closest he'd come to acknowledging the unnecessary delay he'd imposed on Estelle's coming of age. However, the comment was robbed of any hint of apology by his muttered addition. "I would be much better pleased to celebrate it if we had an appropriate betrothal."

"Aefic," scolded his wife. "Can you not put that matter aside for one night?"

"It is an embarrassment to have a daughter unmarried more than half a year past her fifteenth birthday," he said. "She ought to be enlarging the family's honor by allying herself with a powerful province."

"Clearly you can't put it aside, Father," said Eulalia dryly. "But don't ruin this celebration for Estelle. It's not her fault that there are no more provinces in your empire."

"If only our messengers had returned with a more favorable reply," muttered the emperor.

Estelle stared at her father. "Messengers? What messengers? Have you been pursuing a betrothal for me after all, Father?"

Emperor Aefic hesitated as he glanced at her, and she had the impression he hadn't intended to tell her about it. But after a moment, he shook out his long, silver hair, giving a grunt of affirmation.

"I sent messengers to the Dybde Empire a year ago, exploring the idea of a marriage alliance. They returned only days ago, but the response was not encouraging."

"The Dybde Empire?" Estelle repeated, aghast. "But that's so far away! It would take months to get there, if such a perilous journey is even survivable."

"Of course it is," said the emperor dismissively. "The messengers made the swim in only three months, and all but two of them survived. The delay in their return was due to protracted negotiations with the emperor." He scowled. "Who apparently cares little to reopen diplomatic relations with us."

Estelle said nothing, numb with horror over the information that two messengers had died in pursuit of this abhorrent plan for her future. But Eulalia seemed to take the news more calmly.

"It's hardly surprising that they're not interested, Father," said the older mermaid. "It's been hundreds of years since they broke away. I thought we didn't even know if they were still out there."

"Well, they are," said their father shortly. "They settled in the depths, and have apparently made quite a comfortable home for themselves." His brow drew even further together. "And they do not wish to ally themselves with the empire from which they originated."

"The depths?" Estelle repeated the colloquialism through numb lips. "You wish me to move to the depths, probably being eaten by a shark before I could even make it there?"

"Don't be absurd," her father told her. "You would be in no great danger. You would travel with a large pod of guards, as befits your station."

"And how many of them would give their lives on the journey?" Estelle asked passionately. "I'd almost rather get eaten than live in the depths. Father, we're talking about merfolk who've actually chosen to live in the deepest part of the ocean. So far from the sun! You would truly send me there if they allowed it?" She looked appealingly at her mother.

"It is not my wish to have you settled so far from Korallid," her mother said. She glanced at her husband. "Although of course I can see the benefit of an alliance that would so drastically expand our reach."

"Our reach?" The words came out hollow.

"Estelle, be mindful of our surroundings," her mother said sharply.

Realizing how much her voice had risen, Estelle cast a self-conscious look at the guards nearest to them. With a start, she realized that they included Demetrius. She'd forgotten they were so close to Eulalia's guards. Demetrius seemed to be improving in his craft already, because his face was as immobile as a statue of stone, showing no sign that he could hear the conversation, although he surely could.

But any embarrassment Estelle felt at their witnesses was eclipsed by the hurt rocking her. No wonder her father had been so short-tempered with her lately. But how could he be angry at her, when he was the one pursuing this terrible scheme? The revelation of her father's plans for her was more horrible than anything she'd imagined.

"Is that all we are to you, Father?" Estelle asked him, her voice choked with passion. "Opportunities to expand your reach?"

"You speak as though I insult you," said her father impatiently. "But it is the duty and honor of an emperor's daughter to strengthen the empire in this way. None of your sisters ever made such a fuss."

"You never tried to send any of them to the deeps!" Estelle cried. "Father, it's in the very middle of the ocean! Think how cold it would be down there!" A terrifying realization washed over her, regarding her relief at finally being allowed free access to the surface. "There wouldn't even be land in sight, not from any direction," she gasped. "I'd have to travel months to catch a glimpse of it, and I doubt human ships even traverse those waters."

"I've heard more than enough of your obsession with land," said her father, surprising Estelle with the intensity of his anger. "You would reject an alliance with the only other merfolk empire within reach because it's further from the human world? Have you no pride in our kind, in our way of life? In who and what you are?"

"Would I have the option of rejecting it?" Estelle asked, so stunned by the concept that she barely heard the rest of his rebuke.

"Of course not!" her father raged.

"I thought you said they didn't agree to an alliance anyway, Father," said Eulalia placatingly. "So there's no question of Estelle—"

"No question of Estelle contributing anything of value to this family," finished the emperor, still in the grip of his anger.

"That's not what I was going to say," said Eulalia with a scowl.

"If I'm to be burdened with endless daughters, the least they can do is form valuable alliances," the emperor raged. "The rest of you did so effectively. I don't know what we can possibly have done to create such defiance in you, Estelle, or such an unnatural obsession with the humans."

"It's not my fault they rejected the alliance," said Estelle, stung.

The accusation of defiance seemed bitterly unjust to her. She'd been basically compliant all her life, and her father had repaid her for it by trying to send her to the frigid depths of the ocean. Would he tolerate her interest in the human world if she'd been in a position to make a favorable alliance? Or was it the other way around—did he somehow believe that the Dybdeans suspected the offered princess to be unnatural in her interests, and that was why they'd rejected the alliance? Such a concept was nonsense, of course, but she couldn't understand why else her father would be angry with her for the failure of plans in which she'd played no role.

"Of course it's not your fault," said her mother soothingly, shooting a look of irritation at Estelle's father. "Aefic, this isn't the time or place for this discussion. We will simply have to make other plans for Estelle's future. But her coming of age celebration is no place to debate it."

"I've had enough celebration," said Estelle, once again choked with emotion. She wished she could feel the defiance her father ascribed to her. Maybe it would drive away the crushing pain of having it confirmed just how little he valued her. "I think I'll retire early. I'd rather save the energy for tomorrow's ascension."

"Tomorrow's what?" her mother asked blankly.

Estelle stared at her. "I've come of age," she said. "I've had my formal ascension. I'm allowed to go to the surface whenever I wish. I intend to go every day."

"Every day?" Eulalia laughed, the sound a little uneasy. "I assume you're exaggerating to make your point. Surely you don't really intend to go back up tomorrow? It's a long swim to do two days in a row."

"Of course I'm going back up tomorrow," said Estelle. "There's nothing else for me to do, after all. I have nothing of value to offer the empire, so what can it matter how I spend my time?" She cast her father a bitter look. "It seems I might need to make the most of the opportunity while I have it."

"You do not have it," her father said shortly. "Every day, indeed." He shook his head, his silver mane fanning around him. "I allowed the formal ascension today against my better judgment, but I can see that it did not satiate your bizarre obsession with the surface as I was told it would." He cast a meaningful look at Eulalia before his gaze, as hard as stone, returned to Estelle. "Which," he added, "is precisely what I expected. I see my suspicions are correct. You are not ready to be given free access to the surface, and you won't be ready until you overcome this foolish fascination with the humans."

"What?" Estelle felt the color drain from her face, her gaze horrified as it rested on her father's unyielding countenance. "What are you saying, Father? I'm fifteen now, I've officially come of age. You can't deny me my right to break the surface when I choose!"

"I am your father and your emperor," he said flatly. "I can allow or deny whatever I choose."

"Estelle," murmured Eulalia. "I can understand you being rattled by the idea of the deeps, but think about what you're saying. You've seen the surface now. There's nothing exciting there. Surely you don't really want to go up again so soon."

Estelle stared at her sister in disbelief. Nothing exciting? Did Eulalia truly not understand the allure of the world above? Did no one but Estelle? Perhaps she was as much a freak as her father made her feel.

"My decision is final on this matter, Estelle," said the emperor sternly. "You will not ascend while you remain in my household, unless enough years have passed for you to overcome your unnatural obsessions." His voice darkened. "By which time I trust you will have proved your devotion to family and empire by forming a respectable alliance anyway."

Estelle ran shaking hands over her face, fighting the sudden feeling that the coral walls were closing in on her. For a moment she struggled for words, too devastated by the loss of her one comfort to even think straight.

Gentle movement in the water drew Estelle's attention to the space behind Eulalia. An unobtrusive guard changeover was happening, and she saw a solemn-faced, green-tailed merman taking Demetrius's place. Estelle found she couldn't bear for a new contingent of guards to witness her humiliation and distress.

"I need to be alone," she choked out. "I need to retire now. There's nothing left for me to celebrate."

"But, Estelle," her mother protested. "You haven't yet given your public impressions of the surface."

"She will certainly not be doing so," said her father harshly. "Do you think I want her filling more of our subjects' heads with her absurd daydreams about the human world?"

Estelle could barely spare any emotion for her father's rebuke. She had been looking forward to describing her experience to the gathered guests, but she no longer felt any desire to do so.

Without another word, she turned and fled across the room, swimming as blindly as a cavefish in a shaft of sunlight. If her family called her back, she didn't hear them. She suspected her mother would convince her father to let her go. No one wanted a scene in such a public setting.

Blinded by her anguish, she collided with someone in the doorway. A flash of amber scales filled her lowered vision, and she felt embarrassment rush over her afresh as she looked up to realize that it was Demetrius. There was no sign of the other guards who'd been relieved from duty, and she neither knew nor cared why he'd lingered behind. With a murmured apology, she darted past him, painfully aware of his gaze on her back as she swam from the room.

CHAPTER FIVE

Demetrius

Demetrius hovered, indecisive, in the doorway of the ballroom. He was ashamed of his own performance that night. He was supposed to be a guard—stoic, unresponsive to anything but the safety of his charges. So why had he been so rattled by the painful encounter he'd witnessed between the royals?

Princess Estelle's pale, miserable face flashed before his eyes. While objectively he agreed that her situation was unappealing, he refused to let himself feel sympathy for her. That kind of weakness to emotion would make him utterly ineffective as a guard. But there had been something in her eyes that made him pause. She hadn't just looked sad. She'd looked desperate, trapped. He'd seen that look before, many times. He'd aspired to be a guard for as long as he could remember, but he'd still had to assist his father in his chosen vocation throughout most of his childhood. Demetrius's father was a hunter, and Demetrius had traveled far from the inhabited areas of Korallid on their expeditions, hunting all manner of sea creatures.

And if there was one thing he knew, it was the look of a creature that was cornered, with nowhere to go, and no hope of escape. Some creatures in that position would freeze, lacking the intelligence to do more than accept their fate. But others would spring into action, sometimes attempting very desperate things in an effort to escape. Those were the ones he'd always hated to kill, and those experiences were a significant part of what had made him reluctant to become a hunter. He understood that merfolk needed to eat, of course. And he enjoyed the training, and the danger, and the security of carrying a weapon and knowing how to use it. But he figured that as a guard, he could be the one protecting those with fear in their eyes, not creating that fear.

His eyes followed Princess Estelle as she made her way down the corridor with agitated strokes, flanked by two of her usual guards. Her desperation was clear even from this distance, leaving him with one simple question.

What kind of cornered creature was she? One that would hide in her grotto and wait for her inevitable fate, or one whose desperation would drive her to do something foolish, potentially dangerous?

The day before, Demetrius would have guessed the former. But he'd seen her at her ascension. He'd been struck by her eagerness, by the yearning for adventure and exploration he'd seen when she finally reached the world above. Like others, he'd expected her fascination with the unknown to wane as soon as it came within the reach of her experience and lost its mystery.

But it had been clear to him at a glance that nothing could be further from the truth. And her words to her family in the ballroom had confirmed it. Every day? He shook his head slightly, his shoulder-length amber hair swishing against his neck. He'd never encountered such a desire for discovery. It wasn't in the nature of most merfolk.

Reaching a sudden decision, Demetrius swam from the ballroom, turning down the first corridor on his left. He was technically off duty now, but he wouldn't be able to rest with the suspicions that were swirling through his mind. If Princess Estelle came to harm because he'd ignored his instincts, he'd be an utter failure of a guard.

Demetrius emerged into the open ocean, already beginning to hum. His song grew in substance but not in volume as he made his way around the outside of the building. He knew where the royal suites were located, and he came to a stop some distance outside them. He couldn't actually see the windows, as the royal suites all opened onto a private coral garden, its wall curving all the way around in a half sphere that connected with the wall of the palace.

There were regular openings to let in light, and to allow water to move freely into and out of the garden. But Demetrius could hear the songs of other guards, harnessing power to prevent anything from entering the garden through the openings.

Demetrius added his song to theirs, his voice low and melodic as he pulled power from the water around him. He didn't try to block the entrances—others had that task under control. Instead he utilized another type of training he'd received, manipulating the currents to act as messengers. He wanted to sense the movement of any merfolk within the garden.

It seemed no one was currently patrolling the internal area, as at first he felt nothing. Before long, however, his instincts were proved sound when he sensed the vibration of tentative motion. He followed the thread of power, gliding stealthily some distance from the outside of the structure. He didn't want to approach close enough to make the guards on duty think someone was trying to sneak into the private garden. He'd made it halfway around before he saw a slim form slipping through an opening that he wouldn't have thought big enough for a full-grown mermaid.

But there was no mistaking those sparkling blue scales, or the matching hair. As Demetrius had suspected she might, Princess Estelle was sneaking from the palace. The moment she was free from the wall, she darted up through the water with the speed of a startled minnow. Demetrius raced after her, abandoning the idea of going back for assistance out of fear that he'd lose her if he took his eyes off her for a moment. It had been dark now for a couple of hours, and the gloom of the water meant he had to follow close behind to keep her in sight. He considered calling out to her, but she was faster than he'd expected. If she raced off into the night, he might struggle to catch her.

As the princess continued to rise through the water, Demetrius's heart sank. He was fairly sure he knew where she was going, and it wasn't lost on him that she was heading northward. Cleary she was determined not only to break the surface, but to do so closer to the land of the humans than she'd been on her first ascension. Alarm swirled through him as he realized she had a satchel over her shoulder. Just what was she planning to do, and how long was she intending to be at the surface? Perhaps he'd made the wrong decision not to call for help.

Wrong or right, it was too late to change it now. They'd risen rapidly, moving at a diagonal angle, and the palace was far behind them. Steeling himself for a long swim, Demetrius followed the princess for half an hour. He hung back, not wanting her to see him, or hear his song as he occasionally drew on power to repel an approaching predator, or to coax the currents to carry them around some obstacle the princess had failed to anticipate.

He did, however, catch her voice when she at last raised it. She must have felt she was far enough from the palace for her use of power not to draw any attention from the guards who were trained to detect anomalous use. For a moment, Demetrius's strokes slowed, surprised by the sweet clarity of her voice. All mermaids sang, and he'd never heard a voice he considered unpleasant. But Princess Estelle's voice was particularly beautiful. Even in the midst of the anguish he'd read on her countenance, her song radiated hope, and a yearning for life and beauty that no words could ever capture. Embarrassed as he was to admit it even to himself, it moved Demetrius.

His distraction had been poorly timed. Princess Estelle's song had been uttered with purpose. Power swelled around her, the water pushing her upward at a considerably greater speed than her fins could achieve. Demetrius hastened to add his voice, trying to sing quietly as he manipulated the currents in a similar fashion.

In a much shorter time than a fish could swim, Demetrius's ears caught the sound of waves breaking on the surface. He was surprised at how dark the water remained—he'd expected to see the silvery light of the moon before hearing the sounds of the surface. They'd traveled northward as well as upward, and the city of Korallid was now far behind. Demetrius hung back as Princess Estelle broke the surface, taking in the agitation of the water around him. There was a storm above, he realized in surprise. He knew it was summer in the world of the air, and he hadn't expected rough seas. But now he was paying attention, the signs were undeniable. He was doing nothing but treading water, and his own motion was far beyond the normal bobbing of the waves.

Demetrius felt a flicker of interest. He'd been to the surface at night, and during a storm. But never at the same time. What would it look like up there? He could just see Princess Estelle's tail through the gloom, her torso mainly above the waterline. Moving a little distance away from her, he broke the surface himself, fighting the instinct that wanted to keep pulling in breath through his gills.

He realized as soon as he looked around him that he needn't have worried about Princess Estelle seeing him if he came above. The surface of the ocean was nothing like the textured, slightly ridged expanse of the afternoon. He was in a deep valley of wave, able to see very little but the wall of water in front of him.

The swell carried him up and over, and he rode it down the other side, enjoying the storm's chaotic energy. As rain lashed his face, he closed his eyes, welcoming the sensation of powerful water. He received a face full of sea water regularly enough to enable him to take strategic breaths, eliminating the need to dive below.

He opened his eyes only as he once again crested a giant wave, and received a shock. There before him, alarmingly close, was a huge dark shape, riding a rising wave with unsteady speed. He'd never seen one with his own eyes before, but he had no difficulty recognizing a human ship. And it took only a moment to realize it was bearing down on him.

Demetrius dove back under, taking in a steadying pull of water. Suddenly, he remembered what had brought him to the surface in the first place, and his eyes darted frantically around the gloom in search of Princess Estelle. He could see no sign of her, and he struck out in alarm, angling down to give the hull of the ship a wide berth.

"Princess!" he called, no longer concerned about hiding his presence. This was exactly the type of catastrophe he'd feared when he saw her sneaking off. "Your Highness, where are you?"

He heard no reply over the sound of the crashing waves above, and he dove deeper, hoping the princess had caught sight of the ship and fled to safer waters. Based on what he knew of her, however, he doubted it, and his eyes were soon directed up toward the surface again. To his relief, a silvery flash of fins caught his eye, on the other side of the ship.

Demetrius raced up toward it, groaning at how close he had to go to the ship to get to her. If she hadn't been born royal, this mermaid was fearless enough to train as a guard, he thought ruefully.

By the time he reached the point where he'd seen her fins, Princess Estelle was gone. Drawing in a preparatory breath through his gills, Demetrius broke the surface again. The ship was so close he could hear the creaking groan of the wood over the storm. It was cutting through the water at a rapid pace, its sails reefed against the gale, and figures scurrying across its surface.

Demetrius didn't even spare a thought for his first glimpse of humans. He was too busy searching the tossing surface for the princess. With a surge of relief, he saw her, her azure hair plastered against her face as she rode the waves up and down. She was swimming sideways, keeping pace with the ship, and her eyes were fixed unblinkingly on the deck. Demetrius paused, momentarily taken aback by her expression. It was just like the look she'd worn at dinner the night before, when her father announced that her ascension would go ahead. It had reminded him of a child receiving some delightful surprise, and he was struck once again by just how young the princess was.

"Your Highness!"

The shout came from the ship, and Demetrius froze, for one horrified and nonsensical moment thinking that Princess Estelle had been seen and recognized by the humans. But as his eyes found the sailor who'd cried out over the gale, he realized the man's attention was not on the water, but on a lithe figure on deck, leaning over the pitching railing. It was hard to get a good look at him through the driving rain, but he looked young and enthusiastic.

A little like Princess Estelle, Demetrius thought wryly.

"Prince Farrin!" The sailor's shout could again be heard. "You need to get safely below!"

"Farrin, what are you doing?" The new voice came from another young human, this one charging across the deck. "Do you want to drown on your own birthday? We're all supposed to be below deck!"

"I know, I know, I'm coming." The one leaning over the railing turned, his sopping hair flicking as he did. "It's just so fascinating."

"Farrin, you're my brother, and I love you, but sometimes you have about as much sense as a peahen."

The one at the railing laughed, and Demetrius turned his attention back to Princess Estelle, uninterested in the banter of the human brothers. She was watching everything with wide-eyed fascination, and still hadn't even noticed him. He began to swim toward her, intending to get her attention, when a chorus of shouts from the ship brought his head whipping back around, once again concerned the princess had been seen.

But it wasn't Princess Estelle who'd caused the alarm. It was the young man at the railing. The ship had pitched violently, and as Demetrius watched, the human toppled backward over the edge. Limbs flailing, he fell like a stone, straight into the seething ocean below.

"FARRIN!" The other young man was already sprinting toward the railing, only prevented from diving after his brother by the three fully grown men who converged on him, pinning him bodily to the deck.

"No, Prince Emmett!" one cried in clear desperation. "If you go in, you'll be lost, too!"

"Let me go!" the prince screamed. "Farrin! FARRIN!"

Demetrius cast his gaze toward the water, realizing with a jolt that there was no longer any sign of Princess Estelle. He dove below, his eyes rapidly scanning the gloom. A flash of turquoise was visible far below, and he hastened to follow it. As he caught up to the princess, he saw that she was speeding downward as if being chased. His eyes darted ahead of her, and he groaned as he realized that she was the one doing the chasing. The form of the young human was sinking steadily, still thrashing as he tried with no success to find his way to the surface.

"Princess!" Demetrius called, but if the mermaid heard him, she gave no sign. She must have taken some time to find the human prince in the water, because he was still a long way below her, and Demetrius saw his movements begin to slow. He remembered that humans could survive only a very short time under the water, their bodies unable to get breath except in pure air. Clearly it was a lost cause—the princess would be wisest to abandon the whole foolish rescue attempt and return to her own world, where she was safe.

But Princess Estelle showed no sign of giving up. The water was suddenly filled with the sound of her voice, and again Demetrius slowed in spite of himself, captivated by the beauty of the sound. She was harnessing the power in the ocean to slow the prince's descent, and speed herself up. Her technique might be clumsy, untrained as she was, but her song was powerful, he'd give her that. Not many mermaids her age could do both of those things at once in such tumultuous waters.

The human had gone still when Princess Estelle finally reached him, but she didn't let it deter her. Wrapping her arms around his torso, she shot upward, her tail working frantically as she made for the distant surface. Her song was a little panicked now, as she obviously sensed that the human didn't have as much time as it would take her to get him to the air.

Demetrius caught up to her when she was about halfway to her goal.

"Princess, what are you doing?"

Princess Estelle started, her song faltering as her eyes settled on him. She still kept swimming upward, however.

"Demetrius?" she asked. "What are you doing here?"

Hiding his surprise that she'd remembered his name, Demetrius tried to assume the stern expression of a more senior guard.

"Following you to make sure you came to no harm, Your Highness. And I feel bound to tell you, embroiling yourself in anything to do with humans is likely to bring you to harm."

"Well, what else can I do?" she demanded. "Leave him to drown?"

Demetrius gave no answer, but she seemed to read his opinion on his face. He was really going to have to work on that.

"You would truly let him die?" she demanded, her eyes wide with a shock that Demetrius felt more than he cared to admit.

"It's the natural way of things," he said gruffly. "Humans cannot live in water. If they become stranded in the ocean, they die. Just as we would die were we stranded above the surface."

The princess's face set in determination. With a little shake of her head, she sent her blue tresses swirling. "He's not going to die. I'm going to save him." Her expression faltered, a hint of desperation coming through and once again highlighting her youth. "Please, Demetrius. Won't you help me?"

All Demetrius's training—both in terms of the duties of a guard, and the appropriate attitude of a merman toward humans—told him to ignore the appeal in those hopeful eyes. But to his chagrin, he didn't seem capable of it.

Too annoyed with his own weakness to actually articulate his decision, he just began to sing, his voice gruff as he reached for the power around them, using it to propel the swimming mermaid and her burden upward more quickly. Her face lightening in relief, Princess Estelle began to sing again as well, and

Demetrius couldn't help but notice how perfectly their voices mingled together as they shot upward through the water. In moments, they'd reached the surface, three heads breaking into the air.

Princess Estelle's gaze flew frantically around the stormy waters, her eyes alarmed as they latched on to Demetrius's. Struggling to hold the human's head above the water, she submerged her face.

Demetrius did the same, her panicked voice reaching his ears the moment they were below.

"Where's the ship?"

"Long gone by now, probably," he responded impassively. "We were under a while, and the ship was moving fast. I have no idea what direction it traveled."

"But what am I going to do with him?" she demanded.

Demetrius shrugged. "Release him to the fate in which you intervened, I suppose."

"Never," said the princess, with all the passion of a fifteen-year-old. "There's only one thing to do. I'll have to take him to shore."

She bobbed back above, her eyes scanning the human anxiously. Again following her, Demetrius saw that while the prince remained unconscious, he seemed to be breathing. Apparently his body was still capable of taking in air.

Her face once again filled with determination, Princess Estelle started to swim awkwardly backward, hugging the unconscious human's back against her chest as she tugged him along.

With a sigh, Demetrius tapped her shoulder and pointed, indicating that she was going the wrong way for land. Looking disgruntled, she spun around, following the trajectory of his gesture. Restricted to surface level as she was, her progress was painfully slow, and the human kept getting hit in the face with seawater as the princess struggled through the waves.

Demetrius's eyes caught on a rocky outcropping sticking up from the water not far away. Resigned to seeing the rescue through, he once again touched the princess to get her attention. She nodded when she saw where he was pointing and changed course. Soon they'd reached the stone island, and Demetrius helped her drag the prince's form onto it.

"We won't get far on the surface in this storm," he told her, when they'd both dropped below the water again. "We'll just have to stay here until it calms. Then it will be much easier to carry him to shore."

"Will he survive that long?" Princess Estelle asked anxiously.

Demetrius shrugged. "I don't know. If he lives, he lives. If not, we did what we could."

She didn't seem entirely satisfied, but there was nothing more to say. Pulling in a preparatory breath through her gills, she surfaced once again, no doubt to keep watch over her human prize. Demetrius, on the other hand, had no desire to stare at the unconscious human. He was already tired, and it would likely be a long time before he could sleep. Watching someone else while they were unconscious wouldn't help him stay awake.

With that in mind, he stayed below the waves, his eyes fixed on the silver fins of the princess as he wondered just how much he was going to regret his part in her misadventure.

CHAPTER SIX

Estelle

Estelle hovered nervously by the miniature island, her eyes searching the human's face as he lay motionless across the rocks. Farrin, the other humans had called him. Estelle tried the name out when she ducked below to breathe. It had a beautiful sound.

An amber tail came into view, and she realized that Demetrius was hovering closer than she'd thought. Her cheeks warmed with embarrassment when she saw his impatient expression. He'd obviously heard her saying the human's name to herself.

"Still breathing, is he?" the young guard asked unemotionally.

Estelle nodded. "From what I can tell."

He grunted. "It's unusual to have such a violent storm this time of year. I'm guessing it will pass soon."

Estelle nodded again, hastening back to the surface without another word. Somehow the company of the unconscious human above was less confronting than the shrewd gaze of the merman below. Pulling herself as far up the rock as she could, she examined the young man thoughtfully. Was it uncomfortable for a human to have the rain pound his face like that? He was used to being dry, she supposed.

Once he gave a low moan, but other than that, the only sign of life was the steady rise of his chest as he breathed. As the hours slipped by, Estelle struggled with the sleep that wanted to claim her, terrified that if she took her eyes from the prince, he'd slip into the water and drown.

Thankfully, Demetrius's guess proved correct, and the storm blew over quickly. The dawn was still a few hours away when the waters calmed and the sky cleared enough that Estelle could see distant lights in the direction of the land.

She ducked below again, but there was no need to tell Demetrius her thoughts.

"It's time," he said, with a curt nod. "If you're sure you want to do this, there's no more reason to delay."

"I'm sure," she said impatiently. Trying her best to be gentle, she tugged the human prince back into the water. With difficulty, she hoisted him so that his head was above water as she started to swim toward shore.

Her head bobbed below the surface, to be met with the sight of Demetrius watching her, his expression long-suffering.

"Let me," he said, resignation clear in his voice. Taking the human from Estelle, Demetrius maneuvered so that the human was laid across him, back-to-back. Prince Farrin's face remained out of the water, but Demetrius was still able to swim face down. Estelle swam alongside Demetrius, watching carefully to make sure the human's face stayed out of the water.

Demetrius wasn't swimming as quickly as she was sure he could, since he could only use his tail while his hands steadied the human on his back. But he moved steadily toward the shore. Every now and then, Estelle took a turn carrying the human, to give Demetrius a rest. But the merman always retrieved the burden quickly. Estelle wasn't sure if he'd softened to the idea of saving the human's life, or if he was just trying to fulfill his duty as a guard to shield her from unnecessary danger or effort.

For a long time, the land didn't seem to be getting any closer. Then, quite suddenly, it was looming ahead of them.

"They called him a prince," Estelle said, swimming belly up underneath Demetrius, the better to speak to him. "So I suppose we should take him to the castle. I think I caught a glimpse of it at my ascension."

Demetrius grunted. "If you can see it now, lead the way."

Taking the hint that he was flagging, Estelle resurfaced, her eyes finding the elaborate structure perched on top of a cliff. Her eyes widened as she took in the impressive sight, growing sharper in the approaching dawn. It was beautiful, like nothing she'd ever seen underwater.

An insistent splash from Demetrius's fins told her he wanted her attention, and she went back under to speak to the guard.

"We mustn't let anyone see us," he said firmly. "We'll leave him on the shore and go, understand?"

She raised an eyebrow. "Shouldn't I be giving you orders, since I'm the royal and you're the guard?"

His expression was so deeply unimpressed that she couldn't help letting out a gurgling laugh.

"I was only teasing," she said. "I've never given anyone orders in my life." She sighed, her voice dropping to a mutter. "And in spite of what people think, being royal is mainly about taking orders yourself."

Looking up, she saw that Demetrius was watching her with an uncomfortably piercing expression, and she hastened to change the subject.

"I think I saw a sort of cliff jutting out into the ocean on one side of the castle. If we leave him on the far side of that, I doubt anyone will see us."

Demetrius nodded, following as Estelle swam in the right

direction. By the time they rounded the cliff in question, the sky was noticeably lighter. Estelle assisted Demetrius to roll the prince off his back, and the two of them heaved him up onto a sandy beach.

She saw the guard look sharply along the shore, but no one was in sight. Demetrius tugged firmly on her arm, encouraging her to come back under, but Estelle couldn't help lingering. She pulled herself across the sand, draping her body on the shore next to the human as she studied his features. He was starting to stir, which was encouraging. She searched his face, marveling at the differences between their kinds. He had no gills, and his nose arched out from his face much more prominently than hers. There were holes in it, presumably to take in pure air, but there were only two, and they were much wider than gills.

His hair had begun to dry, thanks to Demetrius's clever method of keeping him mostly above water. Consequently, Estelle could see in the growing light that he had golden hair. She glanced down his form, unthinkingly looking for the matching scales of his tail, to be met with the sight of two strong legs, ending in booted feet. Marveling at the phenomenon, she looked back at his face, noting how closely his hair was cropped. The short length—something she'd never seen among merfolk—allowed only the slightest of curls to show. His skin was nearly as pale as hers, and of course she couldn't see the color of his eyes, although she had no doubt they would be beautiful.

Because everything about him was beautiful. He was the most captivating sight she'd ever seen. She'd heard his words on the ship, as well, and his cheerful laughter. He'd been happy, carefree, brave. She'd even seen the light of adventure in his eyes as he leaned over the railing, in defiance of his instructions. Did he yearn for the sea the way she yearned for the surface?

Longing welled up in Estelle, for this handsome human and the world he represented. A world where brothers were so close in age they looked the same, and even as grown men felt no hesitation to express their love for one another. A world where she would be able to feel the light of the sun on her face every day.

The sensation was so intense, Estelle could find no word for it. It was both unbearable and unutterably wonderful at the same time. She stared at Prince Farrin, her heart so full she thought it might burst. She was starting to burn for breath, but she stayed where she was on the sand. How could she bear to ever leave his side?

A sharp tug on her fin forced her to pull her attention from the stirring human. Demetrius had crawled half up the sand, and his eyes were wide in warning as he gestured to her. Following his gaze, she saw a figure walking along the ridge of the cliff above, the section that jutted out into the ocean like a pointing finger. His head was currently hung very low, but if he looked their way, he'd see them for certain.

Estelle cast one last longing glance at Prince Farrin's peaceful face, then yielded at last to the pressure of Demetrius's grip. Wriggling backward across the sand, she slipped into the sea, pulling water in through her gills with a shudder.

"Come on," said Demetrius curtly. "Let's get further out."

She shook her head. "Wait. I want to make sure they find him."

"Your Highness," said Demetrius warningly. "You've taken enough risks."

"We," she corrected him. "You're in it with me now, whether you like it or not. So no more of this *Your Highness* business. My name is Estelle."

"Princess," Demetrius protested. "I'm a member of the royal guard. I can't call you by—"

"Don't take this the wrong way," she interrupted him, "but if you were a proper royal guard, you would have dragged me back to the palace the moment you found me."

Demetrius fell silent, apparently having no answer. Still lying horizontally in the shallows, Estelle turned her attention back to the surface above. She'd just heard a voice cry out, and she peered wistfully through the water.

"Farrin! Farrin, wake up! Talk to me!"

The man from the cliff above had stumbled down to the beach somehow, and he was gripping the prince's form in his arms.

"That's his brother," murmured Estelle. "From the ship, remember?"

"I remember," said Demetrius, apparently unmoved by the touching scene.

"Look how similar they are," Estelle said. "I would have guessed they were the same age."

"It is curious," Demetrius agreed, seeming interested in spite of himself. "I believe human fertility works differently from ours."

"It would be nice, wouldn't it?" Estelle said, her eyes on the forms above the water. "To have siblings close in age like that, and grow up together?"

Demetrius was silent for a moment, and she could feel his eyes on her. "Yes," he said at last.

From the little Estelle could see through the lapping waterline above, Prince Farrin was stirring. His brother seemed almost beside himself with relief, and Estelle felt a rush of gladness that she'd intervened in the grim fate the young prince had been headed toward. Hard behind the thought was the memory of the fate her father had planned for her. Perhaps she was being dramatic—she knew the deeps weren't really equivalent to death—but she couldn't help wishing that her sisters, even her mother, had shown half the inclination to rescue her that this brother had for Prince Farrin.

"Do you think he'll be all right?" she asked Demetrius anxiously.

"That's really not our concern," the young guard said, his tone discouraging.

Ignoring his negative attitude, Estelle lifted her voice, releasing a song of healing and hope. But she could tell it was fruitless. The power swirled readily around her, drawn from the depths of the ocean. But as she sent it out toward the beached prince, she could feel that the power didn't reach him. Like Etta had said during her ascension, it stayed within the boundaries of the ocean from which it came.

"Come on, Prin—Estelle," Demetrius changed course at a look from her.

"I wish I never had to leave," Estelle said impulsively. "I could have looked at him forever. He's so beautiful. Didn't you think so?"

Demetrius gave an incredulous snort. "Beautiful? Didn't you see that protrusion on his face? And the way his hair was hacked away? And those stumps sprouting from his body?"

Estelle gave him a chastising look. "That's how humans' noses are supposed to be. And they're called legs, as I'm sure you know." Her eyes strayed back to the surface. "And I thought his hair looked good that way."

Demetrius actually rolled his eyes. "If you're finished mooning over a human, don't you think you'd better get back to the palace before the whole of Korallid is thrown into an uproar by your disappearance?"

"I wasn't mooning," Estelle said defensively. And unconvincingly.

With reluctance, she turned from the surface, following Demetrius toward deeper water. For several minutes, they swam in silence, and Estelle's thoughts remained on the world above. She'd been so tantalizingly close to the shore, within view of the human castle, and she hadn't so much as caught a glimpse of the trees, or heard a single bird sing. She'd had to abandon the place she most longed to see just as the sun rose to reveal it.

But as the surface faded away and the familiar underwater world pressed in on her, her mind caught up with what Demetrius had said. Was she swimming back into a terrible mess at the palace? Memories flooded back to her of the disastrous celebration hours before, and the things her father had said. When she'd fled her room, intent on nothing but reaching the once again forbidden surface, she'd half intended never to return.

But things had changed now. A sideways glance at Demetrius, swimming silently alongside her, sobered her further. She couldn't just flee into the ocean, not when he was implicated now. How he'd seen her leaving, she had no idea. She'd thought she was being very careful. And why he'd followed her, and helped her rather than forcing her back home, was even harder to comprehend. But she was grateful that he'd done so, and she didn't want to end his career when it had barely begun. If she'd fled, and Demetrius had been in any way implicated, the emperor wouldn't hesitate to banish him, or worse.

Besides, the hours that had passed had calmed Estelle's initial storm of emotion, and she was ready to accept the truth she'd known all along. She wasn't capable of surviving alone in the open ocean. If she truly fled, she would die within the week.

If she could go up on land, of course...

She cut the thought off before it could grow. It was an impossibility, and dwelling on the dream would only make reality more unbearable.

"You were there last night," she said, her sudden speech

seeming to startle Demetrius. "You were floating nearby when Eulalia and I spoke with our parents, weren't you?"

Demetrius met her gaze, his amber eyes, so similar in tone to his scales, once again seeming to see more than she would wish.

"Yes." His expression was hard to read. "I've been assigned to guard Princess Eulalia during her visit."

Estelle nodded. She'd gathered as much. Her insides squirmed at the thought that this capable young guard had witnessed her humiliation. Did he think as her father did, that thanks to the rejection by the Dybde Empire, she had nothing of value to offer her family or her empire? If nothing else, he must think her childish for the way she'd fled her own celebration.

"I suppose you think I'm very foolish," she said, with a touch of defiance.

The guard took a moment to answer, his expression undergoing no change. "Those aren't my words."

This stiff and unconvincing disavowal sent fresh embarrassment through Estelle. Trying to mask it, she tossed her head dismissively, reaching for the power around her as she crafted her song. In moments, she was cutting through the water at an improbable speed, trying to pretend she wasn't watching Demetrius for guidance as to which direction to take.

The guard's voice joined hers, and he kept pace with apparent ease. As the seabed began to look familiar, he paused in his song to address her.

"Do we assume you will have been missed?"

"Not necessarily," Estelle replied. "I told my attendants I didn't wish to be disturbed until late in the morning. I may be able to sneak back in the way I came, with no one any the wiser."

Demetrius nodded, looking relieved.

Estelle cleared her throat, not quite able to meet his eye. "No one but you, that is. Do you...do you intend to tell my father what happened?"

The silence stretched out so long that Estelle was unable to resist stealing a glance at her companion. Demetrius wasn't watching her, his gaze straight ahead, and his lips set in a thin line.

"No," he said at last, his voice gruff.

Relief poured through Estelle, made all the more potent by her surprise. "Thank you," she murmured, not knowing what else to say. Demetrius probably had no concept of how huge a gift he was giving her. She knew that if her father ever learned of her activities that night, the consequences would be dire. She'd be lucky to ever be allowed to leave the palace again, let alone approach the surface.

Demetrius didn't answer, instead raising his deep voice in a quiet song. Estelle had received very little training in magic, but she could feel the power responding to his direction. Knowing he was a guard, she would guess that he was conducting a simple search of the water ahead, checking if the way was clear.

Apparently it was, because they reached the outside of the palace without incident. Estelle hastened back toward the spherical wall of the private garden, noting how Demetrius hovered until she'd made it through. It was early enough that the garden was still deserted, and she was able to enter her room unseen. She sank gratefully into her sleeping hollow, more than ready to finally succumb to her exhaustion. Her last thought as she drifted into sleep was of a pale human face, surrounded by short tawny hair, made golden by the unfiltered light of the sun.

CHAPTER SEVEN

Estelle

It took days for Estelle to fully relax after her midnight adventure and be convinced that her absence truly hadn't been noticed, and that Demetrius was keeping her secret as promised.

Not that she had much attention to waste on fear during that time. She was too caught up in thoughts of the surface, and of the human prince. She dreamed about it every night, the visions a potent mix of memory and longing. She could think of nothing else.

She knew better than to bring up the topic of the surface in front of her family, of course. The family still ate meals all together, although her visiting sisters would soon be returning to their homes. Estelle barely even felt any sorrow at Eulalia's imminent departure. The joys and struggles of the underwater world seemed far away and unimportant in the wake of her all-consuming obsession with the world above.

The emperor, convinced by his advisors to take some time to cool down before sending a further envoy to the Dybde Empire, continued to swim around the palace with short, tense strokes. He never discussed the proposed alliance with Estelle—he barely spoke to her—and she was glad. She had no interest in a future in the deeps, and she didn't think she'd be able to hide her distaste.

Estelle occasionally saw Demetrius, shadowing Eulalia according to his instructions. Although they never spoke, their eyes met from time to time, the knowledge of their shared secret passing between them. The sensation was unexpectedly pleasant, and made Estelle feel slightly less alone.

It wasn't enough, however, to calm the tumult of emotion that was growing within Estelle with each passing day. She hardly knew how she could go on without another glimpse of the surface, and the human prince. Remembering the reunion she'd witnessed between the two brothers, she began to play with an idea, turning it over in her mind. Pursuing her strategy, she went to bed a little later each night, so as to occasion no remark when she slept later in the morning. Beyond the odd chastising comment from her mother regarding her lazy mornings, no one seemed to especially notice. After all, Estelle thought bitterly, she had nothing of value to contribute to palace life, and nothing useful to do with her time. What did it matter if she slept the mornings away?

She didn't actually feel any desire to sleep in. It was all part of a plan which came to fruition a week after her coming of age celebration. She'd retired to bed late, as usual, but although she settled into her sleeping hollow, she didn't sleep. She waited a few hours, until all sounds of palace life had disappeared, leaving only the constant crackling hum of the ocean. Moving silently and cautiously, Estelle slipped from her room into the private garden, then out into the open ocean. Hardly believing her own boldness, she streaked upward into the dark waters, her heart in her throat.

As soon as she considered it safe, she raised her voice, harnessing the power around her to propel her rapidly upward. She had to pause her ascent twice to clumsily attempt to use repelling power when she thought she caught a glimpse of a predator. Whether it worked, or whether she'd been mistaken, she wasn't sure, but she reached the surface without mishap.

Her heart soared as her head broke into the crisp pre-dawn air. She'd timed her ascent well, and the first smudge of dawn could be seen away to her right. In front of her, the land of the humans was visible, the castle perched proudly atop the low cliff.

Moving with eager strokes, Estelle reached the place where she'd left Prince Farrin, settling against a rock just under the surface to watch. To her utter delight, it wasn't long before she once again saw a figure strolling along the clifftops. She was even more overjoyed to recognize the man not as the older prince but as *her* prince, Prince Farrin. His head wasn't bent in sorrow like his brother's had been. He was surveying the ocean with bright eyes, his lips pursed in a sound that reminded her of a narwhal's whistle.

He was beautiful.

Estelle's eyes drank him in, unable to get enough of the sight. What was he thinking? Did some part of his mind remember her, and their frantic nighttime swim? Was he looking out at the ocean with longing, the way she looked up at the surface?

Once again, she felt she could have looked at him forever, but she didn't have that option. By the time he turned back toward his castle, Estelle knew she was cutting it close. She may have trained her attendants to expect her to sleep late, but they wouldn't leave her alone all morning.

The moment Prince Farrin disappeared from sight, Estelle turned, pushing her way through a waving bed of seaweed and darting into a canyon beyond. It wrenched her heart to return to the deeper ocean, but the pain was lessened by the knowledge that she'd be back soon enough.

The meager hours of sleep Estelle managed before she was woken by her attendants weren't sufficient to stop her yawning for half the day, but she didn't mind in the least. At first, she thought no one else had even noticed, but partway through the midday meal, she felt the unmistakable sensation of someone's gaze on her. Glancing up, she saw Demetrius watching her suspiciously. She sent him a small smile, attempting to look innocent, and his eyes narrowed further.

Feeling a flush rising, Estelle returned her gaze to her food, her thoughts defiant. It was no affair of his, after all.

Most inconveniently, Demetrius didn't seem to agree. Estelle was sure he didn't usually fill the duty of Eulalia's guard for both the midday and the evening meal in one day, but it was impossible to miss his lithe upright form when the family convened to eat before bed. As usual, Estelle lingered as long as anyone, and this time, so did the young guard. His eyes seemed to be on Estelle more often than on his charge, and it was all Estelle could do not to fidget.

When she snuck from her room as she had the night before, she moved with more speed than stealth, her main priority to put the maximum distance between herself and the castle as soon as possible.

Her instinct hadn't failed her. She'd barely cleared the area when her skin prickled with the certainty of being followed. Spinning around, she spotted a flash of amber scales approaching through the gloom.

"I knew it!" Demetrius said grimly. "I knew you were sneaking out again."

"So glad you could join me," Estelle said innocently.

His eyes were once again narrowed. "Enough fooling around. You're coming back to the palace now."

"I'm not," she contradicted.

"Estelle," he said sternly, surprising her a little by taking the license she'd given him to use her name. "If you won't come with me, I'll rouse the guards."

"If you do that," she countered, "I'll tell everyone that this isn't the first time you came with me to the surface at night, and that you failed to notify anyone last time."

Demetrius's scowl told her she had him stumped. "Would you really be so vindictive?" he demanded.

"Your threat to turn me in to the guards feels just as vindictive to me," Estelle assured him.

Demetrius considered this in silence for a moment. "How many times have you made this journey on your own?"

"Just once," Estelle told him. Her voice turned eager. "I remembered how Farrin's brother was walking along the shore at dawn that time, and thought maybe it's common for human princes. And I was right! Farrin was there last time, walking all alone."

"Did he see you?" Demetrius asked, clearly alarmed.

Estelle shook her head regretfully. "I stayed below the surface."

"Thank the tides for that," muttered Demetrius.

Estelle let out a sigh. "I wish I could speak to him properly," she said. Her voice dropped to a murmur. "I wonder if Eulalia is right, and there are talismans that would make it possible."

"Talismans?" Demetrius repeated, aghast.

Estelle's eyes snapped to his, regretting her hasty words. "Not that I would really consider using a talisman," she said quickly. "Even if I knew where to find one, which I don't. I know it's an abominable practice."

Demetrius looked visibly relieved and, considering him, Estelle reflected that he might be more willing than her sisters to answer her questions candidly.

"Why *is* it such an abominable practice, though?" she asked.

Demetrius's brow creased a little. "Don't you understand how talismans are made?"

Estelle shook her head, her embarrassment at her lack of magical training eclipsed by the hope of finally getting answers.

"Well, you know that all merfolk can use our song to channel the power of the ocean through our bodies," Demetrius said.

She nodded, eager to demonstrate that she wasn't completely uninformed. "And release it to the purpose of our choice. At least, when we've actually been properly trained," she muttered, regretful over the restriction that required royals to wait longer than everyone else to receive that training.

"We all have different capacities," Demetrius went on. "Some can access power more easily than others, and release it more strongly. It's a partnership between us and the ocean, I suppose. And it's generally accepted that each mermaid or merman can access the level of power commensurate with their capacity. It wouldn't be safe or wise for them to have more than they could handle."

"What does this have to do with talismans?" Estelle prompted, impatient.

Demetrius gave her a look. "I was getting to that. We can only channel the magic in the moment, as we sing, right? Well, to create a talisman someone would have to store the magic, to be used at a different time from when it was accessed. Potentially even by a different individual."

"Hence the black market," Estelle mused. "Merfolk buying talismans that would allow them to use magic they haven't themselves accessed."

Demetrius nodded. "That's right. They're circumventing the natural protections around the use of power, and it's neither responsible nor safe."

"But *how* can magic be stored?" Estelle asked.

"I'm not a criminal, I don't know the process," Demetrius said, sounding a little offended. "All I know is that it's totally separate from channeling power through song. It involves literally mining magic from the seabed."

"Fascinating," said Estelle. "I'd no idea that was even possible."

"Well, now you do," said Demetrius in clipped tones. "All right, I've given you your magic lesson." He angled his body back the way they'd come. "Time to return to the palace."

"Not in a thousand tides," said Estelle flatly.

Demetrius scowled at her. "Don't be unreasonable."

"Demetrius, I'm not going back before I've been to the surface," she said.

The simple and unemotional declaration seemed to convince Demetrius that she was in earnest. The young guard groaned. "Can I really not persuade you to come back?"

"Definitely not." Estelle turned her shoulder on him, propelling herself toward the distant surface. She'd wasted enough time already.

Still grumbling, Demetrius followed.

He did the same the next night, and the next.

Estelle had no idea when he slept, because he seemed to bear the wakeful nights better than she did. For her part, she was a little surprised to find that she didn't mind his company. She also had to acknowledge that his guard training was useful in keeping them both safe during their nighttime swims.

To Estelle's delight, Prince Farrin could reliably be found walking the cliffs every morning, just after dawn. In her daily visits to watch him, Estelle finally got the chance to examine more of the shoreline. The cliffs were low and sandy, nothing like the jagged underwater ravines of Estelle's home. Trees dotted the top of the slope, and birds swooped around the beach in the early morning. It was magical, but it was only the barest glimpse. Estelle found that, far from satiating her curiosity, it only made her eager for more.

"What type of trees are they?" she demanded of Demetrius, as they hovered in the shallows just before dawn, a week after her solitary trip.

"I have no idea," said Demetrius flatly. "And I don't especially care."

Estelle rolled her eyes. "Where's your sense of discovery, Demetrius?"

"Far below the waterline," he responded promptly. "Where yours should be."

Estelle eyed him, unconvinced. "And yet, you join me every morning," she challenged him. "Don't think I haven't seen you examining the land."

"I'm looking for threats," Demetrius said. "For your protection."

Estelle shook her head, not entirely satisfied. But a moment later, movement above them pushed everything else from her mind. "There he is!" she cried.

Demetrius looked less impressed than ever as his gaze followed hers. "I really can't understand what you find so extraordinary about this human," he said. "I suppose he's a prince, but given you're a princess, I wouldn't have thought you would be so impressed by that."

"Him being a prince has nothing to do with it," said Estelle, offended by the suggestion. "It's not his status. It's just...him." She watched Prince Farrin hungrily. "Can't you see it in his eyes? Don't you think he longs for something more, just like I do? I think he might even remember me."

Demetrius's snort brought her back to reality. "Remember you? He wasn't conscious for a single second of the time you were interacting with him."

Estelle scowled. "We don't know that for sure. Why else would he be gazing out at the sea every morning?"

"Because it's a nice view?" Demetrius said prosaically. "Much more beautiful than anything they have on land."

Estelle elbowed him in the ribs, a gesture which drew no reaction whatsoever from the stoic merman.

"You don't have an ounce of romance in you, do you?" she accused him.

That at last provoked a response. Demetrius's eyes were startled as he looked at her. "Romance? Tell me that's not how you think of this prince!"

Estelle bit her lip, regretting her words as she felt heat rising up her cheeks. "I...well...he is very—"

"Very human," Demetrius finished, looking more incredulous than ever. "Estelle, you can't be serious."

Something about his scornful tone sent defiance shooting through Estelle.

"I've never been more serious in my life," she snapped. "I'm in love with him."

Demetrius's mouth actually fell open. "In love?" he repeated. "You've never even spoken to him."

"Yes I have," said Estelle obstinately.

Demetrius's look was painfully pitying. "You've never spoken *with* him, then. If he doesn't hear it, it doesn't count."

Estelle glowered at him, even as she knew her embarrassment was her own fault. She should never have shared her secret. Until now it had been something precious and beautiful, hidden deep in her heart. But now that it was in the open, Demetrius was making it seem childish and foolish.

"You clearly don't understand love," she said, with a weak attempt at loftiness.

"Not that kind of love, no," said Demetrius frankly. "I've never felt it."

"And likely never will, with a heart as cold as yours," Estelle shot back.

Demetrius shrugged. "Maybe." His gaze became stern. "But you don't understand it any more than I do, Estelle, and your mooning over that prince shows it."

"I'm not mooning!" Estelle protested.

"You are." There was no softness in Demetrius's tone. "I'm done with this. I'm not going to help you come up here if that's your game. He's a *human*, Estelle. You can't even breathe the same air as each other." His gaze became confused as it passed over her. "Why would you want to be in love, anyway? From what I've heard, you can't choose who you'll marry."

"Thanks for the reminder," Estelle snapped. Forgetting even to send a wistful goodbye look toward Prince Farrin, she flicked her fins, propelling herself back to deeper water.

Demetrius quickly caught up to her, his voice a little less hard. "I'm sorry," he said. "I didn't mean to upset you. But it's the truth, isn't it? Why would you want to torment yourself?"

"If you'd ever felt this type of *torment*, you wouldn't need to ask," Estelle told him simply.

For a time, they swam in silence, Estelle barely keeping her emotions in check. She was still angry with Demetrius for sullying the one spot of beauty in her dreary life, but she was also curious. And if he was serious about not coming with her anymore, she may not have another opportunity to ask questions without fear of them being reported to her father, as would surely happen with her tutor or another guard.

"Why do you speak so scornfully of humans?" she asked abruptly. "Why does everyone seem to think they're so inferior to us?"

Demetrius frowned as he thought it over. "They just are, aren't they? That's what I've always been taught. I mean, they can't even breathe in the water."

"We can't breathe on the land," Estelle pointed out. "How does that make us better?"

"Good point," Demetrius conceded. "I remember my grandmother talking about humans. Her parents remembered a time when our kind interacted with humans, and what they said suggested a poor opinion of them. She used to say that humans were ruled by their emotions—all heart and no head—and it made them foolish. Merfolk aren't like that." He shot Estelle a sideways look. "Generally."

Estelle's answering glance was long suffering, and she didn't immediately reply. When she did speak, her voice came out far from the confident tones she'd intended. It was closer to pleading.

"Is it so absurd to want love?"

Demetrius considered the question. "Not absurd," he acknowledged. "But unrealistic. It's not *absurd* to wish to eat oysters every night—who wouldn't wish that?—but for most of us, it's still impossible. And we do just fine without it."

Estelle stared at him incredulously. "Did you just compare falling in love with eating oysters? You really don't have a drop of sentimentality in you, do you?"

Demetrius grinned. "Apparently not. But I stand by my argument. It's hard to imagine your soppy idea of love being better than freshly caught oysters. I mean, have you tasted them?"

"Yes," said Estelle shortly. "You forget that, as a royal, I *can* eat oysters every night."

"Oh." Demetrius seemed struck by this point. "Not a good example, then."

"Definitely not," Estelle agreed. "Trust me, it's not as wonderful as you think." She shook her head. "It's a very ironic observation, because the royal status that gives me the luxuries most people want is exactly why I have little hope of pursuing love." Her voice turned wistful. "I've heard that among common merfolk, many do marry for love."

"Some do," said Demetrius unemotionally. "But certainly not all."

Estelle snuck a sideways glance at him. "Did your parents?"

Demetrius nodded. "They did actually. They were unusual in their circle for it. And truth be told, it cost my father the opportunity to expand his operation considerably. My grandfather had an advantageous alliance organized for him."

"How long ago did they marry?"

"Forty years," Demetrius said. "I'm the third-born in my family."

"And?" Estelle pressed. "Are your parents happy, even though they have a more modest livelihood than could have been?"

Again, Demetrius took a moment to consider before answering. "Yes," he said, sounding a little surprised at his own words. "They're among the happiest merfolk I know."

Estelle nodded, satisfied with her point. "I'll be the first to own that my knowledge is woefully lacking in many ways. But take my word for it when it comes to one area in which I'm an expert. Wealth and status do not guarantee happiness the way most merfolk think they do. It can just as easily be the reverse."

Demetrius gave no reply. Estelle thought he looked a little troubled, but knowing what she did of him, she doubted her arguments would have changed his poor opinion of what she felt for Prince Farrin.

"So why did we stop interacting with humans?" she asked after a pause. "Did your grandmother remember that?"

Demetrius shook his head. "She never said why. I think it was a decision made by the emperor of the time, and the rest of our kind just followed." His gaze was a little contemptuous as it traveled up toward the now-distant surface. "I can't see that we lost anything of value in the process."

Estelle ignored the slight on humans, her mind focused on his previous words. "But why did the emperor make that decision? There must have been a reason."

"I imagine so." Demetrius shrugged. "But you would have more idea of that than I do."

He clearly had no concept of the emperor's miserly approach to the education of his youngest daughter, but Estelle didn't bother correcting him. The conversation lapsed, and for a while they swam without speech.

As they drew close to the palace, Demetrius stopped the throbbing song he'd been releasing and pulled Estelle up with a touch.

"I meant what I said earlier," he told her seriously. "I should never have supported this, and I won't do it anymore."

"I don't need your help to go to the surface," Estelle told him shortly.

He shook his head. "I can't let you go alone, Estelle. On my honor as a guard, I can't." A pained look crossed his face. "On my honor as a guard, I should really report to my captain what you've been doing."

"You wouldn't!" Estelle gasped, horrified.

"Not if you agree not to go up alone," he said, no compromise in his voice.

"But if you won't go with me, and I can't go alone, I'll never be able to go," Estelle said desperately.

"You're being dramatic," Demetrius said, unimpressed. "Give your father time, and I'm sure you'll be able to visit the surface again."

"In ten years, perhaps," Estelle said bitterly. "That's not good enough. This is all I live for."

Demetrius's look showed little patience with her exaggeration, but he didn't comment. "That's my offer," he said. "Take it or leave it."

Estelle bit her lip. "I won't go again tomorrow," she said begrudgingly. "But this conversation isn't over."

Demetrius sighed. "Estelle, there's nothing to be gained by staring at some human through the waterline. It makes no difference if he's prince or beggar, he's utterly out of reach."

"I told you," Estelle said hotly, "I don't care about him being a prince."

To her irritation, Demetrius's expression suggested more indulgence than belief. But the young guard gave her no chance to argue her point. He shifted away as the wall of the private garden approached, leaving her to enter alone as normal.

Weary as she was, Estelle struggled to sleep that morning. She didn't know how she was going to convince Demetrius to resume their secret outings, but she knew she had to find a way. Life would scarcely be worth living otherwise.

CHAPTER EIGHT

Estelle

The conundrum of how to change Demetrius's mind filled Estelle's thoughts when she rose for the day, and went about the few activities open to her. When she arrived at the midday meal and caught sight of Demetrius, floating behind Eulalia, she felt a pang of guilt. The wakeful nights were finally beginning to show in his heavy eyes. Her family didn't know it, but they were expecting a lot of him, guarding her at night and Eulalia during the day. Perhaps it was for the best that they took a few mornings off.

The thought occurred to her as she ate her octopus tentacles that Demetrius's schedule would soon become less demanding. Eulalia and her family were due to depart the following day. Once he had fewer demands on his time, would Demetrius again be willing to accompany her to the surface? Or would he perhaps be posted somewhere else, where he would be unable to tell whether she was sneaking off alone?

That second option wasn't as appealing as it should have been. Estelle was surprised to discover that she felt almost as sad about Demetrius disappearing from daily palace life as about Eulalia leaving. Somehow she'd come to see the young guard as both friend and ally, in spite of his near constant disapproval.

For Demetrius's sake, she was glad to see a changeover in guards partway through the meal. Hopefully he was going to eat somewhere himself. Where did the royal guards eat? She'd never considered the matter before.

Once the amber-tailed merman had left the dining chamber, Estelle found that the little interest she'd had in the conversation drained away. Even when one of her nieces broke cheerfully into melody, prompting an unplanned communal song, Estelle could barely focus enough to add her voice. Power swirled around her, and her ears were full of the sounds of her family and the throb of the ocean. But her heart and mind were full of something entirely different, and it pushed everything else away.

Why had the merfolk stopped interacting with humans? Demetrius had shrugged it off, but Estelle's curiosity was properly roused. Some incident must have caused the change. And what had Demetrius's grandmother meant, that humans were all heart and no head? Demetrius had said it like it was a bad thing, but Estelle wasn't so sure. She glanced around at her family, noting the boredom on the face of Emilia's husband, and the perpetually sour expression worn by Eilise's husband. Eilise herself looked half-hearted as she joined in the communal song her daughter had started. Meanwhile, the emperor and empress watched on, too elevated to join in the merriment, but apparently pleased with the thriving family before them. It would have been an endearing sight, if not for the calculating gaze on the face of Emperor Aefic as he looked over his offspring. He looked as though he was assessing the strength of his empire rather than enjoying the company of his family.

Estelle couldn't help but think that merfolk could use a little more heart.

The communal song was still continuing, but Estelle had no more taste for it. Deeming that no one would notice if she slipped away, she swam for the door with unobtrusive strokes. A glance back showed that not one of her family members was following her with their eyes.

Two of her guards flanked her, of course. Estelle sent them a warm glance as she swam down the corridor, unusually grateful for their attention. Her family might have little time or use for its youngest member, but at least her guards took note of her. Like Demetrius, she realized. Perhaps that was why he always seemed to be looking out for her. And she wasn't even the princess he'd been assigned to.

She directed her strokes toward the palace's chamber of history, her thoughts straying to the human brothers she'd seen on the ship. Prince Farrin's brother had done more than just notice his brother's absence. He'd chased him onto a dangerous deck, even tried to dive into the thrashing sea after him, regardless of his own safety. Was that what Demetrius meant by more heart than head? If so, it had been beautiful to behold.

Rounding a corner, Estelle ascended through an opening above, coming out in the cylindrical chamber where the history of the empire was housed. An elderly merman, vaguely familiar to her from lessons years before, looked up at her entrance. His hair was as silver as his scales, and his face was deeply lined. His eyes, however, were clear and sharp.

"Your Highness," the history holder greeted her. "What an unusual honor."

Estelle smiled. "I hope I don't intrude."

"Of course not, Princess Estelle." He gave her an unexpectedly warm smile. "Any member of the royal family is always welcome in the chamber of history. I meant merely that you have not often been a visitor."

Estelle grimaced slightly. "I'm afraid I haven't always been as enthusiastic in my studies as I ought to have been." She paused. "But I'm fairly confident that the matter I wish to ask about today wasn't covered in my studies."

"What matter is that?" the history holder asked.

"How much do you know about humans?" Estelle responded.

The merman folded his hands, considering her thoughtfully. "More than most, I imagine. I was born only a short time after we ceased to have contact with them. In my childhood, it was common to hear them spoken of."

"Did you ever speak with one yourself?" Estelle asked, fascinated.

He shook his head. "No merman or mermaid has spoken to a human in almost three hundred years." His smile was a little rueful. "I am nearing the end of my days, but I'm not quite that old yet."

Estelle gave no reply, not wishing to display a lack of tact. She longed to ask the history holder to tell her everything he knew about humans and their ways, but she was aware that the question would seem suspicious. Already she was worried the conversation might be reported back to her father.

"Why did we stop allowing them to see us?" she asked instead. "Was there an incident which caused it?"

The elderly merman didn't answer straight away, his eyes thoughtful as they considered her.

"Do you mind if I allow my apprentice to answer?" he asked at last. "It is a good training opportunity for her."

"Of course," said Estelle, trying to hide her impatience.

At a word from the history holder, a mermaid swam down from an upper level of the chamber, bobbing her head respectfully to Estelle. She looked to be a similar age to Eulalia, with scales the color of coral. Estelle tried to be patient as the history holder repeated her question for his apprentice. She knew that the training of his replacement was an important process, given he held a great deal of rare and valuable knowledge in his mind, that future generations would need to access. Estelle eyed the other mermaid, wondering who would choose this vocation. From what she understood, the history holder lived an even more restricted life than hers, barely leaving the tall chamber of history. Not only was the task of committing so much information to memory an enormous one, but it was highly important that the history holder remain safe, given how much could be lost were he or she to die unexpectedly.

"Our history with the humans..." the apprentice repeated thoughtfully, clearly exercising her memory. "The relationship between our kinds was never close, given the natural barriers to communication. However, in the time of our ancestors, they did know of our existence. There was a time when their monarchs sought the wisdom of our empire."

"Why did they want wisdom from us?" Estelle interrupted, surprised.

"Because our wisdom is superior to theirs," explained the apprentice comfortably. "Humans are ruled by their emotions and by sentiment, and it makes them foolish. They are always thinking with their hearts, falling in love at the merest breath, abandoning logic in their attempts to feel as much as possible during their fleeting lives."

Estelle nodded slowly, noting that this answer matched what Demetrius had said. But the apprentice wasn't finished.

"The humans believed, correctly, that our substantially greater lifespans give us perspective which they lack."

Estelle frowned, some of her basic learning about humans coming back to her. "They don't live as long as merfolk, do they?"

The history holder and his apprentice exchanged a smile. "There is no comparison," the history holder said.

The other mermaid nodded in agreement. "Seventy years would be considered a generous lifespan for a human."

Estelle stared. "So short! Don't they run out of years long before they tire of life?"

"Indeed," the history holder said gravely. "And their efforts to evade death cause many problems. They care for little else, and most will readily take another's life before allowing their own to be shortened."

"I see," said Estelle, thinking this over. A frown creased her brow as she remembered the scene she'd witnessed on the ship. The behavior of the human brothers contradicted the history holder's words. She didn't believe either had valued his own life above that of the other. Quite the reverse.

"I suppose that's why their fertility works differently," she mused. "With such short lives, if they could only have a child every ten years, there wouldn't be many of them."

"Quite so," said the history holder approvingly. "I see you remember some of your studies, Princess Estelle. They do indeed have children more freely than our kind."

"And," chipped in the apprentice, "due to their sentimentality, family affection can lead them to make unwise decisions which are not in the best interests of themselves or those around them. This risk is particularly egregious when it comes to human royalty, given their position of power. When we had communication with them, that failing had the power to affect even us."

The history holder cleared his throat, his expression not quite pleased as he glanced at his apprentice.

She looked at him, seeming to read his displeasure. "Forgive me if I erred in my answer, Master," she said, dipping her head respectfully. "I thought my information accurately reflected our training."

"You did not err in your information," said the history holder.

The apprentice seemed to be waiting for him to say more, but he didn't. Estelle was fairly certain she understood. The apprentice's words had been true, but her mentor would not have chosen to share the information with Estelle. His critique related to her discretion, not her accuracy, as he would no doubt explain to her once Estelle was gone.

For her part, Estelle was intrigued. She had herself seen evidence of family loyalty among humans, and within the royal family specifically. She had considered it beautiful, and had wished her own family displayed more of it. Why would anyone consider it undesirable?

"So why did the humans cease to seek our wisdom?" Estelle asked, hoping that if she redirected the conversation, the apprentice would keep talking.

"They did not withdraw from communication," the other mermaid said. "We did, once we came to understand their true nature."

"Which is?" Estelle prompted.

"They are untrustworthy and selfish," said the apprentice simply. "They all seek to use others for their gain, from the lowest peasant to the greatest ruler."

Estelle frowned, thinking of the way her father had tried to barter her to expand his empire into the deeps. "And we don't?"

"Princess Estelle," said the history holder, sounding scandalized. "You surely cannot doubt the superiority of merfolk over the manipulative and undiscerning humans?"

"Manipulative?" Estelle raised an eyebrow. "What exactly did the humans do to make my ancestors so angry with them?"

"They showed themselves unscrupulous in exchanges entered into between the royal families," the apprentice said, in the tone of one reciting from memory. "The king of the time is long passed on, but still underwater we live with the results of his dishonesty. If you doubt humans' untrustworthiness, Your Highness, you need only look to the Ocean Miner to see that—"

"That is not a tale for such innocent ears," interrupted the history holder, his voice tight with something that sounded like alarm.

Estelle's eyes passed between the master and the chastened apprentice. "Please, I can handle our history. I want to know what you mean."

"Forgive me, Master," murmured the apprentice, disregarding Estelle's words. "I thought the royal family enjoyed full access to the memories we hold."

"I see we will need to pause in our focus on history to give some attention to the memorizing of regulations," the history holder said, still disapproving. "You have forgotten that access is moderated according to age. Princess Estelle is only fifteen, and as such is still years from receiving full access."

The apprentice's head remained bowed in apology, but Estelle studied the history holder shrewdly. "Is that a new rule?" she demanded. "Did my father impose that because of me, and how irresponsible he thinks I am?"

The history holder's gaze was reproving as he met her eye. "You are to be excused due to your youth, Your Highness, but I would encourage you not to rate your own importance too highly. You must surely be aware that royal life comes with restrictions as well as privileges."

Estelle gave a hollow laugh. "Much more aware than you are, probably." But even as she spoke, she realized the justice of his rebuke. She knew that some age restrictions, at least, had existed long before her father declared her interest in the human world to be a sign of folly and immaturity.

"Is it like the rules around royals being trained in the use of power?" she asked slowly. "How our royal status gives us greater access to the ocean's power, and we must therefore be older and more experienced before it's safe for us to be fully trained in its use?"

"Indeed," the history holder agreed, warming instantly to what appeared to be a favorite theme. "The memories of our ancestors, and indeed knowledge more generally, is every bit as precious and powerful as the magic that emanates from the depths of the ocean. Its potential for both benefit and destruction is just as great, and it is therefore just as important that its access be regulated."

Estelle said nothing, not entirely convinced. She'd often been irked by the restriction that prevented her from being comprehensively trained in harnessing power for decades longer than the average mermaid or merman.

She glanced at the apprentice. The other mermaid had remained silent since her master's rebuke, and Estelle had the sense she was unlikely to let any more promising information slip out. There was probably little more to be learned here on the topic of humans, at least for Estelle.

"Thank you for your time," she said politely, dipping her head to both of them.

Her thoughts swirled with unanswered questions as she swam from the chamber of history. What exactly was the history between humans and merfolk, and who was this Ocean Miner whose mention had brought the conversation to an abrupt halt?

The only certainty in Estelle's mind was that she was far from finished with her inquiries. She would just have to pursue a less circumspect source.

CHAPTER NINE

Demetrius

Demetrius fought a yawn, managing to keep his features straight and his posture upright. Weariness pulled at him, but he was on duty, and a royal family dinner was no place to let his eyes droop.

With an effort, he kept his gaze fixed on the wall over Princess Eulalia's head, where it was supposed to be. The chatter of the family was of no interest to him. His attention was all on Princess Estelle, wondering if she would keep her word about not going to the surface without him. He was still annoyed with himself at how difficult he'd found it to tell her he wouldn't help her anymore. The real question was why he'd ever helped her with such a dangerous and illicit whim. And to that question, he had no answer.

Dimly, Demetrius realized that his charge was speaking about her family's departure the following day. The words startled Demetrius. He'd been so distracted by the encounter with Estelle, he'd forgotten that tonight was his last night assigned to Princess Eulalia. What would he be doing by the following evening? Would he be allowed to continue in the palace, or would he be reassigned to the dull role he'd been filling before, manning a little-used section of the outer wall? Without his permission, his thoughts floated back to Estelle. If he was working elsewhere, would she use the opportunity to go back on her promise, and once again sneak up to the surface to spy on her human prince?

Demetrius only just stopped himself from rolling his eyes. The young mermaid was so absurdly sentimental over that human. At other times he had no difficulty believing she'd come of age, but every time she set her eyes on this Prince Farrin, she became as foolish as a child. She knew nothing of the human, and yet she had utterly convinced herself of his perfection. From where Demetrius was floating, the only thing they'd seen him do was to ignore the advice of his minders on that ship, stupidly and pointlessly endangering his life in the process. And if he really was a prince, that conduct was even less forgivable than in a lesser man, as the impact of his sudden death would presumably be greater.

Why in the seas any of that would make Estelle admire him was utterly beyond Demetrius.

"Estelle."

Hearing the name currently in his mind spoken aloud broke Demetrius's control. His head turned involuntarily to the emperor, who was watching his youngest daughter with a forbidding expression.

"Yes, Father?" Estelle sounded wary, and Demetrius wished he could warn her with his eyes. She was so transparent—surely her father would read on her face that she had a guilty secret.

"I received a report from the history holder today which concerned me."

The young princess's uncertain expression turned quickly to a scowl. "I wasn't aware that a visit to the chamber of history necessitated a formal report to you, Father."

"That is your error, not mine," said the emperor. "I thought I had made my feelings on your obsession with humans clear, Estelle. Do you imagine that interrogating our history holder about them will make me *more* likely to allow you to return to the surface?"

"Since you've assured me you won't allow me to ascend for the next decade, I don't see that I have a great deal to lose," said the young princess, with a boldness Demetrius was sure hadn't been there before her coming of age.

"Estelle." The emperor's voice was low and threatening. "Why were you asking about humans?"

"Because I'm curious!" Estelle burst out. "I want to understand—is that so strange?"

"Honestly, Estelle, it's a little strange," Princess Eulalia chipped in, forestalling their father. "I don't understand why, after having seen the surface, you're still so fascinated by it."

"There's so much more to the world of the humans than a stretch of empty surface," Estelle said, her tone pleading with her closest sister to understand. "And our people used to know it, too. I heard it myself, in the chamber of history. We used to have dealings with the humans. They used to come to us for aid and information. Surely the exchange went both ways."

One of Estelle's adult nephews gave an audible snort. "Both ways? You mean merfolk seeking assistance from humans? Unlikely."

"That's what everyone says, but I've yet to hear a convincing reason why humans are so inferior to us," Estelle said stubbornly. Her eyes were on her father, a recklessness reflected in them. "The history holder wouldn't tell me what happened between our peoples, Father, but I know there's more to the story. Why did we withdraw from the humans?"

"That is not a matter to be discussed over dinner," said the emperor angrily. "Tides above, Estelle, your impertinence grows by the day."

"But Father," Estelle tried desperately, "can't you see that the less you tell me, the more I'm determined to find out? I know it's on your orders that the history holder wouldn't give me a full answer. But I'm ready to know!"

"You clearly are not," said the emperor coldly. "Every word from your mouth convinces me further of your immaturity and lack of wisdom."

"How can I gain wisdom if I'm not given the opportunity to learn from the knowledge of our ancestors?" Estelle challenged. She'd risen in the water, although Demetrius doubted she was even aware of it. "Making me wait half a year for my ascension is one thing, but how does it benefit anyone for me to be more ignorant than the rest of my peers? Why must I wait another decade before being properly trained in the exercise of power? Most of my maids are near my own age, and they've been manipulating power since they were children!"

"Be fair, Estelle," Princess Eulalia interjected reasonably. "That rule was the same for all of us."

"It certainly was," agreed Empress Talisa. "The restrictions regarding royalty learning to use the power of the ocean were in place before your father was even born, and they are there for good reason."

"Perhaps that isn't the best example," admitted Estelle, sounding like she was trying her utmost to speak calmly. "But my education has been miserly compared to others, Father, you know it has."

"I know nothing of the kind," Emperor Aefic said.

"Really?" Defiance once again flashed across Estelle's face, and Demetrius felt a thrill of vicarious fear. While part of him admired the young princess's new boldness, her father's barely contained anger roused all the guard's protective instincts. He didn't like to see the young mermaid placing herself in the path of danger.

"Then perhaps you can explain to me," Estelle went on, rising a little further in the water, "why I'd never heard of the Ocean Miner until the history holder's apprentice let mention of her slip, but my maids seemed to know everything about her when I asked them this afternoon."

Silence fell across the royal family, even the guards' low hum of protective song taking on an uneasy edge.

"Whatever your maids think they know," the emperor said, his icy calm more alarming than open anger, "I can say with certainty that they do not know everything about the Ocean Miner."

"Come, Estelle," chimed in Esteban, and Demetrius's eyes strayed to his friend. The twenty-year-old looked perplexed as he stared at his young aunt. "Are things really so desperate that you're resorting to palace gossip for information?"

"Yes, Esteban, they are," Estelle assured him.

"But surely you've *heard* of the Ocean Miner," Esteban protested. "We all grew up on the stories. I still hear children tell them to one another. She's the monster in the night."

"I didn't grow up on those stories," said Estelle earnestly. "Or any stories." She glanced around at her family. "I don't think any of you realize just how cloistered I've been."

Demetrius felt an involuntary flash of sympathy for the young mermaid. No wonder she was a little naive. It was hard to believe she'd truly never heard of the Ocean Miner. She wasn't exaggerating when she said she'd been cloistered.

"I will not defend my decisions regarding my own family," the emperor said through clenched teeth. His eyes were glinting with fury as they rested on his youngest daughter. "If you have been entrusted with less information than your sisters, you have no one to blame but yourself. You are the one who made no effort to hide your unnatural fascination with the world above water from before you'd properly learned to swim."

"But why is it so unnatural?" Estelle cried desperately. Demetrius saw that her hands had balled into fists at her sides. "Our ancestors didn't think so. They interacted with humans. You're the one who's strayed so far from what used to be. You're the one who—"

"Me?" Emperor Aefic's voice had risen to such a roar that Demetrius saw servants edging back out of the room, clearly sensing that it wasn't a good time to bring in the next course. "You dare to criticize *me*, to claim that *I* have dishonored the legacy of our royal house?"

The already imposing merman had risen well above his family, glaring down at his youngest daughter with an expression that sent another jolt of alarm through Demetrius. He had to fight all his instincts in order to remain in place instead of darting forward to shield the young mermaid.

"*I* am not the disappointment," Emperor Aefic raged. "You have disappointed me from the moment of your birth. Do you think I wanted a *fifth* daughter?"

"Aefic," murmured the empress, her face even paler than usual.

But her husband paid her no heed, his temper fully loose now. "Do you think I want you to remain in the palace?" he stormed on. "Do you think I enjoy the necessity of keeping you restricted, so that you don't endanger yourself or anyone else with your shameful fascination? It is not by my will that you remain here beyond your fifteenth birthday, your very presence displaying weakness." His eyes were hard, and his fins quivered with emotion. "Although it was not what I wanted, I accepted the arrival of each daughter with the knowledge that you could all serve your family by forming alliances that would strengthen and expand our empire. But you have proved incapable even of doing that! You dare to suggest I have failed to remain true to the legacy of my ancestors when you have nothing whatsoever to contribute to your family or your empire? You are nothing but a burden."

The silence that fell over the group at the end of this brutal outburst seemed to make the crackling hum of the ocean twice as loud as normal. It pressed against Demetrius's ears with such force, it was almost painful. Unmoving as he was supposed to be, he couldn't stop his gaze from traveling to Estelle's face. She looked so stricken at her father's harshness, Demetrius could hardly bear to look at her. He could barely comprehend such humiliation, and he felt something stir within him as he watched her, floating all alone, attacked by her own father for things she couldn't control, defended by no one, although her family surrounded her.

At the look on her face, a fleeting memory flashed through Demetrius's mind. It was of his grandmother and her stories about humans. She'd claimed that when their hearts were near bursting with pain or grief, they actually leaked drops of ocean water from their eyes, no matter how far they were from the sea. Crying, they called it, and his grandmother had claimed that it eased the pain ever so slightly.

Estelle looked like she would cry if she could, and Demetrius found himself wishing for her to be granted that release, be it ever so minimal. His gaze passed back to the emperor, and as the feeling that had stirred within him burst into full life, he suddenly recognized it.

Anger. He was angry with the emperor, angry enough to shout at him, if that course hadn't been so unthinkable. The realization rattled Demetrius. He'd devoted his whole life not just to being a guard, but to being a royal guard—a member of that elite force whose entire purpose for existence was to protect the emperor and his family. And now, far from wanting to protect Emperor Aefic, he was feeling a dangerous, unspeakable desire to see him punished.

Demetrius shied away from the idea, unnerved by his own thoughts. Was he destined to fail as a guard? Did he lack the discipline and true protective instinct required? Before he could spiral too far down this depressing path, Estelle's strained voice, quiet amidst the noises of the ocean, brought his mind back to her plight.

"There's nothing left for me to say, Father, except that I'm sorry I'm such a disappointment to you."

Without another word, the young princess turned, swimming from the room with unsteady strokes.

Demetrius knew he should remain in place, knew any deviation from his duty would be reported to his captain. But he simply couldn't let Estelle leave unchecked. Not when he, alone of everyone in the room, knew how effectively she could sneak away from the palace. Would she be on her way to the surface within the hour? Would she ever return this time? He couldn't take that risk, but he wasn't willing to expose her secret to her family. Not after the exhibit he'd just witnessed.

Moving as surreptitiously as he could, he left his post, skirting around the outside of the chamber. He could feel the disapproving stares of the other guards, but he ignored them, trying to look as though he was on a sanctioned errand.

He left the dining chamber just after Estelle, the mermaid's back to him as she hastened down the corridor.

"Estelle," he called, a warning in his voice.

"Leave me alone." Her voice sounded choked, and Demetrius's heart throbbed uncomfortably.

"Estelle."

She gave no response to his second attempt, except to increase her pace. Demetrius put on a burst of speed and easily caught up to her. He gripped her arm, not releasing her even under the admonishing glare of the princess's two attendant guards. He forced his expression to show nothing but stern confidence, willing her to treat his words as the orders of a guard, and not to endanger herself in the heat of her emotion.

"Estelle, you promised. Remember."

She looked at him unseeingly for a moment before he saw comprehension behind her eyes. "I know," she said tightly. "I'm not—I mean, I wasn't going to—"

She broke off, casting a wary look at her guards, and Demetrius released her arm. He fell back, allowing her to swim away unhindered this time. She had seemed genuine in her surprise. Apparently she hadn't left the meal intent on fleeing to the surface.

But Demetrius's unease hadn't lessened at all. On the contrary, he felt considerably more concerned than he had when she'd fled her coming of age celebration in a similar fashion. He'd thought then that she looked as desperate as cornered prey, and that had been nothing to the wretchedness of her demeanor now. Genuine fear streaked through him as he reluctantly swam back to his post in the dining chamber.

Promise or no promise, he would resume his position outside the private garden the moment he was off duty. The princess wouldn't be going anywhere tonight without his shadow.

CHAPTER TEN

Estelle

Estelle propelled herself through the doorway into her own chambers, barely able to hold her emotions in check for long enough to gain privacy. The moment she was shut off from her guards, she dropped all pretense, giving in to the agonizing humiliation. Bending over double, she clutched her torso as her body convulsed in the water.

Her father's words played again in her mind, and she covered her ears, wishing she could silence them. Her eyes were closed, but she could still see a parade of faces before her sight—her mother's discomfort, her sisters' sympathy, her nieces and nephews trying awkwardly to avoid catching her eye. But none of them saying anything, doing anything to defend her.

And Demetrius's face, when he'd stopped her in the corridor. Humiliation washed over her afresh, and she let out a quiet groan at the memory that he'd witnessed that scene. She'd never thought much about the presence of guards during such conversations, but it was an entirely different matter when the guard in question had somehow bizarrely become a friend.

If only he hadn't been on duty. She could hardly bear the

knowledge that he'd heard her father say that she had nothing to contribute and would never be anything but a burden.

She was foolish to let emotion figure in her reaction, though. Demetrius hadn't. When he'd chased her down, he'd been every inch the guard, as always. His concern hadn't been for her. He was just worried she'd break her promise.

That thought stilled her agitation. Lowering her hands, she stared unseeingly at the angelfish darting into the coral that formed her chamber's walls. On reflection, Demetrius's concern made sense. But the idea of fleeing to the surface truly hadn't occurred to her. She'd been too bent on getting away from that scene of humiliation to think where she could go. *Was* the idea of actually leaving realistic?

The immediate answer was no. She had nowhere in the ocean to go outside Korallid. And she had no skills that would fit her for a simpler life, hidden in one of the empire's quieter communities. More to the point, she had no interest whatsoever in that course. There was only one place she'd ever really wanted to go, and that place was irrevocably barred to her.

Or was it?

A strange thrill, half excitement, half fear, washed over Estelle as she remembered Eulalia's words the day of her ascension. Etta had said that there was no way for a mermaid to breathe or speak above water, and Eulalia had responded that they couldn't say for certain that it was impossible, if a talisman was used. At the time, Estelle had agreed with Etta when she said that none of them would ever consider using a talisman.

But dreary as her life had then been, Estelle hadn't yet felt the desperation she felt now. If she did nothing, if she continued meekly as she'd done up until her coming of age, she could foresee nothing but misery ahead.

She'd learned a great deal that day, first from the history holder, and then from the gossip of the castle servants. Estelle was no fool. Once the history holder's apprentice had mentioned the Ocean Miner, it hadn't taken the princess long to draw the connection between the mysterious figure and what Demetrius had told her about how talismans were created. He'd said the magic had to be mined from the ocean bed itself. Clearly this Ocean Miner must be in the business of making talismans.

In fact, from what the maids had said when Estelle asked them, popular belief was that the Ocean Miner was the only one in that business. According to them, she'd been in operation for over two hundred years, and every single talisman had come from her. No one else knew how to mine magic.

If this Ocean Miner was truly responsible for the entire black market that so irked Estelle's father, she could understand why he might be reactive to any mention of her. But it didn't explain the words the history holder's apprentice had let slip. The other mermaid had claimed that the Ocean Miner somehow provided evidence of the humans' untrustworthiness, and it had been that comment which had prompted the history holder to intervene and end the conversation.

But try as she might, Estelle could think of no logical connection between the Ocean Miner and the humans.

Unless...she drew in several steadying pulls through her gills, trying to calm her racing thoughts. Was it possible that the Ocean Miner really could produce a talisman that would allow Estelle to breathe up in the air? To *live* up there? She hardly dared to consider the idea, and yet somehow, the thought kept growing.

The maids had spoken very freely once Estelle got them going. She'd learned not only the Ocean Miner's reputation, but how to find her. Perhaps the information wasn't accurate—if the criminal was so easy to locate, Estelle couldn't imagine why her father hadn't acted against her—but it was at least a place to start.

Thoughts of her father sobered Estelle. He would be horrified if he knew she was even considering trying to access a talisman. It would further convince him of her disloyalty and foolishness. But what did that matter, after all? He'd declared her to be utterly useless, and had done so in front of their entire family, which included influential members of the ruling families of every province. There seemed little point in trying to win his approval, or in following his philosophy regarding the mining of magic. How much further could she really sink in his estimation? Since there was no other province within his empire, and the Dybde Empire didn't want her, she would never have anything to contribute.

Unexpectedly, another question popped into her mind. What would Demetrius think of her musings? She squirmed a little under the imagined gaze of the uncompromising young guard. She was sure he would reprove her for her thoughts. But what did he understand, after all? He might be more tolerant than most, but he was still unemotional at his core, like merfolk were supposed to be. He'd said himself that he'd never experienced romantic love, and he was openly disdainful of her experience of it. She scowled as she remembered his insistence that her attraction to Farrin came solely from his status as a prince.

A thought blazed across Estelle's mind with the intensity of the sun, and she froze, the scowl melting away.

Farrin was a prince. The prince of a kingdom near to, but currently unconnected with, her father's empire.

Hadn't her father declared her only value to be her ability to expand the influence of their family and empire through a marriage alliance? He despised humans, certainly. But that was just because he'd been taught such a sour view of them, like the rest of merfolk. Estelle had seen enough to be convinced that humans were not as inferior as they were made out to be. Surely if she could show her father that, and bring him not just a political alliance, but a royal one, he would be forced to acknowledge that he'd been wrong about her.

She knew the thought was mad, but once it had started, she couldn't stop its growth. Both Demetrius and the history holder's apprentice had said that humans were sentimental and emotional, led by their hearts. The apprentice had said that they fell in love at the merest breath. Estelle knew what that was like—she'd already lost her heart to Prince Farrin. Surely she could make him feel the same way, if she could enter his world and speak to him face to face.

Enter his world. The thought was dazzling. It was the tantalizing idea of actually being on the long dreamed of land that decided her, its potency pushing all thoughts of politics and alliances to the side.

Her mind made up, it was torturous to float idle, but she knew she had to give it time before she could sneak out undetected. She traversed her chamber restlessly, grateful that her guards remained outside her door. If they could see the agitated way her fins were flicking, they'd surely realize she was planning something.

After about an hour and a half, Estelle judged that the meal was probably finished, and all the diners dispersed to their own chambers. A maid came to assist Estelle with preparations for sleep, and the princess submitted to the other mermaid's ministrations uncomplainingly. The sooner the maid was out of the room, the sooner she could count on being undisturbed until morning.

The palace wasn't entirely still when the maid left, but Estelle was done waiting. Moving quietly, she slid a satchel over her shoulder before slipping out of her window as she'd done so often in the past couple of weeks. This time, however, she swam across the private garden before slipping out through a different opening. If her maids were to be believed, the Ocean Miner lived due east of Korallid's capital.

When she cleared the immediate area, Estelle paused, floating in place as she looked carefully around her. She could see no sign of a pursuing guard, friendly or otherwise. She'd become so used to Demetrius being her shadow, that she stopped multiple times to assure herself he wasn't behind her.

Confident that she was alone, Estelle started forward again, traveling well above the normal depth preferred by most merfolk. Once she'd crossed the expanse separating the palace from the rest of the city, however, it was necessary for her to dive back to the seabed in order to follow the directions she'd been given.

She'd never been in the city at night before, and she had to fight a surge of fear as she wended her way above narrow streets. Merfolk moved in and out of stone dwellings carved from the bedrock, emerging after the habitual rest of dusk, when some of the most dangerous predators tended to hunt. She didn't think anyone would be likely to recognize her, but she preferred not to find out.

Even in her nerves, she was fascinated by this glimpse into the lives of ordinary Korallidians. The palace had been quietening down, but Korallid's capital appeared to be waking up for an evening's activity. The hum of the ocean was supplemented by the chatter and noise of the population. Estelle even passed over a night market, the various stalls illuminated by lanterns consisting of luminous jellyfish floating in fishbone cages.

As she continued eastward, the tone of the city changed. Estelle became nervous again as she noticed less chatter and light, and more clandestine movement. This part of the city was still very much awake, but its activities appeared to be of a different nature. To her unease, where the market-goers had ignored her, many of the residents of this area watched her closely as she passed, their eyes seeming to take in every detail.

At first, Estelle was relieved to pass out of the city altogether, continuing eastward across a rocky canyon. But the unbroken darkness of the deep ocean soon created a different kind of dread. For the briefest of moments, she considered turning tail and going home to her chamber, where life might be unbearably dull, but at least she was safe.

Sternly telling herself to be brave, she banished the thought. Instead, she raised a feeble song, trying to copy what she'd heard Demetrius do when checking for predators. It was useless. She was royal, she reflected bitterly, and therefore wouldn't be comprehensively trained in magic for another decade.

That thought filled her with purpose once again. She wasn't spending another decade trapped inside the palace, living for the infrequent visits of her sisters, and crushed under the weight of her father's disappointment.

The canyon was behind her now, a vast reef immediately below her. The coral was colorless in the darkness of the night, her keen eyes picking out the shapes of the fronds. Without the light of the distant sun, they looked dead, abandoned. It would have been unbearably sinister if not for the crackles of life she could hear through the water.

Lifting her eyes from the coral, she caught sight of it at last. A looming cave, the darkness inside its entrance yawning frighteningly. Estelle paused, floating in place as she asked herself whether she really wanted to do this. Every instinct told her that caves like that should be avoided, especially at night. It was the perfect lair for any number of terrifying sea beasts.

But this was the place, no doubt about it. It was a perfect match for the description of her maids. The thought was an unwelcome reminder of the fact that apparently everyone but Estelle knew the location of the Ocean Miner's cave. Still, at least it meant that she knew what lived inside—and it was a mermaid, not a wild beast.

Gathering every ounce of courage she possessed, Estelle swam forward. Upon reaching the opening, she found that it was more tunnel than cave. She followed it for some distance before realizing that she could see a faint glow up ahead. Emboldened, she increased her speed, turning a final corner and emerging quite suddenly into a large open space.

For a moment, Estelle just blinked, her eyes adjusting to the ghostly glow that lit the whole area. The light seemed to emanate from various samples stored around the edges of the room. She saw luminous jellyfish, and some plankton as well, but many of the objects she didn't recognize. Estelle reached toward the closest example, marveling not at the faintly glowing sea snail shell itself, but at its fascinating container. It seemed to have no substance, but it was hard to the touch. Like water made solid.

"Don't touch."

Estelle started at the harsh command, her eyes searching the space for the speaker. She couldn't immediately see anyone, but the voice spoke again. It was so raspy that Estelle winced in sympathetic pain just to hear it.

"Can I help you?"

The tone of that haggard voice robbed the question of any hint of politeness. Estelle cleared her throat.

"I hope so. I...I've come to buy a talisman."

"Have you now?" The voice sounded amused.

Estelle's eyes darted nervously around the shadows, clutching the strap of her satchel. "Where are you?"

A seaweed curtain on the far side of the room shifted, and a form emerged. Estelle had been braced for something frightening, but the mermaid who swam forward was unremarkable to look at. She certainly didn't match the shredded voice that issued from her throat.

"A talisman to do what?"

"Are you the Ocean Miner?" Estelle asked, feeling she'd better get some answers of her own before proceeding. "Am I at the right place?"

The mermaid rested a gnarled hand on the stone bench beside her, surveying Estelle out of indulgent eyes. The servants had told Estelle that the Ocean Miner had been supplying the black market for more than two centuries, and she did indeed look old. Amazingly, though, there were still signs of dull green in the silver of her scales and hair.

"You, little mermaid, are most definitely in the wrong place," said the older mermaid mockingly.

Estelle had to lean forward to even catch her low, hoarse voice, the sound again so painful that it was all the princess could do to refrain from clutching her own throat.

"But yes," the stranger continued, "I am the Ocean Miner." Her eyes narrowed as she looked Estelle over. "I recognize you," she rasped. "Are you the emperor's youngest princess?"

Alarm washed over Estelle, but she pulled herself up proudly. "I don't see what difference it makes who I am," she said.

"If you're a nobody, I won't help you," croaked the Ocean Miner. She began to swim back toward her curtain.

"Wait!" Estelle cried. "I...I am the princess. Princess Estelle."

"Hm." The Ocean Miner stroked her chin, her eyes thoughtful as they rested on Estelle. "Prove it."

"H-how?" Estelle stammered.

"Sing for me," the other mermaid grunted roughly.

"But how will that—"

"I've heard of you," the Ocean Miner interrupted. "I'll be able to tell. They say you have the loveliest voice in the ocean."

"They do?" Estelle stared at the ancient mermaid in astonishment. She had been told from time to time that her voice was lovely, but she'd never imagined she was known for it. She hadn't been encouraged to sing much outside of communal songs, given that it was such a central part of learning to harness power, and she wasn't yet supposed to do that.

"Oh, yes," said the Ocean Miner.

Again, her tone sounded mocking, and Estelle couldn't tell if she was lying. But she lifted her voice anyway, releasing a simple, meaningless song. The water seemed to snatch up her melody, sending it swirling through the space with a substance that was hard to put into words.

A gleam entered the Ocean Miner's eyes, and she straightened in the water. "You are the princess," she rasped. She brought her hands together in front of her, her gaze calculating. "What do you want?"

Estelle swallowed nervously, casting a glance around the cavern. "I don't even know if it's possible," she admitted. "But I heard a rumor that you might have talismans that can make a mermaid breathe and speak above the water."

"For what purpose?"

Estelle frowned at the curt demand. "My reasons are my own."

The Ocean Miner shook her head. "No, no, I can't help you if I don't know what you really want. I might unknowingly give you something that meets your bare description but in fact takes you no closer to your real goal. Tell me your intention."

"I want to live in the world of the humans," said Estelle in a rush. "I want to breathe the air like they do, and..." she shuddered at her own daring, but pushed on, "and have legs. I don't want to be a mermaid anymore."

"My, my," said the Ocean Miner, a smile curving her lips as she regarded Estelle. "The emperor's own daughter, discontent."

"Being royal is not what everyone thinks," Estelle said, goaded in spite of her better sense. "My life is barely worth living."

"Is that so?" The Ocean Miner was still smiling unnervingly. She shook her head. "One ascension, and you're ready to abandon ship."

"What?" Estelle frowned, confused by the unfamiliar expression.

"There's more to it," the older mermaid said, her gaze keen. "You're not just fleeing something. You're chasing something." She leaned forward, enunciating every syllable in that excruciating voice. "What is it you want?"

Again, the words poured out of Estelle, her desperation loosening her tongue. "There's a human," she said. "Farrin. I...I saved his life when he was thrown from a ship. My father is determined for me to make a marriage of alliance, and Farrin is a prince in the world of the humans." She fidgeted with the strap of her satchel. "He doesn't know about me yet, but—but I love him. And I've heard that humans are ruled by their hearts, that they fall in love readily, and..." She trailed off, hearing the absurdity of her words. "I'm a fool, aren't I?" she muttered. "It's the stupidest, most impossible idea anyone's ever—"

"Not at all," interrupted the Ocean Miner, her manner sleek as she floated toward Estelle, but her words still horribly rasping. "What you've heard is true. Humans fall in love as easily as they put one foot in front of the other." She cast an appraising look over Estelle's person. "A pretty young thing like you, looking at him with adoration...I wouldn't be surprised if he married you within a month."

Estelle felt her heart swell with hope, the picture too dazzling to resist. "Do you really think so?"

"Why not?" the Ocean Miner said flippantly.

"So you can help me?" Estelle pressed eagerly. "Is there a way to turn a mermaid into a human?"

"Oh, there are ways," said the Ocean Miner. "But it won't be easy. And I won't do it for free."

"I brought payment," said Estelle quickly. She lifted her satchel. "Every item of jewelry I own. Some of it is very valuable."

"I don't want your baubles," said the Ocean Miner, leaning an elbow back on the shelf.

"But I don't have anything else," said Estelle, crestfallen.

The Ocean Miner's smile grew. "Yes, you do. You have something I want. Something I'd be willing to take as an exchange for what you ask."

"What is it?" Estelle demanded.

The Ocean Miner's eyes were alight with something like hunger as she leaned forward once more. "Your voice."

CHAPTER ELEVEN

Demetrius

Demetrius worked his tail powerfully, propelled as much by fear as by his strokes. Why had Princess Eulalia lingered so long over her meal? Why had Estelle had to sneak out so much earlier than normal?

He'd half thought he was mistaken when his questing song, sent ahead of him, had told him someone was leaving the private garden and heading east. He'd seen no sign of her when he followed the direction, and had considered abandoning what was probably a false lead and swimming the now-familiar route to the surface near the humans' castle. But he reasoned that if Estelle had gone to the surface, he knew where to find her. In that instance, an extra hour or two probably wouldn't make a difference. Whereas if she really had gone east, time might be crucial. With that thought, he'd turned toward the initial path revealed by the questing song.

He'd almost given up when he'd reached the city and found no trace of Estelle. But as he'd swum uncertainly over the tops of the dwellings, he'd remembered the conversation at dinner, and a horrible thought had seized him. Surely she wouldn't go to the Ocean Miner. Young though she was, surely she couldn't be such a fool.

But he'd been unable to feel any certainty on that point, especially when he remembered that Estelle had only heard of the Ocean Miner that day. She likely knew nothing of the rumors that swirled regarding those who did deals with the ancient mermaid. And she'd been so desperate. After the things her father had said to her, was it any wonder if she felt she had little to lose?

Demetrius had put on speed then, but Estelle must have been some distance ahead of him. Any hope he had that his guess was wrong died when he reached the notorious eastern district of the city and made a few discreet inquiries of the residents openly watching his progress. For a small payment, every single one he spoke to described the young mermaid who'd swum over not long before. The one with turquoise hair and scales, and a frightened look on her face.

Terror threatening now to choke him, Demetrius hurried onward, resigned to the fact that he wouldn't be able to catch up to her before she reached the criminal's lair. When the Ocean Miner's cave loomed into view, he didn't hesitate, plunging in as he pulled his slender whalebone blade from the strap fixed over his chest. He sped through the twisting tunnel, pulling up when he saw light ahead, and heard an unfamiliar sound. It took him a moment to recognize the horrible rasping as a mermaid's voice.

"You have something I want. Something I'd be willing to take as an exchange for what you ask."

"What is it?"

Demetrius had no trouble recognizing this second voice as Estelle's, and he groaned internally. Even without the aid of sight, he could hear the eagerness in the scratchy response from the first speaker.

"Your voice."

"No!" Unable to contain his protest any longer, Demetrius flung himself around the corner and into the open space.

"Demetrius!" Estelle's guilty start as much as her gasp confirmed that she knew she was where she shouldn't be.

"Estelle, are you mad?" he demanded furiously. "What possessed you to come here? You're leaving with me right now, and coming home."

Estelle stiffened, defiance flashing across her face. "I'm not going back, Demetrius. Not ever."

"Don't be absurd," Demetrius spat out, annoyed with himself for the fear he could feel just under the surface of his anger. He couldn't let the Ocean Miner see it. "You *are* coming home, and I'm taking you."

"And who is this?" The horrible guttural voice seemed to laugh at him, and he forced himself to look at the old mermaid. Her face was lined, but her eyes were keen, and everything about her filled him with intense foreboding.

"He's no one," said Estelle, sounding churlish. "Demetrius, this is none of your business. Go back to your duties."

"I'm not no one, I'm a member of the royal guard," Demetrius said, eyeing the Ocean Miner with disfavor. "And I won't allow you to take advantage of Estelle, just because she's young and foolish."

"Demetrius!" Estelle protested, her turquoise eyes sparking with anger. "I know what I'm doing. Stay out of this!"

"Ooh, a member of the royal guard," croaked the Ocean Miner. "That sounds important, and very intimidating." She swam forward, her green and silver tail swishing menacingly from side to side as she moved. In form she might be a mermaid, but in manner she reminded Demetrius more of a shark. "You're very informal for a guard, to be calling the princess by her name. Do I sense an intrigue?"

"Don't be absurd," scoffed Demetrius, genuinely incredulous. "Princess Estelle is a child." He glared at the princess. "As this foolish flight demonstrates."

"I'm not a child, Demetrius," Estelle snapped. "Most mermaids would be married by my age."

"Most mermaids aren't this foolish by your age," Demetrius retorted.

He'd spoken without thinking, not intending to echo her father's brutal words. But he saw the pain flash across her face, and was unsurprised when her answering voice quivered with emotion.

"Foolish or not, I'm not answerable to you, Demetrius. Now go away, and let me do what I came to do." She turned to the Ocean Miner, her tone becoming businesslike. "You said you want my voice. What do you mean by that?"

The Ocean Miner sent Demetrius one more mocking glance before transferring her attention to the young princess. "Just what I said. I wish to have your voice, to use it. As you can hear, mine is weary from use."

"But..." Estelle hesitated. Then, casting a self-conscious look at Demetrius, she straightened. "But I need a voice to win the heart of the prince."

Demetrius let out a snort, his gaze unimpressed as it rested on Estelle's face. She was pointedly refusing to meet his eye.

"I understand the dilemma," said the Ocean Miner, in a sympathetic manner Demetrius found entirely unconvincing. To his intense irritation, she was speaking like Estelle's scheme was actually viable.

"Enough of this nonsense," said Demetrius impatiently. "You can't win the human's heart, Estelle. You're a mermaid, he's a human, end of story."

"You show your ignorance," said Estelle with dignity, still not looking at him. "She has talismans that can turn me into a human."

Demetrius went still, fresh horror washing over him. "Tell me you're not serious, Estelle. Dabbling in talismans is bad enough, but trying to change your form? On the baseless hope that some human—a total stranger—will fall in love with you?"

"You said it yourself, Demetrius," said Estelle, suddenly earnest as she turned at last to face him. "He's a prince. And..." she swallowed, color once again suffusing her cheeks as she lowered her gaze, "and you heard what my father said tonight."

"Estelle..." Demetrius's voice softened in spite of himself, but he had no words to ease the effects of the emperor's severity.

Estelle pulled herself together, her expression calm as she met his eyes again. "If Prince Farrin were to marry me, Demetrius, it would be a marriage alliance beyond anything my father planned for me."

Demetrius's mouth fell open. "*That's* your plan? Estelle, it won't work, for so many reasons." He could see the stubbornness on her face, and he scowled. "I thought you said you didn't care about him being a prince. And now you're angling to become the humans' queen?"

"I didn't care about his title," retorted Estelle. "And of course I don't want to be anyone's queen, and I won't be. I'm fairly certain he's the younger of the brothers." Her glower matched Demetrius's. "If I had my way, I wouldn't even be a princess. But I am, whether I like it or not. So don't pretend it's me who cares about titles. I never thought of him that way—it was *you* who put the idea in my head by going on about him being a prince!"

Demetrius groaned, running a hand over his face. "Estelle, every aspect of this idea is poorly thought through."

"You're wrong," said Estelle flatly, turning back to the Ocean Miner. "Is there anything else you would accept, other than my voice?"

The older mermaid shook her head. "That's my price. You don't need a voice to make a human fall in love with you, you know," she added. "It's the easiest thing in the world, especially with a face like yours."

Demetrius growled low in his throat, not sure whether he was more annoyed with the Ocean Miner for her manipulation, or with Estelle for failing to recognize the blatant flattery.

"But if communication is a concern," the Ocean Miner continued, "we can trade voices. I'll give you mine, you give me yours."

"Yours?" Estelle repeated, doubtfully.

The Ocean Miner gave a ragged laugh that sounded genuinely painful. "I know it doesn't sound pretty, but it works, child."

Estelle paused for a moment, considering. "So we change voices, and I become human." Her eyes narrowed in suspicion. "Will it work above water, though?"

"Of course," said the Ocean Miner comfortably. "Your voice will change form with your body."

Estelle was silent again. "And how long will the transformation last? Will it be permanent?"

"Now that's an excellent question," rasped the Ocean Miner. She cast a glance over the various items on shelves around the room. "To make it unconditional would take too much power. But I don't think we'll tie the magic to a specific length of time." Her eyes studied Estelle thoughtfully. "We'll tie it to the success of your scheme. You seem confident enough."

"You mean she fails to make the prince fall in love with her, and she turns back into a mermaid?" Demetrius asked skeptically. "So we're talking about a very temporary excursion above the surface." Perhaps he could salvage the situation after all.

"I'm afraid not," croaked the Ocean Miner indulgently. "What I was going to say is that romantic love is a potent force, one I can work with in my magic. If she succeeds in making the prince love her, that will unleash power that the enchantment will mold to make the transformation permanent."

"Yes," said Estelle eagerly. "I want that."

"What's the catch?" Demetrius asked darkly. "What happens if she fails?"

The Ocean Miner gave a coarse chuckle. "This one is a sensible one." Her gaze was faintly malicious as it rested on him. "If she fails to win his love, she will die."

"What?" Demetrius protested. "Who would make that deal?"

Estelle remained silent, her expression thoughtful. "Is there a time limit to succeed?" she asked seriously.

"Estelle!" Demetrius gasped. "You can't be considering it!"

She ignored him, her eyes on the Ocean Miner as the other mermaid replied.

"No time limit. But his love must be demonstrated by him marrying you. If he marries someone else instead, you will be dead by the following dawn."

The princess was pale, and for a long moment she didn't speak.

"All right," she said at last. "I'll do it."

"Wait," Demetrius interjected desperately. He couldn't let this happen. "Estelle, of all the foolish things you've ever done, this is the most ridiculous."

"What do you suggest, Demetrius?" Estelle demanded, turning on him suddenly. "Do you have any ideas for how I can spend the next three hundred years that won't make me and everyone around me miserable?"

Demetrius didn't immediately respond, silenced by the intensity of the emotion in her eyes.

"Estelle," he tried again. "You must see that this deal is all in her favor."

"Is there something else you'd like to add, to make it more appealing?" the Ocean Miner asked amicably.

"Yes," said Demetrius promptly. "A way out."

"I don't need a way out," said Estelle impatiently.

He turned to her. "Really? If you succeed, wonderful. All your dreams come true." His tone had been heavy with irony, but it became serious as he forced her to hold his gaze. "But what if you fail, Estelle? Are you saying you'd rather die and become nothing more than sea foam hundreds of years before your time than return to the sea and the life you have now?"

She said nothing, but the answer he read in her eyes frightened him more than all the rest. With a hint of panic, he turned back to the Ocean Miner.

"There should be a way out," he said. "Something she can do to return to her mermaid form if she fails, instead of dying."

"Is that even possible?" Estelle asked doubtfully.

"To turn a human into a mermaid?" The Ocean Miner's expression was dark, and hard to read. "Oh yes, it's possible. But that's not what I'm offering."

"Then it's a terrible deal," said Demetrius angrily.

"I wasn't asking you, Demetrius," said Estelle. She turned to the Ocean Miner. "I said I'd do it, and I will."

Demetrius clenched his fist, recognizing that if Estelle didn't fight for a fair deal, the Ocean Miner would have no incentive to make any better offer, whatever he said.

"I'm going to your father," he said shortly. "This has gone more than far enough."

"You are a loyal protector," smiled the Ocean Miner. "Here's what I'll offer. If failure is imminent, you can come to me again, and we can discuss a fresh deal."

"How's she supposed to communicate with you?" Demetrius protested. "You're down here, and she'll be up there."

"Excellent point," the ancient mermaid agreed. Reaching

onto a shelf, she picked up a jar, pulling a conch shell from it and offering it to Estelle. "Speak into this, and I'll hear."

"Very well," said Estelle, still apparently uninterested in the offer of a way out of the atrocious bargain.

"Wait, you have a method of communication that can cross between land and sea just sitting there?" Demetrius asked, skeptical.

The Ocean Miner gave him her unnerving smile. "I have a lot of things just sitting here," she croaked out. "I'm the Ocean Miner."

Demetrius winced at the sound of that horrible voice, and he saw that Estelle did, too. The princess spoke valiantly, however, pretending not to have noticed the voice she would soon carry.

"So the magic in these talismans really is mined from the ocean bed?"

The Ocean Miner cackled. "Use your brain, child—of course it is. Do I sound like I've been singing for magic any time recently?"

Demetrius ignored the words, turning to the younger mermaid.

"You can't do this, Estelle."

"It's done," she told him curtly. Her eyes flicked to the Ocean Miner. "What do I need to do?"

With a nod, the older mermaid turned and swam through a seaweed curtain. Sounds of rummaging issued out to them, but Demetrius ignored them.

"Please, Estelle, don't do this," he said. "Let me take you home to your family."

"My family doesn't need or want me," said Estelle curtly. "You heard it with your own ears, Demetrius." A slight shudder went over her. "None of this is your problem. You were assigned to Eulalia, not me, and no one knows you followed me here. You can go back to the palace and pretend you have no idea why I'm not in my room in the morning."

"I can't," said Demetrius forcefully. "That's nonsense, and you know it, Estelle." Desperately, he cast around for something to persuade her. "You've dragged me into this, and you owe it to me not to embroil either of us any deeper."

"You embroiled yourself," Estelle snapped. "And I'm not looking for your help. Go home and leave me be."

The Ocean Miner chose that moment to swim back into the room, a glass vial in her hands. Demetrius frowned at it, his gaze passing also to the many specimen jars in the room. Glass was rare, and its use was frowned upon by the upper classes. He didn't think he'd ever seen it in the palace. How did the Ocean Miner have so much of it?

"All you need to do is get yourself fully out of the water, then drink this," the Ocean Miner told Estelle, holding up the vial. Looking closely, Demetrius saw that it was full of a clear liquid. It could be water, for all he knew.

"Once again," Demetrius said suspiciously, "you just had it on hand."

"This one I've had on hand for many years." The Ocean Miner said, her raspy voice coming out a hiss. "But I don't begrudge its use."

Her eyes were greedy as they passed to Estelle, and another wave of fear washed over Demetrius. He didn't know what the Ocean Miner's game was, but it was clear that Estelle was playing right into her hands. Could the young princess truly not see it?

"Thank you," said Estelle, holding out her hand.

"Not so fast," the Ocean Miner said, drawing the vial back. "The voice exchange." She held up an elongated shell which glowed faintly. Demetrius hadn't even seen her retrieve it, but she must have done so when she went for the potion.

"Oh," said Estelle, swallowing visibly. "Yes." She sent Demetrius a strained smile. "Goodbye, then, Demetrius," she said. "I suppose this is the last time we'll speak, with me as me."

"You'll still be yourself, child," cackled the Ocean Miner. "It's only your voice you're giving me."

Estelle nodded, swimming forward with an unconvincing show of confidence. Demetrius shadowed her, his fins flicking in his agitation.

"Estelle," he tried again, a warning in his voice.

She ignored him, barely flinching as the Ocean Miner grabbed her shoulder roughly, then laid one end of the conical shell against Estelle's throat. Her excitement was palpable, and the horrible sight compelled Demetrius to make one last attempt.

"Wait," he said. Estelle made a noise of impatience, but Demetrius's eyes were on the Ocean Miner. "This future deal you mentioned, for a way out if Estelle fails in her aim. It's too undefined. I want some guarantees."

"It's not about what you want, young guard," said the Ocean Miner, her own impatience clear.

"He's right," Estelle said suddenly, her voice quavering a little with nerves. Clearly now the moment had come, she was feeling a few qualms, whether she'd admit it or not. "Why have the offer there if it's meaningless?"

Irritation flashed across the Ocean Miner's face, but she quelled it quickly. "What guarantees?" she asked.

Estelle looked appealingly to Demetrius, and he thought for a moment.

"Firstly, a guarantee that if she reaches out through that shell you gave her, you will actually offer her a deal," he said. "Secondly, that it will be something she's realistically capable of doing."

"Yes, yes, all right," said the Ocean Miner, her impatience once again clear.

"And thirdly," said Demetrius, watching her closely, "that if the deal is fulfilled, and she returns to her mermaid form, you'll return her voice to her."

There was a longer pause this time, and he could read on the Ocean Miner's face how much she resented his moderating interference.

"That sounds fair," Estelle said, nodding. "I want those guarantees as well, before we proceed."

The Ocean Miner didn't even look at the princess, her glare still directed at Demetrius.

"Very well," she ground out. "*If* the princess were to fulfill such a bargain, I would return her voice to her."

"Remember that the bargain has to be something she's realistically capable of doing," pressed Demetrius. His eyes narrowed. "You should make an oath."

"An oath?" she exploded, her voice more raw than ever. "Are you an imbecile, boy? Do you not know how binding oaths of power are, how irrevocable?"

"Of course I do," said Demetrius coldly. "That's why I suggested it. If you intend to honor the agreements you've made anyway, I don't know why it would be an issue."

The Ocean Miner's tail lashed back and forth, her silvery-green hair floating around her face like so much rotting seaweed.

"It's a big bargain," Estelle pointed out. "With significant cost to both of us. I think it should be formalized with an oath." She turned to Demetrius. "Can you harness the power for it?" Her pale face reddened slightly. "I don't know how."

Demetrius's jaw worked for a moment. He could do it, of course. But he was reluctant to take any active role in this terrible bargain. Still, he'd already accepted that it wasn't in his power to prevent Estelle from proceeding. Better she did so protected by an oath that bound the Ocean Miner than without any security. And he certainly didn't trust the Ocean Miner to undertake the task of solidifying the oath.

"I'll harness power for the oath to bind her only," he said gruffly, tilting his head toward the Ocean Miner. "I won't provide power for any bargain."

Estelle nodded curtly, turning an expectant face toward the Ocean Miner. With a sigh, the older mermaid bent her head in acquiescence, clearly recognizing that the princess wouldn't proceed without the oath.

Still uneasy with his part in it, Demetrius began to sing. His throat vibrated with the low hum as he called raw power up from the seabed below. He pulled it into the water, not wrapping it around himself, but sending it swirling around the mermaids. Under his supervision, the Ocean Miner repeated the oaths. Demetrius's song changed as he manipulated the power, feeling how it poured into her, binding her inextricably.

When he was satisfied, he let his song die away, and the Ocean Miner turned to Estelle.

"Now for our bargain," she said in her horrid voice.

"Yes." The princess sounded nervous, but she was clearly still determined. "How do we do it?"

By way of answer, the Ocean Miner seized Estelle's shoulder again and jabbed the shell against the younger mermaid's throat. The gesture was so forceful that Estelle gave a grunt of pain. The Ocean Miner placed the other end against her own throat, issuing a curt command.

"Sing. To give your voice to me, you have to sing."

"But I don't know how to use power to do that," Estelle protested.

The Ocean Miner shook her head impatiently. "I'll manipulate the power. You just need to sing."

With an uncertain glance at Demetrius, Estelle did as instructed, her voice starting hesitant, but growing quickly in strength. Once again, Demetrius was mesmerized in spite of himself, lost in the loveliness of the melody. It truly was the purest, sweetest song he'd ever heard. Only when his eyes passed to the Ocean Miner, and he saw the undisguised greed on her face, did his enjoyment dim as he remembered the purpose for which they were there. He could feel the power Estelle was calling up, and sensed the way it was being manipulated by the older mermaid.

Then, quite abruptly, the song went silent. Estelle looked confused for a moment, then she touched her throat, her eyes round and a little afraid, in spite of her bold front.

"Your prize, Princess. Remember, fully out of the water before you drink it." The melodious voice came not from the young mermaid, but from the Ocean Miner. The sound was so wrong for her gnarled old frame, it made Demetrius's stomach curl with discomfort.

The Ocean Miner held out the vial, and Estelle snatched it up eagerly. With a final nod at the twisted old criminal, she swam from the chamber. Throwing the Ocean Miner a dirty glance, Demetrius followed.

"Estelle," he pleaded, as he caught up to the princess just outside the cave. "It's not too late to turn back. She can't be trusted. What if the potion doesn't do what she said?"

"She took an oath." Estelle's eyes widened in shock to hear the scratchy voice coming from her own mouth, and even Demetrius jolted a little in the water. The young mermaid put a slender hand to her throat, her next words the barest whisper. "It hurts."

Demetrius's heart wrenched unbearably, and he felt anger flash through him at the hideousness of it all.

"Estelle, turn back," he said, the words a command. "That

mermaid is evil, couldn't you see that? Whatever her purposes are in making this deal with you, they're nothing good. We should go to your father right now, tell him everything. He'll have the power to force her to reverse the voice exchange, and everything can go back to how it was."

Estelle gave a hollow laugh. "He'd banish me to the deeps forever," she rasped, the words sending a fresh wave of pain over her face. With a little shake of the head, she turned, tilting her face toward the surface. "Goodbye, Demetrius."

It was more whimper than words, and Demetrius couldn't bear to respond. Estelle lingered for a moment, as if waiting for him to try again to stop her, but he said nothing. With another nod, she propelled herself straight upward, heading for the distant surface.

Demetrius hesitated, watching her form disappear into the gloom. Had any guard ever failed more completely in his duty? He was a member of the emperor's elite royal guard, and he'd just watched the princess sign her life away in an illicit bargain with the empire's most dangerous criminal. It was the most horrific mess imaginable. A voice somewhere in Demetrius's mind rebelled against his self-directed strictures, arguing that it was a mess of the emperor's own making after the scene at dinner, and the fifteen years that had preceded it.

But there was nothing to be gained by assigning blame. His only priority had to be fixing the disaster. He had to save Estelle from herself.

Swirling around, he hastened back into the cave, propelled by his anger.

"You," he accused the Ocean Miner, the moment she came into sight. She was right where he'd left her, her arms folded as she watched the entrance with a smirk. Clearly she'd expected his return. "You exploited her naivety, her youth."

"And what of it, guard?" the ancient mermaid purred musically.

The sound of Estelle's innocent young voice coming from that depraved form was so offensive, Demetrius actually turned his head away.

He regretted it a moment later, when the Ocean Miner spoke again, her tones horrifyingly familiar.

"Don't you like what you hear, Demetrius? It is Demetrius, isn't it? But I thought you were fond of the sound of my voice. I certainly say your name with such earnestness, such trust. Surely you could hear the way my tone pleaded with you to rescue me from my folly, even while my words tried so clumsily to send you away."

"Stop it," Demetrius snapped, his hands balled into fists as he forced himself to stare back at the Ocean Miner. He needed the evidence of his eyes to remind himself that it wasn't really Estelle speaking to him. "How dare you do this? Do you think you can get away with it? She's the daughter of the emperor. When he finds out—"

Estelle's bright, musical laugh cut him off. "I'm not in the least afraid of Emperor Aefic," the Ocean Miner said. Her eyes were indulgent as they raked over him. "You're a member of his guard, aren't you? Why don't you swim along back to the palace right now, tell him what happened, and ask if his orders are to kill me?"

Demetrius stared at her, confused by both her words and her confidence. If Emperor Aefic didn't have the Ocean Miner executed after this night's work, he would be utterly astonished.

"Of course," she went on pleasantly, "if you did that, you'd have no hope of catching up to our sweet young princess, as I can see you're itching to do."

Demetrius bit the inside of his cheek to keep the things he

wanted to shout at her inside. Expressing his anger would only waste time.

"That wasn't all of the potion, was it?" he demanded. "You have more."

She smiled benignly at him, not troubling to confirm it aloud.

"Give it to me," he demanded. "She can't go alone."

Her smile broadened. "But what will you give me for it, my dear, kind, *dependable* friend, Demetrius?"

A shudder went over him at the caressing way she said his name. There was no doubt she'd formed her own conclusions about the nature of his interest in Estelle. Wrong though she might be, he still found the experience of Estelle's voice speaking like that to him utterly unnerving.

"I'm not giving you my voice," he said flatly.

She laughed, the girlish sound grotesque coming from her mouth. "I don't want it," she assured him. She studied his face thoughtfully. "I don't object to you accompanying her," she mused. "I might be willing to give you the potion for no benefit to myself. There will, of course, be a natural price attached."

"And what's that?" Demetrius asked darkly.

Her peaceful smile was back. "The potion I gave the princess was incredibly powerful. It was the work of years, and whatever you think, I do not have an excess of it lying around. But I can give you a mimicking draft."

"I'm not versed in the depraved ways of talismans," spat Demetrius, resenting the fact that she was making him draw the information out of her.

"The potion she drinks will leave traces in the vial," the Ocean Miner explained. "If you retrieve the vial before it is washed clean, and pour the mimicking draft into it, it will assume the properties of the previous potion. But," she raised an admonishing finger like she was disciplining a child, "it will be *her* potion you are drinking, not your own. Which means your life will be tied to hers."

"Tied to hers how?" Demetrius asked slowly.

"You will share her fate," the Ocean Miner said. "If she fails, and the prince marries another, you will die just as she does."

"You're forgetting that in that case, she may seek a secondary bargain in order to return to the sea," Demetrius challenged.

"Not at all," she assured him. "That fate you will also share. If she makes a bargain with me, the same terms will apply to you. And, of course, if she succeeds in winning her prince, and remains human forever, you also will keep her form." Her smirk told Demetrius that she knew how utterly improbable that outcome was. "Well, not literally forever," the Ocean Miner clarified. "For another five decades or so, until you die as the humans do."

"What?" Demetrius felt fresh rage wash over him. "You never mentioned to Estelle that her life would be shortened by taking a human form."

The Ocean Miner shrugged. "She should have realized it. The lifespan comes with the form." Her eyes narrowed. "It's not in my control. That's simply how it is." Her expression cleared again as she looked at him. "So what's your decision, guard? Do you race to your emperor, knowing that by the time his forces chase the princess down, it will be too late for them to reach her, and she will be left to her fate alone? Or do you follow her onto land, and share her triumph or defeat?"

Demetrius's fists were balled so tightly now, his nails were digging into his palms. But he knew there was no real choice. However foolish Estelle had been, he couldn't leave her to face the consequences of this terrible bargain alone. Every protective instinct rebelled against the idea.

"Give me the mimicking draft," he snapped, holding out a hand.

With a smile that was uncomfortably predatory, the Ocean Miner unfolded her arms, revealing another vial. Demetrius clenched his teeth, hating how well she'd read him. He wasn't fooled by her blithe words about giving it to him without benefit to herself. She was gaining from the exchange somehow, he had no doubt. But he took it without hesitation, stowing it in the pouch set into the smooth strap over his chest.

"I won't forget this night's work," he ground out. "And I'll make sure you answer for it."

"Of course, Demetrius, whatever you say," crooned the Ocean Miner in that familiar voice. "You're so old and wise, I'll be sure to follow your advice and turn to you for everything."

With a final contemptuous look, Demetrius turned his back on her, eager to put some distance between himself and the old crone's lair. As he streaked out into the water, numb disbelief tugged at him. Was he really about to throw everything away without warning, and take on the form of a human of all things? Was he going to catapult himself into Estelle's misadventure with no idea if there was any way back?

He pushed those thoughts aside, refusing to dwell on all the painful implications of his decision. He'd chosen his course, and there was nothing to be gained by doubting it now. He had to reach Estelle before it was too late to salvage that vial.

CHAPTER TWELVE

Estelle

Estelle stared nervously at the surface above her. She'd come this far, given everything to reach this point, and she was hesitating now? Shaking her head, she broke the surface, closing her eyes and letting the cold air on her skin steady her. There was nothing she wanted more than to live on the land, with Farrin. She'd paid a heavy price, but it was worth it for even the chance of such happiness.

She held her breath as she swam, excitement coursing through her as she remembered that soon that wouldn't be necessary. She'd be able to breathe air once she took the potion. As the land came into view, a smudge of light touched the eastern horizon. It was almost dawn, which meant she needed to hurry. Farrin always walked the cliffs just after dawn, and she didn't want to miss him.

The thought flashed through her mind that her sisters were leaving the capital soon after dawn. She felt a pang at the realization that she wouldn't be there to see Eulalia off when her sister's family departed for their own province. And not just Eulalia—she wouldn't get the chance to say goodbye to any of her family.

The scene at dinner rose in her memory, and she pushed her regret aside. They weren't going to miss her, that much was certain.

There was no one in sight when Estelle reached the beach where she and Demetrius had deposited Farrin the morning after he fell from the ship. The precious vial was still clutched in her hand, and she hugged it protectively to herself as she inched her way through the shallows. The morning air felt cold on her wet skin, but she didn't pause. The Ocean Miner had said she needed to be all the way out of the water before taking the potion. Sticking her head into the few inches of water around her, she drew in one last pull through her gills, then returned her face to the air.

Using her free arm to pull herself along the sand, Estelle moved steadily out of the water. It felt strange when her fins emerged onto sand, the air light and insubstantial against her scales. She was beginning to burn for breath, every instinct screaming at her to return to the water. She ignored her body, however, her hand trembling a little as she raised the vial and pulled out the stopper. Pausing only to reassure herself that no part of her was touching the water, she downed the contents in one gulp.

At once, agony lanced through her. It was so brutal, she was certain for a moment that the Ocean Miner had deceived her, and she was dying. But the next second, she felt a tearing pressure on her tail, and looked down to see her familiar blue scales parting. Much as she'd longed for a human form, the sight was disturbing, her terrified mind reacting instinctively to the sight of her body splitting apart. The two scaled protrusions changed before her eyes, glittering blue scales turning to the same smooth, pale skin that covered her upper half. Her fins—one on the end of each leg—began to transform as well, their silky surface filling out and turning into feet.

A burning ache spread across her face, and she reached up to feel her nose changing. It was pushing out from her face, her gills melding into smooth skin across the protrusion.

Estelle's mind was spinning from lack of air, and without thinking, she drew in an instinctive breath. Amazingly, in spite of the lack of gills, air passed cleanly into her nose, bringing instant relief.

She could breathe pure air. She was human.

The pain was completely gone, a hundred unfamiliar sensations washing over Estelle's body in its place. The air felt so thin compared to the familiar weight of water all around her. And the breeze was cold and refreshing, nothing like the currents that swirled through her old home.

Estelle tried to push herself up, but her new legs were too wobbly. She collapsed quickly onto the beach, and contented herself with digging her toes into the cool sand. Her eyes traveled in marvel over her new form, embarrassment coursing through her as she realized she was completely uncovered but for the satchel slung over her shoulder.

A glance up showed still no sign of Farrin on the cliffs, and Estelle cast her eyes around for something to cover herself with. The section of cliff which jutted straight out into the water wasn't far away, and there was a huge pile of seaweed near the base. She pulled herself quickly across the sand toward it and wrapped the thick, slimy strands around her body. The empty vial in her hand was hampering her movement, and she stashed it in her satchel. The action reminded her that she would probably do well to dispose of the satchel. Its contents were clearly from the ocean, and she'd already decided that her best approach in winning Farrin's love would be to pretend to be a proper human, at least until he got to know her.

Surprising herself with her reluctance to part with it—it was the only relic she had of her home—she hid it in a crevice of the cliff. Hopefully she would get the chance to come back for it, when she had somewhere safe to put it, away from prying eyes.

She'd just begun to edge away from the cliff when she heard it—the familiar cheerful whistling. Estelle's heart leaped into her throat as a handsome figure came into view above her. A potent mix of sensations claimed her, as her new breathing sped up, and her vision spun with excitement at the prospect of properly meeting him at last. This was love, surely.

If only she wasn't at such a disadvantage, though. She felt very exposed and powerless, huddled under her makeshift clothing. She was still debating with herself over whether she should call out to the human prince when his gaze happened to fall onto the beach, and he pulled up in visible surprise.

"Hello?" he called uncertainly. "Are you all right, miss?"

Estelle swallowed, overwhelmed by his full attention. She opened her mouth, not entirely sure what to tell him.

"I—" The word died on her lips, the barest whisper making it out before she cut it off. Farrin wouldn't even have heard it. Estelle clutched at her throat, agony racing through it. If she'd thought it had hurt to speak with the Ocean Miner's voice underwater, it was nothing to how it felt in the air. The pain was genuinely unbearable.

Fear gripped her as she realized that she was effectively voiceless. She hadn't bargained on that. What would she do now? How would she be able to capture Farrin's interest? She swallowed again, every inch of her throat still feeling as though someone had stabbed it.

"Miss?" the prince tried again. "Are you all right?"

Tears welled in Estelle's eyes. She'd intended to show more poise, but she couldn't help herself. In a burst of honesty, she shook her head in answer to his question. Concern lined the young prince's handsome face, and he hastened toward a steep rocky path leading from the cliff down to the sand.

"Are you hurt?" he called, as he neared her. "Is there some way I can—"

He came to an abrupt stop, and for a moment Estelle was afraid she'd somehow resumed her mermaid form. A quick glance down assured her that she hadn't, but also showed her the reason for the prince's evident embarrassment. The seaweed was covering her more than she'd ever been covered underwater, but it must still have been clear that she wore nothing under it.

She saw the prince's gaze travel across the sand, his eyes widening as he caught sight of the tracks she'd left from the water's edge. Were they too clearly caused by a tail rather than legs?

"You were washed up here?" Farrin breathed.

His eyes were full of sympathy as they passed back to Estelle, and she noticed for the first time that they were brown. It was an uncommon eye color in mermaids, and for a moment, Estelle was mesmerized. For some reason, Farrin's eyes reminded her of Demetrius's dark amber ones, although Farrin's were darker.

Thoughts of the merman caused Estelle's stomach to swirl uncomfortably. Where was he now? Had he reported everything to her father? Was he glad to be free of any sense of responsibility for the flighty young princess?

Princess Estelle is a child. His contemptuous words rang in her mind, followed by others which caused pain as acute as that in her throat to cut across her heart. *Most mermaids aren't this foolish by your age.*

She knew Demetrius meant well, and she wanted to believe she could still count him a friend. But it stung bitterly to know that he shared her father's view about her unsuitability to take on the responsibilities of a mermaid who'd come of age.

But why was she thinking about Demetrius, with Farrin

finally before her? Turning back to the prince, she realized he was still waiting for an answer. But her throat still throbbed with the memory of pain, and she couldn't bring herself to try further speech.

"What's your name?" Farrin tried again, his voice gentle. "I'm Farrin."

Estelle opened her mouth to speak her name, then closed it miserably. It was too painful. Perhaps it was for the best, she tried to argue with herself. The horribly scratchy voice the Ocean Miner had given her wouldn't make the best impression, after all.

"I shouldn't be peppering you with questions," said Farrin, contrite. His eyes passed out to the ocean, troubled. "I didn't know there'd been a shipwreck. Or did you get thrown from a ship somehow?" His face softened. "You poor thing, I know what that's like, and it's a terror I wouldn't wish on anyone." Apparently struck by a sudden idea, he stripped off his overcoat, which hung halfway down his legs. "Here." Tossing it to Estelle, he considerately turned his back.

Estelle struggled into it as best she could, trying again to push herself to her new feet. To her relief, the overcoat was big enough to envelop her whole body. She wobbled where she stood, but a moment later, Farrin had appeared, offering his arm for her to lean on.

"You're in a bad way," he said, his voice still full of sympathetic concern. He glanced around. "Are you all alone?"

Throat tight with emotion, Estelle nodded.

"Not anymore," said Farrin staunchly. "I'll take you back to the castle. We'll soon get you cleaned up."

Estelle's heart soared as he put an arm around her, supporting her up the rocky path. Her mastery over her legs was so nonexistent, he practically had to carry her. Even so, Estelle found herself wincing every time her bare feet connected with the uneven slope. The new skin was tender, and her progress was slow.

She didn't mind. She'd come to the land to find Farrin, and here he was. He was every bit as kind as she'd known he would be, and even more handsome up close. His tawny hair glinted in the morning sun, and Estelle was fascinated by it, so different in appearance and motion from hair underwater. A light breeze sent a strand dancing over his eyes, and if her balance had been good enough to lift an arm, she would have been very tempted to clear it for him. As it was, she made no effort to hide her adoration as she gazed up at him, much more interested in the prince than in the castle looming into view ahead.

He was too perfect to be real.

When they reached the top of the cliff, Estelle pulled her eyes from Farrin at last, casting her gaze toward the ocean. She pulled in a sharp breath. It was a stunning sight, the endless expanse calling to her in a way that she couldn't deny. She had to work hard to remind herself that it was neither as beautiful nor as peaceful below the surface as it looked from above. Nothing but humiliation and misery awaited her down there.

Forcing her gaze away, she stared in amazement at the building growing steadily nearer. The castle of the humans was much more impressive up close than it had been from the ocean. The walls were a sandy color, their sides much smoother and their angles much cleaner than any structure carved from the bedrock. The castle seemed to be made up of several joined buildings, each topped with a dome of purple tiles. The effect was beautiful, and perfectly matched the setting. The building looked like it had sprung up from the beach, as natural a part of the scene as the sandy cliffs themselves.

In her distraction, Estelle stumbled over a large stone, and an involuntary whimper escaped her. Her throat throbbed at the sound, and she raised a hand to it, causing her to wobble further.

"Easy there," Farrin said kindly. "Lean on me, that's it."

Estelle's heart swelled again. He didn't even know she was a princess, and yet he was treating her with much more care and consideration than she'd ever received in her own palace. Where was the supposed inferiority of humans?

When they were close to the castle, a low stone wall appeared, two guards standing to attention on either side of the gate. Estelle cast an anxious glance at Farrin, but he just gave her a reassuring nod. Moving with as much confidence as her father in his own domain, Farrin supported her through the gate and across a large courtyard. When they reached the castle's entrance, he sent a servant scurrying ahead of them, with instructions to fetch someone called *the housekeeper*. Estelle barely took in his words, too distracted by staring in fascination at everything around her. Her mind could barely process all the new sensations.

"The head housekeeper will look after you," Farrin assured her, his voice friendly, even while his smile held the awkwardness of a stranger.

We're not strangers, Estelle longed to tell him. *I'm the one who saved your life, I've watched you every day*. The words were held in as much by the knowledge of how foolish they would sound as by the agony of using her revolting new voice.

A middle-aged woman bustled up, with the competent air of a senior servant. Like Farrin, she was clad from head to foot in fabric, although her clothing was very different in style from his. It fell straight down over her legs, instead of molding itself separately around each one. It was also simpler than his, although she looked perfectly neat and respectable.

If only the same could be said for the uninvited guest.

The housekeeper cast a scandalized look over Estelle, who

was wobbling for balance as she clutched Farrin's overcoat close, and whose hair was dripping onto the polished floor beneath her bare feet.

"Your Highness?"

The housekeeper's astonished question made Estelle start, wondering if her identity had somehow been discovered. But of course it was Farrin the woman was speaking to, and her expression bordered on horrified.

"I found this poor girl washed up on the beach," said Farrin confidently.

"But who is she?" demanded the housekeeper. "Why did you bring her here?"

"So she could receive some assistance," said Farrin, as if it was obvious. "She was all alone, and in a bad state. She can barely walk. I think she suffered a misadventure aboard a ship."

"You think, Your Highness?" the housekeeper pressed, her gaze suspicious. "Can't she confirm it?" Her eyes passed to Estelle. "What's your name, child?"

Estelle swallowed, steeling herself. It was time to speak, but what could she say? She could hardly tell them that she'd come from the ocean itself rather than a ship on its surface.

Bracing for the pain, Estelle tried to tell them her name, as a safe starting point. But the first syllable turned into nothing more than a wordless grunt, cut off by the agony for which she obviously hadn't adequately prepared herself.

She clutched her throat, tears starting to her eyes.

"I think she might be mute," Farrin murmured.

"Hm." The housekeeper sounded unimpressed. "She can still nod or shake her head, I assume." She bent her keen eye on Estelle. "Did you fall from a ship, lass? Is that how you ended up on the beach?"

Estelle hesitated, her desire to give a good impression to someone who clearly had influence in the castle warring with her uncertainty about what would be safest to say. She should really have come up with a better plan before drinking that potion. Somehow all she'd thought about was finding Farrin. What came next hadn't even entered her mind.

"I'm honestly not sure she remembers," Farrin said, his voice softer than ever. "I think her mind might be a little overwrought by whatever she's experienced." His tone was a little reproachful as he frowned at the housekeeper. "Surely there's no need to press her."

"But what do you want me to do with her, Your Highness?" the woman demanded.

"Be kind to her," he said mildly. "A hot bath and some clothes would be my first suggestion, but I'm sure you'll know what to do better than I would."

"But we don't even know who she is, Your Highness," protested the housekeeper. "The castle isn't in the habit of taking in nameless strays."

The prince made a scolding noise in his throat, casting an apologetic look at Estelle. "I'm afraid you're not forming a very good impression of Medullan hospitality, miss." He glared at the housekeeper. "I'm sure you'll be happy to change your habits when you've been specifically requested by a member of the royal family."

"Just the one member of the family, Your Highness?" the housekeeper asked dryly.

Farrin sighed. "I'll speak to my parents. You won't be called upon to provide any explanations." He shot Estelle a smile so charming, it sent flutters down her spine. "Perhaps our guest can join us for luncheon, and I can explain the morning's events to my family then." He brightened. "I'm told Emmett arrived home late last night. He can meet her as well."

"Join the royal family, Your Highness?" the housekeeper asked, once again sounding scandalized. "Surely not."

"Of course," Farrin said lightly. "Why not?" He smiled at Estelle once again. "In the meantime, I'm leaving you in very capable hands."

With one more nod at the housekeeper, he strolled away, his hands in his pocket and the same cheerful whistle back on his lips. Estelle stared after him for one longing moment, then let her gaze pass slowly back to the housekeeper.

The middle-aged woman—so much more intimidating than the friendly young prince—was scrutinizing her thoughtfully, and Estelle once again wobbled on her feet. She hadn't counted on being separated from Farrin so quickly. But what had she expected? That he would fall in love with her at first sight, like she had done for him, and wish to never leave her side?

Maybe a little.

Demetrius's scathing words about her plan danced across her memory. *Of all the foolish things you've ever done, this is the most ridiculous,* he'd said. *Every aspect of this idea is poorly thought through.*

In addition to his words, her mind conjured up his face, its disapproving expression seeming to mock her. He'd never shared her faith in what she'd been told about humans falling in love so easily. A horrible fear slashed across her, as sharp as the pain in her throat when she spoke. What if he was right?

Estelle shook off the thought, ashamed of her own fears. It would help nothing for her to lose confidence in herself now. Farrin had been more than kind—his love didn't have to be won immediately in order for her to fulfill the bargain she'd made with the Ocean Miner. It was absurd of her to think it would be that easy.

Scolding herself internally for acting like the foolish child her father thought her, Estelle straightened, meeting the housekeeper's eye. She may seem to the older woman like a nameless waif, but she was the princess of a powerful empire. She hadn't been washed ashore by an unfeeling tide. She'd come to the land on her own initiative, at great personal cost, and whatever Demetrius might think, it had been a calculated risk.

Thoughts of the guard sent a wave of sadness over Estelle, unexpected in its poignancy. She almost thought she would miss the young merman most from Korallid. Bizarre, given how short a time they'd known one another. He'd been the one companion she could be completely honest with. Critical he might be, but somehow it had never stopped her from telling him the truth.

"I suppose you'd best come along then," said the housekeeper, pulling Estelle from her melancholy thoughts. "We certainly need to get you some clothing before anything else."

She started across the entranceway, and Estelle tried to follow. Except she still didn't really know how to use her new legs. They gave way immediately, and she fell with a grunt to the floor.

The housekeeper's face softened slightly as she turned back, clucking her tongue. "Dear, dear, you are in a state, aren't you?" With a firm grip, she helped Estelle up, drawing Estelle's arm around her shoulders. "Lean on me, child, we'll soon get you resting after your ordeal." She made another disapproving noise. "Luncheon with the royal family is taking it a bit far, but a warm bath and some clothes we can certainly do."

Estelle nodded gratefully, although she didn't try to speak her thanks aloud. She would take whatever assistance she could get, and in fact she was inclined to agree with the housekeeper. She wasn't at all sure she wanted to dine with the king and queen in her current state.

At least she was guaranteed to see Farrin again soon.

The thought drew her eyes back toward the doorway through which he'd disappeared, and unease leaked into her stomach. It had all seemed so simple underwater, when she'd pinned her hopes on Farrin himself, without much thought for the family or responsibilities he'd been born into. Everything was much more complicated now she was in his world. Not that her opinion of him had lessened. He was every bit as kind as she'd been sure he would be.

He was the sort of person who would be kind to a total stranger, without any benefit to himself. It reflected well on the prince, but it wasn't altogether encouraging. Because from what she'd so far observed, the one crucial ingredient that was missing was any desire to change her from a stranger into something more.

CHAPTER THIRTEEN

Demetrius

Demetrius swam into the shallows just in time to watch Prince Farrin lead Estelle up onto the cliff. A soft groan escaped him. It seemed he'd been only minutes too late to speak with the princess alone. At least he now knew the potion worked. He wasn't able to get a good look at Estelle to see the minute changes, but clearly she had legs, and the human prince was interacting with her as though she was human.

Demetrius's whole body tensed as he watched the mermaid-turned-human being half-carried by the prince. Estelle had no basis whatsoever for her belief in this Prince Farrin's kindness. For all Demetrius knew, the human could be as predatory as the Ocean Miner. And the princess was now utterly in his power. Demetrius chafed against the barrier that kept him from following, both his personality and his training rebelling against the role of passive onlooker. He hadn't come all this way to float by while Estelle went into danger.

Where was the vial? Had she taken it with her? If so, Demetrius had little hope of retrieving it in time for his mimicking draft to be useful.

He searched the beach with his eyes, seeing the trail Estelle had left in the sand. Why had she dragged herself over to the base of the cliff? A glance up showed that the pair were now out of sight, and Demetrius shifted forward, swishing his tail from side to side as he inched through the shallows. Holding his breath, he dragged himself fully out of the water, his arms tight as he pulled himself swiftly hand over hand across the sand. It didn't take him long to find the satchel Estelle had inexpertly hidden in the rocks. To his great relief, the vial was shoved into it.

Wasting no more time on thought, Demetrius pulled his own vial from the broad strap over his chest, unstoppering it and pouring the liquid into Estelle's empty vial. At once, the solution clouded over, glowing faintly before settling into a substance as clear as water.

Hopefully that meant it had worked.

Demetrius was eager for air by this time, and he didn't delay. Tipping the vial back, he drank it all. Pain assaulted his senses. Mercifully, the transformation was quick, but he was still rattled by the pain. He hadn't expected it to be so intense. Hopefully it hadn't been as bad for Estelle.

When Demetrius looked down at the legs now sprouting from him where his tail should be, and felt the nose protruding aggressively from his face, he hardly knew what to feel. There was surprisingly little emotion in his reaction. Probably because it was all so surreal, he didn't entirely believe it was happening.

He was eager to follow the princess before he lost her trail, but he realized he needed to do something about his uncovered state first. His only garment was the strap across his chest, which constituted the uniform of a royal guard. It was a wide band, and rearranging it around his hips provided a modicum of decency, but he knew he'd have to find something better quickly.

He looked up at the top of the cliff, realizing that he needed to get off the beach. For one unthinking moment, he tried to flick his tail, intending to rise through the air toward the higher ground. But of course, that achieved nothing but making him lose his balance and topple to the sand. Brushing himself off, he struggled once more to an upright position. How shamefully limited this form was! He was confined to the ground, his feet all but tethered to the land Estelle so idolized. What she could see in this life was utterly beyond him.

Resigning himself, he moved awkwardly toward the path he could see zigzagging up the cliff face. His progress was painfully slow, his mind no longer confident in directing his body. He knew he had legs now, but he couldn't stop himself from constantly trying to swish his tail instead of putting one foot in front of the other, and the result was a great deal of falling over.

He eventually managed it, however, and fortunately without any witnesses. His sharp eyes scanned the shoreline on the other side of the protruding cliff and came to rest on a wooden boat. It was a much smaller and simpler version of the vessel from which he'd seen Prince Farrin fall. With several more falls, Demetrius made it tortuously back down the cliff's other side, relieved to reach the soft sand again. A quick exploration of the boat uncovered a wooden box built into its interior. Using his blade, Demetrius forced it open, delighted to discover human garments inside, among other things.

The fisherman would likely miss his change of clothes next time he went onto the water, but Demetrius didn't hesitate to don them, yanking them on according to his best guess. He'd seen Prince Farrin enough times to get the general idea. It was much easier than trying to steal clothes from a human settlement, as he'd feared would be necessary.

In his unwilling surveillance of the human prince each dawn, Demetrius had noticed that Farrin wore sturdy coverings on his feet. Unfortunately no such items were to be found in the boat, so his new feet had to suffer their way back up the cliff. They were cut and bleeding by the time he reached the higher ground, but he disregarded it. He had bigger problems to think about.

Readjusting his strap to a more comfortable position, Demetrius slung Estelle's satchel over his shoulder as well. He'd seen at a glance that in addition to the seashell the Ocean Miner had given her for communication, it was full of expensive baubles. While there was no telling whether what was considered valuable underwater would be of any use on land, something to trade was better than nothing.

It turned out that Demetrius needn't have worried about losing the princess's trail. The castle was immediately obvious once he reached the top of the cliff, its reddish stone seeming to glow in the early morning light. Behind and to one side of it a city sprawled. The bulk of it disappeared northward, although there were also a decent number of buildings stretching eastward along the shore. The closest of these were a short walk away, the simplicity of the dwellings a stark contrast to the opulent castle nearby.

Demetrius's eyes strayed back to the castle. There could be no doubt that was where Prince Farrin would take her. How Demetrius would gain entry was another matter entirely. With a sinking feeling, he realized that pursuing her immediately wasn't the wisest course. If he attempted and was barred entry to the castle, he would identify himself as a potential threat, and be less likely to gain entry at a later time.

Much as it pained him to remember it, Estelle's adventure was not going to be the work of an afternoon. She—and by extension Demetrius—would be stuck on land until she either succeeded in her plan, or was forced to turn to the Ocean Miner for another manipulative deal. Realistically, the latter.

That being the case, Demetrius would be smarter to try to establish himself a little in the human world before approaching the castle. He had little choice but to hope that the royals would do her no harm during that time.

Having reached this conclusion, Demetrius turned toward the simpler dwellings to the east of the castle, figuring that he would stand out less in his disheveled state if he wasn't trying to mingle with wealthy humans. His first instinct was to keep fully out of sight while he tried to master his new body, but he didn't have time for that approach. For one thing, he was no longer confident he'd be able to hunt for food in the water, which meant that he'd have to find a way to acquire human food before long. For another, the need to learn the ways of the humans was equally pressing. And for that, he'd have to be among them.

He'd barely begun his awkward shuffle toward the town when a figure came into view, hurrying along the path that led from the buildings to the shoreline. Demetrius dropped his eyes, hoping to avoid attracting attention, but thanks to his training, he couldn't stop himself from casting a calculating look at the stranger, assessing him for any sign of a threat.

It was a good thing he did, or he might have missed the hasty way the man stowed something into a pocket when he caught sight of Demetrius. His suspicions instantly roused, Demetrius slowed down, listening hard as he attempted to look inconspicuous. Not a feat he was likely to achieve, he thought, watching the confident, steady way in which the other man moved his legs. In comparison, Demetrius felt like a crab with half its legs broken.

The man hurried past him, and Demetrius's eyes followed as the stranger reached the top of the cliff. Demetrius tensed as the man's eyes traveled over the beach. Both his and Estelle's tracks were still visible on the sand. The stranger stood frozen for a moment, then whirled around so quickly, he caught Demetrius watching him.

"Morning, friend," the man said, his cheerful air unconvincing. "I don't think I've seen you 'round the village before."

Demetrius said nothing, gripping his blade against his side, where it wouldn't be visible.

"Been walking on the beach, have you?" the man persisted, coming closer. "I wonder if you've seen my dog. Ran from me not half an hour ago, and I can't find the silly pup."

Demetrius neither knew nor cared what a dog was, but he judged that it would be more suspicious to remain silent than to respond.

"I didn't see any pup," he said. It was the first time he'd used his voice above the water, and the sound was strange. It was his own, no question. But it sounded so shrill in the vast emptiness that was the air. There was no softening water to catch it, no constant sound of seething ocean to envelop it. Demetrius had been too distracted to notice it before, but now he realized that the land sounded oddly empty, the cry of birds and the whistle of the wind so separated from his ears that he couldn't connect with them. It felt like he'd stepped into nothingness, and it was unnerving.

As he wrestled with his new environment, the stranger continued to edge closer. His gaze was searching as he looked Demetrius over from his shoulder-length hair to his bare, scratched feet.

"You don't look so good," he said. "Have you had some kind of an injury? Perhaps I can help you."

"No, thanks," Demetrius said colorlessly. "I'm fine."

His accent was noticeably different from the human's, and he wasn't surprised when the man's eyes narrowed. Demetrius saw the stranger's intention on his face a moment before he lunged, and he pulled out his whalebone blade.

The weapon was no match for the flashing silver dagger that had appeared in the other man's hand, however, and Demetrius's lack of balance did him no favors. It was all he could do to hold off the death blow, and his clumsy attempts to grab at his attacker sent them both toppling to the ground, weapons clattering away across the rocks.

"You're him, aren't you?" hissed the stranger into his ear. "Ocean scum. Where's the girl?"

Demetrius stiffened in alarm. This man knew who and what he was, and worse, knew about Estelle. How was that possible? Humans were supposed to believe merfolk to be a legend. How could one of them have been expecting the pair to appear on the beach?

The two men struggled wildly, the odds evened now they were off their feet. Demetrius's arms were strong, the air offering less resistance to his movement than water would. After a wild tussle, Demetrius managed to yank one hand free and pull it back for a blow. He struck the other man full in the face, and took advantage of the reprieve to plunge his hand into the pocket where he'd seen the human hide something.

The moment his fingers closed around a small, ridged shape, he rolled away, leaving the other man on his knees, holding his bleeding face with one hand. Demetrius lifted his own hand to see a seashell, similar to the one the Ocean Miner had given Estelle. It emitted a faint, unnatural glow in the early morning light. For a moment, Demetrius just stared at it, then his eyes passed to the other man in shock.

"She sent you," he whispered. "To kill us."

"Primarily just you," the man said, spitting out a mouthful of blood. "So I reckon it's time to get it done."

He lunged toward Demetrius, producing another dagger Demetrius hadn't even noticed. Demetrius tried to scrabble backward instinctively, but his hands slipped on the shaley rocks, and he found himself flat on his back. As the other man dove toward him, instinct took over, forgetting his change in form. He tried to lift his tail in a defensive move, and in its place, his legs rose up to meet the lunging stranger. Catching the man full in the stomach, he sent him into the air, his feet carrying the stranger right over the top of him.

With a horrible cry, the human flew past Demetrius's head and plummeted down the cliff. For a moment, Demetrius just stared at his feet and legs, impressed in spite of himself at the strength they clearly possessed, if he could just learn to master their movements. That motion had been no weaker than the equivalent action would be with a tail.

He scrabbled around to peer over the cliff, wondering if he should stay to keep fighting, or flee while he had a head start on his adversary. The true human would undoubtedly move faster than Demetrius had done, but he would still be restricted by the necessity to climb the cliff rather than cruise over it.

But when he caught sight of the man's unmoving form, he stilled. He knew from watching Prince Farrin's accident that falling through air was a very different matter from floating down through water. Still, he wouldn't have guessed that a fall from the height of the relatively low cliff would break a human. Scrutinizing the form below him more carefully, he realized that the stranger's head seemed to have landed on a rock that protruded from the sand.

Demetrius leaned back from the edge, shock warring with his relief. He was glad the man wouldn't be able to kill him or Estelle, but he had no answers, and no way to get them now. His eyes passed to the seashell which he'd dropped in his defensive maneuver. Abruptly, he grabbed a nearby rock and brought it smashing down onto the shell, shattering it. He thought he heard a faint sigh escaping the vessel, but there was no other indication of the magic it had held.

"Hi there! Are you all right?"

Demetrius's head shot up at the call. He gave no response, but he struggled to his feet as another man came running into sight. This new human sprinted to Demetrius's side, dropping a bundle of nets in order to peer over the edge of the cliff. He was stouter around the middle than the first man had been, and he was puffing as he took in the grim scene below.

He gave a low whistle. "That's Davison," he said. "Is he dead?"

"I think so," Demetrius responded gruffly. "I didn't intend to kill him. He attacked me, and while we were struggling, he fell over the edge."

"I know, lad, I saw the whole thing," the man said soothingly. His silver-streaked hair was shorter than Demetrius's, but there was still enough of it to be whipped about by the wind. "I saw him come at you from nowhere, and I'll speak on your behalf if necessary." He shook his head. "To tell you the truth, I doubt anyone will dig too deep. Not for Davison, rest his soul."

"You knew him?" Demetrius pressed.

The man nodded. "Aye, he lived in the village. We're not like the capital over there—everyone knows who everyone is in a small fishing town. But Davison wasn't well liked. Why did he attack you?"

"I don't know," said Demetrius, trying to sound confused. "He asked me to help look for his dog, then he lunged at me."

The human made a tutting noise. "Davison didn't have a dog. He was up to no good. It wouldn't be the first time he'd been caught trying to rob someone." In spite of his words, his eyes passed skeptically over Demetrius's form, clearly wondering why anyone would consider the vagabond worth robbing.

"He'd be too late in my case," Demetrius said, trying to

sound rueful. "Someone else beat him to it while I was on the road here."

"My sympathies!" the man cried, understanding filling his eyes as he once again looked Demetrius over. "Where were you coming from?"

"I was..." Demetrius stumbled over his answer, irritated with himself. "I was coming from further east, from—"

"Ah, I wondered about your accent," the man cut him off mercifully. "From Vadolis, are you?"

Demetrius nodded, wondering what Vadolis was. He would have to do some research to make his assumed persona convincing.

"What's your name?" the man asked. "Do you have anywhere to go?"

"My name is Demetrius," Demetrius said, glad of one question he could answer truthfully. "And I don't have anywhere to go, I'm afraid. I was heading for the capital, hoping to find work."

The man looked him over. "Not in that state you won't find work. Come along to the village with me, we'll see if we can find you some boots, at the very least." He glanced down at the beach below. "We'll have to report what happened with Davison, and get a group out to retrieve the body."

With a grateful nod, Demetrius followed the man along the path, painfully aware of his awkward gait.

"That's quite a limp you've got there," the stranger commented. "Are you hurt?"

Demetrius nodded. "That man, Davison, landed me some solid hits to my legs."

The man tutted again. "He was a rotten egg. He isn't a local, you know," he hastened to add. "Only came to this area a couple years ago. He tried to get work in the castle, I believe, but they didn't take him on. Small surprise. He gave us all a dislike of him pretty quickly, always talking like he was here on some important business, when from all I could see, he never did anything useful with his time."

Demetrius kept silent, his thoughts grim. There was no doubt in his mind who'd been paying the man to loiter around the capital, ready to report on matters relating to the human kingdom. The question was why the Ocean Miner was at such pains to monitor the world above the water. He understood now why she'd been so ready to give him the mimicking draft. Much simpler to dispose of him above the water, where there would be no body, and no witnesses as far as the merfolk were concerned. Had she planned the same for Estelle? At least it was heartening to hear that her spy hadn't been able to get work at the castle. Hopefully that meant Estelle would be safe there for the time being.

But how long would they let her stay there? The humans didn't know she was a visiting princess, after all. Demetrius hoped she would be sensible enough not to tell them who she really was. They would think her mad, and likely put her straight back out on the street.

"Looks like your legs are done pretty bad," the stranger interrupted his musings. "If it's work you're looking for, maybe you'd best try to find a fisherman who might appreciate an extra hand. The smaller vessels allow a great deal of sitting, which might be just what you need." He cocked his head to the side. "Do you know much about fish?"

Demetrius hid a smile, keeping his voice solemn. "A little."

CHAPTER FOURTEEN

Estelle

Estelle straightened her borrowed gown nervously, still not entirely sure she'd donned it correctly. The housekeeper had produced it from somewhere, and she had the impression it belonged to one of the other servants. Which would likely make the meal she was about to share with the royal family even more uncomfortable. She hardly knew whether to be pleased or alarmed at the sight of the young human woman who stared back at her from the tall reflective oval she'd been directed to. A looking glass, the serving girl had called it.

She certainly looked human, she had to give the Ocean Miner that. Her own familiar face was barely recognizable with the prominent nose, and in spite of being covered by the length of the simple gown, her legs changed the shape of her body in a way that was impossible to miss.

Perhaps most bizarre of all was her hair. She hadn't even noticed it on her fumbling journey to the castle, but she saw now that the familiar aquamarine strands had been replaced by hair of a pale yellowish cream color. It wasn't dissimilar to the color of her skin, and it reminded her of the first tentative rays of dawn touching the sky—a sight she'd seen numerous times, thanks to her surveillance of Prince Farrin.

She'd puzzled over her hair when she first caught sight of it, but after some reflection, she'd concluded that blue must not be a human hair color. A change must have been required to make her form fully human.

Although it wasn't quite *fully* human, she thought nervously, reaching up to touch one of the strands of blue that still appeared intermittently among her tresses. Had the Ocean Miner intended to leave them, or had it been an oversight? And would they mark her to the humans, perhaps even reveal what she was under her borrowed form?

"Ready, then?"

The unimpressed voice of the housekeeper broke into Estelle's thoughts, and she squirmed under the older woman's appraisal. The housekeeper had made no secret of her disapproval of Prince Farrin's invitation, but she clearly intended to obey his request. Estelle would have liked to point out that it wasn't her fault Farrin had given the command, since she'd never asked to eat with the royals, but she doubted she would have had the courage, even if she had her voice. At least she could walk without falling, now. She'd devoted the entire morning to practicing the skill, and was relieved to find that as she adjusted to her new body, some kind of instinct kicked in, her mind seeming to know how to make her legs walk just as she knew how to make her tail swim.

The new ability didn't give her much confidence, however. Everything was still overwhelmingly new.

Her chest feeling as tight as if she was trying to breathe above water in her mermaid form, she followed the woman down a wide, airy corridor. Light streamed in through the windows set regularly in walls of the same yellowish stone that she'd seen from the outside. Some kind of decorative fabric was hung at various intervals, some of the patches depicting scenes that Estelle tried to make sense of as she hurried past.

Her guide gave her no chance to linger. Estelle didn't even feel close to ready when they came to a stop outside a large wooden door, every inch of its surface carved with intricate patterns. Estelle reached out a hand and ran her fingers over the carvings, fascinated. She'd seen the odd piece of driftwood, a rare substance that merfolk prized for various uses, but she'd never seen such a large slab, or one so well polished.

"*Guests* don't ordinarily touch the furnishings," said the housekeeper tartly.

Embarrassed, Estelle pulled her hand back, ducking her head in a silent apology.

With a sigh, the housekeeper looked her over, her expression softening slightly. "I don't know what will come of it," she commented. "But it's possible you're not to blame, I suppose." She tilted her head toward the door. "Go on, then."

Estelle cast a glance at the guards flanking the doorway. This aspect of royal life was familiar. The sight of their upright posture brought a certain amber-tailed figure to mind. A pang of sadness passed over her as she remembered the last words she'd shared with Demetrius. He hadn't even responded to her goodbye, too disapproving of her decisions. And now they'd never have the chance to speak again.

Straightening her back, Estelle moved forward, through the door which one guard was now holding open. For a moment, she didn't even see the room's occupants, too enchanted by the stunning vista on display through the windows. There were so many of them that the opposite wall was made primarily of glass, providing a glorious view of the ocean pounding against the cliffs below. The royal dining hall had certainly been well positioned, placed as it was on the seaward side of the castle. Estelle imagined one could live in that castle two hundred years without growing tired of that view.

Then she remembered that humans didn't get two hundred years, and she felt another pang of sadness. Had she been mad to choose this life?

A disapprovingly cleared throat caused Estelle's eyes to whip away from the view, landing instead on a long table of polished wood, at which four figures were seated. They looked small, clustered at one end of the expanse, but Estelle could immediately tell from their indefinable presence that this must be the royal family. She ducked her head respectfully at the middle-aged man, trying to remember the etiquette the housekeeper had attempted to teach her in the short time allowed to them. He must be King Johannes. And the elegant woman beside him, her dark hair streaked with silver, must be Queen Sula.

They were both as intimidating as the undersea ruler must be to strangers, even at times to his own family. Estelle let out a slow breath, relieved once again at the housekeeper's revelation that Farrin was indeed the younger of the princes. She suspected that not even the knowledge of her true identity as a princess—which she hoped to one day find a way to reveal—would reconcile these two stately monarchs to the idea of her marrying their heir.

Her eyes moved with her thoughts, traveling to the third figure at the table. He was such an unsettling mixture of familiar and total stranger, Estelle was momentarily thrown. She'd barely caught sight of him on the ship that stormy night, but there could be no mistaking Farrin's brother. The two were very alike, the main exception being that Crown Prince Emmett's hair was of a dark brown rather than the tawny color of Prince Farrin's.

Speaking of whom...Estelle's eyes slid to the last member of the family, and her heart lifted a little. Farrin was as handsome as she remembered—if anything, the hours of separation had made her forget just how wonderful he was.

"What's she hovering for?" muttered the king in an irritable aside to his eldest son beside him. "Seems the kitchen staff could do with more rigorous training."

"Be kind, Father," murmured Prince Emmett. "I don't recognize her—it's probably her first day."

Farrin looked up casually, his attention caught by the conversation. His face brightened as he noticed Estelle, and he rose from his chair.

"No, she's not a servant, Father. Everyone, this is the young woman I told you about. The one who was washed up on the beach from a shipwreck, in need of our assistance."

Estelle felt herself flushing as four pairs of eyes studied her, and did her best to execute another wobbly bob of respect. Her balance inadequate for the task, she staggered a little, and her heart soared as Farrin hurried forward to help steady her. He was so kind, without having the faintest clue of her royal status.

"Farrin." The queen's voice was long-suffering. "It's hardly necessary—or appropriate—for her to join us at a private—"

"Mother." Farrin cut the queen off, sounding pained. "Surely we can afford to show some hospitality. This poor girl is all alone, and I believe unable even to remember what happened."

"A likely story," muttered the king, and Estelle winced. What a fool she must seem, with no voice to explain herself.

The queen sighed. "Of course we are glad to provide assistance. But I really think the housekeeper can see to the needs of..." She trailed off, raising an eyebrow at Estelle. "What's your name, child?"

Estelle opened her mouth, but the barest hint of noise sent agony slashing across her throat, and she closed it with a snap. Tears of both pain and frustration rising in her eyes, she touched a hand to her throat and shook her head.

"She seems to be mute, Mother," said Farrin. "And I suspect it may be a recent loss."

"That must be difficult," Prince Emmett said with polite sympathy.

"Perhaps she can write her name down," suggested the queen.

Estelle's forehead creased in confusion at the unfamiliar word. Write? What did that mean?

The queen gave her younger son a look Estelle couldn't decipher. "She can't read or write, Farrin. What does that tell you about the appropriateness of this situation?"

"Why is her hair like that?" the king demanded, before his son could respond.

Fear raced over Estelle. Would they realize she was a mermaid in disguise? And if they did, what would be their reaction? Did humans despise mermaids as much as most merfolk despised humans?

"Huh. I didn't even notice the blue earlier," Farrin commented, stepping forward and lifting a strand. He gave Estelle a friendly smile, oblivious to the way his nearness sent a pleasant chill racing over Estelle's air-enveloped skin. "Are you a singer, perhaps?"

Again, she stared in confusion, and the prince slapped his hand to his forehead. "Stupid question, sorry." He frowned in thought. "But perhaps your hair was affected by one somehow?"

Estelle bit her lip, still utterly bemused about what they were talking about. What did he mean, *are you a singer*? Everyone sang, didn't they? For merfolk, at least, it was a central aspect of every part of community life. With a sinking heart, she realized she may well never sing again. It was hard to imagine forcing her raspy, painful new voice to produce anything melodious enough to be considered singing.

A thrill of horror went over her. If she couldn't sing, she

couldn't harness power. She'd be so vulnerable, and worse, she'd never get to learn the magic lore that had been denied her so far. Why did the Ocean Miner's voice have to be so much worse above water than it was below?

"It's all right," said Farrin kindly, and Estelle realized she'd never responded to his question. "Perhaps the memories will come back with time. I've heard of things like that happening."

She smiled gratefully at him, heat spreading through her as he took gentle hold of her arm and guided her toward the table.

"Farrin," murmured his mother reprovingly.

"Surely she can join us for this afternoon, at least," Farrin said. He frowned at Estelle. "Have you eaten since last I saw you?"

She shook her head, and his brown eyes filled with sympathy. "You must be starving. Here, start with a roll."

He picked up something from a plate in the center of the table and handed it to her. Estelle turned it over in her hand, fascinated. It was lighter than she'd expected, and warm to the touch. Tentatively, she bit into it, her face lighting up as warmth and flavor exploded in her mouth. It was delicious.

Farrin's delighted laugh made her flush with embarrassment, but she took another bite all the same.

"I don't know if I've ever seen anyone enjoy bread so much," he said.

Estelle locked the word away, trying to keep up with all the new information. Was it called roll, or bread?

"Where are you from that you're not familiar with bread?" Prince Emmett asked mildly. "I thought it would be familiar in every corner of Providore."

"It's an excellent question," said the king, clearly less than impressed with the uninvited guest. "Do you have someone waiting for you, child? Some family you can go home to? Our people would be delighted to assist you to return to your home."

Estelle swallowed, the bread suddenly feeling thick in her throat. She thought of her father's harsh words, and the passivity of her mother and sisters. Demetrius had been the only one to notice her desperation, and he wasn't even family.

Did she have family? Yes. But family she could go home to?

She shook her head, her eyes on the empty plate before her.

"Well, that's unfortunate," said the queen, her tone managing to convey sympathy while remaining detached. Clearly whatever Farrin had imagined, the royal family were not intending to receive Estelle into their number simply because she'd wandered into the castle.

And why should they? Estelle had never expected that. Farrin seemed to consider her welcome, and that was all that mattered.

"We can consider the future later," said Farrin firmly. "After the poor girl has had a chance to eat something."

Gratefully, Estelle received an array of other food, mostly as unfamiliar as the bread. She was so hungry, she hardly cared what she ate. After trying a number of strange dishes, she saw one thing she recognized—although it was prepared differently —and fell on it eagerly.

Again, Farrin chuckled. "You like fish, do you? I'm quite fond of it myself."

Estelle just nodded, continuing to eat with a speed and eagerness that would have horrified her mother. Tactfully, the prince transferred his attention to his brother instead.

"It's good to have you back, Emmett. How was the ride from Lernvale?"

Prince Emmett shrugged. "Fine. Much the same as always. I'm glad to be home, though. The week felt very long this time."

"And only a few weeks until we lose you again," said Farrin, sounding glum. "It was dull here without you." He brightened.

"Maybe I'll come with you next time. Would we have much luck hunting this time of year?"

"Possibly," said Emmett, considering it. "Not much on the castle grounds, but there's always some kind of game in the forest."

"Neither of my sons is setting foot in the Forest of Ilgal again," said King Johannes, his tone so forbidding Estelle shifted her new feet nervously.

"Perhaps we ought to discuss other matters," interjected the queen smoothly. Her eyes flicked to Estelle, clearly more conscious than the rest of her family members about the stranger in their midst.

Not that she needed to worry, Estelle reflected. She'd barely understood a word of what was being said. A forest, she could comprehend. They had forests underwater, although she imagined the plants were very different. And hunting was a necessity of life for merfolk, of course. But without any comprehension of the context, she had no idea what in the conversation might be inappropriate for outside ears.

And, of course, she could repeat nothing to anyone.

The thought of her enforced silence once again weighed her down, and she momentarily lost track of the conversation as she focused on her food. It was all so new and fascinating. How many questions she would have had if she could have spoken! As a steady parade of servants continued to deliver food, Estelle watched Farrin surreptitiously, taking note of how he utilized the implements placed alongside his plate. It all looked very complicated, and she despaired of ever figuring it out. Mostly, she stuck to the bread, which was plentifully supplied.

"So I sent them back into the forest with twice what I thought I'd agreed to, fool that I am," Prince Emmett was saying, as Estelle refocused on the conversation.

"You should really try to avoid any negotiation with the elves when you're at Lernvale," said the king with a touch of sternness.

"It's not Emmett's fault." Farrin rushed to his brother's defense. "They'll cheat anyone with their murky bargains. That's elves for you." He rolled his eyes at Estelle in a conspiratorial manner that made her heart skip a beat. "Have you ever met one?"

Estelle shook her head. Her confusion must have shown on her face, because Farrin turned fully to look at her.

"You've *heard* of elves though, haven't you?"

Flushing, Estelle shook her head again. *Don't be embarrassed*, she told herself. *They don't know it, but you have very good reason for knowing nothing of the land. If we were speaking of the ocean, you'd know so much they didn't.*

"I wonder if you knew once, but can't remember," Farrin mused, his dark eyes thoughtful. He gave his head a little shake. "Well, elves are different from humans."

"They're about half the size, for one thing," Prince Emmett interjected.

Farrin grinned at his brother. "There's that. But I was thinking of their culture. The obsession with bargaining, and the strict adherence to the rules of magic, even when they've worded their deals so carefully to exploit every loophole."

"To fleece the naive prince, more like," said Prince Emmett ruefully.

Farrin laughed. "You're not naive, Emmett. They're just smarter than you."

Prince Emmett leaned across the table to give his little brother a playful punch on the shoulder. "Show some respect for your future monarch, whelp. The free license I gave you for almost drowning has worn off by now."

"That was quick," said Farrin lightly.

Estelle went still at this mention of Farrin's misadventure in the ocean. If only there was a way to communicate her part in his survival, it might warm the royal family to her. If only she had her voice.

Gathering her courage, she tapped Farrin on the shoulder. He turned to her, his expression as open and friendly as ever, but of course he had no idea what was in her thoughts.

"Oh, right, I was explaining elves wasn't I?" He drummed his fingers on the table. "You couldn't call them unscrupulous, because they stick to their own rules meticulously, I'll give them that. But they don't really know compassion, or generosity. They'll always get the best deal they can manage for themselves, never mind how it affects others. Still, they're not exactly cruel. I'd rather treat with an elf than a giant any day."

"Don't talk nonsense," scoffed King Johannes. "We haven't seen a giant in Medulle for generations."

"And thank goodness for that," his wife agreed emphatically. "If one ever dared show its face this far south, neither of you would be going anywhere near it."

"Yes, I think we can all be grateful we don't have to contend with giants," said Farrin. He smiled at Estelle as he continued his explanation. "Even elves we don't see often here in Port Dulla. But in spite of their devious ways, it's sometimes worth it to treat with them. We have singers who can assist with most magical matters, of course, but there are times when mined magic is more appropriate."

Startled, Estelle dropped the food she was holding, her eyes flying to Farrin's. Mined magic? There were those above water who knew how to mine magic from the land the way the Ocean Miner did from the seabed?

"What is it?" Farrin asked, studying her face. "Which part caused that reaction?"

Estelle swallowed, trying to move her mouth as clearly as

possible without making a sound that would trigger the unbearable pain in her throat.

Mine magic?

"Yes, they mine it," said Farrin carefully, still trying to read her features. "It's a practice specific to elves. Humans don't do it."

For some reason, he cast a shifty look at his brother when he said this, as the king's booming voice entered the conversation with more heat than he'd previously shown.

"I should think not. What the elves do is their own affair—their kind have mined magic for as long as we can remember. But as for the rest of us..." He glared at each of his sons in turn. "Only singers should be able to access magic, because only they can channel it, and therefore control it."

Both princes looked shamefaced, and an instant pall was cast over the meal. For the remaining few minutes, they all ate in silence. When the king rose, so did everyone else, and Estelle hastened to her feet.

It was the queen who thought to take leave of Estelle, however. "I am glad you survived your misfortunes...whatever they were. I trust you will soon be able to return to your home."

"Surely she can stay here, Mother," said Farrin. "We have plenty of room for guests."

"Farrin." The queen lowered her voice, but the air was so thin compared to water. There was nothing whatsoever between the queen's mouth and Estelle's ears, which still caught her words with painful clarity. "I know you mean well, but it is not kindness to elevate someone above the status they can realistically maintain."

"I'm not asking you to award her an estate," said Farrin sarcastically. "She just needs somewhere to stay while she recovers from her ordeal. Hopefully her memory will come back soon." The queen seemed about to speak further, but Farrin hurried on. "It needn't trouble you, Mother. I'll speak to the housekeeper about it."

The next thing Estelle knew, she was being chivvied from the room by Farrin, his brother keeping step.

"Not the most hospitable, are they?" Farrin muttered to his brother.

Prince Emmett said nothing, but the sideways look he gave Estelle suggested that he thought his mother had a point. Frustration again rose up in her. If only she could tell them she was a princess. But of course, she couldn't do that without revealing herself as a mermaid. Would that make them more or less likely to receive her? Impossible to know.

Try as she might to tell herself she was happy about Farrin's kindness, Estelle couldn't deny her growing discomfort as the prince airily informed the housekeeper that a guest suite was to be prepared for Estelle. The housekeeper's evident disapproval was all the harder to take when Estelle knew that Farrin's parents would feel precisely the same. But she didn't see much option other than going along with it all, given she truly had nowhere else to go, and her very life depended on having enough access to Farrin to make him fall in love with her.

Nerves rushed over her at the thought. She had no idea how to make someone fall in love, but she had a niggling sense that she was doing a poor job of it so far. If only she could speak!

The luxuriousness of her quarters brought her no pleasure as darkness fell, and she laid herself down on the enormous item of furniture the humans called a bed. She longed for the cozy comfort of a sleeping hollow into which she could curl. But the room was enormous, and the fabric that a servant pulled closed around her bed did nothing to counteract the chill emptiness of the air. Nothing whatsoever pressed against her ears, and the silence was oppressive.

Of all the foolish things you've ever done, this is the most ridiculous.

Demetrius's voice once again sounded in her head, and Estelle succumbed at last to her emotions. Curling in on herself, she bent her new legs and clutched them to her chest. She received a shock when actual water began to leak out of her eyes. For a moment she was alarmed that her human body was broken somehow, then she remembered a legend she'd heard about humans years before, about crying tears of seawater. It was strangely comforting, feeling the salt water on her cheeks again. It reminded her of having her head out of water, her skin not quite dry from the first touch of the sun. After all, she reminded herself, the surface had been her favorite place in the ocean.

Her mind mercifully empty in its weariness, Estelle drifted at last into sleep.

CHAPTER FIFTEEN

Demetrius

"That's a good catch." The burly fisherman grunted his approval. "You've certainly pulled your weight, lad. You seem to have a knack for knowing where to find the fish."

Demetrius gave a tight smile, his thoughts on the years of his childhood, when he'd helped his father with hunting, and become intimately familiar with the habits of many ocean-dwelling creatures.

Thoughts of home and family were unsettling. What would his parents think when they eventually learned that he'd disappeared from the palace? Better not to dwell on it, since there was nothing whatsoever he could do to change it.

"Reckon we'll head in now," his companion said, glancing at the sun. It was mid-morning, and their nets were full. "I'll be back out again in the evening, though, and would appreciate the assistance if you're still looking for the work."

Demetrius nodded gratefully. "I imagine I will be."

"How will you spend the time until then?" the fisherman asked curiously.

Demetrius gave a shrug. "Walking."

The older man smiled ruefully. "No business of mine, I suppose." He cast Demetrius a sideways look. "I don't mean to pry. But I've heard a rumor you're sleeping rough at the beach. The wife and I have a spare bed if ever you need it."

"Thank you," said Demetrius, surprised. "I'm grateful for your kindness. But I prefer to be beholden to no one."

The fisherman shook his head indulgently. "Age will teach you the wisdom of accepting help when it's freely offered, lad."

Demetrius said nothing. It was strange to hear this man, considerably younger than Demetrius's own parents, speak as if he was getting old. But he supposed that by human estimation, it was probably true.

Once he'd helped haul in the catch, Demetrius nodded a silent farewell to his employer, heading out of the village in the direction of the castle. He hadn't lied about his intended activity. He'd been out of the water for three days, and he'd spent a substantial part of each one walking.

He could certainly do with all the practice he could get, although that wasn't his only purpose. Each day he'd approached the castle, trying to get a sense for the place, and hoping to catch a glimpse of Estelle. So far he'd seen no sign of her, and he was starting to feel anxious. Perhaps it was time to attempt to gain entry to the castle itself.

The walk from the village to the red stone building wasn't long, and it was a pleasant route along the clifftop. Demetrius's eyes drifted out to the ocean, marveling at how still and flat the expanse of water looked from above. No one would guess from that view how much vibrant life teemed underneath.

A thudding sound drew Demetrius's attention from the vista back to the clifftop. He tensed in preparation, his senses establishing that the sound was growing closer before he'd even seen what caused it. The sight that met his eyes was something he could never have prepared himself for, however. A group of sizable beasts—larger than dolphins—were moving along the path toward him, from the direction of the castle. They were sleek and beautiful, with four legs and elongated heads. Long hair flowed out from a line down the backs of their necks as well as in the form of tails. He'd never seen anything like them. Most incredible of all, however, was the fact that each beast had a human perched atop it.

Demetrius was still trying to comprehend what he was seeing when he realized that one of the creatures had broken off from the others and was moving much too fast. The rest of the humans were sitting straight and apparently comfortably, but the human on that animal was bent double, clutching the creature's neck with both arms and seemingly struggling to stay on its back as it plunged rapidly toward Demetrius.

The rider was a young woman, he realized, catching sight of long hair of a pale yellow streaming unrestrained behind her. A strand of blue caught the morning sun, and Demetrius gasped.

Estelle!

The creature had reached the cliff's edge now, turning clumsily and continuing to run much too close to the precipice. Estelle was still clinging on, but she looked like she could fall at any moment. Demetrius sprang into action, turning and sprinting in the same direction as the horse as quickly as his newly acquired legs would allow. He opened his mouth instinctively, seeking to harness power with his song as he'd been trained to do, to slow the animal's movement by manipulating the water.

But of course there was no water, and—more alarmingly—there was no song. When he tried to sing, he simply couldn't. Nothing came out.

Demetrius shoved the problem aside for another time, telling himself he didn't need magic. This feat was just like the times in his irresponsible youth when he and Esteban had shadowed dolphins in this way, using kelp ropes to catch them as they went past and pull themselves on for a ride.

The masterful swimmers had never taken long to shake the mermen off.

He could hear the creature's thundering getting closer behind him, and he focused his hearing. It helped to imagine that the sounds of the creature's approach were flowing to him through water rather than darting so harshly through the empty air.

When it was almost upon him, Demetrius leaped lightly to the side, seizing the rope-like black strap that he'd spotted on the other beasts. Thankfully his arms had retained all their considerable strength in the transformation of his body, and he managed to haul himself up, practically on top of Estelle. The creature's strides faltered for a moment, then increased even more. Clearly he wasn't going to be able to calm or stop the panicking animal. With his own balance as precarious as his companion's, he wrapped his entire body around Estelle's, pulling them both sideways away from the cliff face in an attempt to control their inevitable fall from the creature's back.

They thudded to the ground in a painful heap. Demetrius was still curled protectively around Estelle, so his shoulder and hip bore the brunt of the impact. It was so unforgiving, this empty air! No water to cushion movement. His body felt bruised and stunned, but his mind remained alert. The sound of the creature's flight faded, and Demetrius heard shouts from the rest of the human group. Letting out a breath, he allowed himself to relax. It seemed the immediate danger had passed.

"Are you hurt?" he asked Estelle, anxiety making his voice curt. They'd sustained quite a shock on impact with the ground.

She shook her head, her face hidden by long waves of hair. Demetrius stared at it, amazed by the pale yellow that dominated the occasional blue streak. He hadn't even noticed the change when he'd spotted her on the beach, but now that her hair was dry, it was unmistakable. His own hair had undergone no such change.

Reassured that she was in one piece, he uncurled a little. Estelle toppled loose from his hold, and Demetrius allowed himself to lie still for a moment, sprawled on his back, as he tried to assess the damage to his body. He was aching, certainly, but he didn't think anything was seriously injured. He'd been lucky.

Estelle struggled shakily to her knees, and Demetrius pushed himself up on his elbows. With an effort, he regained his feet and held out a hand to help her up.

Her eyes were full of gratitude as they looked up into his, but the expression changed to shock as she got a good look at him.

Demetrius? The princess's mouth formed his name unmistakably, but no sound came out.

He gave a slow nod, and for a moment they just stared wordlessly at each other, taking in the changes to faces and forms that were once familiar. Then, to Demetrius's surprise, Estelle's eyes began to fill with moisture, and she suddenly threw herself forward, hugging him fiercely around the middle. Stunned, he closed his arms around her, giving her an awkward pat on the back as a shudder went over her frame.

Estelle drew back, making an obvious effort to pull herself together. Her eyes found his again, confusion creeping in.

How? The question was once again clear, although silent.

But there was no time for him to answer. The thudding sound of those creatures' approach could once again be heard, and Demetrius looked up to see the others in the group from the castle drawing close. He had no difficulty recognizing the figure in the lead, and irritation lanced through him as Prince Farrin swung himself down from his animal. The human's face was all sympathy and concern as he hurried to Estelle's side.

"Are you all right? What a tumble!"

Estelle nodded, still not speaking. Demetrius frowned at this prolonged silence. Was she so self-conscious of her scratchy new voice that she'd rather be mute altogether? What foolishness.

"That was entirely my fault," Prince Farrin was saying remorsefully. "I should never have encouraged you to ride a horse alone without checking you knew how. Was that your first time?"

Estelle nodded again, looking embarrassed now. What cause did *she* have to be embarrassed? It was the human prince who'd behaved like an idiot, as he'd acknowledged.

And yet, as the prince hovered around her solicitously, Demetrius could see no hint of criticism in Estelle's gaze. She was clearly still besotted with the human, and the worst of it was, Prince Farrin was being excessively kind given they were near strangers. Demetrius scowled at the other man. If the prince only knew it, his kindness was crueler than a rebuff would have been.

He supposed—begrudgingly—that he should be grateful the prince showed no sign of wanting to take advantage of Estelle's blatant admiration. That was certainly a danger, and one he had no doubt Estelle had never even considered.

On the contrary, Demetrius could see no indication of admiration or romance in the human's manner, which meant he was acting out of the basic consideration of a generous heart. But kindness wouldn't help Estelle overcome her absurd infatuation. It would only have the opposite effect, making her inevitable failure all the more painful. As far as Demetrius was concerned, the sooner Estelle could be brought to realize the impossibility of her scheme, the better. Then they could turn to the Ocean Miner, pay whatever horrible price she would extract for a second bargain, and be done with it. Back to the ocean, back to their lives.

"Thank you." Prince Farrin's earnest voice brought Demetrius's attention to him. "It's a very good thing you were walking there, and that you acted so swiftly. I don't think it's an exaggeration to say that you saved this young woman's life."

Demetrius frowned at the human's failure to use Estelle's name. Just what strange position was she occupying in the castle?

"I was glad to help," he said steadily.

"Yes, thank you," interjected another young man, so similar in appearance to Prince Farrin that he must be the prince's older brother. "Your reflexes and your quick thinking were certainly impressive."

Demetrius bowed his head respectfully, unable to think of anything else to say. It felt strange to be thanked by these human princes, when he certainly hadn't acted for their sake. But he didn't think it wise to reveal his connection to Estelle. They would need to be careful if they wanted to avoid giving away their true origins. And if humans thought half as poorly of merfolk as merfolk did of them, they would be wise to keep their true forms secret.

"I wish there was some way we could thank you," said Prince Farrin. He brightened. "Emmett isn't wrong about your reflexes. I don't suppose you're looking for work?"

"I..." Demetrius faltered, unsure where the prince was going. "As a matter of fact, I..."

"Because I heard the captain of the castle guard saying just this morning that he'll need to recruit again soon. Perhaps you could train for a position with the guard!"

"Farrin," murmured the older prince. "The position of a castle guard is one of great trust. We don't just pluck any stranger from the street."

"I'm not offering him the role," Farrin argued. "I just suggested he might wish to apply. Obviously we won't interfere with the captain's normal recruitment process." He sent Demetrius the ghost of a wink. "Although it couldn't hurt for me to put in a good word, I'm sure."

Demetrius stiffened, his ears suddenly full of the whispers of his fellow guards at the emperor's underwater palace. He hadn't sought any royal favoritism when he applied for that role, and he wasn't about to take advantage of any above water, either. Whatever position he took, he wanted to have earned it.

A cold refusal rose to his lips, but before he could utter it, he glanced at Estelle. She was watching him with a painfully hopeful expression. How precisely she'd managed it, he didn't know. But it seemed that she was installed in the castle, at least for now. And she certainly didn't look like a girl with a plan. She looked adrift and alone, and it was clear in her eyes that she wanted him to accept, so he could be nearby.

Much as he might wish to deny it, his heart was touched, both by her plight and by her apparent confidence in him. Reluctantly, he forced his own pride to one side. He'd come onto the land to watch over her, and he wasn't likely to get a better chance to do so.

"I am actually looking for work," he acknowledged. "And I would be grateful for any opportunity to find honest employment."

"Excellent!" Prince Farrin was beaming. "The captain is always at the training yard first thing. If you come by tomorrow morning, you can submit your name for consideration in the next recruitment. I'll tell the guards on the gate to look out for you, and let you through."

"Thank you, Your Highness," said Demetrius, although his eyes once again traveled to Estelle. "I'll be there."

CHAPTER SIXTEEN

Estelle

Estelle's mind was whirling as the group traveled back to the castle. Even her position on Farrin's horse, clinging onto him to keep from falling once again, couldn't distract her from her astonishment.

How was Demetrius on land? How was Demetrius human? In the first moment, she'd thought she must have been losing her mind, perhaps conjuring up an image of the friend she most wished was there to help her. Surely the human with strikingly familiar features couldn't really be Demetrius. But then their eyes had locked, and all doubt had fled. She'd know that look anywhere. His eyes hadn't changed at all in the transformation, and neither had his hair. Apparently amber was an acceptable hair color on a human.

She could settle to nothing for the rest of the day. There wasn't anything for her to do, of course. Farrin and Emmett were both kind, but neither prince spent their time by her side. They had their own affairs to manage, and their own pastimes to pursue. It had been thoughtful of Farrin to include her in the morning's ride, even if it had been an impractical idea. She should have told him she had no idea how to ride a horse, but she'd been so eager to spend time with him. She'd barely caught sight of him the day before, and she was starting to feel desperate. If she didn't capture his interest soon, the novelty of her arrival might wear off, and she might be sent from the castle forever. Then what would become of her?

Most of the time she wandered the halls of the castle. It was a fascinating place, and so many aspects of human life were new and amazing. But to her own disappointment, she'd begun to feel a familiar sense of being hemmed in. She had nothing to occupy her, and she enjoyed the idleness no more than she had in her own palace. At least there she'd known her place, and so had everybody else. In the human castle, no one knew quite what to do with her, with Farrin treating her like a guest of high status, and the housekeeper dressing her in the borrowed clothes of servants. It was an untenable position, and Estelle knew it.

The morning following the incident with the horses, Estelle was up early, eager to see Demetrius again. However, she had no idea where to find the training yard Farrin had mentioned, and she had no way to ask for directions. She stumbled around for at least an hour without seeing any sign of it. What she did discover during that time, however, was that the castle boasted an incredible garden. It was located on the landward side, sheltered from the ocean breeze by the enormous stone building, so she hadn't seen it previously.

She had no words to describe most of the plants she saw, but her eyes couldn't get enough. She wandered between neat rows of flowers, and explored less cultivated glades of trees. It was the motion that particularly mesmerized her. The land felt so still compared to the ocean, even the wind from the sea sweeping harshly through the barren air toward her rather than rising and falling with the teeming life all around her. But in the garden, it was a different matter. The breeze ruffled the leaves just like the current in a kelp forest, and everywhere she looked, she could see the evidence of its motion. She passed the occasional human tending to the plants, just as she'd cared for her little coral garden back home, but generally she was on her own. Given her struggles to conform to human ways, that situation suited her well.

She could have wandered happily for hours, but then she might miss Demetrius. Forcing herself to turn away, she hurried from the garden, skirting around the outside of the castle, although still well within the low stone wall that formed its perimeter. To her relief, the sounds of tramping feet and the clash of weapons met her ears as she left the garden behind. She hurried as quickly as her still-uneven gait would allow, reaching the entrance to the training yard just in time to see Demetrius emerge.

Instinctively, Estelle opened her mouth to call out to him, only just remembering in time about her voice. She waved a hand frantically, and the movement caught his eye. He stopped, looking as relieved as she felt to have located one another.

"Estelle," Demetrius said quietly, starting back into motion. He gripped her arm and led her around the corner of a nearby building, where they could speak in relative privacy. His general demeanor was that of an adult chastising a child, but Estelle was so grateful to hear her own name again, she hardly cared.

How? she mouthed again as soon as they'd come to a stop, gesturing at his human form.

Instead of answering, Demetrius frowned at her. "Why aren't you talking? Are you so embarrassed about that revolting voice you traded yours for?"

Estelle glared at him, although if she was honest, she found his entirely unchanged manner reassuring.

Painful, she mouthed, rubbing a hand down her throat.

"What?" Demetrius made no effort to hide his impatience.

PAINFUL, she tried again, exaggerating the movement of her mouth.

"Painful?" Demetrius guessed. He rolled his eyes. "You'll mangle your entire body to try to catch the eye of some handsome prince, but you won't go through a little pain to allow you to communicate?"

Estelle's glare intensified. A little pain? He had no idea. She waited until she caught his eye, then mouthed, *feels like*. She reached out to Demetrius's hip and grabbed the ocean-made blade she knew he kept there. Sliding it from its holder, she mimed stabbing her own throat with it, repeatedly.

Demetrius was still frowning at her, but he didn't look irritated anymore. There was something else in the expression, and she found it hard to decipher.

"It's really that bad?" he asked finally. "Bad enough to make it unusable?"

She nodded.

"But you used it underwater," he argued. "You said it hurt then, but you still used it. Is it so much worse up in the air?"

She nodded again, her eyes growing a little wet in spite of herself.

Demetrius sighed, his gaze settled unseeingly on a point over her shoulder. "Well, that complicates things."

No kidding.

Estelle tapped his shoulder to get his attention, then gestured behind him, her eyebrows raised in a silent question.

"The captain?" Demetrius asked. He shrugged. "It went well enough. He's given me a place in the training program. Whether I succeed or not will depend on my own performance, but no doubt your precious prince twisted the captain's arm to get me in the door."

For some reason he looked annoyed rather than grateful about this, but Estelle didn't press. She had other questions.

How? She exaggerated the silent word with her mouth, gesturing again to Demetrius's form.

He met her eye unblinkingly. "How do you think? The same way you did."

Estelle stared at him. He'd made a bargain with the Ocean Miner? But why would she do that? Clearly Demetrius hadn't traded his voice. Fear washed over her—what had Demetrius given up instead? And why would he do that, when he didn't dream of the land like she did?

Why? she mouthed, lifting her arms in a questioning gesture.

"Isn't it obvious?" Demetrius asked incredulously. "To keep an eye on you. Did you really think I'd just let you swim to your death all alone? Clearly you need the assistance."

Estelle's face settled into a glower at his condescending tone, but her irritation was short-lived. Demetrius had always tended toward being critical, and she could handle that. Restraining a groan, she ran both hands down her face. What she couldn't handle was being responsible for him losing the life he'd had—and been perfectly happy with—underwater. Him sharing in her sacrifice was never part of her plan.

"Are you all right?" he asked, his voice a little gruff. "Have you been safe here in the castle?"

Surprised, she searched his face. He seemed to be genuinely asking. She nodded, sadness creeping into her eyes.

I can't sing, she mouthed, using her hand to mime a voice flowing from her throat out into the air.

"Sing?" Demetrius clarified, and she nodded. He scratched his jaw, his expression grim. "Actually, neither can I," he admitted.

Estelle's eyes flew to his, startled.

"I tried yesterday, when that animal was out of control. Nothing came. It worried me, and I asked around in the village yesterday. I've been doing some work for a fisherman the last few days, and he explained it all to me while we were on the water in the evening. It seems magic doesn't work the same on land as it does underwater. I mean," he clarified, "it works the same in that it comes up from the land, like it comes from the seabed, and it's channeled by singing. But not everyone can harness it. Some humans are born with the ability to sing—they're called singers—but most aren't. And it can't be learned. You have it or you don't." He gave her a rueful look. "And apparently, when it comes to the magic of the land, I don't have it."

No magic? Estelle mouthed in alarm.

"No magic," Demetrius confirmed.

Well, Estelle thought, borrowing Demetrius's own words from earlier, that complicates things. They were doubly vulnerable now. She looked Demetrius over, her heart lifting in spite of everything. Actually, she felt considerably less vulnerable than she had a day before, knowing Demetrius was nearby. And as for him...well, the young guard had never shown any indication of vulnerability that she'd ever seen.

She rolled her eyes, not bothering to attempt to communicate her thoughts. It was typical, really, that while she'd floundered for days without making any progress, Demetrius had found work in the village, come to the notice of the prince with his heroics, and secured an opportunity to train with the guards. She had no doubt that he would perform well enough to be granted a position at the end of his training. Demetrius was good at everything he tried.

And yet, she couldn't be annoyed at his success, not when she was so relieved to have him around. She was no longer alone, and that was worth everything.

"How's your mission going?" Demetrius asked, the hint of sarcasm back in his voice. "Have you won the prince's heart yet?"

Estelle sighed, too weary to even be annoyed. She had a feeling from Demetrius's expression that he already knew the answer. She acknowledged to herself that Farrin wasn't falling for her as she'd hoped. Disregarding pride, she'd done her best to make her admiration clear, trying to communicate with her eyes how much she adored him. But she couldn't pretend it was working. He continued to be kind, but there was no hint of the desire for more.

And not everyone was so kind. It was clear from the veiled comments she'd heard that many of the servants were suspicious of her. As she'd gathered from watching him in her mermaid form, the prince could reliably be found walking along the cliffs after dawn each morning. He was well known for the habit, and the story of his near miss when he fell from the ship had also spread widely. Many in the castle thought that Estelle had learned both of those things, then faked her accident in a calculated attempt to win his sympathy. She'd even overheard snide references to her brazenness in shedding her clothing in order to gain more attention.

"Never mind," said Demetrius bracingly. "There's always the Ocean Miner's other bargain. I retrieved your satchel from the beach, and I have the enchanted shell. Shall we use it now?"

Estelle's eyes flew wide, and she shook her head vigorously. Admit defeat and go back to the ocean? Never! She was getting worried, but she was nowhere near that desperate. Besides, the Ocean Miner had said she'd offer a fresh deal if failure was imminent. Farrin not falling instantly in love with her didn't constitute imminent failure.

Demetrius sighed, looking resigned. Clearly he hadn't really expected her to give in so quickly. "Well, I'll be nearby," he said. "My training starts tomorrow, and I'm to move into the barracks this evening. If you come find me, we can talk more then."

Estelle nodded gratefully. If she thought he'd welcome it,

she would have hugged him again, but he would probably just scoff at her. So instead she contented herself with a warm smile before drifting back toward the castle, fresh determination growing inside her. Demetrius thought she was foolish, but her affection for Farrin was genuine. Surely if he could understand how she felt, he'd feel it, too. She would show Demetrius that she wasn't a naive child. She just had to try harder.

To that end, she searched the castle until she found Farrin. Conveniently, when she located him, he was emerging from the royal wing, into which she didn't have access. He looked distracted, and didn't even notice her at first. He had a parchment in his hand, but when he realized she was following him, he stowed it hastily in a pocket.

"Good morning," he said, his friendly tone sounding a little forced compared to normal. "I hope you slept well?"

Estelle nodded, her eyes searching his face. What was he up to? His manner was nothing like his usual lighthearted self. As she plodded along beside him, she saw how his eyes darted back to the royal wing, as if afraid of being caught in wrongdoing. Where was his brother? Farrin and Prince Emmett were often together, but there was no sign of the older brother now.

Something about that backward glance reminded Estelle of the day before, after Demetrius had saved her from the panicked horse. Emmett had said they should turn back immediately, and Farrin had chivalrously agreed, but Estelle had seen him give just such a wistful look toward the shoreline. Once she would have told herself he was dreaming of the sea like she dreamed of the land. But she was under no such illusion this time. He'd had a specific destination in mind, she was sure of it. Where had he been intending to go?

Farrin had seemed in a hurry when Estelle approached him, but now he'd dropped his pace, his movements clipped as he asked her politely how she was. Estelle's ability to reply was limited, but she did her best. If only she could steer the conversation instead of him. She'd come looking for him with a plan in mind, but she had no idea how to implement it. How could she bring up the night he'd fallen from the ship? How could she explain to him that she was the one who'd saved his life? Surely that was her best hope of encouraging affection to grow. Not only would he be grateful, it would also prove to him how much she cared.

Of course, in point of fact, Demetrius had been the one to save Farrin. She wouldn't have gotten the prince to the surface in time without his help, and she wouldn't have been able to carry him all the way to shore.

But she had no intention of telling Farrin that. Demetrius certainly wouldn't have helped without her pleading. A smile curled her lips. Besides which, she had a feeling Demetrius wouldn't thank her for describing him as Farrin's savior.

"Well, it's good to see you smiling," Farrin said in a bracing tone. "After all you've gone through, it's been very understandable that you've been cast down. But things will get better, you'll see." He hesitated. "I don't suppose you've gained any more memory?"

She shook her head. It was strictly true, she argued with herself, even if it was misleading.

"That's a shame," Farrin muttered. "But you'll be all right. Yes, you'll be fine."

In spite of referring to Estelle, he seemed to be speaking more to himself than to her. She felt her brows draw together as she studied his face. He was certainly hiding something. But she couldn't imagine what it was.

"Well, I'm afraid I can't linger at the moment," said Farrin. He waited, but Estelle didn't budge. She'd decided she needed to try harder, and letting him shake her off after two minutes' conversation wasn't going to achieve what she needed. "I think the housekeeper was looking for you," Farrin tried, with an air of desperation. "In any event, I really need to go. Goodbye."

On those words, he hurried away down the corridor, leaving Estelle little choice but to let him go. She didn't believe that the housekeeper was looking for her. That had clearly been an excuse. After a moment's thought, she started moving, following in Farrin's wake.

The prince had just disappeared around a corner, but she managed to catch a glimpse of him before he took another turn. Running as quietly as she could, she pursued him through back corridors she'd never before explored. To her surprise, he let himself out through a side door rather than making for the main entrance. To her even greater surprise, he fished a rucksack out of a large ornamental vase just prior to leaving the building.

Alarm surged in Estelle. What did he need a bag for? Where was he going?

In her haste to keep him in sight, she tripped on the doorframe, falling to her knees on the small stones that made up this particular walkway. Farrin, some distance ahead, turned at the noise. She saw his eyes widen, and he hesitated. But then, a silent apology flitting across his face, he turned and hurried on, disappearing through an archway in the yard.

Frustrated and embarrassed in equal measures, Estelle pushed herself to her feet. She hovered for a moment, then decided that the time for secrecy was past. Disregarding the crunching sound, she ran quickly across the stones. By the time she reached the archway, however, there was no sign of Farrin. A glance around showed that the closest building was the stables, and Estelle directed her steps there. She searched fruitlessly for several minutes, finally catching sight of the prince from a distance as he rode toward the castle gate.

She deflated. No hope of keeping up with him now. A

nearby horse gave a sudden harrumph, and Estelle shied away. She wouldn't be attempting to ride one of those again anytime soon.

For the rest of the day, she was more than usually unsettled, wandering the halls with agitated strides. She didn't usually eat with the royal family, except on the occasions when Farrin happened to invite her. He didn't do so for luncheon, and by dinner, the rumor was spreading through the castle like ink through water—the prince was missing. Or at least, his family had expected him for the last two meals, and no one knew why he'd failed to appear, or where he was now.

Anxiety curled in Estelle's stomach. She hovered around the royal wing until the hard stares of the guards deterred her. Guards! She was supposed to meet Demetrius this evening. Maybe he would have heard something in the guards' barracks. She was hurrying through the castle intent on reaching the training yard when she caught sight of a pair of servants gossiping excitedly behind a plinth. Estelle slowed her steps, hoping to hear the latest news.

She needn't have tried too hard. One of the girls looked around and beckoned her over, probably mistaking her for a servant due to her clothing.

"Have you heard?" she said excitedly. "The queen found a note in her room. Prince Farrin has run away!"

Run away? Estelle just blinked at the other girl. Why would Farrin do that?

"I can't imagine why a *prince* would want to run away from a life of luxury," commented the other servant.

A sliver of guilt cut across Estelle's disbelief. She knew why a royal might wish to escape their life. But surely that didn't apply to Farrin. He'd never shown the least sign of discontent.

She stumbled on from the gossiping pair, her only thought to reach Demetrius. But when she got to the training yard, there was no one to be found. It seemed that the guards were all occupied, and she thought she could guess with what.

Whatever searches they conducted, however, Farrin did not return to the castle that night. After many sleepless hours, Estelle rose with the sun, hurrying toward the royal dining hall in spite of her lack of invitation. A heavy-eyed Prince Emmett intersected her just as she approached.

"Ah, yes." His eyes skated over her, and Estelle had the impression he'd slept little as well. "Good morning." The prince glanced toward the dining hall, then back at Estelle. "I don't mean to be unkind, miss, but I don't think you should join the family for breakfast this morning. My parents are not in the best of humors."

Estelle shook her head vigorously, trying to communicate that she had no desire to impose on their meal.

Your brother? she mouthed as clearly as she could.

"You've heard, have you?" Prince Emmett ran a hand over his face. "Is the whole castle speaking of his disappearance?"

Estelle nodded. She saw no reason to hide the truth from him.

The prince let out a shuddering sigh. "He hasn't returned," he admitted. "He was tracked to the eastern harbor, past the village. It appears he boarded a vessel there."

Estelle was bursting with questions she couldn't give voice to. Thankfully the older prince took pity on her curiosity, perhaps because of the way Farrin had taken her under his fins.

"We don't know where the vessel was going." He grimaced, casting a look around. "Of course, you wouldn't be familiar with the reputation of the eastern harbor. It's not Port Dulla's main port. It's...seedy. We think the ship he boarded was a smuggler's ship. All we know for certain is it's expected back in a fortnight."

Estelle's eyes widened. Two weeks? She was supposed to

wait for two weeks to catch another glimpse of Farrin? What was she to do in that time?

As if reading her mind, Prince Emmett cleared his throat. "We may need to reconsider your...accommodations. Farrin will be gone for some time, it seems, and although I know he meant well with his desire to house you here as a guest..."

Estelle nodded, raising her hands in a gesture of surrender. She was very ready to give up the awkward role of neither guest nor servant.

"Do you have anywhere to go?" Prince Emmett asked helplessly.

She shook her head.

He glanced over her servant's attire. "Would you welcome the chance for employment in the castle?" he asked tentatively.

Estelle gave a more vigorous nod, and the prince looked relieved.

"That much I can do, for your sake and for Farrin's," he muttered. "I'll speak with the housekeeper this morning."

Estelle inclined her head in gratitude, hurrying for the training yard as soon as she was dismissed. There was a great deal to discuss with Demetrius. Not that she could do much discussing, of course.

By the end of the day, the housekeeper had set her to work in the kitchens. Estelle was washing dishes, an uninteresting and exhausting task that was nevertheless perfect in its repetitiveness. Her thoughts circled endlessly around Farrin, wondering where he was, and why he'd fled like that. If only she'd managed to follow him the day before. But wherever he'd gone, he was out of her reach now. So much for her determination to prove to Demetrius that she could win Farrin over.

Demetrius didn't have much to say about Farrin's flight, taking the whole thing philosophically. Maddeningly, Estelle got the impression that the guard didn't think Farrin's absence made any material difference to her chances of succeeding in her plans.

As two weeks turned into three, Estelle began to feel genuinely afraid. Her main concern had initially been selfish, wondering what would become of her while Farrin was gone. But when a fortnight had passed with still no sign of his return, her concerns for him took prominence.

Although she knew it was no longer appropriate given her status as a servant, she hunted Prince Emmett down in hope of answers. He looked haggard, noticeably worse than the last time she'd seen him.

"He's not back," the prince said, not waiting for her to attempt to ask. "The ship didn't return. And inquiries at every major port in Providore have so far yielded nothing. Our contacts at the harbor think the ship might have been lost at sea. But..." He swallowed, seeming to struggle to get the next words out. "But we probably have to accept that we may never know for certain."

Estelle stepped back, horror washing over her. She didn't believe it. It couldn't be true. She turned blindly, fleeing from the ashen-faced prince toward the only haven she had.

Demetrius took one look at her panicked face, and grabbed her shoulders in a firm and unhurried grip.

"Calm down." The words were an order. "Everything will be all right."

In defiance of logic, Estelle felt reassured. She took a deep breath, then attempted to demonstrate with her hands the supposed fate of Farrin's ship. Demetrius frowned on in evident confusion for some minutes before comprehension dawned.

"Are you talking about the smuggling vessel Prince Farrin boarded? I've heard the rumor that it must have sunk."

Estelle nodded, her throat thick.

Demetrius gave a grunt, not seeming especially concerned. "Speculation, Estelle. Castle gossip."

She shook her head, miming a crown.

Demetrius frowned at the gesture. "You heard it from one of the royals?"

She nodded again, and his expression grew more grave.

"What would that mean for us, I wonder?" he asked. "It makes it impossible to fulfill the terms of your bargain with the Ocean Miner, but it also makes it impossible for the prince to marry someone else and inadvertently kill you."

Estelle's eyes widened. The Ocean Miner. A horrible thought occurred to her, and she gripped Demetrius's arm.

Ocean Miner! she mouthed.

He stared uncomprehendingly, and she drew a finger across her throat to signify death.

"The Ocean Miner?" he tried. "You think she might be dead?"

Estelle shook her head impatiently, repeating the gestures, but this time with a crown.

"You think Prince Farrin might be dead," Demetrius translated. "Yes, I know. But what does that have to do with—" He broke off, understanding entering his eyes. "You think she might have somehow sunk his ship?" He thought it over. "It would make sense. That would stop you from succeeding, wouldn't it? Does that mean that if he dies, you're stuck up here as a human for the rest of your life? Neither succeeding nor truly failing in your task?"

Estelle stilled, surprised by how reassuring she found this image. If that was the worst fate she might face, it wasn't so bad. At least she wouldn't have to return to Korallid. She forced the thought down, ashamed of herself for seeing any bright spot in the horrifying idea of Farrin's death.

She looked into Demetrius's thoughtful face, one fact

becoming clear. He'd done more than anyone could ever have asked of him, and there was no reason he should give any more than he already had.

She pointed at his chest meaningfully, then gestured at the ocean, making waves with her hand.

"Return to the sea? Me?" Demetrius guessed.

She nodded, a determined expression on her face.

Demetrius gave her a look. "I can't, Estelle. Not while you're still stuck up here."

She shook her head, pointing at herself. *I'm all right. You go.*

He obviously got the gist of the mouthed words, but his answer didn't change.

"I can't," he repeated. "It's not that I'm unwilling to. I can't."

Estelle's brow puckered in confusion, alarm rising inside her.

"I didn't drink a different vial of the potion, Estelle," Demetrius told her. "I drank a mimicking draft, after pouring it into your empty vial. I transformed because you did—my fate is tied to yours. If you succeed, and win your legs forever, I'll be stuck in the same position. If you fail, and die, so will I." He shrugged. "And I suppose if you remain in limbo, the same will apply to me."

Estelle stared at him, horrified. She'd never planned for this, never imagined she was embroiling anyone else so deeply in her scheme. She thought she'd taken a calculated risk, truly preferring to die for the chance of a life on land than to live a long and miserable life underwater. But she hadn't factored Demetrius into any of that.

And now she'd doomed him as well.

"Demetrius," she croaked, unspeakable agony assailing her throat. Instinctively, she clutched at it, curling in on herself as she fought waves of pain and nausea.

Demetrius drew in a sharp breath, his hand flying out and hovering pointlessly in the air near her throat.

"Estelle, it's not worth it. Don't torture yourself."

"Worth—it," she rasped. "Must...say...I'm...sorry."

The effort of those few words was more than her shredded throat could stand. She let out a whimper of pain, but she didn't regret the exertion. Demetrius deserved that much from her.

"It's all right, Estelle," Demetrius said, his voice gruff and low. For some reason it sent a shiver over her, not entirely unpleasant even in the midst of her mental and physical agony. "You already know what I think of your choices, but I wouldn't change mine if I could. I'm with you until the end of the current."

The tiniest measure of comfort leaked into Estelle's misery. It was truly something not to be alone. But it wasn't enough to stem the flow of her grief, and with a heaving breath, she collapsed to her knees, surrendering to the tears.

TWO AND A HALF YEARS LATER...

CHAPTER SEVENTEEN

Estelle

Estelle dug her hands into the dirt, enjoying the feeling of the moisture on her skin as she turned the soil over. The hyacinths should do nicely here, she reflected happily. Much better to put the daylilies in the smaller garden on the ocean side of the castle. They would have a better chance of surviving the sea breezes. And the hyacinths would still satisfy the queen's request for a cheerful patch of pink along her favorite walking path.

"That looks good, Estelle."

Estelle looked up at the head gardener, smiling in gratitude for the praise. The older man paused, assessing her work with a critical eye. She was pleased to see his slow nod.

"With any luck, the blooms of the hyacinths will be offset with those daffodils just enough to keep a splash of color until this lot come out." He gestured at the next garden bed along.

Estelle nodded, tapping her heart lightly in a gesture intended to indicate that had been her hope as well.

"You have a knack for flowers," said the gardener. "Many of my workers are more comfortable with the trees and hedges. It was a good thought of the housekeeper's to send you out here."

He flashed her a grin. "Plus you don't chatter on like some servants do, disturbing the peace of our haven."

Estelle chuckled soundlessly, taking no offense at the good-natured reference to her supposed muteness.

"I know many girls like yourself aim to become ladies' maids and such," the head gardener went on, "but I hope you'll stay in my team. You've a job in the gardens as long as you want it, as far as I'm concerned." He winked, starting back into motion. "And I'm not likely to retire any time soon."

Estelle ducked her head, color flooding her cheeks at the unexpected assurance. The head gardener was often ready with an encouraging word, but she hadn't realized he rated her services so highly. She agreed with him that the housekeeper had done a good day's work when she'd suggested Estelle help out in the gardens. For the first six months of her time at the castle, she'd struggled away in the kitchens, exhausted and terrible at her role.

Rocking back on her heels, Estelle let her thoughts wander back to those early months. It seemed a lifetime ago. It was hard to believe it had been two years since she'd started in the gardens. Her life was so different now—she was so different now. And if her time in the kitchen felt distant, her years below water were nothing more than a dream. Strangely enough, the memories that felt most real were the times spent in her little coral garden, shaping the rows into the form of the sun, the light of which she'd never even felt.

She wiped a trickle of sweat from her brow with her arm, smiling to herself at the thought. She was very familiar with the heat of the sun now. It wasn't as bad this time of year, but it could be quite oppressive in the summer months. And even now, the air was thick and warm. She liked it. It was comforting, like the land's version of how the water used to press against her when she was a mermaid, cocooning her on all sides. Some of the other servants assured her that in other parts of Providore, the air wasn't thick with heat like in Medulle. Apparently in the far north, where the giants lived, the air was thin, and so cold that everything froze, even the rain.

It was a fascinating image, but Estelle found herself quite content to stay in Port Dulla. It seemed the desire for exploration that had driven her from the ocean had been satiated. Her father would probably be pleased, she reflected, trying not to dwell on the stab of bitterness that came with the thought. She'd had plenty of time to think about her past life, and the decisions that had led her to her present one—gardening was excellent for thinking time—and she'd often wondered if her restlessness had been less about reaching the land and more about escaping the ocean.

But either way, she'd become very fond of this world above the waterline. She returned her attention to the hyacinths, smiling to herself at how ignorant and naive she'd been when she first arrived in the city. She'd assumed the land was one empire, like the sea. She knew now that Medulle, over which King Johannes and Queen Sula ruled, was only one kingdom among four on the continent of Solstice. And that didn't include the island kingdom of Selvana to the southwest, or the island to the east which everyone just called the Reviled Lands. Not that Medulle had contact with either island. Selvana had become cut off from the mainland when its magic went wild generations ago, making the ground uninhabitable. And the Reviled Lands had been rejected by the mainland for some offense Estelle hadn't quite been able to get an explanation for. She could and often did listen in on the servants' gossip, but without her voice, it wasn't always easy to steer the conversation in the direction she might wish.

Her task finished, Estelle brushed off her hands and made her way to the nearby storage shed in search of more bulbs. Her eyes were drawn to the sandstone walls rising not far away, and her thoughts strayed once again to the months she'd spent working inside the castle. She knew the head cook had been eager to get rid of her, but the housekeeper seemed to think Prince Emmett might be upset if Estelle was released. Perhaps she was right—even now the crown prince checked in on her from time to time, in a detached sort of way. She knew Prince Emmett did it for the sake of his brother, who'd been so determined to show her kindness. Probably the proximity between her arrival and Farrin's disappearance created more of a link in Prince Emmett's mind than would otherwise have been the case.

Sadness lanced through Estelle at the thought of the handsome, cheerful young prince who—as far as anyone could tell—had sailed out to his death at only eighteen. That was her own age now, or almost. How grown up and confident he'd seemed to her when she first laid eyes on him! Far from how she felt at eighteen.

Her eyes glazed over, not seeing the chaos of the overflowing shelves before her. Farrin was the kindest person she'd ever known. Her heart still did a strange kind of flop when she remembered how it had felt when he'd touched her in passing, how protectively he'd helped her from the beach that first day, how he'd spoken on her behalf in face of his parents' lack of enthusiasm.

As always happened, her sadness over Farrin's absence was soured by an even worse feeling: guilt. She knew nothing for certain, of course, but the timing of his disappearance seemed too coincidental. If the Ocean Miner really had killed him to ensure the failure of Estelle's plans...

A shudder went over Estelle at the thought of the king and queen's grief when their son had failed to return, of the heaviness that Prince Emmett still carried around with him like a weighted overcoat.

Were her family feeling the same sorrow over her disappearance? Part of her would like to think so, but picturing her father's face when he'd told her she was no use to the empire, she doubted it.

Grabbing more hyacinth bulbs, Estelle made her way back to the garden bed. She'd barely resumed her position, however, when a shout drew her attention to the far side of the garden. Several guards came hurrying around the corner, and Estelle pushed herself to her feet, her eyes instinctively searching for a familiar figure.

Her heart lifted as she recognized the amber hair and upright form of Demetrius. Hurrying forward, she waved to get his attention. It was unnecessary. He was already scanning the gardens, and he tilted his head in greeting when he spotted her. Content to wait, Estelle rocked back on her heels, watching as the guards flagged down the head gardener and conducted a brief conversation. Demetrius would come and find her when he was free. He always did.

She found her thoughts turning once again to the past as she studied his alert posture. Demetrius was ever the guard—in some ways, his ascent to the land had made little difference either to his manner or his lifestyle. It was no surprise to her that he'd excelled in his chosen vocation, even in human form. It had taken only months for his captain to recognize his capability, and less than a year for him to be invited to train for a position guarding the royal family directly. Just like he had as a merman, Estelle reflected, feeling a pang of sentiment as she thought of the sister whom Demetrius had briefly guarded. Eulalia at least would feel sadness over Estelle's disappearance, even if it affected her life little.

What did Demetrius feel about it? The question flitted through her mind, not entirely welcome. The guard wasn't easy to read. He didn't *seem* unhappy, and she'd never heard him complain about his lot. But time hadn't made him softer, either. He had no hesitation in telling her when she was being foolish, and every time he did so, she remembered his words to her outside the Ocean Miner's cave. He showed great forbearance in not saying it, but he must still resent her rash decision, and the life-altering impact on him. They had no new information since their first weeks on land, and every reason to think they were both stuck above water indefinitely.

All things considered, her feelings regarding Demetrius were even more complicated than those relating to Farrin. She felt just as guilty where the former merman was concerned, but she couldn't precisely claim sadness over his fate, like she did the prince. No, the honest, selfish truth was that she remained incredibly glad that he was with her in Medulle. She didn't know how she would ever have coped without him.

One example of his invaluable assistance was the fact that everyone now knew her name. Her lips twitched as she remembered Demetrius's straight-faced performance in the pantomime where they'd pretended he was guessing her name through trial and error. They'd decided early on that it would be wisest not to let anyone know they were familiar to each other, so as to protect their true nature. Therefore Demetrius couldn't just tell everyone her name.

Estelle had also quickly tired of being asked to write it down. It hadn't taken her and Demetrius long to discover that most in the castle could read and write the written language the humans had developed—a marvel that still blew Estelle away at its limitless potential. Demetrius in particular had been concerned that their shared ignorance would be suspicious. But apparently it wasn't so uncommon for those of lower classes not to read. In any event, no one had remarked on it either in the supposed fisherman's son, or in the mute castaway.

Demetrius had found a fellow guard willing to teach him to

read, and then taught Estelle in turn. It had taken many months thanks to the limited free time allowed each of them. But it had been well worth the effort. Quite apart from the invaluable skill, Estelle had found the time spent with Demetrius calming, in spite of him not being the most patient of teachers. With him she didn't have to hide or pretend—it had always been that way, after all, even underwater. And by the end of those months, their friendship was well and truly established among the castle servants, without anyone suspecting them of prior acquaintance.

Some of those servants seemed under the impression that since Estelle didn't talk, her hearing was defective as well. She knew from what she'd overheard that the gossip assigned more than friendship to her frequent interactions with the highly respected guard, and although she'd been embarrassed by the suggestion, it hadn't seemed to faze Demetrius. Nothing much ruffled the handsome young guard. Maybe that was why he was so admired among the servants.

The thought pulled Estelle up. When had she started thinking of Demetrius as handsome? Perhaps she'd just overheard one too many giggling conversations about his quiet strength in the servants' hall. But he was handsome, she acknowledged, as she studied him from the side. It was only partially his features, which were pleasant enough. It was also that he radiated confidence, a quality which most people found irresistible, whether they realized it or not.

At that moment, Demetrius turned his head, catching her eye. He raised a questioning eyebrow when he found her scrutinizing him so closely. Estelle pasted on a quick smile, embarrassed to be caught considering his physical attractiveness, even if he couldn't know her thoughts.

No one much knew her thoughts these days.

The head gardener called out to one of his other assistants

before his eyes scanned the gardens. He saw Estelle watching curiously, and shook his head.

"You can keep working on the garden bed for the queen, Estelle. Two of us should be enough for an assessment."

Estelle nodded sagely, pretending she had any idea what he was talking about. As she'd expected, when the other guards turned away, leading the two gardeners back the way they'd come, Demetrius peeled off. His eyes still searching hers in confusion, he walked up to Estelle with the unfaltering stride that always made everyone assume he was supposed to be wherever he was.

"Is everything all right?" he asked curtly.

Estelle nodded, pointing back at him with raised brow.

He nodded as well, understanding her question perfectly. "Yes, I'm fine."

She tilted her head in the direction of the departed guards and gardeners.

"We were sent to fetch someone to the smaller garden on the ocean side of the castle," he explained. "They think it might be a lost cause altogether, but they're hoping the gardeners might be able to save some of the trees."

Startled, Estelle made a tumultuous rolling gesture with her fists, her expression inquiring.

"Yes, more storms," Demetrius said, once again understanding immediately. "Listen. The waves are pounding the ridge right now. It's as wild an assault as I've ever seen."

Estelle frowned up at the clear, sunny sky. Barely a breeze ruffled the leaves of a nearby willow.

"I know." Demetrius's voice was grim. "It doesn't seem natural." He glanced around, shifting a little closer so that Estelle had to look up to hold his gaze. "I went for a swim again this morning. I went out further this time. I'm not imagining it, and it wasn't some freak anomaly. The tides are changing. They feel...angry."

Estelle bit her lip. Even if her voice had been easy to use, she had nothing helpful to say. Demetrius knew that she shared his confusion about what was happening to the ocean, and his fears about what that might mean for the merfolk. The silence stretched out as Estelle tried fruitlessly to imagine what might be causing the dramatic changes.

"Are you afraid?"

Estelle's eyes flew to Demetrius's, surprised by the abrupt question. Without giving it much thought, she shook her head. It was an honest answer—impossible to feel afraid in the guard's solid, dependable presence, with the attention of those serious amber eyes fully fixed on her—but she realized belatedly it wasn't a very compassionate answer. She should be more afraid for those she'd left behind, and whether the changes in the ocean's behavior were endangering them.

Color flooded her cheeks at the realization of her selfishness. Could Demetrius see it? He always saw her faults with depressing clarity.

"What are you thinking, Estelle?" Demetrius's words answered her question. "Even after all this time, sometimes I still expect you to just open your mouth and tell me what's in your mind."

Estelle glanced up at him curiously. It was unlike Demetrius to share that type of thought. Did he really think about how things used to be—how *she* used to be?

"Do you miss your voice?" he asked suddenly, surprising her again.

Estelle thought it over, then, smiling ruefully, she shook her head.

Demetrius made a noise of disbelief. "That can't be true," he said dismissively. "You must miss it."

Estelle laughed internally, shaking her head more firmly. She held out a hand, motioning the movement of writing, then clicked her fingers.

Demetrius sighed, but he pulled a folded scrap of parchment from an inner pocket. "You're the one whose voice is too ghastly to use," he said shortly. "You should carry around parchment."

Estelle snatched it from him, waiting impatiently while he produced a short length of lead.

Parchment is expensive, she scribbled.

"I know," protested Demetrius. "I'm the one providing you with a constant supply."

Estelle waved a dismissive hand. *You're paid much more than I am*, she wrote.

Demetrius made a long-suffering noise that made her grin, but she didn't needle him any further. Instead she wrote her answer to the initial question, ignoring the impatient tap of Demetrius's foot.

I do miss the ease of simple communication. And sometimes I miss singing. But truthfully, I don't usually miss it because even without my voice, I have more voice here than I ever had in Korallid.

She handed the paper back to Demetrius, watching him as he scanned the three sentences. A frown creased his forehead, and he stayed bent over the words for twice as long as she would have expected him to need. Her eyes were fixed on his face, but she had little success in reading his expression.

"You shouldn't write the name of our empire," he said at last, his voice more gruff than usual. "Who knows how much detail the humans' old stories had—someone might recognize it." He scrunched up the paper and shoved it back into his pocket. "I'll burn that later."

Estelle shrugged, not especially concerned either way. She

returned his lead to him, smiling in a friendly way as she jerked a thumb back toward her unfinished task.

"Yes, I should get back to my post as well," said Demetrius.

But he didn't turn away, and Estelle hovered, wondering what was in his mind. She stared as he shifted his weight from one foot to the other. Was Demetrius fidgeting? It was like he was a young, green recruit again, on duty at the emperor's meal for the first time.

"Tomorrow is your birthday," the guard said suddenly. "You'll be eighteen."

Estelle waited, perplexed. Did he think she'd forgotten?

"That birthday is a rite of passage for humans," Demetrius went on. "That's when they come of age."

Estelle nodded, her thoughts drifting to her own disastrous coming of age. Perhaps if merfolk waited until eighteen as well, instead of committing their mermaids to a life of cold duty at fifteen, she would have been a little wiser, and better able to deal with her family's expectations and her own desires.

"We should celebrate, is my point," Demetrius pushed on. "I assume you've heard about the celebration in the servants' hall?"

She nodded eagerly. She'd been looking forward to it for weeks.

"Well, it seems fortuitous that the event happens to fall on your birthday, and I wondered if I could escort you there," said Demetrius, still sounding brusque. "I'd like to wish you happy birthday before you get too caught up in the frivolity."

Estelle's mouth fell open a little, amazed by this sign of consideration. Amazed and pleased. She nodded, her smile feeling a little more shy than usual.

Demetrius nodded, looking almost pleased himself. Before he could say anything further, however, a voice hailed him.

They both turned to see that one of the guards had come back, looking for Demetrius.

"What happened to you, Demetrius? Did you get lost in here—oh." The guard caught sight of Estelle and his smile grew. "A pleasant type of lost, I see."

Estelle smiled back in a friendly way. The guard wasn't much older than Demetrius. She'd met him before, but his name escaped her. Given she'd seen him with Demetrius a number of times, she assumed they were friends.

"What do you want, Ander?" Demetrius rapped out.

Apparently not very close friends.

"Just to stay and talk to you both," Ander said unconvincingly. He sent Estelle a wink. "Chatting about the dance tomorrow night, no doubt. Going to get all fancied up, Estelle? It is Estelle, isn't it?"

"You can tell the others I'll be with them shortly," said Demetrius, in a tone that left no room for argument.

"No need to be so sour," said Ander, sending the other guard an unimpressed look. To Estelle, he flashed a final smile. "Nice speaking with you, Estelle."

She returned the smile, her shoulders shaking in a silent chuckle as the guard sauntered away. He looked faintly ridiculous.

"Estelle, what are you doing?" Demetrius's harsh voice brought her attention back to him.

She frowned in confusion, wondering what in the ocean she was supposed to have done.

"We're supposed to be keeping our heads down," said Demetrius scoldingly. "Avoiding notice. You do the opposite."

Estelle's mouth fell open, outraged by this unjust accusation. She disagreed with Demetrius's belief in the continued need for great caution, but that was beside the point. She never did anything to attract attention to herself. She didn't even speak!

"I need to go," Demetrius said, his voice again gruff. "I'll meet you here an hour before the celebration tomorrow night. Maybe we can walk in the gardens for a while."

Estelle scowled by way of response, utterly dissatisfied with this redirecting of the conversation without giving her the chance to respond. Demetrius was already walking away, and of course she couldn't call after him. She turned back to her task, grumbling internally over his heavy-handed claiming of her time. There were ways to communicate her displeasure without words. Maybe an hour of waiting in the gardens would help him get the message.

CHAPTER EIGHTEEN

Demetrius

Demetrius let out a quiet groan as soon as he rounded the corner out of Estelle's sight. He'd bungled that whole interaction woefully, and he knew it. He'd intended for the moment to be a happy one, having told himself that Estelle deserved some kind attention on her birthday. She was remarkably uncomplaining about her change in status, and he had no doubt she wouldn't have batted an eyelid at having her birthday entirely disregarded by everyone. He'd figured since he was the only one who knew the status she'd lost, it was up to him to make some kind of fuss. But making a fuss wasn't one of his strengths.

Apparently, making an idiot of himself was.

He hardly knew why he'd reacted so strongly to Ander's flirtation. It was nothing new. Estelle was often the recipient of admiration from the guards. Her unusual hair, with its startling blue streaks, garnered a great deal of attention. Thankfully she didn't hear the way some of them spoke of her—and any of the castle maids they found attractive—and Demetrius made very certain none of them crossed any lines with their admiration. Everyone knew of his friendship with Estelle, and he had enough standing among the guards that no one cared to incite his anger. But it still made him anxious. He considered himself responsible for her safety, and it was a complicating factor that she'd gained the beauty she'd lacked at fifteen while losing the protection of her status as princess.

The frequency of the attention was the problem, he argued with himself. She was always under observation, and she didn't seem aware of it. She must not be aware—how could she be so carefree if she was?

It was an irrelevant question. On this occasion, at least, she'd done nothing to attract undue attention, and Demetrius knew it. He'd reacted out of his own fear, and blamed it on her. He would apologize tomorrow evening, and try to be less critical in future.

Another ability that didn't come naturally to him.

Demetrius felt unusually restless the following day, conscious that it was Estelle's birthday and doubly conscious that they hadn't parted well the day before. When he was released from his duties in the late afternoon, he took the time to change his clothes. He still wore his guard's uniform, of course. Many of the guards were attending the servants' celebration, and all would be in uniform. The majority of the guards didn't come from affluent circumstances, and their uniforms were by far the most formal clothes they owned.

Clad in a fresh uniform, Demetrius surveyed himself critically in front of the single long looking glass the barracks contained.

"What's this I see?" Ander elbowed Demetrius as he jostled for position. "Demetrius preening in front of his reflection? That's a rare sight. The celebration has gone even to your head, has it?"

Demetrius just grunted, checking that his uniform was straight, and his hair—no longer in shoulder-length waves but cut to regulation length—was all in order. He was always neat. It was part of the role of a guard to look uniform and inconspicuous. But tonight he felt a particular desire to present his best. He couldn't explain it to himself, and he certainly didn't intend to try explaining it to Ander.

"Or perhaps it's not the celebration that's gone to your head so much as that sweet little thing, Estelle," said Ander, his tone sly.

Demetrius continued to ignore him, not judging the taunt to be worth a reply.

"She's certainly quite taking," Ander commented, his eyes fixed on his reflection as he straightened his own collar. "If you're not going to claim her, step aside so one of us can."

"Don't be absurd," said Demetrius, goaded into a reply against his better judgment. "She's barely older than a child, and you're—"

Ander's snort cut his words off. "Don't be such a fool, Demetrius. You only have to look at her to know she's not a child. How old is she, anyway?"

Demetrius hesitated, resenting any information shared about Estelle, but unable to think of a good reason not to answer. "She turns eighteen today, actually."

"Today?" Ander turned to him with raised eyebrow. "Planning some kind of declaration, are you?" He cast a critical eye over Demetrius's attire, giving the belt over his chest a firm tug to better position it. "Well, I won't get in your way if it's as dire as all that."

"Of course I'm not," said Demetrius, unreasonably irritated by his friend's assumptions. "That's not what we are to each other. I just wanted to wish her happy birthday before the festivities start."

"In that case," said Ander, with an unconvincing air of innocence, "there's no reason I shouldn't have a try. A man could get lost in those sparkling blue eyes, you know."

"Very funny." Demetrius wasn't in the least amused by the other man's teasing.

"I'm serious," said Ander. "If you don't act soon, you'll miss your chance. Whether me or some other of this worthless lot," he jerked his shoulder to the barracks at large, "someone will cut you out. She's gorgeous, your little friend. The hair, the eyes, that trim figure. And plenty of men like the idea of a girl who isn't going to chatter their ear off." Unmoved by Demetrius's scowl, he gave his friend a quelling look. "And no more nonsense about her being a child. My sister was married with a child of her own by eighteen."

"I thought girls usually married later here," said Demetrius, without thinking. It was one of the things he'd most appreciated about human culture. Girls didn't come of age at fifteen, and he'd yet to see a single one pushed into marriage that early. Probably the difference in fertility had a part to play in that.

Ander threw him a strange look, then nodded in sudden understanding. "I forgot you're half Vadolisian, and grew up over there."

Demetrius just grunted in feigned confirmation of the tale he'd concocted two and a half years before. He'd clearly been foreign, and had needed an explanation, but he'd been concerned that being from the neighboring kingdom might throw his loyalty too much into question to allow him a position in the royal guard. So he'd claimed to have a Medullan father and a mother from Vadolis.

"Well, I don't know how they do it in Vadolis," said Ander, with a final glance at his own reflection. "But in Medulle, eighteen is considered plenty old enough for a girl to marry. So don't drag your heels too long, or she'll look elsewhere."

With that sage advice, he sauntered off, calling to a particular friend of his to join him at the tavern for a drink before the celebration began. Demetrius frowned after the other guard's retreating form. He was irked, but not really at Ander. More with himself. It was hardly the first time one of his fellow guards had insinuated a romantic relationship between him and Estelle, and he'd always just shrugged it off as nonsense before. So why did he feel so rattled now?

He tried to banish the thought as he made his way to the gardens. He was supposed to be apologizing to Estelle for unjustly accusing her the day before. The last thing he wanted was to be awkward before he'd even broached the topic.

He reached the meeting spot punctually, unsurprised to find no sign of Estelle yet. She would likely have finished her duties an hour or two before, and returned to her room in the servants' wing to prepare for the evening. An official, castle-funded servants' celebration was rare, and everyone had been delighted by the prospect for weeks past.

When he'd been waiting for over fifteen minutes, however, Demetrius began to have his doubts. It wasn't like Estelle to be this late. At the end of half an hour, he was forced to conclude that she wasn't coming. Again, it wasn't like her not to show up to an agreed meeting. For a concerned moment, he wondered if something might have happened to her. But as he cast his mind back over their last interaction, he realized she'd never actually agreed to meet him. Truth be told, he hadn't given her the chance to agree or disagree. Clearly she was displeased with him, more than he'd guessed.

His hand slipped into his pocket, running his fingers over the small wooden object hidden there. He felt an utter fool, and the feeling wasn't softened by knowing he was largely to blame.

Irritated, and somehow more uncomfortable than ever, he gave up on the doomed rendezvous. Reluctant to return to the barracks, where Ander might corner him and ask about Estelle, he directed his steps to the castle. It was only half an hour until the celebration was due to begin, and he suspected many servants would already be gathering.

Sure enough, when he reached the servants' hall, cleared of its usual rows of scrubbed wooden tables, he found several clumps of chattering maids and serving men. It took him no time at all to locate Estelle, glowing with silent but happy laughter as she listened to a footman who was entertaining the group with some mundane tale. A flash of annoyance went over Demetrius as he thought of all the time he'd waited fruitlessly in the garden while she flirted with footmen.

The thought drew him up. Where was this resentment coming from? It wasn't like him, and it wasn't fair. Estelle wasn't flirting with anyone. She was just listening, part of a cheerful group. It wasn't her fault that she was the prettiest girl in the room, or that a number of the footmen, grooms, and gardeners were casting her admiring looks. Why was he suddenly so inclined to criticize her for it? She'd often accused him of being critical, but he didn't think her appearance had ever featured in those discussions before.

His thoughts were such a tangled mess, he hardly recognized them, and he ran a hand down his face as if he could wipe his confusion clean. Across the room, Estelle looked up, perhaps alerted by the motion. Her eyes locked with Demetrius, and he saw the involuntary smile that accompanied the flash of recognition. A moment later, it fled in favor of a haughty frown, and the exiled princess tossed her head as she turned back to her companions.

Demetrius hid a smile of his own, heartened by the first instinctive reaction. He was clearly out of favor, and perhaps she had reason. But beneath it all, she was still glad to see him, still inclined to welcome his presence. The situation couldn't be too irredeemable. Recognizing that she was sending a message by ignoring him, he didn't approach her. He picked a place near the doorway and leaned against the wall, watching the room fill around him.

As he'd predicted, the guards all wore their uniforms, but many of the servants were in new clothes, and colors filled the usually muted space. It was nothing to the extravagant display he'd seen at the many balls he'd attended in his role as guard over the last two and a half years. But it was certainly a festive sight. And Estelle stood out among the group, no question. Demetrius couldn't seem to stop his eyes from being constantly drawn back to her, no matter how much he tried to focus on the food or the simple decorations.

He was a little taken aback to realize how much older she looked when not in her usual servants' uniform. She was in a new gown, probably too fine for the occasion, but certainly striking. It was the same sparkling turquoise as her scales had been, with a stiff, beaded bodice, and soft, diaphanous skirts which flowed around her like water when she moved.

Demetrius distinctly remembered when she'd purchased that gown, and even more distinctly remembered his own reaction. She'd returned from a market fair glowing with excitement, and he'd scolded her for her extravagance. He'd assured her it was a foolish purchase which she'd never have occasion to use. His criticism had been based on the false assumption that she'd taken out some kind of loan to afford the luxury item. Knowing that she wasn't paid a great deal, he'd been afraid of the repercussions for her. It had both surprised and impressed him when she'd defiantly scribbled that she had no debt, and had been saving for over a year for a purchase like this. But of course, blockhead that he was, he'd never told her he was impressed, or acknowledged his criticism had been unjust.

Demetrius ran his hand down his face again. Estelle's reaction to his unfair words the day before was becoming more understandable by the moment. And he'd been wrong about the gown. She did have opportunity to wear it, and it was every bit as stunning as she'd no doubt hoped it would be.

A little too stunning, Demetrius thought, shifting uncomfortably as he saw another guard approaching her. Ander's words flashed through his mind. *If you don't act soon, you'll miss your chance.* But he didn't want a chance with Estelle, not that kind of chance. So why did his feet itch to cross the room and cut the other guard out before he could speak to her?

Demetrius curbed the impulse firmly, refusing to give in to the strange compulsions that seemed determined to take hold of him all of a sudden. Ander had gotten into his head, that was all.

The room was full by now, and the king's steward banged on a goblet to get everyone's attention. With the air of an indulgent uncle granting a boon, he declared the celebration open, and invited everyone to partake of the food laid out on a few trestle tables pushed against the walls.

With a cheer, everyone complied, Demetrius unbending enough to claim a chicken wing and a goblet. A dark-haired maid sidled up to him, fluttering her eyelashes coquettishly as she asked after his health. Demetrius replied mechanically, his gaze drawn back to Estelle. She was avoiding looking his way with a little too much determination, but he still couldn't keep his eyes from her. When had she turned into a young woman, and how had he not noticed it happening?

And had she always been beautiful? Had he just not seen it? He tried to recall what she'd looked like when he first met her, but to his surprise, he struggled to call her mermaid features to mind. Her face as it was now—the prominent nose, the frame of golden hair—was just so familiar to him. As familiar as his own.

The noise of the revelers had grown around him as he loitered, cushioning him in a way that was almost tangible. It was comforting. It reminded him of the ocean, and the constant throbbing noise that had always surrounded him in the underwater world. He closed his eyes, remembering how it had felt to sway with the current, surrounded not only by the ocean's sounds, but by the singing of other merfolk as they worked their magic in communal songs. Here singers were so rare.

Demetrius opened his eyes. It was strange to recall how silent and empty the land had felt by comparison, back when he first arrived. That memory felt distant, as did the ache he'd felt for the sea. He still missed it sometimes, but it certainly wasn't a constant struggle anymore. Perhaps it was because he'd come to appreciate the land as well, and to recognize its sounds and rhythms. It was neither silent nor empty as he'd once believed.

Or perhaps it was because something—or rather someone—else had come to occupy his mind so fully, he couldn't ache for a life elsewhere that wouldn't have her in it.

Did Estelle truly mean so much to him? The thought was unsettling, but as he watched her join the dancing, he couldn't deny it. He'd come onto land to keep a close watch on her, and in two and a half years, his desire to do so had only grown. Unlike her, he hadn't been miserable in the life he'd lost, but he still found he had no regrets. If he was making the choice again, he'd do the same.

Finding him uninterested in joining the dance, the maid gave up on him, moving into the throng herself. Servants' dances weren't like the rigidly structured events of the upper classes. Couples didn't dance in polite pairs, all the dancers instead forming a haphazard but festive clump, following the steps of the dance only loosely.

And there was Estelle, shining like a jewel in the midst of the throng. Demetrius wasn't the only one who'd opted to remain on the sidelines, and he clearly wasn't the only one enchanted by the silent princess's dance. Because he was enchanted, there was no sense in denying it. It was a pleasure to watch her spin and swirl, her smile as light as her feet. Unlike the fine ladies who attended the royal balls, Estelle's hair wasn't dressed in a fancy style on top of her head. But the more casual look suited her. The golden tresses, veined with startling blue, flowed freely around her, the movement as fluid as it would be underwater.

And that, Demetrius realized, was what made her stand out so much. The humans around them wouldn't recognize it, but Demetrius did. Estelle was undeniably and completely a creature of the ocean—her every graceful movement communicated the ebb and flow of the tide. And yet, it was somehow as though the air *was* her ocean. She brought all the grace of underwater movement onto the land, where it felt even more natural, at least in her case. He couldn't think of any other way to describe the way she moved.

It certainly wasn't his own experience. It had taken many months for his every step to stop feeling heavy and clunky.

But Estelle...there was nothing heavy or clunky about her, either in form or manner. Demetrius felt his own spirits lift as he took in her delighted smile and the lightheartedness that emanated from her as she dipped and twirled. It was so strikingly different from her demeanor in her underwater life. Here she was a mute servant, and she worked hard—and uncomplainingly—for her keep. In Korallid, she'd been a princess, given every luxury except the freedom and the affirmation she craved.

There was absolutely no contest. She was clearly happier on the land. And somehow, that made everything seem worth it.

Her lightness of step was so entrancing, even the others dancing had begun to notice. Gradually, people pulled back, and before Demetrius knew what was happening, Estelle was dancing alone in the center of the room, watched by everyone with reactions ranging from admiration to open envy. He didn't think Estelle was even aware of the attention, given her eyes were closed. Her smile told how deeply she was enjoying the movement of the dance.

Suddenly, a hush fell over the room, even the musicians bringing their song to a hasty finish. Estelle opened her eyes at last, confusion turning to shock as her eyes passed over the crowd and settled on the doorway. Following her gaze, Demetrius saw Queen Sula standing on the threshold, watching Estelle with an expression of surprised admiration. All around Demetrius, servants bobbed into bows and curtsies, and he did the same, his eyes darting nervously to Estelle. It alarmed him deeply to have her be the center of such exalted attention, given the secrets they both held.

"Your Majesty." The steward hurried forward, bowing low to the queen. "You are gracious to attend."

Queen Sula inclined her head regally. "I must apologize for my tardiness," she said. "I intended to make my visit at the commencement of the festivities, to officially thank you all for the hard work you do to keep our castle running so smoothly. But I was delayed, and consequently I see I interrupt."

"Of course not, Your Majesty," the steward assured her quickly, and entirely untruthfully. "We are honored by your presence."

"Thank you," said the queen, her eyes straying back to Estelle. "I will leave you to your well-earned celebration. But first, I must compliment you on your graceful dancing, child."

Estelle, blushing furiously, lowered herself into a curtsy that wasn't quite as steady as those of the other serving girls.

"Estelle, isn't it?" the queen asked, startling Demetrius. He felt vaguely unsettled that the queen knew Estelle's name.

Estelle nodded again, and the steward murmured in the queen's ear. "Estelle is mute, Your Majesty, or she would of course respond aloud."

"Yes, I'm aware," said Queen Sula calmly. She studied Estelle. "I remember you, child. You have come a long way since the misfortune which brought you to our notice."

Estelle, clearly at a loss for how to respond, curtsied again.

"His Highness Prince Emmett returns to Port Dulla tomorrow," the queen said abruptly.

Demetrius frowned. He'd forgotten the crown prince was due to return. For a moment he was distracted from the situation before him, dwelling once again on the strangeness of the prince's periodic but regular absences. The king and queen always spoke as though it was perfectly normal for their heir to spend chunks of time in the forest-bound castle at Lernvale, in the kingdom's west. But their manner never quite matched the words. Nor did the gossip. The servants whispered about some kind of affliction, a blight suffered by the crown prince since an ill-fated trip he and his brother had taken to the Forest of Ilgal, a few years previously. Demetrius had never gotten to the bottom of it, but the question bothered him.

"There will be a ball to welcome him, and to celebrate his birthday," Queen Sula added. "I would be delighted if you would dance for us all, child, to welcome him home."

Demetrius stilled, alarm rushing over him. It was exactly the type of scrutiny he wanted to avoid, for both Estelle and himself. But how could she say no to the queen? He knew she couldn't.

Sure enough, Estelle nodded before dropping into an even deeper curtsy. When she rose, her face was suffused with color, and Demetrius thought she looked pleased. He felt anything but. As the queen took her leave of the revelers and left the room, Demetrius was assaulted by a fresh fear, one that threw him even more off balance.

There was more than one type of notice Estelle might attract from the royal family. Prince Emmett was unmarried, and judging by castle gossip, he was handsome enough in the eyes of women. He even looked a great deal like the prince whom Estelle had so much admired. When Prince Farrin had first disappeared, Demetrius had wondered whether Estelle's affections would simply transfer to the older prince, proving that it had been the title she'd been enamored of all along. But he was quickly brought to acknowledge that he'd wronged her by even having the thought. She'd shown no sign of considering Prince Emmett in that light, and she'd grieved Prince Farrin with evident sincerity.

But that was a long time ago. Things had changed—Estelle had changed. She was a beautiful young woman now, her increase in confidence just as responsible for the change as her extra years. If everyone else seemed to have noticed, surely Prince Emmett would as well. Demetrius knew the royal family would never see a mute and penniless servant girl as a viable bride for the crown prince, but if they found out her true identity...was there a chance that, instead of reviling her for her mermaid origins, they'd welcome her for her royal status?

Estelle was the center of a hub of gossiping servants now, everyone excited over the queen's invitation. Demetrius could barely pick out her form, and a horrible feeling began to claw at him, as though he was losing her. Again, he heard Ander's voice in his mind. *Don't drag your heels too long, or she'll look elsewhere.* But he had no intention of...he'd never even considered...

Pushing his unfinished thoughts aside, Demetrius strode forward. He still hadn't spoken to her about their tense encounter the day before, or even wished her happy birthday. Logical or not, he was gripped by the fear that if he didn't make it right with her now, he might not get the chance. Elbowing his way through the crowd, he reached her side at last.

"Estelle."

She gave him her best slighted princess nod, but for once Demetrius wasn't inclined to chuckle at her studied haughtiness. With a glance at everyone milling around them, he took her arm, grateful when she responded to his pressure and followed him to the edge of the room.

"You're really going to dance for the royals tomorrow night?" he blurted out, once they were no longer quite so closely surrounded. "Put yourself on display?"

Estelle scowled, and Demetrius could have slapped himself. That wasn't what he'd been planning to say.

"Not that you shouldn't," he said quickly. "I just...hope they're going to treat you with the respect you deserve." He kept his words vague, conscious that they weren't really alone.

Estelle tilted her head, looking a little confused, and Demetrius hurried on while he had the opening.

"What I actually came over to say was I'm sorry. I was unfair yesterday."

Estelle's mouth actually fell open in her surprise, and Demetrius winced.

"Is it so surprising for me to apologize when I'm in the wrong?"

She gave him a meaningful look, and he laughed reluctantly.

"All right, don't answer that. I suppose I can't blame you for leaving me waiting in the garden, since you didn't know I was going to apologize. But I just wanted to wish you happy birthday." His voice had become a little gruff, and he cleared his throat. "It's not much, but I made you this."

He extracted the wooden object from his pocket and held it out. Slowly, Estelle took it, her eyes lighting up as she examined the miniature turtle carved from driftwood. Demetrius had spent many hours on it, trying to make it as lifelike as possible.

Beautiful, Estelle mouthed, exaggerating the word. Her cheeks were a little pink as she smiled up at him. *Thank you.*

Demetrius nodded, suddenly finding himself bereft of

words. "Well," he said at last. "I suppose I'll see you tomorrow night. I'll be there," he explained. "On duty." He waited, but she offered no response. Hesitating, he added, "I look forward to seeing you dance again."

Estelle looked gratified, sending him a smile warm enough to convince him he was forgiven for the previous day's behavior.

But as he strode from the room, having lost all interest in the festivities, he felt no relief. Instead, he felt a certainty that things were about to change. And he had an uneasy feeling that it wouldn't be for the better.

CHAPTER NINETEEN

Estelle

Estelle adjusted her sheer aquamarine skirts nervously as she stepped into the corridor. Demetrius had told her she'd never have an opportunity to wear this gown, and here she was wearing it to the second event in as many days. It had been too fine for the servants' celebration, and she'd known it. Truth be told, it probably wasn't fine enough for the royal ball, but she certainly didn't own anything else appropriate.

The thought of Demetrius's criticism, back when she'd bought the dress, sent a wave of confusion over her. His manner had been so strange the night before. She'd lain awake puzzling over it, trying without success to understand what was behind his apology, and the obvious effort he'd made not to voice his misgivings about her agreeing to dance for the royals tonight.

Perhaps she shouldn't have been so cold to him all evening. She still thought he deserved the lesson, but she hadn't counted on him leaving the celebration so early. She'd thought they would have time to join in the feasting and dancing after her point was made. Once Demetrius had left, she'd found her enthusiasm for the event had faded quickly.

Or maybe that had been because of her nerves about the queen's request, she reflected, casting her eyes down the corridor toward the royal ballroom. If Demetrius had been with her, she would have gladly admitted to him that she half regretted agreeing to dance. It had felt so effortless amongst the cheerful servants. But in a formal ballroom, amidst a host of titled strangers...

Well, there was no help for it now. Estelle hurried forward, trying to muster the excitement she'd felt when Queen Sula first asked her. She knew Demetrius had attended these events before, but unlike a guard, a gardener had no role to serve in a ballroom. Estelle had never seen a human ball, and she was curious to compare it to the celebrations her family had thrown in Korallid. Still threw, presumably.

It would be good to have Prince Emmett back in the castle, as well. She'd heard from another servant that he'd arrived safely back around lunchtime, and everyone was glad of it. The king and queen were always especially somber when their heir was away, the castle feeling muted and empty in the absence of both of their sons.

At least Prince Emmett was never gone for more than about a week at a time, Estelle reflected sadly. If only Prince Farrin had returned so quickly.

But she pushed the departed prince from her mind. The last thing she wanted was to get emotional when she was about to perform for the royal family.

When she entered the ballroom, it was impossible not to feel the magic of the occasion. The golden doors stood wide, and the guards on either side watched her entry with as much respect as they gave every other well-dressed guest. The enormous ballroom was decorated lavishly, hung all over with blooming flowers—many of which she'd helped cultivate—and edged by tables laden with a feast that put the servants' celebration to shame. Guests milled throughout the room, bright colors adding life to the high-ceilinged chamber. She even spotted a few elves among the throng, their diminutive frames the size of human children.

One entire wall was dominated by small glass panes, providing a sweeping view of the shore beyond. The location of the castle had been well chosen, the cliffs near which Estelle had first reached the land having descended by this point to a pleasant, sheltered beach. Estelle could see the waves lapping against the sand outside the window. She knew that there had been concerns in recent months, with the odd adventurous wave actually touching the glass at high tide, something that had never been an issue before. But this evening, all was calm and beautiful, barely a swell in sight.

Estelle turned her eyes back to the view inside the ballroom. The space was steeped in the orange light of sunset, candles already glowing on a thousand surfaces in preparation for the approaching darkness. Estelle's skirts swished softly around her as she walked forward, and for a moment, she felt like a princess again.

The thought added a flicker of discomfort to her wonder. Even though the setting and traditions were so different, there was a very familiar air to the whole event. It was notable in the way the guests moved about the room, giving a respectful berth to the royal family who were at the head of the space, and undeniably at the center of the action. For a moment, Estelle could almost have sworn her father floated there, silver-haired and austere, his brow heavy with the disappointment of her failure. Memories of her coming of age event clouded Estelle's joy, and she felt a shudder go over her. She'd been very happy away from the glamor and pressure of royal status. How had she been thrown so abruptly back into it?

Then her eyes fell on an amber-haired figure standing to

attention on the far side of the room, and she felt herself relax. She'd forgotten Demetrius would be there. She sent him a small smile, and although he didn't break his position to respond, his eyes were fixed on her, and his expression was reassuring. Not that he probably intended to convey reassurance. It was just the effect of his presence. Someone in the room knew her—painful past, present subterfuge, and all. He'd been there at her coming of age celebration, and had still been willing to befriend her. That wouldn't change tonight, no matter how well or badly she danced.

Estelle knew Demetrius wouldn't be at liberty to speak with her, but she still made her way toward him, choosing a place near his post to hover inconspicuously until she was called upon. She gave him another smile, and he returned it as best he could while on duty, his features softening ever so slightly. Turning away from him, Estelle's eyes slid to the sumptuous food. Although she'd long ago become used to human food, she rarely had the chance to sample luxuries like these. But she stayed where she was, unsure if she was allowed to eat. She wasn't a true guest, after all.

The time passed quickly, Estelle enraptured by the sight of arriving guests and the general opulence. It was certainly a far cry from working quietly in the garden, mostly on her own. She studied Prince Emmett thoughtfully while his father welcomed the guests, and formally wished his son a happy twenty-second birthday. Estelle wasn't entirely sure that she agreed with the report that the prince had returned in good health. He was certainly upright and smiling, but he looked worn to her. Something sat heavily upon his shoulders, whether it was the weight of his crown, or the mysterious affliction the servants whispered about. Or perhaps the grief over losing his brother. A familiar stab of guilt went through Estelle at the thought, and she almost missed the queen's invitation for her to approach.

Swallowing nervously, Estelle moved forward, dipping into a curtsy as she faced the king, queen, and crown prince. Recognition sparked in Prince Emmett's eyes, and he smiled encouragingly. It emboldened her. She was sad to see the kind young man so burdened—if she could lighten his heart with her dance, it would be worth the spectacle.

She closed her eyes as the musicians began to play, pretending the crowd wasn't present. It wasn't difficult for her to dance as she had done at the servants' celebration. The movement was as natural as breathing. She'd been swaying and riding currents since her birth—it wasn't harder in the air, not now she had her balance.

Letting the rhythm capture her, Estelle danced with her heart, and her body seemed to follow of its own accord. She lifted her arms above her head, spinning and dipping and stepping lightly across the floor. She could hear admiring murmurs from her audience, but she kept her eyes closed. She could almost feel the water cushioning her like it had once done, holding her weight as she turned where the music led her. When the musicians began to wind down, Estelle opened her eyes. Breathlessly, she sank into another curtsy, both pleased and embarrassed by the hearty applause sounding on all sides.

"Beautiful!" It was Prince Emmett's voice that rang out, and he came forward to take her hand. Raising it to his lips and kissing it with as much ceremony as if he'd known her royal status, he smiled at her. "Thank you for gracing us with your dance, Estelle."

She ducked her head in acknowledgment. *Happy birthday*, she mouthed, and the prince nodded, seeming to understand.

"Thank you."

As soon as she was released, Estelle curtsied again to the king and queen, and backed into the crowd. At a word from the king, the musicians started up again, and couples began to flood into the empty space. Estelle resumed her position behind one of the tables with a sigh of relief. She wasn't entirely sure whether she was supposed to linger or leave now her dance was done.

"Who was that stunning young lady? I don't think I've seen her before, and the queen gave no introduction."

Estelle snuck a glance toward the carrying voice and saw that two young men were standing nearby, considering her over their goblets. Cheeks flushed, she smoothed her skirts, pretending not to hear them.

"She's not a lady, actually," replied the man's companion. "I'd heard she was to dance for us. Apparently she's a serving girl here at the castle. The rumor was she dances like a spring breeze, and I see it's true."

"It certainly is," the first speaker agreed. "Are you sure she's a serving girl? She's very elegant for a servant."

"That's what I've been told," shrugged the second man. "She's the one Prince Farrin took pity on when she was shipwrecked, the mute one."

"Ah, I remember that tale!"

Estelle could feel the man scrutinizing her, and she kept her eyes lowered. Their voices weren't nearly quiet enough to be indecipherable. It was astonishing how often people equated her muteness with deafness. Sometimes it was useful, but on this occasion she merely found it uncomfortable.

"Was it ever established where she came from?"

"I don't think so," the other man said. "I heard she lost her memory with her voice."

"Well, for all we know, she could be a fine lady by birth," said his companion.

Unable to help herself, Estelle glanced sideways at Demetrius nearby. His posture was rigid. He didn't meet her eye, but his expression was as tense as she'd ever seen it. Undoubtedly he also was hearing every word.

"Better if she's not a fine lady, if you ask me."

The speaker's voice was lowered this time, but Estelle could still hear the smirk in his words, and his friend's chuckle. Her eyes remained on Demetrius, and she saw the cloud descend there. She wished he wasn't witnessing this interaction—it would only reinforce his fears regarding her drawing any speck of attention to herself. Honestly, she could hardly believe the men had guessed her noble birth, little as they realized the accuracy of their speculation.

Mercifully, the men made no approach, instead moving away soon after. Estelle relaxed a little, thinking it would probably be wisest to go back to her own part of the castle before someone had to tell her to leave. She was just starting into motion when a much more familiar voice caught her ears.

"Estelle."

She stopped, looking back in astonishment at Demetrius. He'd actually stepped away from his position, reaching out to grip her arm.

Demetrius. She mouthed the word out of habit, although her lips probably moved too quickly for him to catch his name. She gestured back at his post, glancing anxiously toward the royals. He would get in trouble if he broke formation during a public event like this.

"Never mind my post," said Demetrius. Just like back at the servants' celebration, his voice was strangely gruff. "I need to talk to you."

Estelle raised an eyebrow expectantly, waiting for him to go on. But despite his claim, he didn't seem to have anything immediate to say.

"You...you danced beautifully," he said at last, the compliment falling unnaturally from his lips.

Estelle's eyes searched his face, looking for some sign of a jest, or perhaps a head injury. *Thank you?* She formed the silent words slowly enough for him to catch them this time, but in her mind they sounded like a question. What had gotten into Demetrius?

"I uh…" Again Demetrius floundered, but with a shake of his head, he seemed to pull himself together. "Estelle, I've been thinking, and—"

At that moment a side door banged open so violently that the sound carried over the music, which was dwindling in preparation for a new dance. Demetrius sprang instantly to alertness, his posture once again straight and his hand on the hilt of his sword as he searched the room for the source of the noise.

Estelle looked around as well, her eyes latching on to a white-faced castle servant whose name she couldn't remember. The man was sprinting through the guests, eyes fixed on the royal family at the top of the room.

Several guards moved forward, their posture similar to Demetrius's as they stared the man down. He ignored them, coming to a stop in front of the astonished monarchs and throwing himself into a hasty bow.

"Your Majesties, Your Highness." He was panting so hard from his run that he had to pause to pull in a shuddering breath.

"Good heavens, man, don't leave us there," said Prince Emmett mildly. "What's amiss?"

"Not amiss," the man panted, trying heroically to speak through his gasps. "Good news…Prince Farrin…just arrived by sea." He stopped to properly fill his lungs. "I saw him with my own eyes, Your Highness. He's on his way to the castle now."

For a moment there was total silence in the crowded ballroom. Estelle stood frozen in place, hardly able to comprehend the words she'd heard.

Then pandemonium broke out on all sides. Estelle raised a dazed hand to her face, hardly knowing how to feel about the revelation of Farrin's survival. Then her gaze, still riveted to the royal family, saw the look on Prince Emmett's face as he heard that his brother was alive. Of course she knew how to feel, she told herself, with a mental shake. It was the best of good news.

Prince Emmett had been frozen for a beat longer than Estelle, but the next moment he started forward, his every muscle quivering with suppressed energy.

"Where is he?" he demanded, desperation in his voice as he seized the servant's shoulders. "Take me to my brother."

But the servant had no need to do so. The next moment, a cry came up from the corridor outside the ballroom, and a lithe, tawny-haired figure appeared in the doorway.

The queen let out an unladylike shriek that was only partially covered by Prince Emmett's shout.

"Farrin!"

The crowd parted before the crown prince as he sprinted forward, falling on his brother with the force of a tidal wave. Estelle's eyes traveled to Demetrius, wondering what he made of this unexpected development. He looked almost as stunned as the royal family, but his expression was much harder to read.

"Did you miss me, brother?" Farrin's cheerful voice rang out, stilling the crowd. In spite of his light words, the young prince's eyes were full of emotion as they passed from his brother to the king and queen. "Happy birthday is in order, isn't it? I was worried we wouldn't make it in time, but the voyage was uneventful."

"Voyage from where?" Prince Emmett demanded.

"Selvana," Farrin answered, speaking as if it was the most natural destination imaginable.

A collective gasp went around the ballroom at the mention of the island kingdom which was known to be an uninhabitable mess of wild magic, and which had made no contact with the rest of Providore for generations.

"How in the—"

Farrin cut off Prince Emmett's protests with a shake of his head. "All in good time." He stepped back, studying his brother's face. "Are you well, Emmett?"

"I am now," said the other man fervently. "Come."

All this time the king and queen had stood rooted in place. Estelle's impression was that they were struggling to contain their emotion in the public setting. The two princes approached their parents, whispers passing through the room at Farrin's noticeable limp. That certainly hadn't been there when he'd disappeared two and a half years ago.

"Mother, Father." Farrin's cheerful voice was strained, many thoughts and emotions clearly lurking beneath the calm front. But Estelle doubted any of it would be expressed here, in front of hundreds of guests. "I hope you're both well."

"Farrin." The queen's whisper carried across the room, and with something that in a lesser person might have been called a sob, she threw her arms around her son. "You're alive."

"Very much so," Farrin assured her, returning her embrace. He extricated himself gently and turned to bow to his father. "Father."

The king said nothing, but he gripped his son's arm, his jaw working furiously.

With a smile that didn't look quite steady, Farrin cast his eyes over the gathered throng, nodding in greeting as he locked eyes with various guests who were presumably known to him. When his gaze reached Estelle, he paused, surprise and recognition flitting across his features. He smiled warmly at her, taking in her fine attire.

"You're still here," he said, his voice as friendly as it had ever been. "I'm glad to see you so well."

Estelle dipped into yet another curtsy, her mind spinning. She felt rather than saw Demetrius stiffen beside her, but she didn't look at him again. She was too consumed with trying to catch up with the situation. Her mind was too confused to even begin to comprehend what this turn of events would mean for her.

"Estelle," Prince Emmett supplied for Farrin's benefit. "Her name is Estelle."

"Your memory came back!" Farrin said joyfully.

Estelle winced a little, and Prince Emmett considerately answered for her.

"I'm afraid not. But some of the other servants figured out her name."

"Other servants?" Farrin asked, frowning a little. His brother gave him a look tinged with impatience, and Farrin mercifully seemed to realize that it wasn't the time or place to inquire about the working status of his favorite castaway waif.

"Perhaps we could cut the celebrations short, Mother," Emmett was saying. "There's clearly a great deal to discuss." His arm was slung around his brother's shoulder, gripping Farrin as if he never intended to let go.

The reunion of the brothers was heartwarming, and it reminded Estelle of the first time she'd seen them, on board the ship. The unashamed love between them was a significant part of what had drawn her to humans in the first place. She'd been unable to believe they could be as inferior and contemptible as she'd been told.

The memory of that encounter made Estelle feel even more dazed. She could barely find herself in the eager fifteen-year-old mermaid who'd been desperate to win the human prince's love. Even the grief she'd felt at his disappearance had grown distant, even more so now that the guilt over his supposed death was miraculously removed. She realized, to her shame, that a part of her actually felt sad to see Farrin return, because it would inevitably mean change. And she didn't know if she wanted her situation to change. She tried to tell herself how foolish she was being—against all expectation, she'd been given a second chance at her mission. She should take it. Shouldn't she?

Her eyes strayed to Demetrius, drawn by some unexpressed instinct. This would affect him too, she realized. His fate was tied to hers.

She'd been too distracted to hear the queen's response to Prince Emmett's suggestion, but she couldn't miss the new layer of hush that fell over the room. Looking around, she realized that everyone's eyes were fixed on the doorway, which framed a new group of arrivals. Standing prominently at the front of the clump was a striking young woman, her snow-white hair dazzling against her dark skin. She was dressed with great wealth and elegance, and the men hovering around her had the demeanor of guards.

"Ah, Bianca!" Farrin's face lit up as he waved the woman forward. "Everyone, come in, please." He turned to his family, bouncing a little in his eagerness. "There's someone I'd like you to meet." He reached out a hand to receive the white-haired girl, who inclined her head respectfully to the Medullan royals. "Mother, Father, Emmett." Farrin was beaming now. "Meet Her Majesty Queen Bianca of Selvana, soon to be my wife."

CHAPTER TWENTY

Demetrius

Demetrius's surprise had been tinged with alarm when Prince Farrin appeared, but it was nothing to the horror that washed over him at the prince's final words. For a heart-stopping moment time seemed to be suspended, panic rising in him as his mind struggled to process what was happening.

Slowly, his head turned, his eyes finding Estelle's. Did she grasp it yet? The death sentence that had just been pronounced over her? Their gazes locked, many wordless things passing between them, and he knew. She understood. Of course she did—as if she would ever forget the terms of the bargain she'd made with that despicable Ocean Miner.

For the first time since gaining his human form, Demetrius felt true despair. He'd never dreamed Farrin was alive. Clearly they had their answer as to why his disappearance hadn't killed Estelle. Demetrius had been so hopeful that the prince's death had sidestepped the terms of the magic, and that Estelle would at least live a normal human lifespan untroubled by any further conditions.

He knew he should feel ashamed of any hope that involved

the prince's death. But little as he wished Prince Farrin harm, there was no denying that he valued Estelle's life more highly than the Medullan's.

If circumstances were different, he would be glad to learn that Prince Farrin had survived. But circumstances weren't different. The prince's survival and betrothal meant Estelle's death, and Demetrius couldn't bear it. The fact that his own death would follow barely crossed his mind. He'd watched over Estelle for two and a half years, making sure no serious harm befell her here in the human world. Was he really to be powerless now to stop her death?

Her face a mask of shock, Estelle broke eye contact, moving with her usual grace around the edge of the room toward the door. Demetrius hesitated, wondering if he should follow her. But he was still on duty, and it wouldn't do either of them any favors for him to lose his position now. Not to mention he wasn't sure if she would welcome his presence.

The rest of the evening passed in a blur of disjointed thoughts and fears. Demetrius was glad when he was relieved of duty upon the somewhat haphazard completion of the ball, but rest had never been further away. He lay in his bunk in the barracks, mind spinning fruitlessly as he tried to see the best way forward.

He rose with the sun, feeling like he hadn't slept in a week. He was scheduled to have a morning off after serving at the ball, but he made his way straight to his captain, offering his services given the dramatic change in the castle.

"Thank you, Demetrius." The captain nodded. "I am glad of the extra forces." He cast a critical eye over the young guard. "Are you sure you're up to it? You don't look well rested, and I need those watching the Selvanans to be sharp."

"I'm fully alert, sir," Demetrius assured him. "And more than ready for duty."

"Very well," said the captain. "Ander's volunteered for double shift as well. The two of you can join the group assigned to the Selvanan visitors." His voice dropped slightly. "Officially, you're there to provide protection for Prince Farrin's guests, particularly the Selvanan queen. Unofficially, we want you to keep an eye on them, and take note of any suspicious behavior. We want to know for certain why they're here."

"Yes, sir," said Demetrius, standing a little straighter.

It was exactly the task he wanted to do. He wasn't surprised the Medullan monarchs didn't trust the Selvanans, since he felt exactly the same. The island kingdom had been out of contact with the mainland for so long, and no one knew what they'd been doing in that time. The magic of Selvana had apparently run so wild that the ground was lethal to humans, and many had assumed that the island's inhabitants had all died out long ago. Why were they reappearing now, upending everything Demetrius and Estelle had built for themselves? Even though he knew the Selvanans couldn't really be blamed for the effect of their arrival, he couldn't help resenting them.

He found Ander quickly, the other guard full of gossip over the dramatic events of the ball the night before.

"Did you see the king's face when Prince Farrin walked in?" Ander pressed. "I've never seen him so close to actually showing emotion."

Demetrius gave a half-hearted smile. "The return of a supposedly dead son is probably enough to elicit emotion in most fathers." His thoughts flew to Emperor Aefic. If he ever managed to get Estelle back to their home, how would the emperor respond?

The question made him uneasy. When he'd first followed Estelle onto land, he'd been determined to return both of them to the ocean, and as quickly as possible. But it had been a long time since that goal had dominated his mind. He was still as dedicated to keeping her safe, but he was no longer sure that getting her home was the best way to ensure her well-being. Simply put, she was happier on the land. Much happier.

And, somewhat to his own surprise, Demetrius was happy in Medulle as well. He enjoyed his role as guard, still able to fulfill the urge that had driven him to become a guard in his underwater life. And the Medullan monarchs were pleasanter to serve than the undersea emperor. Their castle ran efficiently, and neither they nor their deputies took any nonsense, but on the whole both servants and guards were healthy and happy. The very idea of the crown funding a servants' celebration like the recent one would be unthinkable under Emperor Aefic, for example.

And better yet, while Prince Farrin may have helped secure Demetrius a place in the training program, Demetrius knew that he'd earned his position as a guard through his own performance. And every advancement since was based on merit, not on friendship with anyone royal. He remembered the discomfort he'd felt over Esteban's possible intervention when he was a guard underwater. Returning to that life wasn't as appealing as it should have been.

And if there was a decent chance that returning Estelle to her family would only mean exposing her to bitter anger and criticism along with her former restricted life...

He shook his head. Every protective instinct rebelled against that idea.

But he had to get her back in the water. It was the only choice now. If Prince Farrin was truly to marry Selvana's striking young queen, Estelle would die without the Ocean Miner's second bargain.

Would he be able to convince Estelle to contact the Ocean Miner, though? And would the old miscreant honor her own bargain? He'd never even told Estelle that he'd used the shell once before to contact the Ocean Miner, about a month after Prince Farrin went missing. It had been as hateful as ever to hear Estelle's beautiful young voice speaking the Ocean Miner's words. And even more infuriatingly, the slimy sea snake had agreed with Estelle that the prince's disappearance didn't constitute imminent failure of Estelle's mission. She'd told him that the deal was with Estelle, in any event, and that next time she would only respond if Estelle contacted her.

Demetrius wished he could be sure Estelle would agree to do it.

"Demetrius?"

"What?" Demetrius looked up to see Ander watching him expectantly. "What did you say?"

"I asked what you think the Selvanans want."

"Oh." Demetrius tried to consider the matter, but his own affairs were all-consuming. "I don't know."

"Not very good company this morning, are you?" Ander asked. He slapped Demetrius on the back hard enough to elicit a grunt. "Lying awake dreaming of your pretty little dancer, were you?" He gave a whistle. "I reckon you'll have some stiffer competition to contend with after all the nobles watched her last night."

Demetrius said nothing.

"I saw you speaking with her when you were supposed to be on duty," Ander said, his tone indulgent. "Don't pretend you were oblivious to her charms when she danced. I don't think a man in the room was."

Demetrius shot the other guard a sideways glance, and his voice came out a little gruff. "Saw that, did you? Thanks for not reporting me."

"Reporting you?" Ander sounded outraged. "What do you take me for?" He studied his companion. "You looked worked up. What were you saying to her? Don't tell me she turned you down?"

"Of course not," said Demetrius quickly. Ander's eyebrows shot up, and he hastened to add, "What I mean is, there was nothing to turn down. I didn't make her any kind of offer. That wasn't what I was talking to her about."

"Then what were you talking to her about?" Ander pressed. "What was so important that you abandoned your post?"

Demetrius didn't answer, struggling to explain the lapse even to himself. He hadn't intended to make a declaration to Estelle, of course he hadn't. But honestly, he couldn't say what he *had* been trying to achieve. Ander was right about one thing—when Estelle had danced, Demetrius hadn't been oblivious, either to her appeal, or to the effect it was having on many others in the room. He didn't know what he was going to say to her—he only knew that he'd again been assailed by a bizarre fear that he was going to lose her, and that he couldn't let her go. If he was given to fanciful nonsense, he would have claimed a premonition about the arrival of Prince Farrin.

Because if anything was going to make him lose Estelle, it was the human prince, surely. Estelle had always been foolish over him. Even now, after two and a half years, she didn't like to talk about the deceased prince.

Except Prince Farrin wasn't deceased. He was very much alive, and very much back in their lives. And he was betrothed. Demetrius ran a hand over his face. He hadn't gotten a good look at Estelle when Farrin first appeared, but he'd seen her expression when the prince announced that he was to marry the Selvanan. She'd been horrified. It must have been crushing for her to see the object of her devotion reappear, and gain a glimmer of hope that she might succeed in winning him after all, only to have it instantly dashed. Demetrius had always thought her infatuation with Prince Farrin foolish, but that didn't mean her feelings weren't real. Real and painful, judging by her face the night before.

"Keep your secrets, then." Ander's mild words reminded Demetrius that he'd never answered his friend's questions. "I don't know what you're trying to hide. I already know perfectly well that you've got a bad case."

Yet again, Demetrius didn't answer. A couple days before, he would have had no hesitation in telling Ander that he had it all wrong. But now everything was such a confused mess, he hardly knew what to think.

They'd reached the rest of their group by now, and fortunately no response was required of him. He and Ander listened in silence to their official briefing, then made their way to their posts. Demetrius had expected the visitors to rise late after their grueling journey the day before, so he was surprised upon reaching the royal wing to hear Prince Farrin's cheerful voice approaching from the direction of the entranceway, not the rooms.

"I'm glad you enjoyed it. I used to walk there every morning just after dawn—I was known for it. It's so amazing to share it with you."

"It's amazing for me as well." The soft voice belonged to Queen Bianca, whose startlingly white hair was drawn back into a braid this morning. "I love seeing where you come from. It's very different from the jungle, isn't it?"

Prince Farrin laughed, walking his betrothed to the door of her room. "You've still got some time before breakfast if you want to freshen up. I'd like to speak with my brother before the meal. Meet you in the dining hall?"

Queen Bianca nodded, and after pressing a light kiss to her forehead, Prince Farrin turned away. He was halfway down the corridor when he paused.

"I remember you," he commented, looking Demetrius up

and down. "You're still here!" He gave Demetrius a disarming smile. "I'm glad to see you've done well for yourself."

Demetrius lowered his head respectfully, even while resentment festered inside. "Yes, Your Highness, I'm grateful to have a position among the guards."

"No need to be grateful to me, if that's what you mean," said Prince Farrin. "If you're here, I have no doubt you've earned it. My father's captain doesn't hand out charity, not when it comes to his guards."

Demetrius dipped his head again, not sure how to feel toward the young prince. Not that Prince Farrin seemed as young anymore. The years he'd been away had aged him much more than Demetrius had expected. It wasn't just the scruffier look he sported, or the beard spreading across his chin. It was in his eyes, and the way he carried himself. Demetrius's gaze followed the prince as he strode off down the corridor, his limp pronounced. What precisely had he been through in the years of his absence?

Demetrius wasn't assigned to the prince, or to the foreign queen. His morning was spent following other members of the Selvanan delegation as they explored the castle and shoreline. They seemed amazed at everything they saw, and Demetrius often heard them exclaiming about the convenience of walking on the ground. Clearly the rumors about Selvana's toxic ground had some truth in them.

Using all his training in being inconspicuous, Demetrius kept close watch on the visitors, looking for any signs of duplicity or subterfuge. He was a little irked not to detect any, and had the decency to feel ashamed of his response. He shouldn't be hoping for nefarious intentions among the Selvanans.

In spite of his vigilance, his thoughts were never far from Estelle. How was she taking this development? Was she hard at work in the gardens, trying to put her approaching doom from her mind? Or was she curled in a ball somewhere, weeping the seawater to which she'd hoped never to return?

The thought made Demetrius feel powerless, and it wasn't a feeling he coped well with. He'd become a guard to protect others from harm, and he'd given up everything in his old life to protect Estelle specifically. Once he'd thought her obsession with Prince Farrin to be merely a sign of her naivety and foolishness. But he didn't think her foolish now, and he hated the knowledge that there was nothing he could do to protect her from being crushed by heartbreak.

"Who is that stunning girl? Is that *blue* in her hair? Is that common on the mainland?"

The words brought Demetrius's gaze whipping round. He was accompanying the Selvanans as they climbed up from the beach, intent on reaching their luncheon at the castle. Someone at the front of the group had reached the cliff above, and their voice carried back down to Demetrius's position.

He had no doubt whom they were speaking about, but he still hastened up the path to see for himself. Sure enough, Estelle was sitting some distance down the arm of cliff that jutted out into the ocean. They could see her profile, but she didn't seem to have noticed them. Her hair was flowing freely around her, the wind whipping it back and forth as she gazed unmoving out at the ocean. In the sunlight, the blue streaks in her hair stood out even from their distance. The unknown Selvanan was right. Even clad in her simple servants' garb rather than the dazzling dress of the night before, Estelle was stunning.

Her posture tugged at Demetrius's heart, speaking so clearly of longing and loneliness. He'd never seen her staring out at the sea like that before. Was she remembering the past, or thinking of the future? Neither prospect held much happiness, and that broke his heart. An image flashed before his eyes, of Estelle dancing the night before. Dancing with such abandon, expressing with her motion all the things her voice could no longer say.

But she'd been expressing herself clearly for years, in spite of her silence. Last night had been a more flagrant example of it, but to anyone paying attention, her demeanor always spoke volumes. Demetrius had no trouble reading it—he saw with perfect clarity how beautiful and happy and hardworking and graceful she was. Had he really once thought her foolish? He was the foolish one, to fail to see how perfect she was. Estelle as a mermaid, privileged but cloistered, inquisitive but constantly pushed down, had been compelling. Her plight had called to him, even while he'd been impatient with her youth and naivety. But Estelle as a human, confident and happy, kind-hearted and uncomplaining in the face of hard work and restrictions...

She was breathtaking. She was everything.

The truth broke over Demetrius without mercy, so that his mind felt as tumbled as seaweed on the beach. Had he really not realized it, or had he known all along and refused to look it in the face? He honestly couldn't tell, and it hardly mattered. It was enough to know that he loved her now.

It was absurdly difficult to force his feet to keep walking away from her, following the Selvanans back toward the castle. But it was for the best. He was nowhere near ready to talk to her. He was still in the grip of the most bewildering surge of emotions he'd ever experienced. The most laughable of his impulses was a reason-defying desperation to protect her. He'd been doing that for years, without any strong emotion involved. But it was different now. There was no calculation of risk, no heroic sacrifice. If he had to give his life to save hers, he'd do it readily, and duty wouldn't factor in the decision. Her well-being *was* his well-being. He could never be happy living without her, knowing it had been in his power to save her. Such a life would be unthinkable. Unlivable.

Demetrius continued to wrestle silently with his revelation as he shadowed the group to the castle. He hardly knew what to make of the unfamiliar state of his mind. He'd always cared about Estelle, but now it consumed every corner of him. On the one hand, he wanted everyone to know, he wanted it to explode out of him. On the other hand, it was too intimate and precious to be shared with anyone. He'd never felt more adrift.

As he stood in the royal dining hall, watching the visitors eat lunch with the royal family, his mind traveled back to that lone figure on the cliffs. His emotions regarding Estelle were so intense, it was genuinely painful to dwell on them. And yet, he couldn't gather the tiniest interest in dwelling on anything else.

A memory flashed through his mind, of a forlorn fifteen-year-old Estelle. It was shortly after he'd discovered her clandestine trips to the surface to watch Prince Farrin walk along the cliffs. He'd demanded to know why she would even want to be in love when she couldn't choose who to marry. *Why would you want to torment yourself?* he'd asked.

Her reply came clearly to his mind. *If you'd ever felt this type of torment, you wouldn't need to ask.*

She was right. Even back then, in her foolish teenage years, she'd known something he didn't.

Being in love was torment. And he wouldn't trade it for anything in the world. Was this how Estelle had felt about Prince Farrin all along? If so, he should never have belittled it.

Reluctantly, Demetrius let his eyes travel to the young prince. He was deep in conversation with his brother, his expression serious as he discussed some matter pertaining to diplomatic relations between Medulle and Selvana. Demetrius couldn't bring himself to care about any of it. But he forced himself to study Prince Farrin, to give the human prince a chance.

Was there any justice to the scorn Demetrius had sometimes felt for the Medullan? If he was being honest, he had to say probably not. He'd resented the prince's interference in his life from the start, but none of it had been Prince Farrin's choice. He'd undoubtedly been foolish to get himself pitched off the ship the night Estelle first saw him, but it was absurd to blame him for the startling consequences of that moment in both Estelle's and Demetrius's lives. The human could never have predicted any of that. Even now, he knew nothing of it.

And could Demetrius really criticize Prince Farrin for showing Estelle kindness? If the prince had been cruel, or worse, taken advantage of her admiration, Demetrius would be much more critical.

It was true that Estelle hadn't really known the human when she'd decided to fix her affection on him. For all she knew, he could have been an unscrupulous or weak-minded person. But as it had transpired, he wasn't. It brought Demetrius little pleasure to admit it, but Prince Farrin was a good man.

An inkling of a possibility came to Demetrius, almost against his will. He'd thought the only path forward was to go to the Ocean Miner and brace themselves for whatever terrible price she'd extract for another bargain. But perhaps there was another choice. Maybe Demetrius should put his own feelings aside and try to help Estelle win Farrin's heart. He wasn't married yet, and for all Demetrius knew, the betrothal might be motivated by the desire for a political alliance to make up for the pain he'd caused his family when he disappeared. Hadn't Estelle chased Prince Farrin partly for similar reasons? If the prince knew that Estelle was a princess herself, would he feel differently? He'd never really had the chance to get to know

Estelle before he left for Selvana, but surely if he did, he would realize her appeal.

The thought sent a pang of pure agony through Demetrius, but he pushed it aside. If he loved her, he would do what was best for her. If she loved Prince Farrin, and wanted to marry him, then she deserved to win him. And that way, she wouldn't die, and wouldn't be forced to return to a life of misery in the ocean.

Demetrius's own future looked bleak in that circumstance. He would win his human form forever, but he knew his life on the land would be robbed of much of its joy. Still, he could remain a guard, and make sure Estelle stayed safe. And at least she would be able to live, and live happily.

When Demetrius was released from duty after lunch, he found himself walking through the castle with Ander. The other guard had been part of the group assigned to the Selvanan queen, and was eager to discuss what they'd each observed.

"She was with Prince Farrin all morning," he said. "They barely leave each other's side."

Demetrius fidgeted with his belt. There was no way the prince could really prefer the unknown Selvanan over Estelle if he truly knew them both. It was impossible.

"I have to say, I couldn't see any sign of duplicity, either from her or the others in her delegation."

"Neither could I," acknowledged Demetrius.

"No need to sound so disappointed about it," chuckled Ander. "It's a good thing, surely." He stroked his chin thoughtfully. "The prince is different though, isn't he?"

"Is he?" Demetrius asked gruffly, wishing the other man would leave him alone with his thoughts. "I'd barely started with the guards when he disappeared."

"Oh, I'd forgotten that," Ander said vaguely. "Well, take my word for it. He's changed. He's cheerful enough on the surface—

probably putting it on for his family—but underneath he's more serious. Whatever happened in those two years, it sits heavily on him."

Demetrius just grunted, not acknowledging that the observation tallied with his own, more limited reflections on the returned prince. "I didn't realize you were so insightful, Ander," he said, emerging from the castle on the way to the barracks.

The other guard grinned at his dry tone. "I'm a fount of wisdom, my friend." He clapped Demetrius on the shoulder, squinting in the afternoon sunshine. "I knew you were in love with Estelle before you did, didn't I?"

Demetrius remained silent. He had no answer for that, little as Ander might know the dramatic change in his thoughts since they'd last spoken.

"Speaking of which..." Ander trailed off suggestively, and Demetrius looked up to see Estelle a stone's throw away, hands deep in the dirt of a garden bed.

Sometime during the luncheon, she'd returned from the cliff and resumed her duties, but her demeanor still gave the impression that she was gazing off into an uncertain distance. Demetrius drew in a breath, steeling himself.

"I should speak with her," he muttered. If they were going to change Prince Farrin's mind, they would need to act quickly.

"That's the spirit," Ander said brightly. He gave Demetrius a shove in Estelle's direction, disappearing toward the barracks with the ghost of a chuckle.

CHAPTER TWENTY-ONE

Estelle

A shadow fell over her garden bed, and Estelle looked up, surprised. She'd been so lost in her thoughts, she hadn't heard anyone approach.

At the sight of Demetrius's tall figure, she shot to her feet. His general appearance was as ordered as ever, but his eyes told a different story. He looked almost anguished, and it cut Estelle to the heart. She shouldn't have run out the night before without talking through the drastic change to their situation. Farrin's betrothal would affect Demetrius as much as it would affect her.

"Are you all right?" Demetrius asked, his voice much softer than she'd expected it to be.

Hesitantly, she nodded. It was true. She was all torn up in one way, but underneath it all...somehow she was all right. She pointed back at him.

Demetrius gave her a smile that was hard to read. "I'm fine." After a moment's hesitation, he took her hand, mud and all, and drew her to a bench set by a large pond nearby. He waited for her to lower herself onto it, but didn't seem able to still himself enough to sit. Putting one foot on the bench beside her, he leaned against his knee.

"This is a bit of a development, isn't it?"

Estelle gave a silent laugh, raising a hand in a helpless gesture. Her eyes slid to Demetrius's face, studying it. He wasn't reacting at all how she expected. She thought he'd be surly, probably remind her of the folly that had gotten them into this mess. She'd been certain he'd say it was time to go to the Ocean Miner. But he expressed none of that. He was different somehow, but she couldn't put a finger on it.

"I've been thinking, Estelle." Demetrius cleared his throat, and she tilted her head questioningly. "Thinking about you and Prince Farrin. I...I know I was always disparaging about your admiration for him, but I acknowledge that he's never given me cause to think badly of him." He swallowed visibly, and Estelle's eyes followed in astonishment as he tugged at his collar. "It's not for me to criticize your heart," Demetrius added in a rush. "I want to help you win him. You...you deserve it."

Estelle stared at him in blank amazement. She couldn't decide what was more bizarre—Demetrius's words, or the vicious stab of disappointment she felt at his offer. What was wrong with her? Wasn't his proposal exactly what she'd always wanted? Why should that disappoint her? Besides, it wasn't reasonable of her to expect anything different from Demetrius. His very life was tied to the success of her mission, after all.

Even that consideration, bitter as it was, didn't change her answer, though. She reached out a hand, waiting while Demetrius dug parchment out of his pocket. She always liked it when he had a fresh sheet ready. It suggested he'd been expecting—maybe even hoping for—private conversation with her.

I appreciate the offer, she wrote, her hand flying over the parchment as she tried to make her complex thoughts succinct.

And I know none of this is fair to you. But I'm not going to try to steal Farrin from his betrothed.

"Steal?" Demetrius read skeptically. "They're not married yet. For all we know, it's a political arrangement."

Estelle gave him a look before bending to add, *Demetrius, use your eyes. It's not political. They're in love.*

He bit his lip, remembering the scene he'd witnessed that morning, when they returned from the cliffs. "It does seem that way," he acknowledged. "But the heart can change."

A wave of sadness, tinged with something sweeter, washed over Estelle. *Yes*, she wrote. *It can.*

"You're sure that's how you feel?" Demetrius pressed. "You're sure you don't want to pursue him, and try to fulfill the original bargain?"

Absolutely sure, Estelle wrote.

"Well, then." Was that relief in Demetrius's voice, or disappointment? Impossible to tell. "There's only one option left. We need to use the seashell and talk to the Ocean Miner."

Estelle looked down at her lap, fidgeting with her simple skirt. She saw the wisdom of the course, but she was reluctant, to say the least. Smoothing the parchment out, she wrote more slowly.

I suppose we have to. I don't know what else we can do. She looked up, gazing unseeingly at the pond for a moment before bending once more over her lap. *I'm so sorry I dragged you into this, Demetrius. If it was just me, I think I'd let events play out.*

"What do you mean?" Demetrius demanded. "You'd die when the prince and the Selvanan queen marry."

Yes, she wrote. *I suppose so. But I'd still be glad to have had a happy life, however short.* She shook her head, flipping the covered parchment onto the clean side, and scrawling the words with more determination now. *But that's neither here nor there. You're in this, too, and your situation reminds me how little I consid-*

ered the impact on others when I made that rash bargain. I'm sorry, Demetrius. I was wrong.

She looked him full in the face, wanting him to know how sincerely she meant the words. His eyes held hers, no reproach in their depths. She couldn't think when she'd seen him so serious, but at the same time, he felt closer than ever before, reachable in a way she couldn't ever remember.

"You were wrong," he agreed, the gentleness of his tone robbing the words of any sting. "But you were also wronged. I was there, Estelle. I saw your life in the palace. I heard the things your father said to you that night. I'm sorry I judged you so harshly. And I was wrong as well." He gave a twisted smile. "I'm sure I seemed old and wise to you back then, but I was very young myself. Looking back, I can see how badly I mishandled the situation. I practically drove you into the Ocean Miner's arms with my criticisms and my commands for you to stop, when we both knew I had no authority over you."

Estelle gave him a sad smile, unable to think of any reply. They both knew it all. They knew what happened, and how little either of them had really been in control of the events that unfolded.

"Estelle." Demetrius's voice was husky, and he wasn't meeting her eye. "Are you truly certain you don't want...I mean, you're really not going to see if Prince Farrin might..."

Estelle flipped the parchment back over, pointing calmly to the place where she'd written, *Absolutely sure.*

Demetrius drew in a long breath, letting it out through his mouth as he lowered himself onto the bench at last. Estelle watched him, fascinated. She'd really never seen him behave like this.

"I..." Demetrius ran a hand over his face. "There are things I need to say to you, Estelle, but I'm not good at that." He gave her a wry smile. "Even with my voice, I'm much worse at expressing how I feel than you are."

Estelle felt her brow furrow in confusion. How he felt? What was he getting at?

"It's just so stark," Demetrius blurted out. "There's nothing to cushion my words. Do you ever feel that way? That it's just so empty and silent up here, and every sound is blunt and unmusical?"

Estelle gave a silent chuckle. *I used to*, she scrawled. *Not so much anymore.*

Her gaze slid past Demetrius to the pond behind him, and a thought occurred to her. A glint of mischief in her mind, she stood, taking Demetrius's hand and tugging him up beside her. He came readily, his hand closing around her as if it was instinctive. Ever cautious, he snatched up the parchment she'd been writing on and stowed it back in his pocket. When he realized where she was dragging him, he paused.

"I'm off duty, but aren't you still working? And I don't think the pond is intended for swimming."

Estelle gave him an exasperated look, lifting her shoulder in a gesture intended to say, *What do we have to lose at this point?*

Demetrius seemed to understand. With a grunt, he started back into motion, only pausing to strip off his boots. Estelle didn't even do that, simply sliding into the water, uniform and all. Her body instantly relaxed, the cool refreshing and the substance of the water cushioning her reassuringly. She might think she'd fully adjusted to life on land, but she was still a creature of the water after all.

Demetrius joined her just as she spread out, floating on her back with perfect balance. She closed her eyes, kicking her feet lazily to stay in position. It was incredibly relaxing.

"You're right." Demetrius obviously couldn't talk underwater in his human form, but his voice still came to her muffled, given her ears were now submerged. "This is better. Not as good as the ocean, but better."

Estelle just smiled, still not opening her eyes. She knew what Demetrius meant. In the sea, she could not only hear nearby sea creatures, but could *feel* the ocean life stretching into the unseen depths of existence. The pond didn't have the same crackling pressure, but the water still swished audibly around them, the pops of little frogs breaking up the steady rhythm.

"Estelle." Demetrius's tone told her that he was returning to whatever topic he'd found so hard to broach while dry. "I don't know if you want to hear this. I don't know if there's even any point when our time might be so limited. But...I've been a bigger fool that I realized."

Estelle opened her eyes at last, perplexed by his pained voice. What she saw caused her to splash upright, all the calm fleeing at once. The queen's face—both astonished and disapproving—loomed over her. Whatever Estelle had implied about having nothing to lose, she hadn't actually expected to be caught frolicking in the pond by the queen herself.

Coughing and spluttering, Estelle hurried to the edge of the pond, tugging surreptitiously at Demetrius. He came upright quickly as well, his neck darkening with embarrassment.

"My word." The mild exclamation was tinged with laughter as Farrin appeared behind his mother, his betrothed at his side. "I'd say that looks like an excellent way to cool off, except the weather's already cold."

"I wouldn't say cold," Prince Emmett added dispassionately, courteously looking anywhere but at the miscreants.

"Compared to Selvana, this is freezing," Farrin assured him.

Estelle and Demetrius scrambled from the pond, not looking each other in the eye. Under her embarrassment, Estelle felt a definite sense of frustration. What had Demetrius been going to say? Why did people have to keep interrupting them?

"I'm sure I don't need to tell you this is highly inappropriate," the queen said, clearly displeased at being required to deliver the rebuke herself.

Estelle winced. No doubt the head gardener would hear of the incident, and the formidable housekeeper as well.

"Your Majesty," I apologize, said Demetrius quickly, bowing. "I'm at fault, not Estelle."

"No harm done, Mother, surely," said Farrin. "I'm just glad Estelle isn't too afraid to go in the water after her previous experiences."

He sent her the ghost of a wink, and she smiled faintly. If anything, his heavier air and more rugged appearance made him more handsome than before, and he seemed to be just as kind. But somehow, the charm was gone. Or, at least as far as she was concerned. The Selvanan girl beside Farrin clearly thought differently.

"Farrin told me about your misfortune," the Selvanan queen said, her voice kind. "I'm sorry you had such a terrible accident, and I'm glad to see you've landed on your feet."

Estelle shot a look at Demetrius, the hint of a smile curling both their lips at the unknowingly apt description. She dipped into a curtsy by way of thanks, her skirts and hair dripping.

"Having experienced something similar myself, I'm extra sympathetic," Farrin commented. "The ship on which I sailed to Selvana is nothing but a wreck at the bottom of the ocean, I'm afraid."

"It's become quite a habit with you," Prince Emmett said dryly. "Let's not forget your eighteenth birthday, when you threw yourself off the ship into a raging storm."

"Not on purpose," Farrin protested. He gave his brother a

playful shove with his elbow. "I was just following in the family tradition."

"Family tradition?" Queen Bianca asked curiously.

Prince Emmett rolled his eyes. "He's talking nonsense, as usual. Our tutor told us a legend when we were boys, and predictably, it captured Farrin's imagination. Something about an ancestor being lost to the sea."

"Not lost," said Farrin, in a voice of mock solemnity. "Surrendered. Sacrificed to the ocean, never to be seen again."

"What absurdity," said Queen Sula impatiently. "A foolish legend, as Emmett said. As I recall, that tutor was dismissed for telling you tall tales."

"It really wasn't the man's fault," said Prince Emmett mildly. "I thought it was very unfair to let him go just for giving in to Farrin's incessant nagging. It was all Farrin's fault, really."

"True," Farrin acknowledged. "He's right."

"Of course he is," said Queen Bianca brightly. "Older siblings always are wiser, you know."

That provoked an outraged protest from Farrin, and as the conversation threatened to devolve into lively banter, Estelle sent Demetrius a meaningful look. Could they sidle away, go in search of dry clothes?

"Such behavior from grown men," Queen Sula scolded, no real heat in her words. "And one of you a week from being married."

Estelle froze, feeling Demetrius do the same beside her. A week? Was that all the time they had?

"Mother, we've been over this," said Farrin, sobering at once. "That was never part of the deal when Bianca accompanied me here."

"I thought you said Bianca specifically wanted to wait to marry until you had your family's blessing for the union and the alliance," said Queen Sula with dignity. She nodded to the young queen. "Greatly to your credit, if I may say so."

"Yes, I did say that," Farrin said impatiently. "But that doesn't mean we planned to marry here. We're supposed to have a big state wedding in Sel, after we return."

"It's all right, Farrin," said Queen Bianca. "I don't mind."

Farrin turned to her, surprised. "Are you sure?"

"Of course I am," she said. "I don't especially want to wait any longer."

That brought a spark to his eyes, a fact which Estelle noted had no effect on her heart whatsoever.

"But what will your people think?" Farrin demanded.

"They've only just put on a big coronation six months ago," Queen Bianca pointed out. "And we can certainly have a formal celebration when we return. I think we should celebrate our marriage as many times as we can get away with."

Farrin was positively glowing now, and Estelle deemed that the royals were unlikely to notice if the two misbehaving servants made themselves scarce. Moving discreetly, she and Demetrius began to inch around the edge of the pond, back toward the bench where they'd been sitting. The last thing she caught as they moved out of hearing range was Farrin's excited voice.

"One week away it is, then."

CHAPTER TWENTY-TWO

Demetrius

Demetrius parted ways with Estelle at a side door to the castle, recognizing that the moment for declarations had fled. Hopefully there would be another, and hopefully he wouldn't be so useless next time. She must be wondering if he'd lost his mind. He smiled to himself as he watched her hurry into the building, dripping wet and casting shifty looks around. It had been a ridiculous but thoughtful idea, submerging themselves in the pond to give him courage to speak. How many of the schemes he'd called foolish had really been endearing if he'd only had a better understanding of his own heart?

His steps were heavy as he made his way to the barracks. The information that they had only a week before Prince Farrin's marriage was sobering, to say the least. But that wasn't actually the aspect of the overheard conversation which stuck the most in Demetrius's mind. The passing reference to an ancestor surrendered to the sea had struck him as strange and sinister. Even more striking than the tale itself was the queen's reaction to it. She'd spoken airily, but she'd seemed uncomfortable to Demetrius. And had the tutor in question truly been dismissed for sharing the information? That seemed like the sort of thing Emperor Aefic would do. It wasn't in keeping with the more open atmosphere Demetrius had generally observed in the human castle.

Certainly food for thought.

When Demetrius entered the barracks, Ander was there, he and another guard taking advantage of the captain's absence to engage in a game of chance, a pastime generally frowned upon. Ander cast one look at Demetrius's dripping form, and his mouth fell open.

"Don't ask," Demetrius said curtly.

Ander's eyes sparkled with laughter. "Looks to me like she pushed you in the pond," he commented. "Ah well, old fellow, at least you tried."

Demetrius just rolled his eyes, heading for his own belongings to retrieve dry clothes. Once he was respectable again, he made his way back to the castle. He wasn't entirely sure what he thought was behind the tale of the royals' ancestor, but he felt certain *something* was behind it. And given it related to the sea, he particularly wanted to know what it was.

The castle had a records room, but although Demetrius had stood guard at the door more than once, he'd rarely had cause to enter it. He was pleased to see that the guards currently on duty outside it were known to him, and inclined to be friendly. They didn't question his interest, letting him enter without any searching inquiries. They wouldn't have stopped him—the majority of the room held public records—but they might report his movements up the chain of command if they considered him suspicious. He would prefer that not to happen.

Demetrius wandered into the room, at a loss for where to start. It wasn't on the ocean side of the building, and a large window commanded a pleasant view of the gardens. Dust drifted lazily through the air in the afternoon sunlight, the shafts falling on shelf upon shelf of scrolls and parchment.

"A guard in the records room. That's a rare sight." The cheerful voice greeted Demetrius from a corner, and he turned to see a man in servants' garb stepping forward, rolling up a scroll with relish as he did so. "Not that I mean to suggest you're not welcome," he added. "I'm always delighted to have visitors." The man, who looked to be in his thirties, smiled widely. "People often assume that those who work with records must prefer their own company, but it's not so in my case. Historians can be sociable people as well. It gets blasted lonely in here, honestly."

Demetrius blinked, unsure what to say in response to this tide of friendly chatter.

The other man's face dropped at the look on his face. "Don't tell me. You're not here for the records at all, just carrying a message or something."

"No, I'm off duty," said Demetrius quickly. "I'm here for the records."

The historian brightened at once. "Excellent! How can I help you—what was your name again?"

"Demetrius."

"Demetrius?" the man repeated, squinting. "Why is that familiar? Ah, I know! You're the one who was learning to read a few years ago. One of the other guards came in here regularly to borrow records with simple language, which I thought might be useful for you while you were learning."

"Oh," said Demetrius, taken aback. He'd never thought about where the documents had come from, but he should have. "Thank you."

"My pleasure, my pleasure," said the other man airily. "And now that you can read, a world of discovery is open to you. What in particular are you looking for today?"

"The history of the royal family," said Demetrius.

"Well, there's plenty on that," the man responded. "In fact, we have a whole section on the genealogy of King Johannes's line. The monarchy has been unbroken for more generations than any other kingdom in Providore," he added with a touch of pride.

"Impressive," said Demetrius politely. He glanced at the section the servant had indicated. Noting the sheer volume of records, he decided he'd do better to be more direct. "I'm actually curious about a specific story I heard, regarding an ancestor of the current king who was sacrificed to the ocean, or something along those lines."

The other man's expression was long-suffering now. "Has that old rumor resurfaced? Strange how these things never die, no matter how little truth there is to it." He shook his head. "Given Port Dulla has been the seat of the monarchy for some seven or eight generations—prior to which Medulle's capital was in Lernvale, incidentally—the sea has been part of the daily life of the court for a long time. Of course there have been some tragic drownings, even among the royal family. But I think I know the one you mean. The tale has become more sensational in the telling, and you won't find it in here. This is a place of truth, and the truth was fairly unremarkable."

"What happened?" Demetrius pressed.

By way of answer, the other man strolled over to one of the shelves he'd indicated and rifled through a stack of paper. He pulled out a parchment and held it out for Demetrius's inspection.

"That's the one, I believe."

Demetrius frowned over the simple entry. It was the name of a person, Princess Regina, with a date of birth and death some twenty-five years apart, and a notation that read, *tragically drowned.*

"Drowned?" he said. "In the ocean?"

The historian nodded. "She fell from a ship apparently. They couldn't recover her."

Demetrius narrowed his eyes, looking again at the dates. "This is what...two hundred years ago?"

The other man nodded again. "It was the topic of a lot of gossip a couple years back, when Prince Farrin fell overboard and was believed lost. That was before he went missing, I mean. People raised it again when he disappeared, of course. There was talk about the ocean's curse on the royal family, or some such nonsense. Before that, I think it had been forgotten altogether."

Clearly not altogether if the princes asked their tutor about it when they were children, Demetrius reflected. But he didn't share the thought aloud.

"What did she look like?" he asked.

"Who?" The other man seemed confused.

"This Princess Regina."

The historian stared at him. "How should I know? She lived—and died—two hundred years ago."

Did she, though? "There isn't a portrait of her or anything?" Demetrius pressed aloud.

The other man shook his head. "Not that I'm aware of. You called her the king's ancestor, but she wasn't. She was the sister of a former king, not in the line of succession herself. If her portrait was taken, it's no longer around."

"What else do we know about her?" Demetrius asked. The vague suspicion dancing in his mind was almost too absurd to entertain. And yet, he couldn't shake it.

"Not a great deal," the man shrugged. "I once read the official tribute written after her death. It was full of glowing praise for her, but that doesn't mean much. Whenever her death comes up, the rumor goes that she was a nuisance, even that she tried to dabble in magic in spite of not being a singer. They say no one was sorry to see her go. Some even claim that the royals had her pushed overboard, which is where the story of her being sacrificed comes from. But there's absolutely no evidence to support that."

Demetrius was silent, thinking it over. He certainly didn't have evidence. But he had questions, ones that tugged uncomfortably at his mind, demanding to be answered.

"Thanks for your time," he said lightly, taking his leave of the records room.

He spent the afternoon mulling over the information, and by the time he made his way to the evening meal, he had decided on his course. Estelle was already in the servants' hall, eating her meal in a subdued silence that was a stark contrast to her usual cheerful demeanor. Demetrius slid onto the bench beside her.

"We need to talk."

She turned to look at him, her expression faintly hopeful. It fell at his next words, however.

"About the Ocean Miner."

Estelle gave a reluctant nod, casting a glance around her.

"Yes, we should go somewhere more private," Demetrius agreed. "Are you almost finished eating?"

Estelle frowned, gesturing at the empty place in front of him.

"I'm fine," said Demetrius impatiently. "This is more important."

With a sigh, Estelle pushed herself to her feet, following him out of the dining hall. Demetrius led her down several corridors and into an abandoned storeroom, closing the door behind them. The servants ate early, and light still reached feebly through the windows. He pulled off the rucksack he'd been carrying and laid it on a nearby table, before turning to Estelle.

"Do you remember what the princes said about some royal ancestor who was sacrificed to the ocean?"

Surprise flitted across Estelle's face at the random topic. She thought for a moment, then nodded.

"Well, I found out more about her today. She was a princess, and her name was Regina."

Estelle raised her eyebrows expectantly, clearly waiting for the information to become relevant.

"The official story is very tame, but the rumor is that she was a bad clam, that she dabbled in magic, and that she was pushed into the ocean on purpose, with everything hushed up afterward. This all happened two hundred years ago."

Estelle just blinked.

"Two hundred years ago, Estelle!" Demetrius said impatiently. "Doesn't that make you think of anyone? Someone who's been in the ocean, up to mischief like that, for two hundred years?"

Estelle's mouth fell open. *The Ocean Miner?* She mouthed the words so clearly, Demetrius could almost hear them.

He nodded. "I know it sounds mad, but what if it's her? What if she didn't die, but was somehow turned into a mermaid instead?"

Estelle's eyes widened, and she gestured frantically for parchment. Demetrius handed her the same one she'd covered earlier, mostly dried out from being submerged in the pond, and she scribbled on a corner.

She specifically said it's possible to turn a human to a mermaid.

"She did!" Demetrius had forgotten that detail, but it came back to him once Estelle mentioned it. "She also said something strange to me, after you'd left. I tried to threaten her with what your father would do when he found out about your bargain, and she taunted me. Laughed in my face. She said she wasn't afraid of him, and suggested I ask him directly whether his orders were to kill me."

Estelle frowned, scrawling over the top of other words so Demetrius had to squint to make it out. *She's protected somehow?*

"I don't know," he said. "But it seemed that way."

Estelle gasped, her hand flying to her throat.

"What is it?" Demetrius asked anxiously. "Does it hurt?" She hadn't even spoken.

Estelle shook her head impatiently, patting her throat once again.

"Your voice?" Demetrius asked. "Her voice," he realized. Thinking it over, he thought he understood. "You think that's why her voice was so scratchy and awful? Because it was a human voice?" He frowned. "No, that can't be right, because it's even worse up here. She said the voice changes form with the body." He met Estelle's eyes, his own expression serious. "I don't know exactly what's going on, Estelle, but whatever it is, it's gone far enough. It's time to use this." He reached into the rucksack and pulled out the shell. It looked perfectly ordinary, but felt unnaturally warm in his hand.

Estelle looked at it with distaste, her nod reluctant.

"It has to be you," Demetrius said apologetically. "Because the bargain was with you."

Grimacing, Estelle took the shell. She swallowed twice, then raised the talisman to her mouth.

"Ocean Miner."

The rasp sounded so painful, even Demetrius winced. Estelle curled in on herself, her free hand flying to her throat, and an involuntary tear escaping one eye. The sight was like physical pain to Demetrius as well, and he slid an arm around her shoulders in support.

"Is that my own sweet voice? I can't say I've missed it."

Both of them started at the sound of Estelle's youthful voice wafting from the shell. Demetrius had forgotten how melodious it was. Estelle was silent, looking rattled. It must be very strange to hear her own voice for the first time in years.

"She's proved she's here, now I assume I'm allowed to talk," he said gruffly.

The voice in the shell laughed. "Ah, Demetrius. The faithful guard, still at your post. Such a shame my agent turned out to be woefully incapable."

Anger burned in Demetrius. "So you acknowledge that you attempted to have me killed the moment I arrived here?"

"All part of the game, dear child, no need to get your scales all rubbed backward. But I'm sure you didn't contact me to discuss that old incident."

Demetrius glowered at the shell, even though he knew the Ocean Miner couldn't see him. "We're here because the prince is to be married. You agreed that if failure of Princess Estelle's plans was imminent, you would offer another bargain."

"So I did," the carefree voice replied. "A way out, I believe you called it. Do you wish to return to the sea, my little mermaid?"

To Demetrius's surprise, Estelle spoke again. "No," she croaked. "But let Demetrius—"

"Estelle, stop," Demetrius said, unable to bear either the signs of her agony or the content of her words. "That's not the plan. If you're not going back, I'm certainly not."

Estelle met his eyes desperately, her own pleading with him to see reason. But he just glared back at her, unwilling to budge on this point.

"This is all very touching," said the Ocean Miner through the shell. "But I'm confused. When last we spoke, I thought you said the prince was gone forever."

Estelle cast a startled glance at Demetrius at this reference to his earlier conversation with the Ocean Miner, but he didn't stop to explain.

"He's back," he said curtly. "And he's betrothed. So what's the new bargain?"

"Hm, I'll need some time to think about it," the voice said dreamily.

"We don't have time," Demetrius ground out. "You agreed that if she reached out to you through this shell, you would offer her a deal. You took an oath—you're bound by the magic."

"Indeed I am," she mused. "Things are under control here... what could you do for me up there? It's disappointing that the royal family had their lost son returned to them. Clearly I need to take a hand in punishing them since fate won't do it."

"Under control?" Estelle could barely rasp out the words, but she persisted valiantly. There was no point, however, as the Ocean Miner just laughed.

"Why do you want to punish the royal family?" Demetrius asked suspiciously.

"I have my reasons," the voice replied.

Demetrius was growing more certain by the minute that he knew what they were.

"What would an *Ocean* Miner care for the world up here?" he pressed. "Or should we be calling you Princess Regina?"

There was a moment of silence before the voice responded.

"What did you call me?"

The tone of the Ocean Miner's whisper told Demetrius he'd struck a nerve. "So did they really push you into the ocean? Clearly you made quite a nuisance of yourself."

"Don't speak of matters you don't understand," she hissed, her voice sounding less like Estelle's and more like her own. "They'll pay for their part in the crime, just as your pathetic emperor will pay for his."

Estelle's eyes flew to Demetrius's in alarm, and he gave her a reassuring squeeze. Whatever the Ocean Miner said, no amount of mined magic could ever hope to rival the power that the undersea emperor could channel through his song. With the authority of his royal blood, he could harness the whole ocean if he chose.

"You want a deal?" the Ocean Miner growled. "I'll give you a deal. Kill every member of the human royal family, and I'll change you back."

Estelle gasped, and again Demetrius squeezed her shoulder.

"No," he said. "That's not reasonable. You agreed that the task would be something Estelle is realistically capable of doing. There's no way she could achieve that—the royal family are well guarded at all times. Even if she managed to kill one member, there's no way she could get the others before she was stopped."

"She could with your help," the Ocean Miner pointed out.

Demetrius considered it dispassionately. "I doubt it," he said. "It *might* be possible, but I doubt it. It doesn't matter, anyway. The deal was with her, not me."

"Demetrius!" Estelle's protest sounded like it cost her as much emotionally as it did physically. "You can't be considering it...kill the royals? Kill *Farrin*?"

The Ocean Miner's chuckle sounded through the shell. "Still infatuated, child? And now he's to marry another. Well, well. To love is pain, is it not? You always had the heart of a human, weak and driven by emotion. I just made your body match. If it's too difficult to kill the whole family, you can just kill Prince Farrin. Here's your achievable task—put his blood on your feet, and they'll return to fins. And *you* must be the one to plunge the blade in him, no one else."

Estelle gave a wordless protest, but the Ocean Miner didn't stay to listen.

"That's my bargain, take it or leave it," she said sweetly. "Now, do excuse me. I have business to attend to." Demetrius expected the shell to fall immediately silent, but instead a beautiful sound filled the air. He was so stunned to hear Estelle's glorious song, he almost dropped the talisman in his shock. Before he could think of any response, the sound cut off.

He looked slowly over at Estelle, seeing his horror reflected in her eyes.

"She can sing," he murmured.

Estelle swallowed. She started to speak, but cut herself off, agony washing over her face. Snatching at the parchment, she wrote. *She said she didn't sing.*

"Not with that voice, she couldn't." Demetrius's own voice was grim. "I should have realized she would be able to once she had a better voice, but somehow I didn't think about the implications of that."

Estelle bit her lip, looking worried.

"I assumed she couldn't sing because her voice was so old and worn," said Demetrius, thinking it over. "But it makes more sense now I know she was human once."

Estelle frowned, clearly not following.

"Well, my voice is fine up here," said Demetrius. "But I still can't sing as a human. My voice changed with my form, but that couldn't change my essence—I'm a creature of the sea, and I don't have the ability to harness the power of the land. Not all humans have that, only those born as singers, which is a select few. I suppose, as a human from the land, the Ocean Miner couldn't harness the sea's magic even after she changed form." He shook his head. "She must be the only mermaid who can't."

Estelle lowered herself into a chair, her face even more pale than usual. Demetrius stared unseeingly at her, fear pricking at him as he put the pieces together.

"Surely she can't...I mean...I know it's technically your voice," Demetrius went on, his lips numb. "But she isn't really you. She doesn't have your royal blood. Having your voice in her body wouldn't allow her to access the level of power that royals can harness, would it?"

Estelle stared helplessly back at him. She didn't need words to tell him she had no answers. She hadn't even received rudimentary training in magic, let alone education in the complexities of royal power, and the technical reasons behind the restrictions placed on royal singing. Her fool of a father had seen to that.

"If she can," he said, his voice troubled, "who knows what havoc she could be wreaking down there? She could do much more damage with your song than with mined magic."

He saw the fear in Estelle's mind and knew she was thinking the same thing he was. The freak storms, the changing tides. Was that the work of the Ocean Miner? What was she doing to the underwater world?

"We have to stop her," he said.

"But how?" Estelle's rasp was like fingernails on slate, and Demetrius gripped her shoulder.

"Don't put yourself through it," he said quickly. "Write it down."

Eyes still wet with unshed tears of pain, Estelle flipped the parchment over, looking for an empty space. Demetrius had to lean close to read her words, the light fading rapidly around them.

We can't stop her from up here.

"I know we can't," said Demetrius impatiently. "But if you make it back to the ocean, she has to return your voice to you. She swore it. Then her reach will be severely lessened."

Estelle gave him a desperate look before lowering her head back over the parchment. *But I can't. The only way is...*

"To kill Prince Farrin," Demetrius repeated hollowly. "I know."

For a long minute they just stared at each other, as night fell outside the window, and hope died in Demetrius's heart. He'd pinned everything on this last resort, this way out. But he had to admit the Ocean Miner had outmaneuvered them. Because the task she'd given, while technically possible, was beyond the capability of the sweet-hearted girl beside him.

Forget her own fate, or his—even with the entire underwater world at stake, he didn't think Estelle could ever find it in her to murder Prince Farrin.

CHAPTER TWENTY-THREE

Estelle

Estelle moved through the castle in a daze, barely aware of her surroundings. For five days she'd been going through the motions of life, her mind an ocean away from the quiet garden haven her body occupied. It was a shame, really. If these days were to be her last, she wanted to savor every familiar sight, sound, and scent of her life in Medulle. But she couldn't focus on anything. The Ocean Miner's words repeated constantly in her head, the memory all the more chilling because they'd been uttered in Estelle's own voice. She'd almost forgotten how it sounded—the way the water cushioned the noise, the carefree sound of her laugh.

The voice she carried, by comparison, had lost none of its garishness in the year or so since she'd last pushed herself to use it. It had taken two full days for the pain in her throat to fade away after the encounter with the Ocean Miner through the shell.

She could hardly believe she'd actually used the shell to speak to the ancient mermaid after all this time. It was all too surreal. She half expected to wake in her bed in the servants' quarters to realize she'd had a nightmare of the sort that used to plague her when Farrin first disappeared.

Farrin. Good, honorable Farrin, whom she'd once believed to be perfection itself. Farrin, who'd returned with a heavier spirit and a limp, but just as kind and true a heart, at least from what she could see. There was no possible way she could bring herself to kill him. He didn't deserve to pay the price for her mistakes.

It wasn't that she was in love with him. She wasn't, although her mortification at how foolishly infatuated she'd been was softened by the evidence that Farrin was deserving of admiration. Many young girls had surely chosen worse targets for their dreams.

But he'd been nothing more than a dream, as she could now clearly see. She'd known it for a long time, although she'd never had cause to articulate it even to herself, given he was supposedly dead. It was just that his absence had long since ceased to hurt in the personal, intimate way it did at first. As she got caught up in castle life, forming friendships with other servants, learning to read with Demetrius, discovering the joy of gardening, Farrin's central place in her mind had shrunk and shrunk until he was barely there at all. And that part he did occupy mainly contained guilt over all that had passed.

Except now he was back. The guilt over his death was gone, thankfully, but plenty more guilt rushed in to take its place every time she thought about Demetrius. It was just too horrifying for words that due to her own folly, Farrin's upcoming marriage would mean Demetrius's death.

Of course, a stubborn part of her tried to argue, she hadn't forced Demetrius to tie his fate to hers. She hadn't even asked for it, hadn't even wanted it. He'd made the choice himself.

But the argument brought little relief, because it rang false. She might not have asked for it, but it wasn't true to say she didn't want it. She'd been glad of his presence every day for the last two years and more. She could never have done so well without his assistance.

Estelle reached her own little room, and performed a mechanical wash of her hands and face before the evening meal. Her mind drifted back to that moment in the pond, when Demetrius had been nerving himself to speak. He'd never finished the thought, although there had been several opportunities since. The revelation about the Ocean Miner's origins, and the new bargain she'd offered, had pushed everything else to the side.

Had it been possible he'd been going to tell her he cared for her? It seemed unlikely—not brutally honest, no-nonsense Demetrius, who knew better than anyone what a fool she'd been. But his manner had been so strange she could believe anything.

She made her way to the servants' hall, her eyes scanning the space automatically for Demetrius. She didn't decide to do it, it was simply a reflex she performed any time she entered the communal space. He wasn't present, so he must be on duty.

What if he had been going to say something of that nature? She pondered the question as she lowered herself onto a bench and began to eat. How would she feel about that?

The idea of Demetrius seeing her that way was so foreign, it wasn't easy to predict what she'd feel. She'd never imagined he would consider her romantically. She could still remember the look on his face when the Ocean Miner had accused him of an intrigue with the princess.

Don't be absurd, he'd said, his lip curling in disdain. *Princess Estelle is a child.*

It had stung at the time and every time Estelle had thought of it since. Which, she realized on reflection, was more often than she'd acknowledged to herself. But when she pictured his expression after her dance at Prince Emmett's ball, when he'd told her she danced beautifully, she found that the old memory no longer pained her. He hadn't spoken to her of romance on that occasion, but he certainly hadn't looked at her like one looked at a child.

She'd changed monumentally since that night in the Ocean Miner's cave. Was it so strange to think that he had changed as well?

Estelle shook her head, dislodging the thought. None of it mattered, anyway. They had no future, because she'd doomed them both to death.

Unless...

No. Estelle shuddered, ashamed that any part of her was even considering the other possibility. She couldn't kill Farrin. She wouldn't.

For a moment she let the certainty buoy her, feeling empowered by the one choice she could make. But her certainty was soon crowded by despair. It wasn't just about her own sacrifice anymore. If she didn't kill Farrin, and she consequently died, the Ocean Miner would get to keep her voice forever. She could have another hundred years to wreak destruction with it under the sea. Would anything be left of the Korallidian Empire by the end of that time?

And clearly the Ocean Miner's thirst for revenge didn't stop at the waterline. She wanted to punish the Medullan royal family for whatever had happened, that much was clear from the repugnant task she'd set for Estelle.

A task Estelle could never complete. But how could she fail, when failure might mean the deaths of her entire family, and everyone she'd known in her underwater life?

It was an impossible situation, and Estelle had never felt more powerless. She knew that if she was going to do anything, it had to be soon. The wedding was set for the next day, which meant she'd be dead by the dawn after that.

And her death would seal the doom of Korallid.

Why did it have to be her? Why couldn't the decision rest with Demetrius—he would be sure to make a wiser choice than her. But that was selfish. She shouldn't wish this burden on him, no matter how capable he was. He hadn't even reproached her over any of it. No hint had passed his lips that he remembered his own life was on the line as surely as hers was.

But he remembered. She could see it in his eyes every time she looked at him.

The dining hall was still crowded, the air full of cheerful chatter, but Estelle found that she had no appetite. She rose from the table and passed into the corridor on silent feet. She was a long way from sleep, however, and her steps led her away from her rooms. Even the gardens offered no solace anymore. Hard as she'd tried to flee it, her path had led inevitably back to the ocean, and that was where she needed to go to think. She'd barely reached the entranceway when a voice hailed her.

"Estelle!"

Surprised, Estelle turned to see Farrin himself coming toward her.

"I'm glad I caught you. I wasn't really sure where to find you. Are you well?"

Estelle nodded mutely. There was nothing wrong with her body, after all.

"Good, good."

Farrin was beaming, and it was no surprise. He was to be married in the morning, to a beautiful young woman with whom he was clearly desperately in love. The thought brought an unexpected pang to Estelle's heart. For a moment she lost track of the prince's words, wondering why she would suddenly feel jealousy, after deciding for certain that she was no longer in love with Farrin, if she ever had been.

Without conscious prompting, her mind threw another face before her thoughts, a less cheerful face, with a brow that showed a tendency to furrow, an unflatteringly shrewd gaze, and a mane of amber hair. Perhaps it wasn't the prince's love she coveted, but his certainty of a future with the one he loved.

Estelle shied away from the thought. She couldn't face what she might or might not feel for Demetrius. Not now.

"...so basically, it was all at risk of becoming unbearably enormous and tedious," Farrin was saying brightly, when she brought her attention back to him. "Which is how we came up with the idea of having the wedding on board a ship."

He seemed to be waiting for a response, so Estelle smiled mechanically. Did he really think that there was a single servant in the castle who wasn't aware of the details of his wedding ceremony the next day?

"Anyway, I know there's no particular role for a gardener on a ship," he went on. "But I've requested for you to be included in the contingent of servants joining us." It was impossible not to find his warm smile disarming. "It may have been purely a coincidence of timing, but you're still linked in my mind with the whole adventure that led me to Bianca."

Estelle didn't know how to respond, taken aback by the unexpected invitation. She appreciated the thought, but it made her nervous. Farrin didn't know it, but it could be dangerous for him to have her on that ship. Was it a sign? Was restraint the wrong choice? Was she valuing Farrin's life too highly when set against the whole of the underwater empire?

Feeling lightheaded, she sank into a curtsy, relieved when Farrin took his leave. She hurried out of the castle, making for the cliffs near which she'd first emerged from the sea. She'd been sitting atop the cliffs often lately, but she found her steps leading instead down the little path to the beach. Kicking off her boots, she let the soft sand squelch between her toes. The water lapped gently on the shore, giving no sign of the freak storms that had been concerning everyone so much. Estelle walked right to the wave line, lifting her skirts and stepping into the water. It felt cold and refreshing, and a childhood's worth of memories assaulted her. It hadn't been all bad in her underwater life. If the cost wasn't so unthinkable, she would likely choose to return to the ocean rather than die. She had a feeling she'd be better at pushing back against her parents' plans for her now than she had been two and a half years ago.

But it wasn't an option. At least, not one she could consider.

A splash drew her attention, and she looked toward where the water met the cliff's edge, expecting to see a bird flapping across the surface. She almost forgot her abused throat and let out a cry when she instead caught sight of a familiar face, framed by purple hair, sticking out of the water.

Eulalia!

It didn't seem possible, but there was no mistaking her sister. Eulalia lifted a hand, beckoning frantically for Estelle to come. Disregarding her clothes this time, Estelle splashed obediently toward her. The mermaid wasn't far—still shallow enough for Estelle's head and shoulders to remain out of the water.

Eulalia dove back under the water as Estelle approached, and she realized she would have to put her own head under if she wanted to hear her sister speak. Taking a breath, she submerged her head, her eyes searching the gloom of the water for her sister's face. The salt stung her human eyes, but she kept them open, desperate to see her sister.

"Estelle!" Eulalia sounded like she wasn't sure whether to laugh or cry. "Estelle, is it really you? At first I thought it was a stranger, you look so different."

Estelle tried to smile, although the expression didn't feel natural.

"You can't talk under here, can you?" Eulalia said.

Estelle just nodded. For a moment the two sisters regarded each other in silence. Eulalia looked the same, except perhaps for the worry lines that creased her face. How was her family? Her youngest would be past infancy now. Estelle longed to ask Eulalia those and many more questions, but her voice was as silenced underwater as it was above.

"I hardly knew whether to believe it when the Ocean Miner taunted us with your decision," Eulalia said, her voice little more than a whisper. "Did you really do this willingly?"

Estelle acknowledged it with another nod. She was almost grateful for the enforced silence. How could she possibly have found words to explain to her sister the convoluted mixture of guilt and defiance inside her? She deeply regretted anything Eulalia had suffered due to her decision, but even after everything, it was hard to make herself regret what she'd done. She wished she'd found a way that didn't involve giving the Ocean Miner her voice, of course. But she loved her life above the surface, and had never been either happy or useful under it.

"Do you know what's happening in Korallid?" Eulalia asked, her voice stilted now. "Do you know what the Ocean Miner is doing?"

Estelle shook her head, her eyes full of desperate questions. Holding up a hand to tell her sister to wait, she lifted her head above the water, taking a deep breath before plunging below again.

"She's taking over, Estelle," Eulalia said in a rush. "She's destroying everything our family has built. And just destroying the city in general. She wants to be empress, and I'm beginning to be afraid that she'll manage it."

Estelle gestured frantically at Eulalia, then herself, then

traced a circle in the water with her hand in an attempt to refer to the family that connected them.

Eulalia frowned. "Me? You? What about us?"

Estelle went to mouth the words, but realized in time that she couldn't open her mouth underwater. And of course she couldn't write it down, because the written language was a mystery entirely unknown to Eulalia.

She repeated the gesture more slowly, hoping the fear in her eyes would do the talking.

"Our family?" Eulalia suddenly realized. "Yes, everyone's in one piece so far. We came for a visit weeks ago, and it hasn't been safe for us to travel home. I'm taking a risk even coming here, but I had to speak to you. I've been trying every day, in the hope you'd come to the shore. It wasn't easy to get away unseen. Every available guard is defending the palace." Her voice was heavy. "Except the ones we've already lost, of course."

Estelle winced, thinking how easily it could be Demetrius losing his life to defend her family from her mistakes.

"Estelle, you have to get your voice back. Is there any way to do that?"

Hesitantly, Estelle nodded.

"Then please, Estelle. Please, do whatever it takes. We can't let her win! She'll kill all of us, and make Korallid as barren as the depths."

Estelle's eyes stung from more than just the seawater. She surfaced again, the fresh air she pulled in seeming insufficient to fill her lungs. She felt as though she was being steadily crushed. What was she going to do?

Her sister surfaced as well, searching Estelle's eyes as they floated face to face. It was strange to see Eulalia's features. It had been so long since Estelle had seen any merfolk. The flattened, gilled nose seemed all wrong, now, and even the purple hair was startling.

With a tug, Eulalia pulled her back under.

"I have to go, Estelle," she said. "I hope it won't be the last time I see you."

She pulled Estelle in for a hug, but there was no comfort to be found in it. Not with the situation so dire.

"Please save us, Estelle," said Eulalia seriously. "I don't pretend to understand why you did what you did, and I know you were upset with Father at your coming of age. But it's such a long time ago. Surely you don't want to see us all die over it?"

Estelle shook her head frantically, desperation rising inside her.

"I can't stay." Eulalia was agitated now. "But I know you'll do what's right." With a final squeeze of Estelle's arm, she turned, her tail flicking powerfully as she dove toward deeper water.

Estelle surfaced at once, pulling in another shuddering breath. She hurried from the water, shivering as she retrieved her boots. Darkness had all but fallen while she was in the water, and the air was chill against her wet clothes and hair.

It was so simple in Eulalia's mind—save the underwater world at whatever cost. But if there was a right course, Estelle couldn't see it. Everywhere she looked was death and disaster.

CHAPTER TWENTY-FOUR

Estelle

The day of the wedding broke quietly, with Estelle awake to see the sun rise over the eastern cliffs. She'd slept little, but she didn't feel weary. Her mind was wide awake, her body tauntingly full of life and energy. Would she and Demetrius be dead by this time tomorrow? Would all her family share their fate before long?

Given the nature of her role at the castle, Estelle had no real task to perform as the food and other supplies were loaded onto the boats. But she assisted anyway, preferring to be active rather than to dwell on her thoughts. When the servants boarded the ships, about two hours before the royals and guests were to arrive, Estelle caught sight of a familiar amber-haired figure marching onboard with the rest of the guards.

Tears sprang to her eyes. She'd had no chance to tell Demetrius that she'd been invited to attend the wedding. Had he been scheduled to serve on the ship anyway, or had he discovered her involvement and negotiated to be by her side? It would be like him.

Having been dismissed for the moment by their captain, the guards joined the group of servants awaiting final instructions.

Demetrius came to stand beside Estelle, moving with a total confidence that suggested separating from the rest of the guards was exactly what he was supposed to be doing.

Estelle looked up at him, and as their eyes met, he gave her a reassuring nod that seemed to say, *I won't be far away.* Estelle nodded back, her throat tight, then started when she felt the unexpected sensation of his hand sliding into hers. His expression underwent no change as he gave her hand a quick squeeze, and Estelle tried to keep her emotions inside as well.

She understood his message—he would stay with her to the end. She sent him a watery smile in return, not regretting her lack of voice since she had no words to convey how much it meant to her to know that she wasn't alone, however much she might deserve to be.

"Are we going out deep, do you know?" The nervous whisper came from a maid standing a short way behind Estelle.

"First time on a ship?" another servant asked sympathetically. "Not to worry, it's not a true voyage—we're not actually going anywhere. Land will be in sight the whole time, I believe."

"Then why go on the ship at all?" the first servant asked.

A third voice answered, and Estelle didn't bother to check who it was. "It's just a picturesque setting for the wedding. And it's supposed to be neutral ground, symbolizing that this marriage will be a union between two kingdoms. Or so one of Prince Farrin's personal servants told me."

"Do you think we'll be in danger?" the first maid asked, still sounding uneasy. "Will we be far enough out to run afoul of sharks or sirens or anything?"

Her words were greeted by a general laugh.

"How do you imagine sharks will get on the ship?" chortled someone. "And sirens are an old sailors' tale, lass."

"My grandpa swears he's seen them," the first voice said defensively. "He was a sailor, and he said anyone who works on a ship knows they're out there. They're like people on the top half, and fish on the bottom."

Estelle stiffened, her eyes flying to Demetrius's. His posture remained calm, and he sent her the hint of a warning glance. He was right—her reaction would be suspicious if anyone was watching.

"They're supposed to be stunningly beautiful, with voices like pure music," the girl went on. "To look on them is to love them, so my grandpa tells it."

Estelle realized Demetrius's gaze was still on her, and she stilled, arrested by the look in his eyes. Heat rushed up her skin, and her heart sputtered. It reminded her of how she'd felt when she'd first laid eyes on Farrin, and yet it was nothing alike. Farrin had dazzled her, but Demetrius wasn't in the least dazzling. He was comfortable and familiar, often exasperating, always dependable. He wasn't prone to excitement, and he certainly wasn't demonstrative in the way she'd seen Farrin be at times. His face was naturally stern rather than cheerful, and his lips were more likely to offer maddeningly honest feedback than flowery words. But she trusted his word implicitly because of it, and never hesitated to turn to him for help—which he'd never once failed to give.

No, it was impossible to be dazzled by Demetrius. She knew every line of his face, every tone of his voice, every look in his eyes. He was her closest friend—perhaps it was more a statement of the loneliness of her former life than anything, but he'd been her closest friend almost since their first meeting. The affection she felt for him was undimmable, deeper than emotion. It was settled somewhere at her center, where it remained untouched by their arguments, by the mundane reality of doing daily chores together, even by his lack of chivalry in pointing out when she'd behaved foolishly. None of it mattered in the big picture, because little as she could explain why, she somehow knew that none of it changed his opinion of her, or his value for her. He was her Demetrius, and would be no matter what trials they passed through.

Her Demetrius? Where had that thought come from? What exactly did it mean? Why was her heartbeat continuing to pick up speed? It was absurd to entertain any thought of Demetrius and romance. As she'd been reminding herself for days, he was fond of her as one might be of a foolish younger sister, but he thought her too childish to ever consider her in that light.

And yet...their eyes were still locked, and she found herself revising her earlier conviction that she knew his every look. Surely he'd never looked at her like that before, with such a powerful mix of affection and fierce determination. She would have remembered. She would have asked herself some very important questions before now. She would have—but it didn't matter what she would have done, because they were out of time to do any of it.

"But their beautiful voices are how they lure you," the maid added earnestly, breaking Estelle's attention from the charged moment with Demetrius. "Once you're in the water, their song takes hold of you, and they drag you down to be drowned."

A snort sounded from one of the other servants, and Demetrius looked like he wanted to join in. Humor danced in his eyes, dispelling the intimacy of the moment before. Estelle shrugged half a shoulder, not entirely inclined to laugh off the maid's tales as ridiculous. She knew plenty of merfolk who'd probably consider a drowned human preferable to one afloat. After all, even Demetrius had thought they'd do best to leave Farrin to his fate back when he first fell from the ship.

What a lifetime ago that seemed. Demetrius no longer thought humans inferior now, any more than she did. How could he, when they'd lived among them all this time, and seen the truth of their intelligence? He'd even been humble enough to admit his error to her, but she hadn't needed the confession. She could see it in the way he interacted with his friends, in his unswerving dedication to his role as a royal guard. He would give his life to save that of his charges, as he would have underwater, and that wouldn't be the case if he thought humans of no worth. She had no doubt that in the same situation now, Demetrius wouldn't hesitate to save Farrin's life. Not by the slightest look had he suggested that she kill Farrin to save them both.

Of course, he didn't know what Eulalia had said. He didn't know how high the stakes truly were.

Time passed quickly enough before the guests arrived, but once the festivities began, it crawled. Estelle kept out of the way as much as possible, too afraid and conflicted to feel any appreciation of the lavish, heartfelt ceremony. Farrin was devastatingly handsome in his formal attire, and the bride was more stunning than anything Estelle could have imagined. Her hair was braided back into a crown of its own, and the bright red flowers tucked into it were a match for her red lips. The splash of color against the white provided another striking contrast, like that of her hair—as white as the layers of her elaborate gown—and her dark skin. Even with the much greater variety in hair color to be found in the underwater world, Estelle had never seen anyone to equal her.

The vows were exchanged with obvious adoration on each side, and Estelle's heart knew a flicker of warmth underneath the cold dread. How could she ever consider ending this beautiful tale before it had properly begun? She couldn't. Surely she couldn't.

She wrestled with herself throughout the celebratory supper that followed the wedding, wishing she was on one of the other ships full of interested spectators rather than so close to the newlyweds. She wanted to believe she would do the right thing, but every now and then she felt a horrible impulse to just close her eyes and attack, for the sake of Korallid and all its inhabitants. If only she could be absolutely and unequivocally certain what the right thing was.

Darkness had fallen by the time the festivities began to slow down. The ship would soon be heading for shore to allow everyone to disembark, and once they were back at the castle, she would be much less likely to be in close proximity with Farrin. Estelle's window of opportunity was closing. And that was a good thing.

She was almost sure.

"Are you all right?"

Demetrius's quiet voice made Estelle start. She hadn't even heard him approach across the deck. She was standing at the stern of the enormous vessel, one hand clenched on the wooden railing as she gazed unseeingly on the dark ocean. They hadn't begun the short voyage back to the city yet, but the crew were bustling about, beginning to prepare the vessel.

She closed her other fist over the small wooden object she'd taken to carrying around everywhere before turning and giving Demetrius a hopeless look. She had no idea how to answer his question.

"I assume you can feel it, too? In your chest, I mean." Demetrius's voice was calm, and Estelle's eyes flew to his.

Slowly, she nodded, her heart breaking a little at this evidence that he truly was going to share her grim fate. She had indeed been feeling a growing pressure in her chest since the moment Farrin and his bride exchanged their vows. It was increasing gradually, making her breaths feel more labored. She didn't know how long it would take to crush life from her completely, but by the Ocean Miner's words, it would be before dawn. It was in keeping with all the Ocean Miner's nasty tricks, she reflected dully. Estelle had assumed death would be instantaneous, that her life would just be snuffed out right before dawn broke. But she should have guessed it would be slow and torturous. A shudder passed over her. Just how painful would it be before it was over?

Demetrius seemed to see her shudder, because he took hold of her shoulder, turning her gently to face him. Every line of his frame communicated calm confidence, and Estelle felt her rising panic start to ebb. Demetrius's eyes traveled down to her closed fist, confusion marring his features. Estelle opened her hand slowly, and for a moment they both stared down at the beautifully carved turtle. From the start she'd thought it a surprising gift, one which would have required Demetrius to put in hours of effort in addition to the thought. And now, she realized with a little pang, it had become the most precious treasure she had.

Her eyes traveled slowly up to meet Demetrius's.

He didn't say a word, just searching her face for a moment. Then his hand shifted up from her shoulder to cup her cheek. The gesture was reassuring, but also so comfortable and intimate that it brought tears to Estelle's eyes.

Pitching forward more from impulse than thought, she threw herself against him, her face pressed into his chest. He'd donned the formal overcoat of the guards as the evening progressed, and she slid her hands inside it, circling them around his sides until her hands were clasped behind his back, the turtle between them.

Demetrius's arms went around her as well, not pulling her close, but enfolding her so that his warmth was on all sides. Estelle's heart picked up speed again, and she tightened her own hold. Her cheek was still laid against his chest, and she could hear the steady rhythm of his heart. Steady, but a little faster than normal, she thought.

He'd held her like this the day they'd discovered Farrin

wasn't coming back and realized that they were stuck on land without him. She'd felt like her world was ending then as well, and Demetrius's arms had been just as comforting. Why couldn't she just stay inside their circle forever, where she felt safe, and nothing was expected of her?

Her arm brushed against a thick patch in his uniform, and she smiled. Even when on duty at a wedding, he remembered. He always remembered.

She drew her arms back, slipping a hand into the pocket as she did so. It emerged with a folded wad of parchment and lead. Grasping her intention, Demetrius released her, taking the turtle to free her hands and passing it rhythmically between his fingers.

Shouldn't you be at your post? Estelle scribbled, leaning the paper on the railing.

"That depends whose definition of 'should' you're using," Demetrius said. "If my captain's, then yes, I should be. But if mine, definitely not. If we only have hours left, there are other ways I'd rather spend them."

Estelle swallowed, as overcome by the intensity behind his calm words as by the enormity of the situation.

What if we didn't only have hours? she wrote, barely breathing.

Demetrius's eyes darted quickly from the parchment to her face. "What do you mean?" he asked sharply. "Are you considering doing it?"

Estelle made a hopeless and indecisive gesture.

I wasn't, she scratched out. *Not really. But Eulalia came to the shore yesterday evening. My sister.*

Demetrius's eyes widened. "She knew how to find you? What did she say?"

She said the Ocean Miner is using my voice to take over, destroying my family and the city in the process. People are dying.

She begged me to get my voice back if there's a way, and to save them all.

The paper was nearly full now, but Estelle didn't flip it over. What more was there to say? Demetrius understood all the implications of the situation.

"I see," said Demetrius softly. His gaze was searching. "That can't have been easy, hearing your sister beg you to do something you're so determined not to."

She didn't know what I have to do to change back. Even in writing, Estelle could almost feel the defensive tone of her words.

Demetrius said nothing, and Estelle didn't meet his eyes this time. Most likely he was thinking the same thing she was.

The truth was, she had an uncomfortable feeling that any member of her family, even Eulalia, would tell her that the solution was very simple. They wouldn't see killing Farrin as greatly different from killing a fish for supper. Most likely they would feel betrayed to know that she was even considering holding back when their very lives were at stake.

"What are you going to do?" Demetrius asked at last.

Estelle ran a hand over her eyes, bemoaning once again that the decision fell to her. One life for so many. It seemed an acceptable exchange when stated like that, but there was nothing acceptable about it. Her gaze fell on Demetrius's belt. She'd disarranged his overcoat with her embrace, and something white was now visible, glinting in the moonlight. Slowly she drew it out, and they both stared wordlessly at the whalebone blade.

Members of Medulle's royal guard didn't use blades like this. Demetrius must have carried it with him since his transformation from merman to human. It felt cold in Estelle's hand, and a terrifying rush of power went over her. For the first time, she grasped that she really could kill Farrin. It was possible.

She was so frightened by her own reaction, she almost

dropped the blade onto the deck. But her hand closed over it instead, some instinct unwilling to let go of the empowering feeling of having a choice, having control over her fate.

"Estelle, there you are."

Prince Farrin's voice startled Estelle so badly, she almost sliced her own hand with the blade. Shoving her hand roughly behind her back, she turned. The prince was approaching, his new wife by his side.

"I'm glad you could be here," said Farrin. "I hope they didn't make you work too hard."

Estelle shook her head, unable to help smiling at the happiness radiating from the prince. Her gaze, a little shy, slid to Queen Bianca, and she sank into a curtsy.

"Congratulations, Your Majesty, Your Highness," said Demetrius, offering the words she couldn't say.

"Thank you," said Farrin, slipping an arm around his bride's back. There was a hint of mischief in his eyes as he looked between the pair of them. "Isn't there some saying about one wedding inspiring more?"

Demetrius said nothing, and Estelle could practically taste the grief rolling off him. Tears suddenly clogged her own throat as she thought of the future that was about to be stolen from both of them.

But if they were free, if there was no deadly bargain hanging over them, what then? She lifted her eyes to Demetrius's, surprised to find him already watching her. As their gazes met, every doubt fled. She knew with absolute certainty that if she had a future before her, she'd want to spend every minute of it with Demetrius.

What a cruel irony, to discover how she felt just as time ran out. They'd had two and a half years living in close proximity, and they'd never even tried to explore the connection between them, not comprehending how precious was every second.

Farrin and Queen Bianca were both looking between the two of them awkwardly, clearly grasping that the groom's light words had triggered some intense and unpleasant response in each of his listeners. Estelle looked out to sea, all of a sudden unable to bear the sight of the happy couple whose marriage meant not only her own death, but that of the person she cared about most in the world. She reminded herself that it wasn't Farrin's fault—he didn't know what she'd done all those years ago, and what this day's work meant for her and Demetrius. But his joy was suddenly as painful as salt in a wound.

Before she knew what she was doing, she found her grip tightening on the blade behind her back. Farrin was standing so close, she could reach out and touch him if she chose. Her hand was halfway out when her mind caught up. Horrified, she raised the whalebone blade slowly before her eyes, staring at it. Had she really been considering it? Was she really such a monster?

Locked in her own battle, she ignored Farrin's startled cry, only vaguely aware of the way he shifted to stand in front of his new wife. An image of the Ocean Miner flashed before Estelle's eyes. Whether human or mermaid in form, in truth, Princess Regina was a monster. With the thought came the certainty Estelle had been chasing for a week. She knew, without doubt, that if she were to kill Farrin in cold blood, no matter what her incentive, she would be a monster, too.

The whalebone blade clattered to the deck, falling from numb fingers. Dimly, Estelle realized that there was a commotion around her, as guards hurried toward them from across the deck, and Demetrius attempted to shield her. But none of it mattered. In that moment, not even her impending death mattered. All she felt was unutterable relief. She'd fought her battle, and she'd emerged victorious. Her knees gave out, and she fell to the deck, her eyes rising slowly to meet Farrin's astonished and confused gaze. Shame washed over her that any part of her had considered killing the good-hearted young man who'd shown her such kindness.

"I'm...sorry..." she rasped out, the words like fire in her throat. "I...would never...hurt...you."

Farrin's mouth actually fell open in his shock, and he started forward a step.

"Did you just speak? Estelle, what's going on? Are you all right?"

Guards hurried forward, but the prince waved them back, apparently no longer concerned that Estelle was a threat.

Estelle didn't answer, her hands on her throat as tears pooled in her eyes. It was agony, the pain somehow intensified by the growing pressure in her chest. The pressure of her approaching death.

She reached one hand out blindly, and a strong grip found it, Demetrius suddenly on his knees beside her.

"It's all right, Estelle," he said, his own voice unusually choked with emotion. "There's nothing you need to explain."

"I...want...to," she insisted, barely able to get the words out. "Tell...them."

He stared at her, alarm in his eyes. "What do you mean, tell them?" he murmured. "You mean...everything?"

Estelle nodded, tears running down her cheeks without her permission. It was her body's involuntary response to the pain in her throat rather than any strong emotion. She actually felt quite calm now, more at peace with herself than she had been since Farrin reappeared.

When Demetrius didn't speak, she gestured impatiently. What did they have to lose now?

"What's the meaning of this?"

King Johannes's voice broke into the group, and Estelle looked up, taking in the scene properly for the first time. There was a crowd gathered now, largely guards standing tensely at the ready on either side of Farrin and his bride. The king and queen had just arrived, their eyes passing in alarm from their son to the blade on the deck, where someone had kicked it out of Estelle's reach.

"I said, what's the meaning of this?"

Estelle could hear the fear behind the king's anger—how many times did this poor man have to go through the fear of losing his son? She could see Prince Emmett hurrying across the deck toward them, but she didn't wait. She gestured again to Demetrius.

"I think we're about to find that out, Father," Farrin said, offering Estelle his hand.

She looked him in the eye, giving a slow nod of acknowledgment as she took the offered hand and let him pull her to her feet.

"If it's really what you want, Estelle," Demetrius said. "I suppose it hardly matters now." He cast a look over the assembled group. "I'll speak for both of us, as it's excruciatingly painful for Estelle to use her voice. But I don't know how much time we have, so I'll try to keep it short." His gaze moved to the king. "We're both here in Medulle under false pretenses, Your Majesty, but not with any ill intent. The truth is, it was Estelle who saved Prince Farrin's life when he fell overboard two and a half years ago."

Estelle elbowed Demetrius meaningfully, and he sighed.

"All right, it was both of us, but I helped under protest, so I don't expect any credit. Anyway, Estelle was very...taken with you, Your Highness. She was only fifteen, and she was, well—"

"Foolish," Estelle croaked, then regretted it as pain assailed her.

Demetrius laid a hand on her arm, and she put her own over it, squeezing gratefully. She would let him do the talking.

"I don't understand," Farrin interrupted. "How did you save me? Were you on the ship?"

Demetrius shook his head. "We were in the ocean, Your Highness. We're merfolk by nature. These forms are not our original ones."

His matter-of-fact revelation didn't have the effect Estelle was expecting. Instead of gasps of shock, she saw lots of shifty glances, and heard a few snickers.

"They're out of their minds," muttered one onlooker audibly.

The royals were just staring in blank astonishment, and Demetrius pushed on, giving no sign he'd heard the derision.

"Estelle approached an unscrupulous mermaid with a great deal of magic, and made a deal to gain a human form. The terms were that Estelle exchange her voice for that hag's ghastly one, and that her fate would be tied to her mission to make Prince Farrin fall in love with her."

Farrin and his wife exchanged startled glances, and Estelle felt her face heat with embarrassment. But it was no time to worry about her pride.

"The terms were that if she won his love, she would stay human forever. But if she failed, and he married someone else, she would be dead by the next dawn. And my life is tied to hers." His eyes dropped to Estelle, his voice softening to a murmur. "Which is the only way I'd have it."

Estelle could barely handle the intensity of the emotions that were coursing through her, but Demetrius had already broken the connection, his eyes back on his royal audience.

"Like everyone else, we thought Prince Farrin was dead when he mysteriously disappeared. We seemed to still be alive, so we went about our business. Then he reappeared, betrothed, and we realized what would follow. We were offered another deal—if Estelle were to kill him, and put his blood on her feet, they'd turn back into a tail and she could return to the sea."

His voice turned fierce. "Estelle is no murderer. She would never kill another to save her own life. But we've discovered that the mermaid who made the bargain has been using Estelle's voice—which in addition to being the most beautiful sound you could ever hear, carries a powerful song which can harness a great deal of the ocean's magic—to destroy our home and kill our people."

There was a moment of tense silence, which no one seemed eager to break.

"So she's been in a terrible position," Demetrius added. "But she was still unwilling to hurt Prince Farrin, as you've all seen, because her heart is pure in spite of everything she's suffered."

Again, there was silence, and Farrin's eyes found Estelle.

"I'm sorry," he said softly. "I didn't know...about any of it."

Estelle ducked her head, regretful of the blame he was unfairly placing on himself, but unsure what words would fix it.

"You called it a bargain." It was Queen Bianca who spoke this time, her voice thoughtful. "Forgive me if I'm way off the mark, but does this matter involve elves in any way?"

Demetrius shook his head. "No, Your Majesty, but the mermaid in question mines magic, similarly to the way elves do on land."

"Hm." The young queen's eyes were fixed on her husband, but she seemed to be lost in her own thoughts. "It's just that I've had a bit to do with elves, and in their case at least, the wording of the bargains is crucially important. What exactly did this mermaid say Estelle had to do in order to get her mermaid form back?"

"Uh..." Demetrius glanced at Estelle, and she scrunched up her face in an effort of memory. What exactly had she said?

"I think she said Estelle has to kill him," Demetrius said slowly.

But Estelle shook her head. That wasn't actually correct. The Ocean Miner had certainly talked about killing Farrin, but those weren't the words of the bargain. She snatched up the paper she'd dropped on the deck, and Demetrius produced some spare lead.

She said "here's your achievable task—put his blood on your feet, and they'll return to fins."

Demetrius read the words aloud. "Yes, that sounds right," he agreed. "She also said that it has to be Estelle who plunges the blade into him. I remember that particularly, because she said it with such relish."

A disapproving rustle went around the gathered guards, but Queen Bianca actually looked hopeful.

"It sounds to me like she might have been careless with her words. Do you think it's possible that Farrin's blood could do the trick without him being killed?"

Estelle stared at the other woman, her mouth falling open in her astonishment. She'd never thought of that. And was the bride really proposing so casually that the groom be cut open to fulfill Estelle's foolish bargain?

Could it be possible she was right, though? Estelle hardly dared to hope.

"I doubt it," said Demetrius brutally. "She definitely intended for Estelle to kill him."

Queen Bianca shook her head. "It's not about what she intended. It's about what she actually said. That's how magical bargains work, at least with elves."

"Excellent thinking, Bianca!" Farrin sounded pleased as well. "No harm in trying it." He held out his arm expectantly.

Protest arose on all sides, his family pressing forward as determinedly as his guards.

"Surely you don't believe this nonsense, Farrin!" King Johannes demanded.

Farrin shrugged. "I don't know if it's true, Father, but it certainly answers all the mysteries surrounding Estelle's appearance. And I'd rather be foolishly gullible than be responsible for someone's death through my skepticism. Losing a few drops of blood won't hurt me."

"What if it's a trick, or some kind of magic is involved?" Prince Emmett protested. "You don't know what might be on that blade."

"There's no magic on it," Queen Bianca said. "I'm a singer, remember? I'd be able to tell, and I can't sense any at all."

"I don't like it," the king said, but Farrin had already picked up the whalebone blade, and was offering it to Estelle.

"Thank you for saving my life," he said, his smile open and untinged by embarrassment. "If I can return the favor, I would very much like to."

Estelle took the blade with trembling hands, shooting Demetrius an uncertain look.

He was holding himself very tensely, but he nodded encouragement. "Like he said, it can't hurt to try."

With a deep breath, Estelle laid the blade against Farrin's exposed skin.

"No." Demetrius shook his head. "She definitely said *plunge*."

"Yes, best to do the thing properly," Farrin agreed cheerfully.

A shudder went over Estelle, but she forced her distaste down, swiveling the blade so that it was point down into the crook of Farrin's arm. She drew it back slightly, then pushed it down as gently as she thought the word plunge could allow. She wanted to gag at the feeling of it breaking the skin, but Farrin barely flinched. And when Estelle pulled the blade back, still feeling sick, she saw red beginning to pool on the wound.

"Go on, then," Farrin urged her.

Kicking off her shoes to be safe, Estelle tentatively grasped the prince's arm. She turned it, placing one foot underneath. A tiny trickle of blood flowed down Farrin's arm, dropping onto Estelle's bare foot. She swapped feet, releasing Farrin as soon as both feet had splotches of red on them.

Everyone seemed to be holding their breath, and disappointment washed over Estelle in a crushing tide when nothing happened.

"Like I said, lunatics," muttered someone out of sight.

Estelle's eyes met Demetrius's, the grief doubly potent for the moment of false hope.

Then, quite suddenly, she felt a prickling begin to spread down her body. It started gently, but quickly became as painful as if she was being pierced by many sharp knives. She fell to the ground, and just as she let out a gasp of pain, she felt her legs spring together as a sensation of great cold rushed over them.

Then, abruptly, the pain was gone. Barely aware of the screams of shock around her, Estelle gazed down on her own familiar tail emerging from her servant's gown, her aquamarine scales glinting in the light of the lanterns.

CHAPTER TWENTY-FIVE

Demetrius

Demetrius darted forward, hardly able to draw breath. It had actually worked! Estelle would live!

Estelle was staring up at him with a look closer to panic than relief, and when she clutched at her throat with both hands, he suddenly understood. Kneeling, he scooped her into his arms, struggling to his feet and moving toward the railing.

"Hold on! Where do you think you're going?" King Johannes demanded.

"She can't breathe pure air anymore," Demetrius grunted. "She needs to get into the water or she'll drown."

"She'll...what?"

The humans seemed absurdly confused, but Demetrius ignored them. He looked down, suddenly grasping the fact that he held Estelle cradled in his arms. Her face was both strange and familiar, the nose almost completely flat and once again scored with gills. But he'd know her anywhere.

"I'll meet you below," he murmured, telling himself not to get lost in the moment when she couldn't breathe. With a grunt, he heaved her up and over the railing, watching as she turned his clumsy toss into a graceful dive. With a flash of fins, she disappeared into the water.

"This is outrageous," the king was blustering, as most of the guards milled around, clearly unsure what to do in such an unprecedented event. Some had hurried to the railing, but no one seemed inclined to follow the fugitive mermaid into the water.

"You should know," said Demetrius, speaking quickly given he didn't know how long he had, "we believe the Ocean Miner—the mermaid who made the deal with Estelle—is actually Princess Regina, the sister of your ancestor, the one rumor says was surrendered to the ocean. I know it sounds like nonsense, but merfolk live up to three hundred years, and she told me herself the life span comes with the form. We think she wants to punish your family as well as the merfolk, and that's why she suggested Estelle kill Farrin. Not that she ever really thought Estelle could do it. She wanted to ensure Estelle never returned to the ocean, but that's another story. Anyway, we think she's behind the unnatural storms and changing tides."

King Johannes stared at him in horror. "Princess...Regina?" he repeated stupidly.

But Queen Sula didn't seem to have followed Demetrius's rapid speech. "I thought she was suspicious from the start," the older woman commented, her eyes on her younger son. "A homeless waif angling to marry a prince of Medulle?"

Demetrius glowered as he stooped to retrieve his blade, which Estelle had dropped on the deck. "She might have been homeless when she came to you, Your Majesty, but she was far from a waif." A tingling started in his feet, and he sped up, knowing he would soon lose the ability to speak above water. "She is Princess Estelle, youngest daughter of Emperor Aefic and Empress Talisa, rulers of the Empire of Korallid, which stretches across half the known seas." He gripped the railing, preparing to vault over as pain assaulted his legs. "And quite frankly, she's much too good for Prince Farrin." His eyes found the newly married prince, who had his hand pressed against the superficial wound on his arm in order to stop the bleeding. "No offense, Your Highness."

A slow grin was spreading across Prince Farrin's face, but Demetrius didn't stay to hear his reply. Pushing through the pain, he swung himself over the railing, feeling his legs turn to tail—shredding his uniform in the process—as he entered the water.

His first true comprehension of his change in form was the pleasant cool of the water. He knew that if he was still human, it would have been freezing. But against his scales, the sensation was soothing.

He had scales again! He twisted slightly in the water, staring at his amber tail. Flicking his fins experimentally, he propelled himself forward. It was nothing like when he'd had to learn to walk. It had been a long time, but his body instantly remembered how to navigate the water. And, thankfully, the pressure that had been slowly crushing him since Prince Farrin said his vows was now completely gone.

Demetrius spun in a slow circle, his eyes scanning the darkness as he called out. "Estelle?"

It was strange to once again speak underwater, and to pull in breath through his gills. Demetrius would have expected to feel delight at being restored to his original body, but it didn't feel right anymore. The ocean pressed against his ears, filling his mind with too much sound, and he felt an illogical panic rising as he tried in vain to locate Estelle. There was just too much happening between his ears and any sound she might be making.

Then he felt something stir the water, and he spun around to see a familiar form streaking toward him. Estelle's hair—now fully blue again—was fanning out behind her, and her eyes were wide with relief at the sight of him.

"It worked for you, too," she croaked out. The sound was as horrible as it had been on land, but Estelle's wince was much milder than the agony she'd always shown when she spoke above water.

"Yes, it worked," Demetrius said. He searched her face, once again taking in all the changes. "You can speak, it seems."

She nodded. "It still hurts, but not nearly as much. I suppose the constant presence of the water soothes it."

"I'd hoped your voice might automatically return to you once you changed back," said Demetrius.

Estelle sighed. "That would have been nice. But too easy, I suppose. She didn't work the return of my voice into her enchantment. She just made an oath to return my voice to me if I fulfilled the bargain she'd set. It looks like I'll have to claim it from her."

Demetrius frowned. He didn't like the idea of a confrontation between Estelle and the Ocean Miner. Especially while the latter still had Estelle's voice, and with it Estelle's ability to harness the power of the ocean.

The power of the ocean! Sudden realization came to Demetrius, and he opened his mouth, urging his voice to respond. To his delight, he was able to sing again. He felt the power gather around him as he drew it toward himself, reveling in the feeling of strength it gave him.

"I'd forgotten how beautifully you sing."

In spite of her harsh voice, there was something so gentle about Estelle's words, Demetrius found his focus slipping from his work. His song died out, and for a charged moment he and Estelle just looked at each other. There was so much he wanted to say, but he didn't know how to say any of it. And their troubles were far from over yet.

"It's nothing to how you can sing," he told her. "I know neither of us expected to make it this far, but against the odds, we've not only survived, but gotten our forms back. Let's go get your voice back, too, then you can do more than sing. We'll be able to end this."

Estelle nodded, but she didn't look enthusiastic. As she angled her body downward, Demetrius caught the wistful glance she sent up toward the surface above them.

Demetrius turned away from her, using his song to call power around them and send them flying through the water. He knew Estelle well enough to understand what was in her mind. A return to the water had been his original aim, but it had never been hers. Determination filled him as he swam, sending power ahead to help find the way toward Korallid's capital. He wasn't just determined to protect Estelle—and the rest of the merfolk—from the Ocean Miner. He was equally determined to protect Estelle from a return to the miserable life she'd known the last time she lived underwater. She wouldn't be alone anymore when she tried to stand up for herself.

The night drew on as they made their way downward. Demetrius had forgotten how deep the darkness could be, far from the light of the moon above. Every now and then he caught a glow of luminescence, but his main guide was the power he was disseminating through the water rather than anything his eyes could discern. Estelle swam silently beside him, her demeanor giving little away.

As they neared the capital, they exchanged a glance. Their sight was restricted by more than darkness now. The water had become so murky, they could barely see one another's forms.

"Was it always like this?" Estelle asked. "Have I just forgotten?"

Demetrius shook his head, his voice grim. "No, it wasn't like this. Something's changed."

It was true. Korallid had been built on a clear section of ocean bed, and it was basic manners not to swim so close to the bottom that your passage would stir up sand. The water was usually as clear as crystal. Now, it was a muddied mess.

It wasn't just the murkiness, either. He could feel the magic swirling through the water, powerful and unstable as it created chaos from the normally predictable rhythms of tide and current. Demetrius's own magic could barely find a way through it in its attempts to guide him to the palace. Every now and then he caught a glimpse of the city below, once thriving coral gardens dead and bleached, stone buildings crumbling away under the unnatural erosion, merfolk darting in and out of sight with fear evident on their faces. More than once a rotting fish carcass floated past him.

They proceeded more slowly, wary of swimming into something or someone with such limited vision. When they neared the palace, a throbbing, many-layered song reached their ears. It filled the water around them and made the ocean pulse with power. Shortly after, a web of merfolk came into sight, floating in formation in a loose dome that stretched out of sight in the gloom.

"Guards," Demetrius said. With a cry of recognition, he darted forward, his eyes fixed on the closest merman. "Axel!"

"Demetrius!" The young guard broke off his song. "We thought you were dead!"

"Not yet," said Demetrius. "Where's the emperor, and his family?"

"They're in the..." The guard trailed off, his mouth falling open as he caught sight of Demetrius's companion. "Is that Princess Estelle?"

"Yes, and she needs to get to her family," Demetrius said.

"But...I thought she was the one who..." The guard

exchanged glances with his fellows, none of them making any move to relax their formation.

Unease swirled through Demetrius. Their reaction wasn't an encouraging sign regarding the reception Estelle was likely to receive from her family.

"Are you going to forcibly prevent a princess of the empire from entering the palace?" he asked tartly.

"Of course not." The guards still looked hesitant, but they parted to allow the pair through. Inside, the water was much clearer, and Demetrius could feel magic at work, different from the protective songs of the guards.

"The palace yard is empty," Estelle rasped from beside him. "They could fit so many merfolk inside this sanctuary. Why is no one here?"

Her tone made it clear she didn't expect an answer, and Demetrius didn't offer one. He had nothing constructive to say about the emperor's decision to hide away in the safety of his heavily guarded palace while outside the gates his people grappled with the chaos the Ocean Miner was creating.

The guards at the entrance to the building seemed just as shocked as those at the boundary, but they also let them pass unhindered. Demetrius hailed the first servant they passed, demanding to know where the emperor was. The other merman barely looked at him, his astonished gaze fixed on Estelle as he told them that the royal family were sheltering in the interior courtyard. They swam tensely around the curved corridor, neither speaking. Demetrius cast a glance at the familiar route as they passed. The coral walls weren't dead here yet, but there was a noticeable lack of sea life darting in and out of them. The Ocean Miner's influence was reaching into every inch of the empire.

When the doorway drew into sight, Estelle spoke unexpectedly.

"This is where we first met," she commented. "At least, where we first spoke." She tilted her head toward the two guards floating on either side of the doorway into the interior courtyard. "You were on duty there, and I stopped to speak with you. Do you remember?"

Demetrius was silent for a moment, his gaze steady as he searched her face. "Yes," he said at last. "I remember."

With a nod, Estelle swam forward. "My family is within?" she asked imperiously.

The guards stared at her, their eyes wide and horrified at the sound of her scratchy voice. Estelle seemed to take their silence as confirmation, because she pushed through the seaweed curtain and out of sight.

Demetrius hastened to follow, emerging into the large open space. It was ringed by a wall of guards, several layers deep, most of their eyes fixed on the water above their heads. In the center of the ring, a large group of merfolk floated. Demetrius caught sight of Esteban, along with his parents and siblings, but it was Emperor Aefic who really captured his attention.

The silver-haired merman was floating a few inches above the rest of the family, armed with a spear and glaring about him as if angry with the world.

"Estelle!"

The gasp came from the empress, but Demetrius's eyes were still on Estelle's father. He saw the moment the emperor's gaze fell on his youngest daughter, and the expression there caused Demetrius to swim to Estelle's side with purpose. It was time to make good on his determination not to let her be bullied by her family any longer.

"Estelle!" Princess Eulalia's cry was joyful, but not many of the others seemed to share her sentiments. "You found a way back!"

Estelle swam forward, a strained smile on her face as she accepted her sister's embrace.

"Yes, I found a way," she croaked out.

Her family visibly recoiled at the sound of her voice. The anger that flashed in their eyes told Demetrius that they had at least some idea of the exchange Estelle had made with the Ocean Miner.

"Why did you return?" Emperor Aefic's voice was as cold as the depths. "How dare you show your face here after what you've done?"

"I've come to help fix the damage I unintentionally caused," Estelle rasped steadily. "And I came because I owe you all an explanation."

"We've received all the explanation we need," the emperor responded. His eyes passed over Estelle's human clothes—her servant's dress still floated around her. "We've known for years that you prefer the company of the humans to your own kind, and in light of that information, I see no reason for you to ever return here."

"Aefic." The empress's voice was miserable, but Demetrius noticed she'd made no move to embrace Estelle as Princess Eulalia had. Clearly they all blamed Estelle for what the Ocean Miner had done.

"You knew I was with the humans?" Estelle said, something in her voice causing Demetrius to give her his full attention. "I assumed when Eulalia came to the surface that she'd only just found out...but are you saying you knew where I was all along?"

"Of course we knew," snapped the emperor. "You'd barely been discovered to be missing when the Ocean Miner arrived to gloat openly of your betrayal."

Pain passed across Estelle's features, and Demetrius felt his hand ball into a fist.

"Why did you never try to contact me?" Estelle whispered.

"Contact you?" The emperor's voice was a roar. "Did you think we would come begging for the pleasure of your company to be returned to us?" His chest swelled. "Why would we wish to have contact with you when *you* did this to your own people?" He gestured toward the sea beyond the palace, where turmoil still swirled.

Demetrius could stay silent no longer. "With respect, Your Majesty," he said, his words crisp where Estelle's had been croaky, "*you* did this."

"How dare you?" The emperor's voice was low and deadly, but Demetrius was undaunted.

"I began serving as part of your royal guard not long before Estelle left this palace, and I saw the way she was treated. You told her to her face, and in front of near strangers like me, that she had no value to you or to your empire. All because someone else rejected your plans for her, in which she had no say, and which she did nothing to compromise. You saw that she was fascinated by humans, but instead of giving her the opportunity to safely explore that interest, and learn what most merfolk know of them, you pushed her down at every turn, made her feel like she was betraying her kind even to ask questions, and in so doing ensured that her fascination would only grow."

"She *was* betraying her kind!" the emperor said furiously. "And she completed that betrayal when she gave her voice to our greatest enemy!"

"I'm sorry, Father," Estelle rasped out. "I truly am. I didn't know—I didn't understand that my voice would allow her not only to sing, but to harness the ocean's power like one of royal blood. If I'd known that, I never would have done it."

"How could you know?" Demetrius agreed. "You'd intentionally been taught nothing of how your voice works, or how to harness power." He turned back to the emperor. "It was your decision to withhold trust and information from your own daughter that put the blade in the Ocean Miner's hand, before Estelle ever heard of her."

"The practice of delaying the education of royal children regarding power was not of my creation," the emperor growled. "It was put in place by my forebears specifically as a result of the foolishness which led to the Ocean Miner!"

"Then your forebears were wrong, Your Majesty," Demetrius said simply. "The truth would have served everyone better than the deceptions which drove your own daughter straight to the arms of a monster."

"Demetrius." Estelle's scratchy voice was soft as she laid a hand on his arm. "I appreciate what you're doing, but I can't just reject all blame. I didn't mean to do this, but I did it nonetheless. I made the choices that led us here."

Pride swelled inside Demetrius as he looked down into her face. She'd grown so much since they'd met—she had long ago ceased to be the foolish child he'd called her. In acknowledging her errors, she showed more grace and maturity than her father, who by Demetrius's count must be around eighty years of age.

"I respect that," Demetrius assured her. "I just wanted to point out that your choices weren't the only ones that led us here."

"Enough." Emperor Aefic was clearly livid, his fins quivering as he fixed his eyes on Demetrius. "I am your emperor. I have no need to explain myself to you. You claim to be a member of my royal guard? You are a disgrace to that position. Consider yourself dismissed with dishonor, and barred from ever serving in my guard again."

"I already considered myself to have left your service," said Demetrius calmly. "Having guarded Estelle for two and a half years, I don't believe I could ever again serve someone for whom I hold so little respect."

"Demetrius."

The pained protest came from where Crown Princess Etta's family floated, and Demetrius turned to the speaker.

"I'm sorry, Esteban. I didn't mean to include you in that statement. I will always be honored to have called you a friend. But I can't support a regime that takes no responsibility for its mistakes."

"You speak of what you don't understand," said Crown Princess Etta bitterly. "We have already paid more than enough for the mistakes of our dynasty. We have less control than you imagine."

"What does that mean?" Estelle demanded. Her eyes passed to her parents. "No more secrets, please. Just tell me the plain truth about what's going on."

The emperor still looked too angry to be reasonable, but Estelle's mother floated forward. "It was a little over two hundred years ago that it all began," she said in a rush. "Long before your father was born, or his father. It was during the rule of his great-great-great-grandfather, who died well before his time as a result of the unrest he caused. He was a greedy emperor, discontent with the abundance of riches the ocean had to offer. He wanted more, and he became obsessed with the wealth of the land, both in resources and in information."

She glanced at her husband, who was glowering at his youngest daughter. Demetrius looked at Estelle also. What did she think of this revelation? It provided some background to her father's unreasonably intense reaction any time she showed interest in the human world.

"At that time, the human rulers had a problem," Empress Talisa went on. "One of their princesses was dabbling in things she shouldn't have been."

"Princess Regina," Estelle said. "The sister of the current king's ancestor."

"Was that her name?" The empress raised her arms helplessly. "I never even knew that much detail. Her name was lost to our history. The humans wanted to be rid of her, but family affection wouldn't allow them to actually kill her. On her deathbed, the king's mother had made him swear not to harm or imprison his sister, or something to that effect. He was left with a dilemma."

"One our ancestor was only too happy to exploit," said Crown Princess Etta angrily.

Her mother nodded. "The emperor of the time made a deal with the human king. As emperor, he had access to enormous power thanks to the vast wells of it that can be found in the depths of the ocean, and over which his royal blood gave him great control. He agreed to take the human princess into the ocean, using that power to change her form so that she could live down here among the merfolk. In exchange the human king gave the emperor great riches from the land."

"Most of which are long gone, since they don't survive well underwater," Crown Princess Etta interjected. "And you left out the key point, Mother. The emperor swore an oath that neither he nor his descendants would harm or restrain the human princess. She was to be left to live out her days in peace. The king must have believed this would honor the promise he'd made to his own mother."

"And she's living here still," Demetrius mused. He looked at Estelle, who appeared to be deep in thought.

"That certainly answers a great many questions," she croaked at last. Her eyes passed to her father. "And are you still bound by that oath, Father?"

For a moment, he hesitated, his gaze sullen as it passed between her and Demetrius. Estelle half expected him to refuse to discuss the matter, especially after Demetrius had offended him. But whether because he realized his wife's willingness to explain made his silence pointless, or because the crisis of his situation had stripped away some of his usual restraint, he relented and answered.

"We all are." His voice was bitter. "It was an oath of power made by the ruling emperor—it had the full force of the ocean behind it. It can't be broken. For two centuries she's been creating mischief, mining magic from the ocean bed and encouraging all kinds of crime. And none of us can touch her. She could continue for another hundred years for all we can do about it. Even with the power of the ocean at my disposal, I can do nothing but act defensively. I can't stop her attack, I can't even order my guards to arrest her. I've tried many times, believe me. I'm incapable of giving the instruction, because it would still be my action, and it would breach the oath."

"Well, then," said Demetrius briskly. "It's fortunate that you've dismissed me from my position among your guards. Any action I take now is entirely my own."

Everyone swiveled to face him, Estelle included. The emperor looked unconvinced.

"I don't know if it will work. I've tried everything I can think of. I can't offer a reward for her capture, I can't send a civilian, I can't stir up resentment against her in the populace indirectly. Nothing works. So even though I haven't directly instructed you, even suggesting by implication that I wish you to—"

"Be easy on that score, Your Majesty," said Demetrius tonelessly. "I'm not under your authority. Nor am I acting out of any desire to do your bidding, or based on anything you've told me. I re-entered the ocean with the express intention of bringing the Ocean Miner down, before I heard anything of the oath that binds you."

The emperor considered him thoughtfully. "Acting purely on your own initiative, you're not prevented by the oath from mounting an attack against her, of course, any more than any civilian would be." His tone turned dismissive. "But you'll never beat her. Do you think she hasn't made any enemies in all her years? Do you think no one's ever tried to do her an injury on their own account? Even defended only by her mined magic, she was too powerful. Now that she has a royal's voice at her disposal, you won't stand a chance."

"He will once I've played my part," Estelle said firmly. She turned to Demetrius. "Let's go."

"You're royalty, Estelle," the empress said anxiously. "You can't fight her any more than your father can."

"I'm not going to fight her," said Estelle simply. "I'm going to hold her to the oath she made to me."

"Which was?" The emperor sounded unimpressed.

Estelle looked him full in the eye. "That if I managed to return to the ocean, she would give me back my voice."

CHAPTER TWENTY-SIX

Estelle

The mood of the room instantly shifted, everyone straightening where they floated and every eye flying to Estelle's face.

"You can reclaim your voice?" her father demanded. "Why didn't you say so immediately?"

Estelle saw hope flicker behind the emperor's angry expression. He was trying to hide it, but he felt as desperate as she'd done all those years ago. Trapped, even. She felt a reluctant surge of sympathy for him. Not as much as she might have felt if he'd been willing to show even the tiniest hint of vulnerability. But he'd never seen her as someone to be honest with. She wasn't family to him, just another moving piece in the service of his empire.

"Because I felt there were things we needed to say to each other first," she said, her throat raw and throbbing from the pain of her scratchy voice. She sighed, resignation coloring her tone. "But clearly you don't feel the same way."

Her eyes shifted to Demetrius, full of purpose. "We're the only ones who can end this. Let's go."

Demetrius gave a curt nod before propelling himself straight upward.

"Estelle, wait."

Warily, Estelle swiveled in the water to face her mother. She wasn't sure she could handle more recriminations, not if she was going to be focused enough to take on the Ocean Miner.

"I missed you," the empress said, her eyes sad as she looked her youngest daughter over. "You've grown."

Estelle returned the smile as naturally as she could. "Thank you, Mother."

Finding nothing else to say, she simply embraced the older mermaid. As much as she appreciated the words, she couldn't help but remember that while her mother supposedly missed her, she'd made no effort to contact Estelle in the last two and a half years, despite knowing all along where she was.

"Do we send guards to protect them?" Etta's words carried clearly through the water to Estelle, but she didn't pause. She kept swimming, her father's reply coming to her more faintly.

"I don't know. I don't know what the magic of my ancestor's oath would allow."

He sounded helpless and uncertain, and conversely Estelle took heart from it. He wasn't as confident and implacable as he tried to appear.

Dismissing her family from her mind for the moment, she followed Demetrius up out of the courtyard. A solid wall—or rather, ceiling—of guards hovered above them, but they parted to let the pair through.

"Why would they choose to hide here?" she wondered aloud. "There's no ceiling to protect them from above."

"There's also an additional escape route," Demetrius grunted.

Estelle nodded. She hadn't thought of that. "Where do we go?" she croaked, once they were through the guards' defensive barrier. "Do you think she's in her cave?"

Demetrius gave her a look. "No, I think she's very close by."

He must have seen Estelle's confusion, because he explained himself—and did so much more patiently than in times gone by, Estelle noted with a private smile.

"It's well and truly night time now, Estelle. I doubt your family are hovering in that courtyard all day and night. If they've been gathered there with such a huge number of guards around them, I'm guessing it's because an attack is currently underway. Can't you feel the aggression of the magic in the water?"

Estelle paused, testing the ocean around her. He was right, she realized. They were still cocooned inside the protections the guards had placed around the palace, but if she focused on the power itself, she could feel that it was under siege. Other forces were battering against it constantly. She'd been so distracted by the confrontation with her family, she hadn't been paying attention to the magic around her. And she hadn't even thought about how strange it was for the entire family to be gathered in the courtyard in the middle of the night when the palace hadn't been breached.

"You're good at this," she commented. "You should be a guard."

Demetrius rolled his eyes, but she didn't miss the hint of a smile that softened his lips. For a moment her gaze lingered on that feature, noting how they'd become slightly blue once again. She'd almost forgotten merfolk's lips looked like that. She'd become so used to the warmth and color of Demetrius's human form.

A pang went through her at the life she'd lost, but she pushed it back. She'd been selfish in her flight to the surface, but even then she hadn't been selfish enough to buy herself a life on land at the cost of the whole underwater empire—not knowingly. Now that she'd learned the effect of her choices, there could be no priority above righting the wrongs she'd caused. She had to get her voice back.

They swam across the palace surrounds in silence, neither speaking again until they'd passed through the loose net of guards and back out into the open ocean. If anything, it was murkier than before, and now that Estelle was paying attention, the attacking power hit her with the force of a battering ram the moment she emerged from the protective bubble.

"She's not far, all right," Estelle grunted out. "Can you feel the way the ocean is bending to her will?" She gave her head a little shake. "I can hardly comprehend that I apparently had that much power at my disposal."

Remembering her own choices as a fifteen-year-old, she reflected that perhaps her ancestors had been right that young and immature members of the royal family shouldn't be trained in the use of their formidable power until they'd been mellowed by age. If she'd had this much power, she could only imagine how much her father could wield as emperor, and he'd never been prone to excesses in the use of magic. But she was inclined to agree with Demetrius that there was no justification for withholding the information as well as the training. In her case at least, that had done much more harm than good.

"I feel it," Demetrius said grimly. "When we passed over the city, it felt like the currents were fighting one another with no predictable rhythm, making the water churn and throwing everything into chaos. I couldn't sense any purpose or target other than to cause maximum damage. But here, next to the palace, it's different."

"It's definitely an attack," Estelle agreed. "And it's worse than when we passed through on our way in."

She could even see the strain on the faces of the closest guards, their features contorted as they tried to keep singing. It seemed as though the water itself was pressing against them, constricting them, trying to crush them. Was this how some of the guards had died, as Eulalia had said? Estelle shuddered, unnerved by the strength with which the water was pressing against her own ears.

A low, throbbing hum joined the hubbub of the water, and she turned to watch Demetrius as he sang softly. He broke off quickly, nodding as if in confirmation of his thoughts.

"It's a constant barrage in every direction. I don't think it will be difficult to follow the power back to its source—or rather, the point where it's all being channeled." His expression was serious as he met Estelle's eye. "I suspect you're the only one who can hold her to her oath, but once you've got your voice back, get to safety as quickly as you can. I'll challenge her as soon as you're clear."

"There is no way in the oceans that's happening," said Estelle blandly. "I'm not fleeing like a startled minnow, Demetrius. Once I have my voice back, I'll be much more powerful than she is, right?"

"But you can't attack her—you're bound by the magic of your ancestor's oath," Demetrius argued. "I have to do it. I'm the only one who can."

"You're not the only one who can," Estelle said, exasperated. "Anyone can, as long as they're not a member of the royal family or acting on the royal family's orders." She gestured toward the city, not visible through the murky gloom. "In theory, anyone in there could have gone after her as soon as she started attacking the city."

"The problem with that theory, as you're well aware, is that she has the power of the ocean at her back," Demetrius said dryly. "Anyone who went up against her would be sea foam in moments. But once she's relinquished your voice—"

"Then the two of us working together should be able to bring her down," Estelle agreed firmly.

Demetrius moved forward abruptly, surprising Estelle as he took her hand. "Estelle, please let me protect you. It's what I do. I can't stop now. I could never live with myself if I failed to keep you safe."

"I thought you were dismissed as a guard," Estelle said, with a twisted smile.

"As a guard of your father's," said Demetrius. "As far as I know, I still have a position with King Johannes's guard."

Estelle gave him a look. "Protecting me isn't part of that assignment."

"Protecting you was never my assignment," Demetrius assured her, his voice low and serious. "It was always my choice."

The simple words thrummed with sincerity, and Estelle hardly knew how to respond. She squeezed his hand, wishing they had time to say all the things they'd never been bold enough to put into words.

"While we're speaking of your choice," she said softly, her voice cracked and hideous, "you also made the choice to tie your fate to mine. As far as I'm concerned, it goes the other way as well. We do this together, Demetrius. We're at our strongest when we're together. We always have been."

Demetrius searched her eyes for a long moment, finally surrendering with a nod. With one final squeeze, Estelle pulled her hand from his, closing her eyes as she tried to focus on the power beating down on her.

She could feel its irresistible pressure, and it took every ounce of her energy to fight against it, to swim upstream along the surging, invisible torrent. She could feel Demetrius at her side, following the closest current of power. Estelle had expected to go upward, perhaps to find the Ocean Miner floating above the city, where she could gaze down at the palace from which she dreamed of ruling her stolen empire.

But instead, the torrent led them down, its potency increasing as they descended. Before long, they entered a ravine to the south of the palace. Estelle was familiar with the area, although she'd never explored it. The water was colder down here, deep below the surface, far from the warm touch of the sun. They said that even during the day the ravine was almost as dark as night. Estelle had never had any interest in going there, and she felt reluctant even now. The ravine was the first place that had sprung to mind when she learned that her father intended to send her to live in the depths.

Not that she'd expected to be able to stay away indefinitely. She knew that the oldest of her sisters had spent extensive time down there during their training in harnessing power. The ocean's power poured from the depths, and it made sense that the Ocean Miner would have based herself as deep as possible. She would be accessing the sea's power more directly.

Estelle was therefore unsurprised that the potency of the magic was nearly suffocating by the time she heard a familiar voice cutting through the water. For a moment her strokes faltered as she listened to the song. The voice she'd once called her own was beautiful, there was no denying it. If only she'd valued it when she'd had it. Because now its beauty was twisted and unearthly, turned to a purpose she would never have chosen.

"Ocean Miner!" she cried, the harsh grating of her raised voice sending agony slashing across her throat. "Princess Regina! You have an oath to keep."

The song died abruptly, and a figure appeared through the swirling eddies of sand.

"Impossible," murmured the Ocean Miner, her eyes narrowed to slits as she took in the pair of merfolk improbably attired in human clothing. "You can't have killed him. You didn't have it in you."

"Perhaps you underestimate me," said Estelle coldly. She felt no compunction to reveal the means by which she'd gotten around the evil mermaid's bargain. It had worked, which meant the magic was satisfied.

"It seems I have." The Ocean Miner rose in the water, her gnarled form swelling with anger. "But it won't matter when you're dead."

She rose her voice in a shrieking cry that was more shout than song, but which caused power to swell violently around her nonetheless.

"Stop!" Estelle tried to inject her rasping voice with authority. "Enough of this. Give me back my voice."

The Ocean Miner let out a snarl that suited her old voice better than her acquired one.

"Do you think you can just take it from me?" she demanded. "Do you know how long I've waited for the power to sing, what I've been through to acquire it?" One of her wrinkled hands curled into a fist. "When I discovered that all mermaids could sing, and yet it was denied me in this form, I was enraged. My life above water was stolen from me by my traitorous snake of a brother, and even below I was to be restricted?" She seethed with remembered fury.

"It didn't take long to learn that the skills I'd developed for mining magic from the land—skills my narrow-minded family were incapable of appreciating—could be turned to good account below. The seabed is even richer in magic than the ground in the magic-saturated Forest of Ilgal."

"And yet," Demetrius said contemptuously, "your knowledge of magic was clearly inferior. No consideration could make you sing under the water, because although your form may be that of a mermaid, you are a creature of the land. It took us very little time to ascertain that ourselves, when we discovered that even with my own voice I couldn't sing on the land. I can't harness the power of the land—my voice will only ever connect with the power of the ocean."

"Don't think to patronize me," the Ocean Miner scoffed. "You are a mere infant. You know nothing of the magic I've acquired. You have no idea what I put myself through in my attempts to give my voice access to the power of the ocean."

"I have some idea," Estelle rasped dryly, wincing as pain lanced through her throat.

The Ocean Miner smirked, touching a hand to her own throat. "Of course you do, child. How could I forget?" Her eyes narrowed again as they darted to Demetrius. "Clearly you're mistaken when you claim that nothing could make me sing underwater. You've heard it with your own ears. I carry a new voice now, and I have no intention of surrendering it."

"You have no choice—" Estelle started, but before she could finish her sentence, the Ocean Miner raised her voice in a sudden, furious song.

Water swirled around the older mermaid, pulling a hundred spiny sea urchins from the bedrock below her. Before Estelle could blink, the urchins had exploded, hundreds of needle-thin black spines flying toward her. She raised her arms instinctively, but another voice sounded from beside her, a deeper note that sent the approaching water swirling violently to the side, so that the urchin spines spun aimlessly, losing enough momentum that Estelle could dart out of the way.

With her eyes, she sent a silent thanks to Demetrius, but she wasted no more time with her words. Clearly the other mermaid was trying to silence her forever before she could activate the broken oath. Raising her ghastly voice, she spoke to the Ocean Miner.

"You swore an oath of power, and you are bound by it. I claim what was promised—you must return my voice to me."

The Ocean Miner let out a cry of rage that cut off abruptly mid-scream.

The chaos of the currents, which had been considerably slowed by the Ocean Miner breaking off her song to deal with her uninvited guests, ceased completely. The ocean was still again, nothing but the familiar gentle rocking motion at work.

For a moment Estelle just watched as the former human clutched at her throat in silent fury. Then the shout recommenced, this time scratchy and painful to hear, just as Estelle felt a rush of energy shoot up her throat.

All the pain disappeared, and with a gasp, she let out a cry of her own.

"Demetrius!" The name slipped out without thought, the sound joyful and pure. Her frame shook as she turned to him, hardly able to believe that she truly had her voice back.

"Estelle." Demetrius's gasp was so full of emotion, she hardly recognized his voice. Their eyes locked, and for a moment she half expected him to take her in his arms. She understood. She hadn't felt this whole in a long time.

But it was no moment for sentiment, and they both remembered it in a hurry when the Ocean Miner's growl took on words.

"You think I'm finished?" The rasping voice was horrible to hear, but Estelle felt nothing but relief at the reminder that it was no longer issuing from her own throat. "You have no idea how to use that voice—you could never do with it half the things I've achieved."

"I wouldn't want to try," Estelle said simply, relishing the ease with which the words came out and the total lack of pain.

The Ocean Miner lunged toward her, but with a flash of fins, Demetrius appeared from nowhere between them, his blade raised. The older mermaid paused, looking calculatingly between them.

Estelle started to sing, calling power to herself. Her efforts were clumsy compared to what the Ocean Miner had been achieving, but she could still feel the deep wells of power responding to her guidance. She'd never unlocked a fraction of the power available to her before, and it was a heady, overwhelming sensation. She didn't know how to use raw power to attack, but she tried to send a jet of water toward the Ocean Miner, hoping to throw her off balance.

The water responded to her prompting, but as soon as it neared the Ocean Miner, the invisible current split, shooting harmlessly around her.

Estelle's song petered out. It was as her father had said. She couldn't harm the Ocean Miner.

The twisted old mermaid knew it, as well. She'd obviously sensed the magic Estelle had tried to use, and she gave a gleeful cackle. Pulling a small pouch from the satchel slung over her chest, she loosened the tie. A black substance, similar to squid ink, seeped out. It began to disseminate through the water, and although she couldn't guess at its function, Estelle could sense the magic oozing out with it.

His voice low and urgent, Demetrius began to sing, the water vibrating to his melody. But the black liquid wasn't as easy to redirect as the urchin's spines had been. It billowed out toward them, only some of the growing cloud fading as Demetrius sang. Estelle added her voice to his, relieved to find that the oath of her ancestor didn't prevent her from defending herself against the Ocean Miner's attack.

As soon as she opened her mouth, however, she caught a flash of movement from their adversary. The Ocean Miner had produced a shell that Estelle recognized. It was conical, and it glowed faintly in the water. The Ocean Miner laid it against her own throat, and although she made no sound, Estelle could feel something trying to grab at the power she was manipulating.

"Stop singing," Demetrius said sharply. "She's trying to steal your voice back."

"Can she do that?" Estelle gasped.

"I don't know," said Demetrius, "but let's not find out."

He resumed his song, but the pause had cost them. The substance had almost reached them, and they were forced to scatter. Estelle swam rapidly upward, keeping the Ocean Miner in sight as she fled from the inky black liquid. The ancient mermaid was pulling more talismans from her satchel, and Estelle could feel shockwaves going out through the water. Clearly the Ocean Miner had plenty of damage to cause even restricted to her mined magic. And Estelle was powerless to stop her, prevented by the oath from attacking directly, and afraid to sing for fear of her voice being snatched away again.

She saw Demetrius circling behind the Ocean Miner and realized the only way she could contribute. She needed to distract their enemy.

Softly, Estelle started to sing, keeping her voice low as if she was hoping to evade notice. Sure enough, the Ocean Miner's head whipped instantly toward her, and she advanced through the water, an evil smile on her face.

Undaunted, Estelle continued to sing, her voice growing louder as she drew power from the depths of the ravine. She didn't try to send it against the Ocean Miner, instead wrapping it in a protective layer around Demetrius. He was moving along the ocean floor like a sea cucumber, his eyes on the mermaid floating above him. Estelle tried not to look at him, continuing to sing as the Ocean Miner was lured further into her trap.

Perhaps there was some truth in the sailors' legends of the siren's song.

Estelle increased the volume of her voice, trying to inject an edge of panic to the sound as the Ocean Miner reached her. It wasn't hard, given the way her heart was pounding. She hoped it would seem like she was still trying fruitlessly to circumvent the oath that bound her.

Her voice wavered slightly as the Ocean Miner once again placed the shell against her wrinkled throat. Demetrius was almost on them, but the need for stealth meant he had to move slowly.

"No mistakes this time," the Ocean Miner rasped, reaching one gnarled hand toward Estelle's throat.

With a cry, Demetrius moved at last, but his eyes were on Estelle, not their enemy. Estelle's song faltered as he propelled himself frantically through the water, bypassing the Ocean Miner completely as he threw himself between Estelle and the danger she hadn't even seen coming.

The creeping black cloud enveloped him, the substance clinging to his form in a way that wasn't natural. He went instantly limp, and terror rose in Estelle's heart.

"Demetrius!" She clutched at him, momentarily forgetting about the Ocean Miner's advance. He was utterly unresponsive in her arms, his blue lips silent, and his eyes closed.

An irritated grunt sounded from Estelle's other side, and she whipped around, Demetrius still grasped against her.

"Interfering nuisance," muttered the Ocean Miner. Her eyes narrowed as they rested on Estelle. "But there'll be time enough for your turn. Now sing if you don't want everyone you care about to end up like him."

Estelle quivered with fury as she pulled Demetrius against her. She understood what the Ocean Miner had been doing. She'd intended to snatch Estelle's voice then immediately kill her, to ensure she never came back for it. And Demetrius had thrown himself in the way of the attack, once again sacrificing his own life for the sake of hers. This time literally.

For a moment the horror of it threatened to overwhelm Estelle, but she knew she couldn't fall apart yet. Regretfully, she let go of Demetrius's form, which floated beside her, its only motion that of the current. Raising a defiant face to her enemy, Estelle hissed, "I will never give you my voice."

"Listen here, you little sea snail." The Ocean Miner lunged forward, seizing Estelle by the throat. "I'll take what I want from you, and I'll see both your little kingdoms fall before my—"

She never finished the sentence, her words cut off by a hideous gurgling splutter. The still form beside Estelle had suddenly sprung into fluid motion, Demetrius's arm whipping out to reveal the whalebone blade he'd carried since his brief days in Emperor Aefic's guard. He plunged it straight into the Ocean Miner's heart—her eyes widening for the briefest moment of comprehension before they went blank—and her blood poured into the water as thickly as the ink that had coated Demetrius.

The moment he'd struck, Demetrius's arm went limp, and he floated gently down through the water, leaving his blade behind in the lifeless mermaid's body.

"Demetrius!" Estelle screamed, diving down to stop his descent into the ravine. She put her arms around him, pulling him softly to a nearby ledge of rock where they could rest. "Demetrius, talk to me!"

The familiar amber eyes flickered open. "Not my...finest... moment," he said, grunting with the effort of speech. "Played dead like...a lemon shark." The black ooze was gone, but the damage was clearly done, his movement sluggish and his face turning slowly blue. She was losing him.

"It was brilliant, Demetrius," Estelle choked out, her eyes stinging with the tears her mermaid form couldn't shed. "You did it. You saved us all. Now you're not allowed to die."

Demetrius gave a low, labored chuckle, the sound painful to hear. "Didn't know I needed...royal permission."

"Demetrius, please," Estelle sobbed. Terror threatened to

overwhelm her. She was losing everything, and she was still powerless to—

Her eyes widened as realization hit. She wasn't powerless anymore. With the Ocean Miner dead, there was no more reason to fear using her voice. And her song could harness the very power of the ocean.

Soft and low, she began to sing. She wasn't trained in healing, but what she lacked in expertise, she made up for in raw volume of power. She could feel it surging up from the deeps, swirling around her and Demetrius with an eagerness that was almost violent. Desperately, she poured her whole heart into her melody, closing her eyes to better focus on the sensation of the magic. She could feel the mined magic attacking Demetrius, tearing at him from the inside out. She focused her mind on that power, willing it to obey her song. It was foreign and vile, but it had been mined from the seabed. It had once been ocean power, and ocean power was under the control of her voice.

Making up the words as she went, she commanded the power to respond, drawing it from Demetrius like poison out of a wound. Slowly at first, then more steadily, it began to retreat from him, leaking out of every pore and back into the water, where she sent it diffusing harmlessly out. It felt like an eternity, but it was less than a minute before his eyes flickered open again, their expression now clear as he cast his gaze around in confusion.

"Estelle?" he asked warily, his eyes finding hers. "Am I alive, or are we both dead?"

Estelle released him, an unsteady laugh escaping her at this matter-of-fact response to his brush with death. Relief flooded every inch of her, and she raised a shaking hand to cover her face.

They'd done it. It was over.

CHAPTER TWENTY-SEVEN

Demetrius

Demetrius pushed against the rocky ledge beneath him, floating back to an upright position. Estelle hovered before him, her hands over her face as she struggled with whatever emotion had her in its grip. His eyes passed around them, taking in the gruesome sight of the Ocean Miner floating nearby in a cloud of her own blood.

Well, at least that was over.

The water was clear everywhere else, free of the malicious influence of the Ocean Miner's stolen power. It was even showing the first signs of lightening. Dawn must have broken far above them.

Demetrius took stock of his own body. He wasn't sure what precisely Estelle had done, but he felt completely well and whole, no sign of the crushing paralysis that had spread through him from the moment the black ink touched him. He gave his tail a flick, satisfied that no lingering damage remained.

Then he turned his attention back to Estelle. She was still hiding behind her own hands, but more importantly, she was unharmed. Or more accurately, she was glorious. Her scales glinted through the water, a cloud of aquamarine hair billowing around her head. Her servants' uniform floated around her, utterly out of place in the underwater scene, but somehow endearing.

That was the Estelle who was more familiar to him. The human who loved her garden, and glowed under the light of the sun. An image flashed into Demetrius's mind, of the way Estelle would close her eyes and turn her face up to the sun anytime she exited a building into sunlight, smiling as though she'd just received her heart's desire. He felt a pang at the loss of that life, but more importantly, he felt a burning desire to look at that beloved face.

He went to straighten the jacket of his guard's uniform, then laughed silently at himself for the very human gesture. Abandoning dignity, he swam forward, one of his hands taking gentle hold of Estelle's, and lowering it from before her eyes.

"Are you all right?" he asked softly, his eyes searching her face.

She smiled tremulously. "Better than all right, thanks to you. You saved me."

"And you returned the favor," he pointed out.

She nodded. "But my life wasn't on the line when I saved you—you were truly ready to give yours for me, weren't you?"

"Of course," said Demetrius simply. "I always have been, even when we hardly knew each other. Did you think I would be *less* willing once I realized I was in love with you?"

Estelle's mouth fell open at the unemotional declaration, and Demetrius winced.

"I didn't do that very well, did I?" he said apologetically. "Estelle, I'm not good at this sort of thing. I'm not a romantic hero like your prince. I just—"

"Not a hero?" Estelle's indignant protest cut off his ramblings. A smile was growing on her face, and she moved closer to him. One of her hands was still clasped in his, but she lifted the other to lay it against his cheek. "You're the most heroic hero I know." She gave her head a little shake. "Your protectiveness is such a part of you, you can't see it for the wonder it is. You were willing to give up everything to protect me even when you had no personal stake in it, even when my sufferings were fully self-inflicted."

"You were never fully to blame," Demetrius contradicted. "I was so hard on you, and I ascribed all kinds of motives to you that were never there. I saw that in our life on land. You never sought status, or vanity, or even luxury. You were content to make an honest living as an unknown servant, without even your voice. I know you thought you were chasing romance, but the truth is that all you wanted was freedom, and it was beautiful to see your joy when you had it."

"Our life on land." Estelle repeated the words in a soft whisper. "It was a good life, wasn't it?"

Demetrius's heart ached at the sadness in her voice, but she was already turning her face back up to his with a smile.

"We weren't talking about my supposed qualities. We were talking about yours. Your willingness to give your strength to protect others is one of the things I love most about you. I always admired that protective instinct in both Farrin and Prince Emmett, and it took me far too long to realize I'd been drawn to it in you before I knew either of them." Her clear blue eyes seemed to sear into Demetrius's soul as she added simply, "I became used to being mute, but the real question is how I could have been so blind as to not see that it was you I loved all along. I should never have thought I needed to go on land to chase happiness—what I needed was at my side the whole time."

Too overcome to find words, Demetrius caught her into her arms, searching her face earnestly. Moving uncertainly at first, then growing in boldness, he slid his tail through the water toward hers. They both jumped a little as their scales connected, twining their tails so that their fins were intermingled.

"You told me once that the love you felt for Prince Farrin was torment, but you seemed to want it anyway."

His arms tightened around her as he tried to straighten out his thoughts. She seemed perfectly content to float in his arms, her face turned up to his as she waited.

"I didn't understand it at the time," he went on. "I thought it was foolish and dramatic."

"It was," Estelle interjected.

Demetrius shook his head. "No. When I realized I was in love with you—after you bewitched me with that dance, and after the prince came back and I thought I might lose you—I finally understood. I'm sorry I mocked you when you told me what you felt. You were much braver than I would have ever been, to open your heart like that. I was the foolish one, thinking love was nothing more than a children's story. I just didn't know it was possible to feel this way."

"What way?" Estelle asked, her voice little more than a whisper, and her body warm against his in spite of their scaled forms.

"Like I'd gladly die to keep you safe, but I'd much rather live so I can spend every second at your side," Demetrius told her.

Estelle's face glowed so much, he could almost believe she'd moved into sunlight.

"I feel the same way," she murmured. "And please believe me when I say that was never truly how I felt about Farrin. I came to see a long time ago that my obsession with him was never just about him. I was equally fascinated by the world he represented, but I didn't know how to separate the two once my fancy fell on him. It wasn't love. It was an infatuation, based on my unhappiness about my own life. It was never really about who he was or wasn't." Her hand stole up to press against

Demetrius's chest, causing his heart to pick up speed. "But with you..."

A shout drew both their attention to the side, and they fell apart quickly at the sight of half Estelle's family floating barely two tail lengths away, staring open-mouthed at the pair. They must have felt the total cessation of the Ocean Miner's attack, and come to investigate the source. The group was ringed with guards, and Demetrius realized that the cry had come from one of them. The merman had discovered the Ocean Miner's body some distance away, and his fellows soon swarmed around him, dealing with the unsightly display.

"What's the meaning of this?" the emperor demanded, his voice dangerous.

A snort greeted his words. "I would have thought that was fairly obvious, Father." It was Princess Eulalia who spoke, her gaze not unfriendly as it assessed Demetrius. "Have you been up there with her all this time, then?"

"Just how long were you all listening?" Estelle demanded, seeming flustered.

Demetrius shifted subtly, floating to her side in a silent show of support. She seemed to appreciate it, her shoulders relaxing slightly.

"Long enough to get a fairly good idea of where the current's flowing," Princess Eulalia said frankly.

"Were you really so unhappy in your life here?" The soft question came from Empress Talisa, and Demetrius couldn't help but be moved by the depth of emotion in her eyes.

"Yes, Mother." Estelle's voice was gentle but unapologetic. "I was very unhappy, and I foresaw nothing but unhappiness in my future." She glanced at her father. "And although you'll probably despise me for admitting it, I was happy on land, as a human. When Farrin disappeared, and I thought I'd doomed myself to be trapped on land forever, I didn't truly regret any of it. Not once I'd gotten over the shock. The truth is, I preferred a shorter, less pampered life under the sun than a long and miserable one locked away in an underwater palace."

"Any parent should be proud of how Estelle conducted herself in the human kingdom," Demetrius interjected. "She was a credit to you in her cheerfulness and her hard work." His eyes softened as they rested on Estelle. "And she truly was happy. I'm sorry that life is lost to you, Estelle. I don't think there's anything unnatural about your desire to live under the sun, and I wish I could give its light back to you."

"Is it lost to her, though?" Princess Eulalia asked thoughtfully. Her eyes moved to her father. "Estelle's guard may not be able to give her the light of the sun, but that doesn't mean it's impossible. If the Ocean Miner could do it with illicitly mined power, couldn't the true ruler of the ocean do it even better?"

"We know from the Ocean Miner's history that our ancestor could do it the other way," Crown Princess Etta agreed. Her gaze flicked to the defeated mermaid. "And that clearly worked."

Demetrius glanced at Estelle, his heart hammering. She looked as though she was hardly daring to hope. He couldn't stand to see her dreams dashed. But he couldn't imagine what would convince her father.

"The humans are not the uneducated boors our history tells us they are, Your Majesty," he interjected. "I think our people would have much to gain and nothing to lose from reopening communication with them."

"Do you?" Emperor Aefic sounded unimpressed.

"He's right, Father," said Estelle. "They're much like us, just...warmer."

"Probably the effect of the sunlight." Esteban nodded sagely.

Demetrius ignored his friend's helpful contribution, his eyes fixed on the emperor. "The monarchs of today are not like the one who exploited your ancestor's greed. I've served in the king's guard for two years, and I can say with confidence that they are honorable, and attempt to do right by their kingdom and their neighbors."

The emperor's eyes narrowed in thought. "It was a human prince who started all this folly, wasn't it?" He was looking at his youngest daughter, but he didn't seem to really be seeing her. "The Dybde Empire never did bend. I never considered an alliance with a kingdom of the land—why would I? But perhaps—"

"No, Father." Estelle's voice cut through the water, clear and determined. "You're too late. Prince Farrin was married yesterday, to the queen of another land kingdom. We witnessed the ceremony ourselves."

The emperor looked put out. "Didn't our intelligence say there's another prince? The heir?"

"I'm not marrying Prince Emmett, either," said Estelle with finality. "I won't be married off to expand your empire, Father. And I have no interest in any princes of any kingdom. I'll flee into the deeps and live there in exile first."

"No need to get excited," said Princess Eulalia mildly.

Estelle turned to her sister, her expression unusually ferocious. "There's every need to get excited. Father's little better than our ancestor who started all this mess. His greed just takes a different course."

"Estelle." The emperor sounded furious, but Estelle didn't back down.

"No, Father, it's true. But I'm not wealth to be bartered for your gain."

She turned a defiant face to Demetrius, and he saw the vulnerable emotion behind her bold words. He slipped his hand into hers, hoping the pressure of his touch would steady her. Estelle studied his eyes for a moment, then her posture relaxed slightly, and she turned back to her parents.

"I've told you that I was happy on the land, and wished I could stay there. But I'd rather never see the sun again than be forced to marry someone against my inclination, to serve some purpose in which I have no interest."

Crown Princess Etta cleared her throat. "Let's not let emotion blind us." Demetrius thought there was the hint of a warning in the glance she sent her young sister. But it was gone as she raised her face to the emperor's. "As I've argued many times, Father, a marriage alliance may not be the only way Estelle can contribute to our family and empire. If we're to consider reopening communication with the humans, no one could be better placed than Estelle to serve as an ambassador. She knows our ways, and now she knows theirs more intimately than any other merfolk alive can claim." She glanced at Demetrius. "Except perhaps this young guard."

He stilled, wondering if he was understanding the direction of her thoughts. It hardly seemed possible that he and Estelle might be allowed to have everything they wanted.

"If it's what Estelle wants, Aefic," Empress Talisa said, her words soft and a little sad, "then I think we owe it to her. In light of how the Ocean Miner got power to wreak such havoc, she may not be well received down here anymore. And I agree with Etta that she could be of great service to the empire on the land." Her eyes passed slowly to her daughter. "And she might have the chance to be happy."

"But you'd only live another sixty years," Princess Eulalia protested. "Are you sure, Estelle? Do you really wish to be human for the rest of your life?"

To Demetrius's surprise, Estelle shook her head. There was a hint of wistfulness in her voice, but her words were confident. "No, I don't. I mean, I would wish for that if circumstances were different." Her eyes traveled to Demetrius's, the smile that curved her lips so intimate that he wished her family elsewhere.

"But I'd rather be underwater with Demetrius than above without him."

His heart swelled. "You don't have to make that choice on my account," he said. "I don't know if it's possible," his eyes darted to the emperor, "or if I could ever be considered worthy of the use of such an unmeasurable volume of power. But if I could choose any future, I'd choose one on land with you." He dropped his voice, wishing once again that they were alone. "I want to see you light up from the feel of the sun on your face again," he told her. "I'd give anything for that sight. You know what I feel. I'd rather a short and happy life together than three hundred years without you."

"Demetrius," she whispered, clearly moved.

"This is absurd," blustered the emperor.

Estelle turned to her father, making no attempt to hide her hope now. "What will you do with me if not this, Father?" she pointed out. "You've said yourself you have no way for me to strengthen your empire from below the waterline. Why not let Demetrius and me try to strengthen it from above? He's well-respected in King Johannes's castle. And we can read and write like the humans do, now. Who knows what sharing of resources we could negotiate? The empire could become as strong under your rule as it was before your ancestor let his greed bring it to ruin."

Demetrius could see that the emperor was beginning to be swayed. He wished he could be sure it was because he wanted his daughter to be happy, or even because he saw the wisdom of the arguments being put to him, rather than because he wanted to be rid of his troublesome youngest child. But if the emperor granted their request, Demetrius supposed they shouldn't quibble about his motivations.

"Very well," said Emperor Aefic. "I will consult the history holder and discover whether records remain of the method used by my ancestor to achieve the feat of transformation. And I will send agents to surveil the coastline, to confirm whether the details you've provided are accurate. But you'd best never give me cause to doubt your first loyalty, and—"

Demetrius didn't even hear the rest of the emperor's strictures. He was too focused on Estelle's face, lighting up as surely as the sky far above, where the sun was continuing to rise.

They were going home.

CHAPTER TWENTY-EIGHT

Estelle

Estelle floated impatiently in the internal courtyard of the palace, her Medullan servants' uniform slung over her arm. She felt her tail flicking, and told herself to settle down. It had been a long week, and she was eager to be above water again, but she didn't begrudge Demetrius the time with his family. She could still barely believe the sacrifice he was making to be with her. And, most incredibly of all, he didn't seem to even consider it a sacrifice.

"So desperate to be off?" Eulalia's voice was a little sad as she floated through the seaweed curtain that separated the courtyard from the corridor. "So eager to leave us?"

Estelle turned to embrace her sister as the other mermaid approached. "Of course not," she said, her musical voice sending a thrill over her, even after so many days. "It's not that I want to leave you, Eulalia, and I'm not desperate, not anymore. Last time I was fleeing from something, but now I'm swimming toward something. It's my future I'm eager to reach."

"I know," Eulalia assured her. "I can see it when I look at you, and it's beautiful." She studied her sister's face. "The only other time I've ever seen you excited about the future was before your first ascension." She gave a dry chuckle. "I really thought you'd lose interest in the surface once you'd seen it."

Estelle laughed as well. "Every species has its freaks."

"You're certainly not that," Eulalia told her firmly. The seaweed curtain shifted, and they turned to see the rest of the family entering. The emperor looked as forbidding as ever, but he truly did seem resigned to Estelle's course.

"We'll miss you, child," Estelle's mother said, swimming forward to enfold her youngest daughter in her arms. "Do you have the shells?"

Estelle nodded, nudging the satchel slung over her shoulder. Of all the treasures that had been discovered when the emperor's guards had raided the Ocean Miner's abandoned cave, these were most precious in her eyes. A whole stash of shells to allow communication from a distance, even across the barrier of the waterline. Estelle would be able to communicate with her family at will. It would aid in her attempts to commence diplomatic relations with Medulle on behalf of the Korallidian Empire, but it would also ease the separation on a more personal level. Her mother, Eulalia, and Etta all carried shells that would keep them connected with her, and one had been sent to the home of Demetrius's family.

Speaking of Etta, Estelle noticed that her eldest sister wasn't present. She'd barely had the thought when the middle-aged mermaid swam into the room, her eyes warmed by a smile. "He's on his way," she told Estelle. "He'll be here any minute."

Estelle's scales rippled with anticipation. No one bothered asking who Etta meant. They'd all quipped Estelle often enough over the last week about her restlessness in Demetrius's absence. She couldn't help it, she'd explained simply. For the last two and a half years, not a day had passed when she didn't lay eyes on him. He was as crucial a part of her life as her own breath.

The merfolk around her always fidgeted uncomfortably when she said anything sentimental like that. But she didn't let it trouble her. They could say and think what they chose. Unlike them, she'd lived among both kinds, and she unequivocally preferred the human attitude toward love, however foolish and emotional it might be.

"Do you really think I'll be able to sing?" she asked her father, even as her eyes strayed to the doorway.

"You are of royal blood," he said shortly. "Your voice can harness the power of the ocean on a level unattainable for other merfolk. No change in form will take that away."

"I don't think you'll be able to harness the power of the land like these human singers you've told us about," Etta chimed in. "I think your voice will be forever tied to the sea, and the magic that comes from the depths."

Estelle nodded. She supposed it might come in useful to pull magic up from the depths of the ocean, given she would be living close to the shore. But that wasn't her main interest. She just wanted to be able to sing for the joy of it.

The seaweed curtain fluttered again, and her heart soared as a familiar figure swam through. Demetrius. The week since she'd seen him had felt like an eternity. Sometimes she'd feared he wouldn't return, that his family would forbid it, or he would become distracted somehow. But watching his upright form approach, she wondered how she could ever have doubted him. He'd never failed to come through for her before.

His eyes found hers immediately, and she saw the way his posture relaxed. He'd felt it too, the wrongness of their separation. His family didn't live in the capital, and they'd had no contact since the day the Ocean Miner was defeated.

"Are you sure you want to do this?" The question came from Etta, and was directed to both Estelle and Demetrius. "With the amount of power involved, you won't be able to just change back tomorrow if it doesn't work out."

"We know," Estelle assured her. "We intend to make a life up there."

"But you'll only live for a short human lifespan," her mother said sadly.

"I know, Mother," Estelle said gently. "But it's the life I choose." Her eyes strayed to Demetrius, and she saw no conflict there. He was as set on their course as she was.

"We don't know for sure whether the human sovereign will receive our message favorably," Etta reminded her. "He may not offer you a position in his court as ambassador, as we hope. What will the two of you do if you're stuck up there without means or status?"

Estelle and Demetrius exchanged a look, and she could see her own humor reflected in his eyes. "Don't worry about us," she told her sister. "We'll land on our feet, regardless of how King Johannes responds."

"You'll what?" Everyone present looked confused, with the exception of Demetrius, who was no longer trying to hide his smile.

"Never mind." Estelle smiled as well. "Let's go."

Only a select few had chosen to accompany them to the surface, so Estelle said most of her goodbyes in the palace. The journey was completed mainly in silence, Estelle feeling a strange mixture of excitement and wistfulness. She would miss her family, especially Eulalia. But after all, she reminded herself, she would be closer to them than she would have been in the depths of the Dybde Empire. Much closer.

She was a little disappointed that Demetrius didn't swim alongside her, but when she saw that Esteban had joined the group, she understood. Demetrius would want a chance to say goodbye to his friend.

When they reached the familiar beach, the rest of the merfolk hung back. After a final embrace for her closest sister, Estelle pulled herself hand over hand through the shallows. Demetrius followed, his guard uniform—the pants of which he seemed to have mended during the last week—slung over his arm. When they were shallow enough that they had to duck to keep their heads under, they spun around.

"Are you ready?" Emperor Aefic's voice carried clearly through the gently lapping water.

Estelle and Demetrius both nodded, pulling on their human clothes.

"Then goodbye, Estelle."

Without another word, Estelle's father began to sing. His voice was deep and throaty, and Estelle could rarely remember hearing him use it with such force. She could feel the magic that swirled toward them, reaching eagerly up from the depths to chase them to shore. It was significantly more potent even than the power the Ocean Miner had harnessed with Estelle's voice. It swept over her and Demetrius, and the change was instant. A prickling started in her fins, spreading up her scales. It was much less painful than the Ocean Miner's potion, and acted more quickly.

Before Estelle knew it, she was pushing up with her feet, her lungs eager to take in pure air. She could feel her nose stretching back into its former position, and when she pulled a lock of hair in front of her face it was once again blond, only the occasional streak of blue remaining.

Demetrius followed a moment later, having paused to don the trousers of his guard uniform. Estelle stuck her head back in the water to see her family turn away, scales glinting in the noonday sun as they began the swim back to the palace. If all went to plan, she would see them again in a few days.

Once they were out of sight, she withdrew her head from the

water, turning slowly to face Demetrius. The air felt fresh and cold against her wet face, the cries of the gulls harsh in her ears with no water to soften the sound. She was back on land, with endless possibilities before her.

And one man beside her. A man who was gazing at her with such warmth it sent a pleasant shiver over her new form.

"Estelle." There was so much in the simple word, and in those amber eyes. For a moment Estelle was so overcome, she hardly knew what to say.

"Are you truly sure?" she asked him, feeling suddenly shy. It was incredible to hear her own voice above the water for the first time, but she pushed the thought to the side. "You're giving up everything, and—"

"It's a little late to ask me that now," he said, in his usual blunt way.

Estelle bit her lip anxiously, but his face relaxed into a smile.

"Of course I'm sure, Estelle," he said. "I'm not giving up anything I can't live without. If I stayed underwater without you, I would be."

He strode through the shallows toward her, stopping mere inches away. Reaching out, he lifted one strand of her hair between strong, calloused fingers.

"There you are," he said, searching her eyes. "There's the Estelle I fell in love with." The expression in his eyes was something more than warm now as his gaze rested on her face. "I've missed you."

"I could barely breathe this last week, I missed you so much," Estelle said in a rush. "I was so afraid you wouldn't come back, and I don't think I can do any of this without you."

Demetrius suddenly shifted, and abruptly, she found herself in his arms, looking up into a face that was only a breath away from hers.

"Not come back? Estelle, land or sea, wherever you are is

where I'm going. I'd follow you through a thousand tides. I love you, Estelle. However long or short, I want a life by your side."

Emotion surged through Estelle, raw and overwhelming. When she thought of the life she'd tried so clumsily to chase, she could hardly believe her good fortune. How had she evaded marriage to a kind but uninterested prince and instead landed the most selfless, truest heart in land or sea? She pushed up, her bare toes sinking into the sand of the shallow seabed as she raised her face to Demetrius.

He lowered his to meet her, their newly raised noses colliding abruptly.

Estelle pulled back a little, laughing. "How do humans kiss with these things in the way?"

"I'm guessing something like this," Demetrius said, his voice as low and intense as the throbbing of the ocean. His hands were suddenly cupped around her head, and he pulled her toward him as he angled his face. The next thing she knew, his lips were pressed to hers, and stars exploded before her eyes. Demetrius kissed her so thoroughly, she lost track of time and space, unable to remember whether she was floating in the water or basking in the sun. It felt like some combination of the two, and she never wanted it to end.

Far too quickly, he pulled back, breathing hard as he rested his forehead against hers.

"Why didn't we do that sooner?" she demanded, dazed.

Demetrius gave an unsteady chuckle. "Because we were both too blind to see what was before our eyes." His voice softened. "But we've got plenty of time to make it up to ourselves." He lifted his head, searching her eyes. "I'm not a prince, Estelle. I don't know if I'm even a guard anymore. Whatever your form, you remain a princess of a powerful empire, and I have neither wealth nor status to offer you. But will you take me anyway? Will you let me be your husband

and give me the right to protect you and to stand by your side?"

Estelle's breath was so short, she could almost believe she was trying to take in pure air through gills.

"Demetrius," she whispered. "You know I will."

She reached for him again, kissing him with a heart in danger of bursting. This time she was the one to break the kiss. "We have a job to do," she reminded him regretfully.

He nodded, pulling himself together and leading the way out of the water. The climb up to the castle felt surreal after all that had passed. Estelle half expected to be barred entry, but the guards on the gate let them through, one of them dispatching a message to the royals as the pair were led into a small audience room.

"Estelle!" Farrin burst into the room with his new wife right behind him, his face alight with excitement. "Thank heavens you've come back! I thought we'd never get answers!"

"And we're very glad to see you both unharmed, of course," Queen Bianca added courteously.

"That too," Farrin agreed. He slid an arm around his wife, pulling her to his side. Marriage seemed to agree with both of them. "I do have a great deal of questions, though. The explanation on the ship was woefully inadequate."

"I know," Estelle said repentantly, and the prince started at the musical sound of her voice. "But I think we should wait for the others before we tell the whole story."

"I agree," Queen Bianca interjected. "But there is something I want to say right away." She leaned her head against her husband's shoulder. "Thank you, to both of you. You saved Farrin's life when he fell from that ship. Without your intervention, I would never have even met him. Which, in addition to being unthinkable," she added, "would mean I was dead by now for certain."

Estelle looked between them curiously. She never had heard the full tale of Prince Farrin's adventures in Selvana.

"I'm glad you're both still here," Demetrius chimed in. "I agree that you're owed an explanation, and I was afraid you might have returned to Selvana by now."

"We delayed our departure in light of certain dramatic events," Farrin said with humor.

The door opened at that moment, Prince Emmett entering with his parents close behind him. Estelle wasn't surprised to see half a dozen guards follow the royals into the room.

After the initial exclamations had passed, Estelle cleared her throat and curtsied to the monarchs. Savoring the painlessness of it, she spoke at length, giving the background to her adventures on land and describing the defeat of the Ocean Miner. Once her tale was told, and all immediate questions were answered, she passed on the formal message from her father regarding his desire to open communication between their kingdoms once again.

"He wishes to send you as an ambassador?" King Johannes repeated, sounding a little dazed as his eyes passed over the gifts Estelle had brought from her father. She had presented only a few treasures of the deep which could fit in her satchel. She knew her father intended to offer more in future, and had his own requests in return.

"That's right, Your Majesty," she confirmed.

The king exchanged a look with his wife. "I'll be honest, Princess Estelle, if I hadn't seen you transform with my own eyes, I would think you'd lost your senses."

She chuckled. "Then it's a very good thing you did see it, Your Majesty, although it wasn't my most dignified moment."

The king's gaze passed to Demetrius. "And what about you?"

Demetrius drew himself up. "Princess Estelle and I are to be married, Your Majesty," he said, with as much confidence as if he was a king himself. "As soon as possible. Whatever role she takes, I will be at her side to support her."

"It seems congratulations are in order," the king said mildly. He eyed Demetrius. "Given you're to marry a foreign ambassador, I suppose it won't be appropriate for you to resume your post with the royal guard."

Demetrius bowed his head. "I had assumed as much, Your Majesty. I regret the necessity, but in any event I had no expectation of my captain welcoming my return given my deception."

Farrin gave a snort of laughter. "I don't think he's too troubled by that. I personally told your captain that I'd seen you turn into a merman and disappear into the ocean. He gave this irritated grunt and said, 'Does that mean he's resigning his post? Shame, he was one of my most promising guards.'"

That account drew a smile from the normally serious Demetrius. "He's a good captain, Your Highness," he said. "I've never known him to allow himself to be distracted by any unnecessary nonsense."

"Evidently," King Johannes said dryly. He ran a hand over his chin, his eyes still on Demetrius. "I have also discussed these events personally with your captain, and he spoke in the highest terms of both your ability and the loyalty you displayed during your time with the guard."

"I'm flattered, Your Majesty," Demetrius said, again lowering his head. Estelle thought he sounded taken aback by the praise.

"I've been thinking about it, actually," said Farrin brightly. "It might be a bit much for you to be on the royal guard if you're basically an ambassador, but there could be another option. The captain has been speaking for some time about the royal guard sponsoring a training program for the city guard. I believe there's even discussion of extending the city guard to include a coast guard. You'd be perfect for that."

"I would be glad to be considered for training in the

program," Demetrius said, not completely succeeding in hiding his eagerness at the idea of retaining some kind of guard position. He'd certainly found his calling, and Estelle hardly dared to hope that he might be allowed to pursue it in spite of the drastic changes to their circumstances.

"That's not quite what I meant," said Farrin, sounding amused. "I suggested to the captain that you would be an ideal candidate to help train new recruits, not to be a recruit yourself. He agreed."

Demetrius was silent, looking astonished and, unless Estelle was mistaken, a little moved. She beamed at Farrin, her heart swelling at his kindness to the person who was everything to her. Her fifteen-year-old fancy had alighted on a good-hearted man, even if she no longer had any interest in him being her man.

"There's a great deal to be considered," King Johannes cut in briskly. "For all of us."

"Of course, Your Majesty." Estelle dipped into another curtsy. "My father has requested a joint audience in three days' time, at the shoreline. Communication will be hindered by the differing forms, but not impossible. I hope our two peoples can reach a better understanding for the future than what we've known these last few hundred years."

The king nodded again, and Estelle and Demetrius took their leave. The royals would need some time to talk it all over.

"As soon as possible, is it?" Estelle teased Demetrius once they were alone.

He smiled. "I have to act quickly, before any more dreamy princes cross your path."

"I never said dreamy," she protested. But she felt no real annoyance as she leaned against Demetrius. "As soon as possible works for me," she said. "I don't feel the need for any great fanfare. I'd rather a simple ceremony on the clifftop than an elaborate display in a throne room."

"Then that's what you'll get," Demetrius assured her, pressing a kiss to the top of her head.

She grinned up at him. "Will you think me childish and foolish if I say I want to go to the kitchens now? I'm dying to see the reaction of the housekeeper and everyone to the information that I'm a mermaid princess."

Demetrius laughed. "Just the right level of foolish. I wouldn't want to see your ambassadorial role make you too stiff and serious." His tone sobered. "On that topic, how do you feel about me being a guard again, with this training program? If you think it will interfere with your duties..."

"Of course it won't," said Estelle quickly. "I have no idea what to expect from this role. For all I know, I may be called upon to communicate between the two sovereigns only very rarely. If that's what you want to do, I think it would be wonderful. Could we live off your wages, do you think? I like the idea of not being dependent on whatever provision my father considers appropriate for his reluctantly appointed ambassador."

"Well, we won't be able to live in a palace," Demetrius told her. "But assuming the pay is similar to what I received as a member of the royal guard, a modest home here in the city would be very achievable."

"With a garden?" Estelle pressed, smiling up into his face.

He gave her a squeeze. "Most definitely with a garden."

She laid her head against his chest and let out a contented sigh. "That sounds like the best life anyone could have, in either land or sea."

Nothing in the following days did anything to dim that impression, the meeting between the sovereigns going as smoothly as could be anticipated, and the captain sponsoring Demetrius for a role with the training program with a minimum of fuss. Demetrius moved temporarily back into the barracks, and Estelle was grateful to be granted a room in the castle while she and Demetrius made their quiet wedding preparations.

True to what she'd told Demetrius, she rejected all offers to facilitate a lavish celebration. She was pleased, however, to accept Farrin and Bianca's offer to extend their stay further, so as to attend the event. When she expressed concern that it might be an inconvenience to them, Demetrius told her to stop undervaluing herself. Besides, he reminded her, quite apart from the personal history, given she was the princess of a newly rediscovered empire, it was appropriate to have the royalty of other kingdoms represented.

The morning of the wedding, two weeks after their return to the land, Estelle rose early and slipped from her room out to the gardens. She paused to breathe in the sweet air, reflecting that she would miss working with the soil. Perhaps the head gardener would let her help out unofficially when she was in the castle for her ambassadorial role. He'd been a little more shocked than Demetrius's captain at learning her true form, but he'd continued to be kind to her nevertheless.

"Good morning."

Estelle turned at the greeting, delight overtaking surprise as she caught sight of Demetrius leaning against a nearby tree.

"What are you doing here so early?" she demanded.

"I could ask you the same," he pointed out.

"I was going to take a walk along the cliffs before the day began," she told him.

"I guessed as much," Demetrius said. "I'd like to join you if I may." She was about to eagerly assent, but he wasn't finished. "But first, there's something I want to show you."

Intrigued, she took his offered hand, following him through the gardens and out through the castle gate. They walked in companionable silence for about twenty minutes, skirting the outer ring of the city, with the ocean on their right. Demetrius came to a stop before a small sandstone dwelling, perched comfortably back from the ocean road. A trellis arch marked the entrance to the property, tenacious roses climbing across it.

"Why have we stopped here?" she asked.

"So I could ask you what you think," Demetrius said. "I've just entered an agreement to lease it, but if you don't like it, it's not too late to back out."

"Oh, Demetrius!" Estelle's heart swelled, eagerly scanning every inch of the building with fresh eyes. "I love it. It's perfect for us. Close to the ocean and close to the castle, but not too close."

"With a garden," he reminded her.

She laughed. "Yes, with a garden. I must say, those roses are doing well to survive in this salty air. A bed of daylilies below them would be just the thing."

"The garden and the home are yours to do with what you like," Demetrius assured her. He pulled her close. "Just like my heart."

Estelle couldn't help laughing. "When did you become so sentimental?"

"It's this human form," he said ruefully. "I can't seem to help it."

"Well, I like it," she assured him, nestling into his chest for a moment before pulling briskly back. "No more time for sentiment right now, though. I have things to do today."

Demetrius released her with a chuckle. "So do I, as it happens."

The walk back to the castle felt more like floating in water than trudging on soil, Estelle's heart almost unbearably full even when they parted ways at the gate.

Or at least she'd thought it was unbearably full. She realized a few hours later, as she walked along the cliff toward Demetrius, that she hadn't known the half of it.

His eyes were blazing with love so intense it was fierce as he watched her approach. Her simple white gown flowed out behind her as smoothly as water, and her hair was unrestrained. The occasional flicker of blue whipped into her sight as the wind blew it about. Farrin, Bianca, and Emmett all beamed at her from among the small group of attendees, most of whom were servants and gardeners who'd become friends to Estelle during her years at the castle. A contingent of guards also lined the clifftop, Demetrius's friends elbowing each other as they grinned at the emotion on the usually stoic guard's face.

And in the water behind Demetrius, Estelle could see a row of familiar heads, her family gathered to watch the ceremony. She could see Eulalia's purple hair, and Etta beside her, with Esteban and a few others from her family. Her parents were further back, but still present. It warmed something deep within her to see them there, accepting the path she'd chosen even if none of them quite understood it.

The humans were all facing her, watching her approach, and hadn't yet seen the merfolk. She had no doubt there would be quite the commotion when they did, but she didn't care about that. All she cared about was the upright figure at the end of the jutting expanse of cliff, his eyes fixed on her, and his expression telling her he would never leave her side again.

Without even thinking about it, she raised her voice in a song, soft and low. She saw Demetrius's eyes light up at the musical sound, and felt the power that stirred beneath the surface of the water. She wasn't trying to call on it, though. She was just enjoying the freedom to sing her song of the sea up on the land that had become her home.

She heard Queen Bianca's voice join hers, quiet and unobtrusive, and to Estelle's delight, lilies began to bloom along her path. It was more perfect than any gift the wealth of a royal treasury could buy.

When Estelle at last reached Demetrius, and slipped her hand into his strong one, she felt as though her very heart was singing. It hardly seemed possible that after everything, she could have reached that moment. The land had welcomed her, and the sea was safe from the Ocean Miner forever. She had her voice, her freedom, and the future of her choosing. And, most precious of all, she had Demetrius, by her side for the rest of whatever years their lives would hold.

No foolish dream of her fifteen-year-old heart could have imagined an outcome more perfect. She had everything she needed for the happiest of lives. Now all that was left to do was live it.

NOTE FROM THE AUTHOR

Thank you for reading *Song of the Sea*. I hope you enjoyed returning to the world of Providore. I would be so grateful if you would consider leaving a review on Amazon—it would really make a difference!

If you want to learn more about what's really going on in Providore, and what the deal is with the giants, check out *Song of Winds*, the next installment of *The Singer Tales*. You'll find more adventure, fantasy, mystery, and hard-won happily ever afters!

Join up to my mailing list at deborahgracewhite.com to be kept up to date on new releases, specials, and giveaways, such as bonus chapters. You'll receive some great freebies, too, including *An Expectation of Magic*, a novella which is a prequel to my completed YA fantasy series *The Vazula Chronicles*.

Plus, you'll receive *Dragon's Sight*, an 8,000 word prequel to my completed YA fantasy trilogy *The Kyona Chronicles*.

Again, thanks for entering the world of Providore! I hope to see you back again.

ALSO BY DEBORAH GRACE WHITE

The Kyona Chronicles: YA Fantasy

The Kyona Legacy: YA Fantasy

Also by Deborah Grace White

The Vazula Chronicles: YA Fantasy

The Kingdom Tales: Fairy Tale Retellings

The Singer Tales: Fairy Tale Retellings
(releasing throughout 2023)

ACKNOWLEDGMENTS

Huge thanks to my fabulous team for doing their thing to make *Song of the Sea* so much better than it would have been without them.

Ray, for once again diving into a mermaid world with me, and giving such helpful feedback. My betas for their awesome contributions and encouragement: Adrian, Mel W, Dad, Steph, and Mum. And Dad for developmental editing. Thanks also to Shae for the excellent job proofreading. Any remaining errors are definitely my own.

Thanks to Karri for the gorgeous cover, and to Becca for the beautifully-drawn map.

To you, the reader, thank you for giving me the privilege of being an author.

And most importantly, to God, who gives us new life.

ABOUT THE AUTHOR

I've been a reader since I can remember, growing up on a wide range of books, from classic literature to light-hearted romps. The love of reading has traveled with me unchanged across multiple continents, and carried me from my own childhood all the way to having children of my own.

But if reading is like looking through a window into a magical and beautiful world, beginning to write my own stories was like discovering that I could open that window and climb right out into fantasyland.

I cannot believe how privileged I am to actually be living that childhood dream and publishing my own novels. I do so from my hometown of Adelaide, Australia, where I live with my husband and our three little ones.

I've never outgrown my love of young adult stories, so the genre of young adult fantasy was always going to be my niche. Feel free to email me at deborah@deborahgracewhite.com and introduce yourself! Or subscribe to my mailing list at deborahgracewhite.com for free giveaways, sales, and updates.

CPSIA information can be obtained
at www.ICGtesting.com
Printed in the USA
BVHW081154190223
658756BV00001B/132